MINDTOUCH

MINDTOUCH
BOOK I OF THE DREAMHEALERS

M. C. A. HOGARTH

STUDIO
MCAH

Mindtouch
Book I of The Dreamhealers
First edition, copyright 2013 by M.C.A. Hogarth

M. Hogarth
PMB 109
4522 West Village Dr.
Tampa, FL 33624

ISBN-13: 978-1490450339
ISBN-10: 1490450335

Cover art by MCA Hogarth

Designed & typeset by Catspaw DTP Services
http://www.catspawdtp.com/

For Liana
I didn't know what I was supposed
to learn from what happened to you
so I asked

TABLE OF CONTENTS

CHAPTER 1

"**I**'M HERE FOR MY ROOM assignment, please," Jahir said.

The woman behind the registration desk glanced at him and barely concealed her surprise. He supposed not many people stood tall enough to look over the desk at her. Either that, or it was because he was Eldritch.

"New or returning student?" she said, stumbling back onto her checklist. Her fingers swiped through the display hanging mid-air before her, gathering data like a mage out of legend at work on a spell. He found it unlikely and mesmerizing, the Alliance's interface with its technology.

"New," Jahir said.

"Name?"

"Jahir Seni Galare," he said.

Tiny chimes accompanied her data entry. She nodded. "First year, Xenopsychology." She paused while she scanned his information, hesitated. When he canted his head, she said, "You're . . . a bit older than our usual freshman." She cleared her throat. "Do you have a data tablet?"

He fetched it from the bag at his feet and set it on the counter for her, wondering anew what purpose the desk's height served. Most people would have trouble with it. Was it meant to intimidate incoming students? There might be a paper in it.

The thought amused him, and his slight smile bought him another covert glance, one he wasn't supposed to notice. Her ears and cheeks flushed bright pink. Jahir didn't remember which of the foxine races had the mostly humanoid faces, but she was entirely believable despite her improbable origins. From what he understood, most of the Pelted were Earth's engineered children.

"We don't get many Eldritch," she said as she took the tablet, one ear sagging and the other upright.

"I don't mind," Jahir said, and didn't. Stares were the least of his issues.

Her smile brightened and she set the data tablet back on the counter. "First year information is on your tablet, along with your room assignment and your roommate's name. Dorms are outside and to the—"

"Roommate?" Jahir frowned. "I thought I specified I wanted a single occupancy room."

"We're full this semester," the foxine said. "No one gets a single until some space frees up."

"Perhaps there is a misunderstanding," Jahir said. "I paid for a room alone."

She nodded. "Your refund is processing," she said. "I'm sorry, Mr. . . . err, Galare? But this semester everyone's rooming with someone else."

Jahir shook his head, stifling the first surge of panic. "A room to myself is a medical necessity. I'm afraid I must insist."

"A medical necessity?" She paused, and once again her fingers swayed over the display. A few moments later, she said, "I can't find anything on your file. Did you indicate your medical needs on your application in the appropriate space?"

Jahir set his hand on the counter. "No," he said, drawing the word out.

"You didn't," she said flatly, eyeing him.

"No," Jahir said again, wishing he'd thought of it. He hadn't expected the need, and he certainly hadn't wanted to discuss the limitations imposed on him by his race's mental abilities with the university staff.

"Is this an elective medical need?"

Yes, there was asperity there. Caught between lying and exposing his weaknesses, Jahir considered his options. "No, I'm afraid not."

The woman's ears flipped back. "I'm not sure we'll be able to help you this semester, Mr. Galare."

"And I'm afraid I can't compromise on this, madam," Jahir answered. "Perhaps you should fetch your superior."

She sighed, and left.

Jahir leaned against the counter while he waited, pressing his fingers to the bridge of his nose in a vain attempt to banish the headache lurking there. He had not been on Seersana even six hours, and he'd already been smothered several times by the overactive minds of aliens. Having to stand so close to them in lines, shuttles and ground transports inevitably resulted in accidents, some of them so intense he'd had to find someplace to sit until the impressions faded. He'd been treated to grocery lists, silent tirades against unfaithful lovers, wistful sexual yearnings, fears and grumbles about work situations so byzantine he couldn't believe he could learn so much from a few seconds' contact . . . just six hours, and he already needed at least one to regain his equilibrium and rebuild his fragile globe of psychic shielding.

He was weary in bone and joint, in a way he hadn't at all been anticipating. He could not, absolutely not, spend an entire semester without a place he could barricade himself into to recoup.

The woman's superior turned out to be a Phoenix of a gender Jahir couldn't discern, an amazing creature with metallic plumage, a beak as long as Jahir's forearm and enormous eyes the clear blue of cornflowers. It tilted its head at him far enough to study him with one large avian eye, shuffled the wings that depended from its humanoid arms.

"May I help you, Lord Seni Galare?" it asked, without trace of an accent.

"I require a single room," Jahir said. "For medical purposes."

Maintaining sanity counted, he assumed.

"Nanette informs me you did not flag this medical necessity in your application," the Phoenix said.

"That is correct," Jahir said.

"We take the health of our students very seriously, Lord Seni Galare. We are not well-served by students arriving with unmentioned medical needs that immediately disrupt the processes of the university. Do you have any other mysterious needs you declined to share with us on your application?"

The creature's straight delivery of this speech gave Jahir cause to wonder if it was trying to shame him or if this was some mystery of Phoenixae behavior. These were the kinds of idle thoughts that had driven him here, to this marble floor in front of a too-tall-for-everyone-else registration desk, where an alien was, he thought, reprimanding him. "None, no," Jahir said.

The Phoenixae's feathers ruffled. "We have no single rooms this semester. Apologies, but we cannot make an exception. There is a simple issue of physical space. It cannot be reasoned with, you understand. The laws of the universe."

"Surely—"

"No," the Phoenix said, in a manner so alien Jahir wasn't sure whether it knew that interruption was rude. Its brassy crest lifted, spread, feathers shining beneath the sun streaming in from the overhead windows. "I am so sorry, Lord Seni Galare. If this medical need truly is necessity, we will attempt to make alternate arrangements for you outside the university." A pause, then.

"I'm sorry, I must insist," Jahir said. He didn't miss the slight quiver and drop of the foxine's ears.

"Very well," the Phoenix said. "But in the future, you will disclose such information to us, or we will not be held accountable for any harm that comes to you."

"Of course," Jahir said to its back as it departed. He glanced at the foxine.

"I'll see what I can do," she said in a low voice. "When I have more information, I'll push it to your tablet. You may have to stay in one of the auditorium conference rooms until we find something."

With a frown, Jahir looked at her, and she finished, "Apartments fill up quickly, Mr. . . . er, Lord. The semester starts in a few days. We may have issues finding something appropriate. Particularly if you have preferences about how far you wish to walk, or how much more than your deposit you want to pay." She cocked her head. "You don't have any preferences, do you?"

"I'd call them parameters, but. . . ."

Her ears sagged further. "Naturally. Well, tell me now. And don't leave anything out this time."

They spent the next fifteen minutes in that discourse, and by the end of it the foxine's ears were pinned to her head and her face had stiffened into a polite mask. Jahir wished he could spare her the trouble he'd evidently created for her, but there was no way he could stay sane in a double.

Shouldering his bag, he left the administration building, boot heels clicking on the stone tiles. Once outside, he squinted at the yellow sun and its shroud of fine clouds as pale as his own skin, felt the weight of the hours that had passed. He found a bench in the courtyard and claimed it, relieved to be able to sit. How strange it was to finally be here! After so many years, and few of them planned . . . he'd never intended to leave home, for as the heir to the Seni Galare he'd had work, even with his mother still active in the management of the estates. But he'd been educated on the use of the Well feed to the Alliance, one few Eldritch would have known about, and in his off hours had chanced on the university's open enrollment. He'd take first one class . . . and then another . . . and soon enough found himself longing to actually see the world he'd been reading about.

He'd been expecting his mother to object to his plan to leave; instead, she'd put him in contact with the Queen's courier service herself and told him to write her as he had the time. He'd left his isolationist world without a single qualm. Jahir was done with seclusion, or so he'd thought. He hadn't realized how much he'd been counting on having a private space to retreat to when the alienness of it became overwhelming. Even tightly shielded and clothed from throat to gloved fingertips and down to booted feet, he could sense the vibrant life of the campus. Scattered students wandered across the courtyard's paths, their essences whispering to his mind. He was not especially talented for an Eldritch, but even so it threatened. Most of his kind, on sensing the presence and feelings of others, closed themselves off completely.

Sensing the feelings of others had set Jahir on this path.

A path that led to a roommate.

He sighed, trying not to envision himself sleeping on a conference room table in an auditorium for a few days. He focused instead on a creature shaped like a giant bird with horns as it walked past in the company of another one of the foxlike humanoids. Curiosity brushed aside the unease in Jahir, as it always had. He could remain here, to obsess over his data tablet and occasionally step into the building to see if the woman needed further urging . . . or he could spend the rest of the day investigating the campus. Inevitably, he headed for one of the locker rental units.

⁓∞⁓

According to the research Jahir had done through the Well feed, Seersana's university had preceded even Karaka'A's prestigious institute as the first in the Alliance, just as this solar system's two worlds had been the first settlement for the Pelted fleeing Earth. Its renowned medical colleges had been the product of necessity, for the first generations of the Pelted had been forced to re-engineer themselves to remove the flaws humanity had bequeathed them. As the Pelted encountered the first aliens, the medical curricula grew to encompass them. Seersana's xenopsychology school was also the oldest in the Alliance, another reason Jahir had selected it.

Now that he was here, its unalloyed beauty offered an additional lagniappe. Ancient trees guarded the campus's walkways, nodding over the broad lawns that separated the buildings. Tiny fountains nestled in secluded copses, their commemorative plaques written in Universal rhyme, Seersan glyphs, or, as one might expect of the race that carekept the Exodus records, both and a multitude of other languages besides. Jahir traced the engravings with his fingers. His own tongue was never one of those other languages, of course. His people would never have allowed it.

Every place he walked, he saw great effort employed in the preservation of the existing flora. The path leading from the School of Healing-Assist to the Rhone Medical Library wended through what could only be called a small forest, where a series of metal arches prevented the trees from draping their leaves onto the shoulders of passersby.

It was a disappointment to reach the edge of the medical campus and discover an empty lot, so finding a centaur wrapped up in a rope and surrounded by six squealing girls was a decided improvement. Jahir stopped on the edge to stare.

The creature tangled in the ropes had four legs and two arms in the configuration of a centaur. He also had a tail and two smooth wings attached lengthwise to his lower back. His black and white pelt suggested a permanent formal suit, with white stripes down his black back, a white chest and white toes. His face was some amalgam of animal and human, with a short muzzle and floppy black bangs over brown eyes. Instead of ears, he had feathers arranged in sprays, like the back of a woman's hat. Jahir had never seen anything like him.

The Eldritch walked forward before he could think better of the plan. "Pardon me. May I assist?"

The centauroid glanced at him; all the little girls glanced at him. In the silence, Jahir was suddenly the center of attention.

"What is that?" one of the girls asked.

Another said, "It's a human in white paint!"

"No, no," the centauroid said, laughing. He had a pleasant voice, a warm tenor with a furry timbre. "That's an Eldritch, kara."

"Those are the ones that never leave their world, right?" another asked.

"I guess not," the centauroid said with a grin.

"You sure he's not a painted human?" the first girl asked again. "Or maybe he's like one of those animals that's born without skin color?"

The centauroid laughed. "I'm certain. If he were human he wouldn't be so elongated. He's an Eldritch, sure as I'm fuzzy."

"So that means he has secret powers!" This from a human girl with ragged pigtails of dull brown hair and eyes bright as a sparrow's. "He can read people's minds, and he has a treasure trove of gold, and he has a dragon protecting his ancient palace, and he's probably a prince!"

"A lord anyway," Jahir said, laughing. "But a very, very minor one. Tell me, gentles, what are you doing to yonder man?"

"We're teaching him to jump rope," she said.

"Trying, anyway," another said.

"And he's not a man," said the third. "He's a Glaseah."

"He's doing okay for someone with so many legs," one of the girls untangling him said. She had small limp ears, naked and set on a bald head. Jahir wondered what strange aesthetic had prompted the coif.

"And wings."

"And arms!"

"I see," Jahir said.

"Ladies, a little more help, please?" the Glaseah said, for the discussion had distracted them. "I can't reach some of those tangles, you know."

"Oh! Sorry!" The human and two of the others went back to picking the rope from around the centauroid's tail. Jahir watched, fascinated. He had never heard of jump rope, but he couldn't fathom how they'd managed to tangle the Glaseah up so completely.

"What are you looking at?" another girl asked, the shortest of the six. "You asked if you could help, so come help!"

"He's not supposed to touch people," the centauroid said.

"Not at all?" the bald girl asked. "But why?"

"Because if he does, he'll lose his virginity!" a different human girl said.

Jahir and the Glaseah stared at her. The other girls simply looked puzzled.

"What does that mean?" the shortest one asked.

The human shrugged. "I don't know. I heard one of the nurses say it while she was watching the news. She said one of her friends was guarding her virginity like an Eldritch would. I guess that's something important."

The Glaseah's mouth twisted into an amazing pucker, chest shaking with withheld laughter.

"Is it true?" the bald girl asked him.

"What's a virginity, anyway?" another asked.

Jahir opened his mouth, then closed it.

"I believe," the Glaseah said, glancing at him with sparkling eyes, "that the reason you can't touch him is because if you do, you will force your thoughts on his. His mind is very sensitive, you see."

"Oh. Is that what a virginity is?"

"No," Jahir said firmly, determined to steer the conversation away from the whole topic. "But I will get that knot up yonder." He pointed at the one on top of the centauroid's wing.

"Okay," the children said. They returned to their labors, leaving Jahir to approach the centauroid with caution. The Glaseah's eyes had not lost their sparkle, but they also held a note of curiosity, one that Jahir was familiar with. He'd seen it in the silvered glass a few too many times at home. It had led him here, to the task of untying an alien in bondage to six little girls. Wonders never ceased.

The knot had looped around the top of the wing, which Jahir studied with great interest. The front of the wing resembled another arm with an elongated forearm. The rope was caught in something that resembled a thumb with a claw at its crest.

Not caught. Held. Jahir stared, taken aback, when the thumb lifted and dropped the rope into his palm. When he looked at the Glaseah, he received a solemn wink . . . and then a nod at one of the children. Jahir chanced a look past one shoulder and caught the flash of a metal-lined port nestled in the base of one neck.

Then the rest of the scene fell into place. The lot with its sleek, small-occupancy vehicles, meant to receive visitors from outside the university. The simple gowns, gaily patterned but all cut to the same design. The bald head . . . the ragged hair on the human . . . the sallow skin. The building across from him had to be—and was, he saw, squinting to read the plaque—a children's hospital.

"Did you do your part?" the human girl interrupted. "'Cause we're done."

Jahir stepped away. "All free," he said. "I'd love to see this jumping rope. There's no such thing on my world."

The Glaseah added, "Maybe I should watch you again. I'm obviously missing something."

The girls nodded and rearranged themselves, one at either end of the rope and the other four in the middle. The two girls on either end sang out a count, and on the beat the four in the middle jumped. Over and over the rope struck the ground with a smart *thap*.

"Vasiht'h," the Glaseah whispered. He had seated himself on his lower haunches beside Jahir, leaving only barely enough space to separate them. Jahir didn't spare the dangerous closeness much thought, though. His sorrow for the sight consumed him. He would live over a thousand years, fifteen hundred if averages held, had already lived over a hundred and fifty, and yet these children would probably not see two decades. He knew little of Alliance medicine save for the rumor of the power of its technology, its knowledge. What diseases remained to afflict small children must be grave and virulent.

"Pardon?" he said.

"My name," the centauroid said. "Vasiht'h. I'm a xenopsych student."

"Oh!" Jahir exclaimed, then lowered his voice. "I am, as well. First-year. Jahir Seni Galare. Do you do this often?"

"Oh, no. I was wandering today and here they were. They needed to laugh."

The girls had barely been jumping a few minutes and Jahir

could see how they flagged. Their pleasure slipped away with their stamina, and took their grace with it. For there had been grace in the display, the grace of exhilaration and bare feet, the grace, briefly, of children. Fatigue aged them before Jahir's eyes.

"I think I'm ready to try again!" Vasiht'h said, before exhaustion reduced them completely.

Jahir stood next to Vasiht'h. "I as well."

The centauroid glanced at him, then grinned.

Together they tangled themselves in the rope, tripped over their own feet and apologized profusely before making their second tries. The game itself was simplicity, but Jahir found that the rope wasn't long enough to accommodate the entirety of Vasiht'h's length as well as his unusual height. He crouched as he jumped, which sent the girls into paroxysms of giggles, some so intense they had to stop the lesson altogether.

Jahir spied the healers-assist first, searching for their charges on the hospital lawn. He caught Vasiht'h's eye and glanced their way.

"One more time," Vasiht'h said. "I promise we'll get it right this time."

"Okay, okay," the girls said, and began again.

Vasiht'h tucked in his wings and tail and danced over the rope, and Jahir went with him, still crouched.

"Yay, they got it, they got it!"

"Oooh, go-go manylegs!" They revived their chant, the same they'd used for themselves and sang as the two males danced to the *thap-thap* of the rope.

The game ended soon after. The girls' nurses retrieved them, chiding them for leaving their biogems behind so they could not be tracked. The human girl stopped as she was being led away.

"Will you come visit?" she asked, addressing them both. "Maybe we can teach you other games."

The harried nurse made a strangled noise. Jahir cleared his throat and said to the girl, "Perhaps something a little less strenuous? I've worked up quite a sweat . . . I could fairly faint."

Vasiht'h nodded sagely and whispered to the girls, "Eldritch have very fragile constitutions! Maybe we should do card or board games next time."

"Ooh! I know some!" one of the girls said.

"Me too!"

"Soon, then," Vasiht'h said.

Their glee lasted long after the nurses herded them away. Jahir could tell even without touching them, so strong was their joy. It hung in the air like a trail of perfume.

"That worked out well," the centauroid said, hands on the join between torso and lower body. "I hope you want to come back."

"Absolutely," Jahir said. He smiled down at the other male. "That was well done of you."

"You too." Vasiht'h grinned. "So, first-year xenopsych, ah? I'm second-year. It's good to meet a colleague. Where are you staying?"

"I don't know," Jahir said. "I had paid for a single, but . . ."

"But they wouldn't give you one, I bet," Vasiht'h said, nodding. "I heard about their being full. Enrollment this year is high. Do they know where they're putting you?"

Jahir folded his hands behind his back. "Unfortunately not. They're supposed to offer a selection of places off campus presently."

Vasiht'h squinted. "Am I reading your body language correctly when I guess you aren't thrilled by that? I've never met an Eldritch before. You don't seem to move much."

"We like to minimize the possibilities of accidental contact," Jahir said.

"Ah, that makes sense," Vasiht'h said. He began strolling back toward the campus core. Bemused, Jahir fell into step alongside, leaving enough space in case the Glaseah's body-talk involved his wings. Far be it from him to resist the lure of the alien, particularly when it came in such a bizarrely painted package. That Vasiht'h did not seem to emanate the same agitation and disorder characteristic of so many other aliens didn't hurt. Come to the thought, Jahir had bumped into him several times during their comedy routine. What had he sensed? A stillness, a competence. Mild concerns for the children, pleasure at the unexpected partnership. All gentle feelings, held in a calm mind.

"So, you'd prefer being on campus?" Vasiht'h asked.

Jahir glanced around at the trees, the grass, the broad sky. He took a long, measured breath, chest barely rising. Part of that was habitual control . . . the other half, a vague weariness. "Yes," he said on the exhale. "This is a new enough experience without adding the complexities of navigating a new city. Still, I would not prefer to sleep in a conference room for the duration of the semester."

Vasiht'h tilted his head. "My roommate just graduated. They've probably already assigned me a new one, but I bet we could get them to move you in with me, if you wanted. I have one of the older residential apartments. You'd have a room to yourself—not a big one, but there's a door."

Jahir hesitated.

"And if it doesn't work, you can always pack up and move off campus," Vasiht'h said. "It's easier to find apartments a few weeks after the semester's started, when people decide to drop their classes or find alternate arrangements."

Jahir glanced at him. "I've only just met you."

"That's better than not having met me at all," Vasiht'h said, "which is the situation most people are in when they get on-campus housing . . . !" He smiled. "We're in the same program. We could compare notes, study together. And I like to cook."

Why had he come, if not to take risks? And as the alien said, he could always leave if it didn't work out. "Would they let you switch your current assignment thus?"

"I don't know," Vasiht'h said. "Let's go find out."

The woman behind the registration desk actually flinched when she saw Jahir coming, but her expression was nothing to the one that blossomed when Vasiht'h reared and hooked one forepaw over the desk, leaning over it with his torso.

"These desks," he muttered, "are far too high." More clearly,

"My roommate graduated last semester, which means I have an opening. I'd like to room with this student."

"You can't choose your—"

"Ma'am," Vasiht'h said, "I presume you know this man?"

The woman glanced at Jahir, ears flicking back. "Yes," she said, drawing the word out.

"And he made trouble, didn't he."

She said, "I'd rather say he was surprised by the fact that we didn't have any single rooms available."

"He'll probably make trouble again," Vasiht'h said. Jahir opened his mouth to object, and the centauroid pointed. "See? He's about to start." Vasiht'h leaned toward her. "We can all spare ourselves frustration if you just switch the room assignments. Take whomever you were planning to put with me and move them into whatever room you had the Eldritch in and I'll take the Eldritch home. You'll be happy. Your supervisor will be happy. I will be happy. And the Eldritch will be happy. You will solve every problem! Surely that's better than trying to find him a conference room to malinger in."

The woman stared at him and then started to laugh. "Fine, fine. I'll arrange it. What's your name?"

Vasiht'h gave her the pertinent information, received the promise of a mailed confirmation and smiled at her. "Thank you, alet."

"You're welcome," the foxine said, shaking her head.

Vasiht'h dropped off the desk and turned to Jahir. "So, let's go get your baggage."

Jahir couldn't help a laugh. "Just like that."

"Just like that," Vasiht'h said. "You forget, I've been attending here for a year already. I know how it works." He peered up at Jahir. "You see, that's why you need someone like me. Like a native guide."

"And will my tour also include cultural explication?" Jahir asked.

"As much as you want," the Glaseah said. "Let's go get you settled in."

CHAPTER 2

A N ELDRITCH! VASIHT'H CHANCED a look at the man walking
beside him, one long stride for two of his own. He'd been
on Seersana for almost six years now, attending the university,
had seen members of all the Pelted species and almost all the
aliens besides, including humanity. He'd listened to the sound
of multiple languages, struggled through the customs of at least
three major races, and considered himself cosmopolitan for one
of his race. But never in his life would he have thought to meet
one of the Eldritch. They weren't just rare, they were . . . well . . .
mythical.

But he was being paced by one, and nothing about this Jahir
Seni Galare dispelled the fairy tale feel of the stories of the reclu-
sive species. He was taller than any humanoid Vasiht'h knew, at
least a head and a half taller than Vasiht'h himself (and probably
closer to two). Though he shared a similar face and body to the
humans Vasiht'h had met, the Eldritch's frame was more attenu-
ated, and his movements had a finish that suggested training:
dance, maybe, or deportment? Except that his body language was
so minimalist it drew the eye immediately, like a puzzle begging
to be finished.

He wore clothes not unlike some of the plantigrade Pelted,

but unless Vasiht'h was mistaken those garments had never seen a genie: someone had hand-stitched them, he was sure. There were other signs of wealth too: a jeweled ring on one long hand, a strand of gems braided into the hair—and there was a lot of the hair, a straight satin fall to the Eldritch's ribs—even the messenger bag slung from shoulder to hip looked expensive.

In anyone else, Vasiht'h would have wondered if this was some pampered lord. But not in someone who'd faced him across a jump rope with eyes that made a lie of his mask-smooth face, eyes that had sparkled at the chance to delight a group of children. And even now, walking down the sidewalk toward the library and the apartments there, the Eldritch was looking around him with too much interest for a jaded personality.

No, this was something special. And Vasiht'h had stumbled right into it. Truly, the Goddess loved a good coincidence.

The apartments came into view far too soon. Or maybe not soon enough. Vasiht'h couldn't decide what excited him more, the thought of having a chance to get to know this alien in a quiet apartment over a cup of kerinne, or taking him all over the campus and deciphering the subtle signs of curiosity and wonder on that reserved face. Speaking of which, the Eldritch was wearing a look like that now.

———— ∞∞∞ ————

"It's because the campus has grown," Vasiht'h said. When Jahir glanced at him, he said, "You've got this . . . look in your eye. Like you're puzzled. Am I right? Your facial expressions are really minimalist compared to Pelted or human norms."

"I—yes." Jahir stopped, looked down at the other. "How . . ."

"I've been in the xenopsych program for a year already," Vasiht'h said. "It's part of what I'm supposed to be learning, right? Humanoid body language. They'll teach you too, you'll see." He resumed walking up the lane. "It's up here, we're in apartment four. Anyway, the campus used to be smaller, but it's grown a lot, and as it has they've added more housing. That's why it's scattered all over campus. This was one of the first built for the medical campus, so it's the closest to a lot of the buildings." He grinned. "Everyone fights to get into these. I won the lottery last year."

The apartments were astonishing things, by Jahir's standards: stripped of any ornament save large windows, they were single-story buildings, each with two entrances. He could divine nothing of the interior from the exteriors, which were block-shaped and obscured by climbing vines; he found the architecture mysterious, accustomed as he was to the Eldritch's rococo styling.

Vasiht'h approached the door and then paused. "Here, see if they've set the code for you yet."

"The code?" Jahir asked.

"Try to open the door . . . do that by waving your hand in front of it."

Determined not to make the puzzled face again, Jahir offered the door his hand. It opened for him with a chime, and he pulled his hand back, surprised.

"It recognizes your biosign," Vasiht'h said. "Which is good, means they processed the housing change already. Anyway, go on in . . . your room's on the left. Cadia left several weeks ago so it's already empty."

Jahir stepped directly from the door into a high-ceilinged great room that segued into a kitchen, set off by a counter/bar. The back wall of the kitchen was composed entirely of a bank of windows, floor to very high ceiling. To the left he found a hall broad enough for another of those windows, and built into it was a reading nook, complete with bookshelves. The door at the end of the hall opened on a small room with a bunk on the right and a desk on the left; after the opulence and echoing emptiness of his family home, he found the room's size strangely appealing. It was barely the size of an Eldritch closet, but it felt more complete somehow, in itself. He set his bags down and thought he could be quite content here.

"The bathroom's shared," Vasiht'h said, peeking in. "I'll show you."

The bathroom was indeed shared, off the great room to the right. A skylight, rather than a window, illumined a sunken tub; there was some sort of cube as well, with falling water—Jahir paid attention to the controls as Vasiht'h explained them, hoping he'd remember how to use the thing—and indoor plumbing as well, something he'd come to expect from the Alliance on the trip here. It still struck him as miraculous, how everything always worked when used, and how none of the Alliance's citizens expected it could be otherwise.

It was a small suite to be sharing with a stranger, but Jahir found it oddly comfortable. The great room had a short couch, a chair, and a strange nest-like arrangement of pillows on the floor, all arranged facing a fireplace, and it felt cozy, even though the kitchen not fifteen feet away was flooded with sunlight. How they'd partitioned it so effectively without walls, Jahir had no notion. But he was glad to sit and rest a moment.

"So, house rules," Vasiht'h said. "You can come in my room, but knock first, and if you borrow something please put it back when you're done. I like to cook, but I won't do all the work—the person who cooks doesn't do dishes or do the grocery shopping. Cadia and I used to switch off with that every other day. And your friends are welcome anytime. Just tell them to keep the noise down, we share a wall with another duplex."

Jahir said, "I'll bear that in mind."

"Overwhelmed a little, I'm guessing?" Vasiht'h said, and smiled. "Don't worry, it'll sort itself out. As my grandmother used to tell me, one paw at a time." He stretched. "Thirsty?"

"A little, yes," Jahir said. "Have you anything warm? It's a touch raw out."

"We have kerinne, hot cocoa, tea—mostly herbals, I haven't checked lately—and I might have some coffee left. Cadia was a bigger coffee drinker than I am."

"Kerinne is . . . ?"

"A cinnamon drink made with cooked cream," Vasiht'h said. "I was going to make myself some, you can try mine."

"Thank you," Jahir said. "I'll have the coffee, then, and a taste of what you're having."

He closed his eyes, heard the Glaseah pad off the round braided rug and onto the wooden floors. The weather was cooler than he'd expected, and a little more humid to boot, but he hadn't expected to be quite so tired so quickly. It was probably the excitement of the new situation, and the worry over the housing issue. No doubt a good night's rest would put paid to it.

He smelled the coffee before he heard Vasiht'h's footfalls approaching and sat up to receive the cup.

"I put it here . . . right?" Vasiht'h said, setting it on the little table next to the chair. "Because we're not supposed to touch."

"Yes, thank you," Jahir said, surprised.

"And a little kerinne," Vasiht'h finished, adding a glass cup alongside it. The drink was an appealing pale orange, and smelled fragrantly of spices. Jahir sniffed it, sipped, felt the hairs rise along the back of his neck. Vasiht'h chuckled at his pause. "Too strong?"

"I . . . wasn't expecting it to be quite so rich," Jahir admitted. "You can drink an entire mug of this?"

"I can drink two or three, I'm afraid," Vasiht'h said, feathered ears fanning downward. "Which isn't such a good thing, since after two or three even I begin to feel a little like I've eaten a lead weight. Some people water it down, but it's supposed to be made like this. Oh, I forgot to ask . . . do you take milk? Should I have brought honey or sugar? Or a lemon?"

Jahir chased the kerinne down with a sip of the coffee. "This is fine." He smiled. "So. Second year in xenopsychology?"

"Starting next week," Vasiht'h agreed, settling back down on the cushions.

"And have you any advice for this first year student?"

Vasiht'h huffed, disturbing the steam over the cup. "Have a better idea of what specialty you want to pursue before you get too far into the program. I've spent most of two semesters trying to figure that out and it's not doing anything for my academic career."

"What did you think, initially?" Jahir asked.

"That's the problem," Vasiht'h said ruefully. "I didn't think, at all. I just started taking whatever classes looked interesting to me. If I'd been more focused, I'd have finished my degree within three years. As it is, it'll be more like three and a half . . . if I can decide what I want . . . !" He sipped from his cup. "What about you? Do you have any ideas?"

"Not entirely," Jahir said. "I am under the impression they will assign me an advisor during orientation?"

"They will, yes," Vasiht'h said.

"Then I imagine I will discuss it with him."

Vasiht'h nodded. "Tomorrow, then." He rubbed his fingers on the handle of his mug. "About the children . . . we left them with the impression—"

"—that we'd be visiting?" Jahir said. "Is there any reason we can't?"

"I don't know," Vasiht'h admitted.

"Then we'll have to find out."

The Glaseah studied him, head tilted. "And . . . you want to do that. Go back. Play cards and board games with some children you haven't met before. Terminally ill ones, even."

"Don't you?" Jahir asked.

Vasiht'h paused, then laughed. "All right. Yes, that was well said." He grinned. "I think we're going to get along pretty well, we two." He got up. "I'll let you unpack and rest. I'm sure it was a long trip in."

"Thank you," Jahir said, and the other left him to the quiet, and the contemplation of the cold hearth. Did anyone use it, he wondered? It was clean, and there was no wood stacked next to it. He'd have to ask. If the weather was this cool in early fall, he could only imagine what it would be like in winter.

After a time he stood and brought his cup to the kitchen, rinsing it in a sink that magically seemed aware of his hands without the use of any handle or control. From there he repaired to his room and began to unpack, mindful of his fatigue. Clothes, the least ornate or leading he could find: he'd studied the prevailing fashion of the Alliance Core in the viseos provided during his distance studies and it was far less ostentatious than anything the typical Eldritch would wear. A few precious books, one entirely of musical scores . . . he had not brought any instruments, guessing he wouldn't have the time to use them, but reading the scores would allow him to replay the songs in his mind. One weapon: the House dagger, the only part of the set that by law he could not leave behind.

It was very little, really, to have brought for all that he'd abandoned. His mother had not fought him when he'd revealed his plan to leave; she was a Galare and too aware, perhaps, of the boldness and curiosity that seemed to come with the blood-line. That it left her alone on the homeworld had not seemed to disturb her, either—when he'd asked, she'd said only that he and his brother were more likely to come to harm at home than they were in the Alliance. Certainly the Alliance's medicine could have saved their father's life; Eldritch died regularly of things that would probably appall Alliance healers.

Such things were part of what had spurred him on his way. What did the rest of the Galare line know about the Alliance that he had not yet learned, skimming an education off the palace's Well feed? Of all the Houses on his world, the Galare had produced the majority of those who'd dared to leave. His own brother had left decades ago, despite being younger than Jahir. His cousin Sediryl, likewise, was already living on some far-flung starbase. The Queen most certainly had been off-world, or he would never have had passage himself, for he'd been sped on her courier service.

What was it about the Alliance? That the Eldritch fostered ties to it so carefully, and denied them with its second breath? His mother thought it safer than home; the rest of his race thought it so dangerous they'd joined with past queens to require a Veil of lies and silences between their world and their ally.

Jahir had no idea which notion was right. Preparing for bed, he thought the answer was most likely both.

CHAPTER 3

"AH, YOU'RE A MORNING PERSON," Vasiht'h said, rubbing his eyes as he padded into the great room.

"Tolerably so," Jahir said, still searching the cabinets for something he could use to make food. He glanced across the room at the Glaseah, who looked rumpled despite being naked—was the term proper, he wondered, for someone who had a centauroid conformation? Strange to realize he didn't perceive Vasiht'h as naked despite his lack of clothes. "I found the mugs, but I fear I've not had any luck with anything else."

"Food, you mean," Vasiht'h said. "I haven't been to the market yet this week . . . I was off-world visiting family during intersession." He yawned. "If you're willing to wait for me to shower, we can walk to breakfast. I can drop you off at orientation on my way to my major professor's office."

"That sounds fine," Jahir said. "You should teach me the use of the appliances, though. At your convenience."

"At mine, you mean, if I don't want to be constantly doing things for you?" Vasiht'h said, amused. He joined Jahir in the kitchen, scratching his back where his torso joined the centauroid lower body. Unwashed Glaseah smelled interesting . . . a little musty, like an old book, but warmer. Jahir thought of horses and found the association pleasing. "You found the mugs. The coffee's here . . . and this thing will press it for you."

"I am surprised there is no magical device that makes fresh food from thin air," Jahir said, watching the Glaseah's hands. In person, three fingers and a thumb looked both more natural and less than it had on viseo.

"Oh, there is," Vasiht'h said, pushing the press over. "Go ahead, try it. But genies aren't terribly energy-efficient. You see them a lot on starships, they've got those massive engines and power's easier for them to come by than space. But even they supplement with stores." At Jahir's stare, he said, "When I was an undergrad I roomed with a Seersa who was retired Fleet. He was here for a second education."

"I see," Jahir murmured.

"There," Vasiht'h said. "Coffee. I'll be out in fifteen minutes."

"Very good," Jahir said, and poured himself a cup. He occupied himself with carefully disassembling the press and rinsing it. It was strange to do his own chores, but calming. The principles of stewardship had been inculcated in him from early childhood, and cleaning helped him feel he was caring for the suite—and that made it his, in some part, in a way that the invisible processes of the university could not.

———

"So, one thing I should warn you," Vasiht'h said as he stepped out of the apartment, now clean, brushed, and wearing a short red vest and a pair of caramel-brown saddlebags on his lower body.

Jahir followed him into a cool, clear day with a wet breeze that tousled the edges of his pale hair. "What's that?"

"Not too many espers enter the program," Vasiht'h said, starting down the sidewalk. Jahir followed at a measured pace. He was sore today, though he didn't remember doing enough walking to merit it. "In fact, I was the only one until you came along. That makes some of the staff a little nervous. Not like they're worried you're going to go reading your patients' minds

or anything, but . . . there's not really much written down, proce-
dure-wise, for dealing with people like us."

"You?" Jahir asked, surprised. "Read thoughts?"

"Almost all Glaseah can," Vasiht'h said. He grinned. "Don't
worry, I'm not reading yours."

Jahir snorted. "I should hope I could tell."

"You could," Vasiht'h said. "Anyway. They're going to know,
looking at you, that you're an esper because . . . well, you're
Eldritch. Be ready for that to fluster them."

"I assure you, I am already acquainted with the typical reactions of Alliance citizens," Jahir murmured.

Vasiht'h snorted. "I bet you are. Tired of being stared at
already, I'm sure."

"A touch. Perhaps."

"We'll have to take you shopping then," Vasiht'h said. "Your
clothes don't help. They're good for the climate—I'm guessing
you get cold? No fur and all that?—but even people who can't
recognize hand-made work can tell when something looks higher
quality than the norm."

"And have you divined everything about me just in half a day
of knowing me?" Jahir asked, unsure whether to be alarmed or
intrigued.

"I haven't even gotten started yet!" Vasiht'h said with a
laugh. "But tell me at any point if I get annoying. I don't mean it.
I'm just as intrigued as anybody else, I'm just doing my best not
to be quite so obnoxious about it. Which reminds me . . . are you
attached?"

"Am I what?" Jahir asked, bemused.

"Attached," Vasiht'h said. "Married, engaged, entangled . . .
you know. Involved."

Jahir folded his arms behind his back to disguise his discomfort with the question. "No."

"Are you interested?" Vasiht'h asked, a question Jahir would
ordinarily have found appalling, save that from his roommate's
expression he wasn't asking from some prurient curiosity.

"Why are you worried?" he asked.

"Well, you're going to be awfully pretty to a lot of people here," Vasiht'h said. "If it hasn't occurred to you yet, I thought I'd warn you."

"You mean to tell me people will find me attractive?" Jahir asked, startled. "I'm not even the same species as anyone on campus."

"That won't matter one bit," Vasiht'h said, shaking his head. "In some cases, it will just make you more attractive. Especially if you're not interested."

For several strides, Jahir said nothing . . . only stared at the sidewalk, the foliage, the thin blue sky. "I think . . . perhaps . . . I should have somewhat fewer shocks for a bit. Tell me where we're going to eat."

"Ah . . ." Vasiht'h smiled. "It's called Tea and Cinnamon. You'll like it."

———— ∞ ————

Tea and Cinnamon was nestled into the corner of one of the medical buildings, a narrow space with wooden floors and paneling, and a second floor tightly wedged above the counter where delectable pastries sat on doilies in display cases. The furniture and tables differed wildly from one another, and from the patrons lounging, sitting, standing or perching at them Jahir imagined they'd been designed for a multi-species campus.

The scent of cinnamon did in fact form the prevalent aroma of the shop, though the wood and sunlight also added to the perfume. He found it entirely charming. The food was also good: he had some sort of egg baked into pastry with diced herbs, a cup of mint and honey tea, and tried, at Vasiht'h's insistence, some sort of sweet mousse made from pureed nuts that reminded him of chestnuts.

"Eat more," Vasiht'h said, pushing half the mousse over. "You'll be doing a lot of walking and you're a stick as it is. Are all Eldritch so stretched out?"

"Are all Glaseah so compact?" Jahir asked, amused.

Vasiht'h patted his withers. "Comes with the genome.

Anseahla's a bit heavier gravity than some of the other Core worlds, so we were engineered with that in mind. As best the RaGEs could manage, anyway." At Jahir's lifted head, he said, "Racial Genetic Engineers. If you haven't gotten through the history of the Alliance . . . well, they won't teach you that in grad school. But I've got a few good books if you want to read about it. You'll probably want to if you end up working out here. Which I imagine you will be?"

"Have I said so?" Jahir asked.

"No, but you're in school for xenopsychology," Vasiht'h said with a grin. "And on Seersana. I have to imagine you didn't come all this way to learn about alien behavior just to leave."

"No," Jahir said. "No, that would be somewhat of a waste."

"Exactly," Vasiht'h said. "Eat the rest of that, please."

He did so, to be polite, and because he found it didn't fill him as much as he'd expected. It also allowed him to be silent while his new roommate talked, and that suited him . . . for Vasiht'h's question had caught him off guard. He had never really contemplated the aftermath of his education. He'd come to the university to learn, certainly. But learning did not necessarily imply application. By his family's standards, he already had work: he was the heir to the Seni Galare. He wouldn't be needed in that capacity for some time, God and Lady willing, but at some point he would be recalled to become the steward of his family's lands, people and fortune.

In fact, until Vasiht'h had suggested it, the thought that he could do aught else—that he had the time to be any number of things—had never occurred to him, and was so stunning he was relieved for the distraction of the food and the tea that the Glaseah refilled for him. He would have several Pelted lifetimes to fill with a vocation, before he had to return to discharge his responsibilities.

What could he do, with several mortal lifetimes?

What did he want to do?

------⊗⊗⊗------

After concluding their breakfast, Jahir followed the Glaseah out of the building into a cool, damp morning, now advanced. Vasiht'h squinted against the light, pointing. "That building there, in the distance? That's where you'll be going. Orientation starts with a walking tour, then they'll bring you back to the admin building to meet some of the program directors and assign you an advisor. You'll probably be done by late afternoon."

"Sounds promising," Jahir said. "And I thank you for the directions. And breakfast."

"You can pay next time," Vasiht'h said, grinning up at him. "Once I teach you how to use money here."

"I take it the process is as enigmatic as the one that permitted a woman behind a desk halfway across campus to teach your front door to open to me."

"Exactly so," Vasiht'h said, and laughed. "I'll talk to you tonight."

"Go well," Jahir said, and tasked himself to the same.

———⚬⚬⚬———

Orientation involved more people in one space than Jahir was accustomed to seeing in such close quarters. At home, a crowd this size would have required a hall three times the breadth of the auditorium they were herded into. He hung back near the wall, watching the students milling together. Some two hundred of them at least, at a guess, and of varying species: mostly Pelted, but some number of humans as well. He saw none of the true aliens of the Alliance, but from what he'd read they were rare . . . less so than Eldritch, but nonetheless.

He was careful to keep himself apart. He'd had his share of accidental contacts on the trip to Seersana and had no desire to invite more of them. There were students who glanced his way, but he kept far enough back to seem just another humanoid shape . . . a little taller than average, but not worth more than a glance. That wouldn't hold once they started walking, he thought, but it protected him for now.

Orientation began, as he had half expected, with a speech

by the associate dean of the College of Medicine, of which the xenopsychology school was a part. He was one of the Seersa, the foxine Pelted who'd given the world its name, a lean and grizzled elder with salt-and-pepper fur and the intensity of a medic. Jahir listened to his monologue while marveling that he was actually here . . . sitting in a chair in an auditorium filled with aliens. The woman in front of him had silk-furred ears that were trembling from the effort of catching every word. The ends of the rows had spaces for centauroids to recline, or the more avian aliens to perch. He was, very definitively, no longer home, and if the stress of his danger at being so crowded was giving him a head- ache, well . . . it was worth it, for the newness of it. There was nothing new about home. Not for him, not for the generations before him. The Eldritch were dedicated to the preservation of their chosen ways. One did not deviate. It was uncouth.

For the walking tour, the mass was split into ten groups of a manageable fifteen to twenty students each. Jahir's guide was a staff member, another of the shorter Pelted races, the feline Karaka'A. He tried to stay in the back of the group, but was very aware that he garnered at least as many stares as the landmarks their guide was describing. He did his best to ignore their curios- ity. It helped that the campus was broad and beautiful and, most importantly, fascinating. The Rhone medical library, a branch of the university's larger system, was taller than a cathedral and had the stained glass windows of a church. The administrative building, where he and Vasiht'h had gone to eat breakfast, had mosaics depicting all the Alliance homeworlds—not counting his own, of course. The classrooms had been designed in honey- combs around gracious gardens or courtyards, rising above them to overlook a lake with a bridge that led to the teaching hospital and the children's hospital, where he and Vasiht'h had met.

What would it be like, to find all this familiar instead of new? Within a few months, this place would no longer look strange to him. The thought was astonishing.

The advisor to whom he was assigned was another of the vaguely vulpine Seersa, a woman this time. Despite the fact that she was most probably a third his age, her brown pelt had already gone partially gray. Her eyes were a luminous sap green, and she glanced at him with them, then flicked her ears sideways. "Well, here is something new in the universe. Have a seat. Lord Seni Galare, your file says? How do you prefer to be called?"

"Jahir will do," he said, sitting across from her. He would have thought the technologically-advanced Alliance would have put paid to papers, but her desk was cluttered not only with data tablet and displays, but books and slips and notepads.

"Jahir then," she said, glancing at what he presumed must be his student file on one of the floating displays. He could just see an image of himself from the shoulders up in reverse, a translucent rectangle in white and blue. "I'm Khallis Mekora, and barring any catastrophe I'll be your graduate advisor until you've completed your education here." She peered at him past the display, ears flicking forward again. "You can request a new advisor at any time, of course."

"That not being one of the catastrophes," he surmised.

She chuckled, a warm, husky burr that he decided he liked. "Not unless you want it to be. But I'm used to dramatics, being surrounded by young people all day. You'd have to work hard to make it rise above the general noise level."

"I'm not fond of displays," Jahir said. "So no fears, Missus Mekora."

"Please, Khallis is fine," she said, scanning the rest of his record and then sitting back in her chair. "So, Jahir. First year student. You've gotten the basic information on the program, presumably?"

"I have," he said. "But I would appreciate a précis from someone with more experience delivering it."

"Right," she said, and split the display with her hands, pushing them apart and making a stirring motion with a finger until its orientation switched to face him. It truly was uncomfortably like magic, these intangible projections. "The xenopsychology program is part of the College of Medicine here, which is not always how it's done. We do it that way, though, and it affects how the program's run. There are three concentrations: clinical, research, medical. They all share a common core of classes in the first semester, but by the second semester they start forking . . . so you'll want to have a notion of where you're going by then. Clinical track will require a single year internship before graduation; you can take that in parts or all at once. Once you're done, you'll have fulfilled the license requirements for practice as a therapist on the core worlds; all you have to do is apply for the certificate. The research track doesn't require practicum, but you'll have to write a thesis; students completing the research track are expected to continue on into the doctoral program.

"The medical track requires a two-year residency at the conclusion of the coursework, and at the conclusion to that you have to take a separate test to be licensed as a healer-assist, at which point we also graduate you. That's a bit backwards from how the healers handle residencies, but it works for us." She spread her hands. "In general, I tell students: if you want to spend most of your time with people in a cozy office, take the clinical track. If you want to spend most of your time in a lab or in front of a display, take the research track. And if you want to spend most of your time in a hospital, take the medical track."

"But I don't have to decide yet," Jahir murmured.

"No," Khallis agreed. "Though it's easier on you if you know sooner rather than later. All students have a graduation term limit—for our program, you have five years maximum—so you don't have an indefinite period to horse around. Plus, the registration for internships can get competitive, so it's good to know in advance what you want to apply for."

"I see," he said. "I'll give the matter serious consideration."

"Good," she said. "In the meantime, let's see about signing you up for your first few classes. I hope you like working hard, alet."

"I assure you, ma'am, I did not come here to do otherwise."

"So, have you made a decision yet?"

Vasiht'h sighed, blowing the forelock up off one eye. "Would you be surprised if I said no?"

"No," Sehvi said with a laugh. "That would be just like you."

He was sitting in his room facing the wall, which had a virtual window open on his sister's room on Tam-ley, where she was studying reproductive genetics. Sehvi was one of his eleven siblings, and the closest to him; despite the expense, they tried to find opportunities for real-time communication at least once every other week. Vasiht'h was an avid letter-writer and kept in communication with all his extended family, but Sehvi was special.

"I still have time," Vasiht'h said. "To decide, I mean. There's no rush."

"So you have made a decision," she said. "You want to be an eternal student. Mother would approve."

"Mother would most certainly not approve," Vasiht'h said, making a face. "Given how often we've heard the 'students who never leave the university, using up resources' speech." He sighed. "I'm still planning her route. More or less."

"Third generation professor," Sehvi said. "You can be Dami's heir and I'll be Tapa's." She cocked her head. "Except I never really saw you as a professor, ariihir."

"I could do it," Vasiht'h said. "As long as it wasn't pure science, like our father. I don't have patience for that. I like people."

"Maybe so," she said. "But I can't imagine how much use a psychology professor with no real-world experience would be. You should go out and do something with your degree before you start chasing tenure. Don't you think?"

"Maybe?" Vasiht'h sighed and rubbed his face. "To be honest, Sehvi, I haven't thought that far ahead." He made a face. "It really is true what Bret'hesk said to me at my going-away party . . . I'm the least deterministic of the family. Even Hatti has more of a notion what to do with her life at fifteen than I do now."

"Try to take Bret's comments in context," she said. "He's so focused he's positively grim . . . and he takes his responsibility as the eldest of us seriously. He just wants you to be happy."

"And well-off," Vasiht'h muttered.

"Having enough money to eat is not a bad thing!" she said with a laugh. "Especially once you start feeding kits—" At his expression, she held up her hands. "No pressure! We're both underage for that."

"Goddess," Vasiht'h muttered. "I'd like to know what I'm doing with my life before I start having children I need to advise on the matter."

"Well, like you said, you have time," she answered, grinning. "A little anyway. How's everything else going?"

"Fairly well. In fact . . ." He smiled and shook his head. "You won't believe who I got for a new roommate."

"This ought to be good," she said, putting her cheek in her hand. "Tell me."

"An Eldritch!"

"A . . . what?" she said, sitting up. "You're not pulling my tail?"

"No!" he said. "And yes! That was my reaction too. I found him in a hospital parking lot—"

"And you took him home like a lost peltsnake?" she said, laughing. "Oh, Vasiht'h."

"I know," he said. "I have a talent!"

"You do, I think," she said. Her reply was so considering he began to ask her to elaborate, but then he heard the door. "That's him now, actually. I should go be sociable. Catch you in a couple of weeks, ariishir?"

"Absolutely, ariihir. Kisses."

He smiled and waved the connection closed before padding to the door and peeking through it. His new roommate was setting down his bag. "Hey, hello," Vasiht'h said. "How'd Orientation go?"

"Well enough," the Eldritch said, straightening. "A bit tiring, perhaps."

"It can be a long walk," Vasiht'h agreed, entering the great room. He squinted up at the taller male. Reading Jahir's face was difficult, given his self-possession, but something about the tension in his jaw and around his eyes suggested discomfort. "Are you entirely sure you're all right?"

"I should be," Jahir said. "Though I should probably eat."

"I'll get you something, just sit—"

"I had better," Jahir said, sounding confused as he swayed and then grabbed for the arm of the chair.

Vasiht'h paused, then lunged for him as he fell. "Goddess!"

It was like watching some amazingly tall tree collapse, and he was too late to brake the Eldritch's fall. Vasiht'h heard an alarming thump and then saw a sprawl of white limbs and hair on the dark rug. "Emergency channel! Get me a healer!" He dove for Jahir's side and stopped when he realized he shouldn't be touching the Eldritch. Except he was unconscious. How was that supposed to work?

The door opened too many moments later for two Seersa in the uniforms of emergency personnel, along with Lucrezia from next door. He almost didn't notice her while answering the barrage of questions from the technicians, who examined the Eldritch with instruments before gently turning him onto his side.

Lucrezia crouched next to him and whistled. "Wow. A real live Eldritch. Congratulations, Vasiht'h. I might even be jealous."

"You aren't," he said, trying not to fidget. "Is he okay?"

She glanced toward the technicians, then flicked her ears back. "If he was in serious danger they'd be moving a lot more quickly, and there would be a lot more red tags on the sensor readings. I don't see any from here." She nudged him with an elbow. "When were you planning on telling me?"

Vasiht'h wrinkled his nose at her. "Luci, I'm a little distracted?"

She laughed. "Relax. Look, he's coming around now."

—————◆◆◆—————

Jahir was not entirely sure he'd woken when he opened his eyes; his mind was clouded with unfamiliar thoughts, memories edging against his, overlapping, giving him a medical knowledge he didn't have. He squinted and twisted his head away, as from a too-bright sun.

"Mr. Seni Galare? Can you say something?"

"Stop touching me," he managed in a rasp.

"If you won't fall forward—"

"Let go of him." That voice he recognized at least: Vasiht'h, sounding agitated.

The hands left him, and took with them the primacy of their thoughts. Jahir shook them off with difficulty and evaluated himself. He was . . . on his side. The rug was flush to his cheek, brown and rust and yellow ochre braids. He closed his eyes for a moment, breathed in. "I appear to be on the floor."

"You fainted," one of the strangers said.

"And bumped your head on the way down," Vasiht'h added, worried.

"I fainted," Jahir repeated, finding the possibility astonishing.

"You're not built for this gravity," one of the strangers said, packing his instruments. "You should make an appointment so they can instruct you on proper acclimation techniques."

"Failure to do so can result in more serious injury," the other added. "We encourage you to report to the clinic at your earliest convenience."

"He fainted because of the gravity?" Vasiht'h asked, ears flicking down. "You can do that?"

"It's the exertion," said a woman sitting beside him on the floor. "You can get light-headed because you're working harder than your system was designed to."

"If you have any other symptoms, check yourself into the clinic," one of the strangers said.

"I'll consider it," Jahir murmured, and they left. He sat up cautiously, touching his head. He wasn't sure if the ache there was the fall or the intrusion of other people's minds. There was a tension in his wrist that belonged to someone using an instrument he'd never touched. He twitched his shoulders and made a face. "Vasiht'h?"

"Here, alet," Vasiht'h said, beginning to rise and then sitting again abruptly, digging his paws into the rug. "I'm sorry, I . . . I probably jumped for you too late. I wasn't sure if I should touch you, and then you smacked the chair arm on the way down—"

Jahir held up a hand to still him. "No harm done."

"For now," the woman said. "But you absolutely should get to the clinic." She grinned. "Lucrezia. I'm in the building next to you."

"She's a second-year medical student," Vasiht'h added. "Um, maybe I should make tea. Coffee? Wine?"

"Do you have wine?" Lucrezia asked, dry.

"No," Vasiht'h said.

"Good," she said. "Because I wouldn't give it to someone who'd just hit his head."

"The wine's not for him," Vasiht'h said. "It's for me!"

"Tea," Jahir murmured. "Sounds very good. Thank you."

"I'll get it," Vasiht'h said, scrambling to his feet.

Lucrezia, sitting across from him, looked like a leopard made bipedal, with all the sensual beauty of the creature, ragged black spots on lemon-yellow fur. She had large dark eyes, heavily lashed, and a tilt to her mouth that made her look perpetually amused. Harat-Shar, he thought, if he remembered right. The Alliance's hedonists? He wouldn't have imagined one in a medical profession.

"I'm not going to eat you," she said, showing teeth in her grin.

"I didn't imagine so," Jahir said, and carefully sat up with his back to the side of the sofa. He stretched his legs out and closed his eyes, head back.

"But I meant it, about going to the doctor," she said, voice serious. "If they're right about the diagnosis, you're going to be susceptible to problems unless you take precautions."

"Could I not learn those precautions from a search on the u-banks?" he asked, eyes still closed.

"You could," she said, and he could almost hear her scowl. "But it wouldn't be the same as receiving trained medical advice."

"Am I correct in presuming that such personnel would be

required to keep a medical file on me?" he said, opening his eyes.

"You're in the Alliance," she said. "They've already got a file on you."

A file, he thought, that was subject to constant editing, though she wouldn't know that. It had been work to get the student record to stick—the readings the two technicians just took would probably only last a few hours before the censors required by the treaty found them. There were very few Eldritch abroad, and all of them were being followed by those censors . . . the only place they couldn't easily reach was Fleet's record data-base. The Eldritch Veil had a long arm.

"I'll consider it," he said.

She sighed out, exasperated, and stood as Vasiht'h came by with two tea cups. "Going already?"

"I have studying to do," she said, glancing at Jahir. "And since I doubt he's going to let me seduce him, I might as well do something productive with my night."

"I . . . don't think there's any hope of that, no," Vasiht'h said, ears flipping back.

She shook her head, poked him gently. "Talk him into it, will you? It's important."

Vasiht'h stared after her as she left, then sat across from Jahir, careful not to touch him as he set the tea cup by his side. "Talk you into what? Going to the doctor?"

"Or some such," Jahir murmured, thinking that would be the end of the matter. So he was surprised at his roommate's outburst, perhaps as surprised as Vasiht'h himself.

"You are going, aren't you? Because if you don't, I'm not sure what I'd do. I'd never be sure if you're about to collapse, what to do about it if you do, whether I can even touch you if you're unconscious—"

"—don't do that," Jahir said.

"You see?" Vasiht'h said, agitated. "If you don't go to the clinic, you're going to pass out again at some point because you won't know what to do to keep from having these problems. And then what? Next time you fall and crack your head for true and put yourself in a coma."

"That sounds unlikely," Jahir murmured, but the residue of the touch of the technicians whispered in him, hissing distracting objections.

Vasiht'h just folded his arms.

"I have worried you," Jahir said.

"Yes!" Vasiht'h said.

Jahir suppressed a sigh. "Very well, then. Tomorrow."

"Early tomorrow," Vasiht'h said.

"Early tomorrow," Jahir said, resigned. And because Vasiht'h glowering was unpleasant, he said, "For now perhaps you can tell me about our neighbors while we make dinner."

"While I make dinner, and you sit here and rest," Vasiht'h said.

"While I sit here and rest," Jahir said, and left the Glaseah mollified. How strange these outworlders were, to often be so . . . straightforward. He would have to remember that, to seriously entertain the notion that what they said and showed on their faces might actually be true.

CHAPTER 4

THE FOLLOWING MORNING, Jahir accepted directions to the clinic and reluctantly set out to follow them. Intellectually he knew any medical records the clinic accumulated would be erased at some point, but he still felt it was his duty to maintain the Veil. So it was with every one of the few Eldritch who'd left the homeworld, as had been patiently explained by members of the Queen's government.

It made him wonder, somewhat, that the Queen herself had not been present at any of these explanations, despite the rarity of one of their number leaving the world and the supposed importance of maintaining the secrecy about their species.

No, he wouldn't have gone, but that Vasiht'h's comment had struck him deeply. It was a grave discourtesy to the alien to ask him to live with the uncertainty of a roommate with an untreated medical issue. Jahir had been so deeply trained to bow to duty that he found it hard to deviate from it. And part of duty was consideration for others. That he was not sure yet how to express that consideration to people with alien needs did not excuse him from trying; and certainly if he was told outright he had no excuse.

So he took himself to the clinic, stepping into its waiting area with a sense of trepidation . . . and wonder. How clean everything was. How spacious. The chairs were all in perfect condition, the cushions without wear, the people friendly and professional. The Hinichi who took his name seemed to know not to touch him. He was escorted without noticeable delay to a private room with an examination bed, several chairs, and a display for his use if he needed distraction, which he didn't. Or rather he did, but from his own curiosity, not from boredom. Doctors on his own world made house calls, and rarely had much aid to give those in their care.

The door opened for a youth in a coat designed to make her look polished and trustworthy—that much was common to both their cultures, he supposed, even if the Alliance version was less fussy. She was one of the felinesque species, the shorter Karaka'A, a lovely one with a gray mask on cream fur and pristine blue eyes, pale as opals.

"Lord Seni Galare," she said, betraying her youth only by the slight hesitation before addressing him. "My name is Healer Shelbie Narrows. I'm an intern here at the university health clinic. I see you've come in following an incident with the emergency medical service?"

"That's right," he said, fascinated by her professionalism.

"Healer KindlesFlame will be in to go over your case with you in a moment," she said. "Would you mind telling me about the incident, in your own words?"

KindlesFlame, he thought. What an astonishing name. Folding his hands on his knee he proceeded to relate his experience to her, what little of it he could remember. When he had finished, she said, "And prior to this, did you have any other similar symptoms? Fatigue? Dizziness?"

"Fatigue," he said. "I thought nothing of it. New experiences are often tiring."

"Yes, they are, aren't they?" she said, with a suddenly lopsided smile that made her look all her few years. He found it endearing and disarming, the reminder of how young everyone off his world was. "Could you sit here so I can check your readings?"

He obliged her, watching the display change and wondering what she was divining from the graphs. Like another language, he thought. His curiosity, never far from the surface, rose at the suggestion.

"Thank you," she said. "If you'll wait here a moment, I'll return with Healer KindlesFlame."

"Very well," he said. Once she had gone he pushed himself off the bed and studied the readings more carefully. They were labeled: blood pressure, saturation of gases in the bloodstream, pulse and respiratory rate, body temperature . . . weight, height, body fat composition, so many statistics, in fact, that he was still reading them when the masked Karaka'An returned with her senior. KindlesFlame was one of the tall foxine Tam-illee. He had a distinguished, self-contained air, a thoughtful face, shrewd eyes that did not quiet conceal their kindness.

"Lord Seni Galare," he said. "I'm Lafayette KindlesFlame, the director of the clinic. Thank you for coming in."

"Pardon?" Jahir said, bemused. "Have I done something that deserves gratitude?"

The Tam-illee chuckled. "You have given my staff a great deal of delight. We have seen all the known races and species in space, save two . . . and now, we can reduce that count by one."

"What species remains?" Jahir asked.

"The Chatcaava," offered the intern.

"And it'll be a cold sun in the sky before we'll see one of those, given the likelihood of one enrolling at the university," the healer said. "May I sit?"

"Of course," Jahir said.

KindlesFlame sat on the edge of the bed, one foot on the floor, the other drawn up. "Doctor Narrows tells me you're having issues with the gravity here."

"So I've been told," Jahir said.

"You're just on the cusp of body type that I'd be comfortable leaving unmedicated," KindlesFlame said. "So I'm going to prescribe you the drug regimen we give to light-worlders. It'll help build your bone density and deal with the cardiovascular issues.

You'll be on the course for six months; that's usually long enough to complete the adaptation."

"Six months," Jahir said, astonished. "That short a time?"

"That's actually a long time for an adaptation regimen," KindlesFlame said. "While you're on it, I'd like you to be mindful of your fatigue level, and rest when you're tired. You'll also need to eat more frequently. Healthfully, of course, but you'll need more fuel. An extra snack twice a day should be sufficient."

"More food," Jahir repeated. "Less exercise?"

The healer held up a hand. "Not necessarily. As your body changes, you'll be able to build more muscle, and your body will need regular exercise to complete the cardiovascular changes. But you will want to go about that judiciously. Begin with normal activities, like walking. Within a year you should be ready for more strenuous activities if you care to undertake them. Explain your aims to one of the counselors at the gym, they can design a program for you. I recommend something with low wear on the joints. Swimming, or low-g sports."

"I see," Jahir said.

"I will also issue you a prescription for an anti-inflammatory, for days when the joint pain is bad. You don't have to take them, but they're useful to have if you need them. Healer Narrows, will you put together the pharmaceuticals? And update the case file? Also, put together some information for Lord Seni Galare on the common side effects of the adaptation regimen."

"Yes, sir."

After she'd left, Jahir observed, "You have sent her away."

"I have," KindlesFlame said. "You're a special case which I had to research before entering . . . thus the delay, for which I apologize by the way." He resettled himself on the bed. "The records the emergency technicians had on you are gone already. I assume that's not an accident."

"I'm afraid not," Jahir said.

"I'm not sure you're aware our medical oaths require us to privilege patient autonomy and privacy above many other considerations?" KindlesFlame continued. "We can lock your file, if you're concerned—"

Jahir hesitated, then said, "It is not my decision to make, I fear."

"I see," KindlesFlame said. He inclined his head. "Will this cause you to avoid future visits to the clinic?"

"I . . . will try to avoid it," Jahir said. "Not entirely because of privacy issues. I should prefer not to be ill."

"Of course," the Tam-illee said with a chuckle. "I ask because if that's an issue, I will make you an offer."

"That being?"

"That you call me directly," he said. "And I'll make time for you outside the clinic."

Jahir sat back. "Because . . . ?"

KindlesFlame lifted his brows. "You're a student here, doing masters-level work if your college record's any indication. Tell me your suppositions."

"Because I am the only Eldritch on campus," Jahir said. "Because you're curious about me. Because you suspect if something were to befall me it would cause political difficulties as well as medical and administrative ones."

"Very good," KindlesFlame said, pleased. "You only missed one."

"What's that?" Jahir wondered.

"Why do people become healers, Lord Seni Galare?"

"I . . . presume it's to cure disease and succor the dying," Jahir answered.

"I don't like it when people suffer, particularly if that suffering can be prevented," KindlesFlame said. "If you'll avoid the clinic because of whatever privacy concerns have been mandated, then we'll have to find some other way to keep you healthy."

Such a simple statement, to be so vast and shocking. And beautiful, like poetry, that also. Jahir was not accustomed to altruism on a level so broad it could be applied to strangers. It was not something rewarded among his kind.

"If that's so," he said at last, "perhaps we might be served by . . . a regularly scheduled meeting."

"Lunch, maybe, once a week," KindlesFlame said. "One old man and one young one, talking medicine. We'll let the spectators guess at which is which."

"I'd enjoy the opportunity," Jahir said, realizing he meant it.

"I'll drop you a message, then." KindlesFlame stood. "Healer Narrows will see you out. You shouldn't need to give any additional information to Reception before leaving."

"Thank you," Jahir said.

At the door, the Tam-illee said, "Xenopsychology, ah? Have you chosen a track yet?"

"Not . . . quite," Jahir said.

"Mmm," KindlesFlame said. "They're all good programs. I'm sure you'll get something out of whichever you choose."

After leaving the clinic, Jahir found a bench beside a pond and watched the shadows of leaves sway on the pavement. Such an incredible notion. Only in the Alliance, he thought, was there luxury for such expansiveness of feeling: to be open to strangers, to care for their welfare, to devote oneself to principles. And he was here, in its midst, and there was no need for him to go home anytime soon.

--- ∞ ---

"This," Doctor Palland said severely, "is not a course schedule plan, Vasiht'h. This is not even an attempt at one."

"I know," Vasiht'h said, chagrined.

The Seersa sighed. "Do you even want to graduate? And I mean graduate with a license to practice, because if you keep veering all over the course catalog this way they're going to graduate you just to get you off campus, and you'll have spent five years here with nothing to show for it."

"I know!" Vasiht'h said, ears flattening. He resettled himself on the pillows scattered on the floor in the seating area in his major professor's office. Said professor was behind his desk, as usual, and nearly hidden by stacks of books and data tablets, also as usual. He was one of the natives, a Seersa with a ruddy pelt and champagne-colored ears that had escaped the graying that was beginning to show around his mouth and eyes.

"You know, but . . . ?"

"I know, but everything looks interesting," Vasiht'h finished, lacing his fingers together and trying to look contrite.

Palland pointed at him. "You are not interested in everything. You're not interested enough in any single one thing. And you know that."

"Guilty as charged," Vasiht'h muttered.

Palland sighed and came around the desk, pulling up a chair beside the table. "I don't mean to harangue you, Vasiht'h. You're a hard worker, a good student, and you have a fine brain in that skull. And it's not atypical for students not to have a clear idea of what they want out of their degrees. But usually by the time they've been in school four years they have *some* notion of what they want."

"My sister thinks I need some real world experience," Vasiht'h said, rueful.

"Which one?" Palland said, leaning back and drumming his fingers on the table. "The younger one?"

"Yes," Vasiht'h said.

"Sehvi, then? Is telling you to live your life before settling into it," the Seersa said, smiling crookedly. "You know you have trouble when your younger siblings are more on top of things than you are."

"I know," Vasiht'h said, setting a paw on top of the other to keep from chafing them against one another.

Palland leaned forward. "What is it you're really thinking? And don't show me that course schedule you sent me. That's not thinking, that's grasping at straws."

"I . . . am really thinking that I don't want to leave the university?" Vasiht'h guessed, rueful.

"I'd buy that for a fin and call it a bargain," Palland said. "Is it true?"

"I don't know," Vasiht'h admitted. "You know my family's got a history of producing professors."

"Before you can teach, you have to have a degree," Palland

said, smiling.

"I know!" Vasiht'h said. "I know. Maybe it's just a lot of pressure. To do what my family's done. What if I don't want that?"

"What if you don't?" Palland said. "There's nothing forcing you to stay here after you graduate. Get your degree, go practice. You'll enjoy it."

"What if I'm wrong about what I want?" Vasiht'h said.

"Then you don't enjoy it, you give up the practice, and you come get your doctoral degree and become a professor like your mother and grandfather," Palland said. "Vasiht'h . . . you've got time. Even if you spend ten years outside the system, living a life, even if you spend those ten years, fifteen, traveling the Alliance and doing nothing specific . . . you'll still have time to make changes in your life. Don't treat every decision like it's your last."

"Is that what I'm doing?" Vasiht'h wondered.

"I don't know what in the Speaker-Singer's silent hells you are doing, but it's as good a guess as any to explain this schedule of courses you've turned into me. Which reminds me . . . let's do some surgery on them while you're here, ah? While you still have time to drop/add."

"All right," Vasiht'h said. And sighed. "Thank you."

"Nonsense. It's what I'm here for. Let's start by asking why you're taking a doctorate level assessment course when you haven't finished the suggested prerequisites."

———— ⌘ ————

Vasiht'h plodded back to the apartment, head bent and shoulders curled inward, wondering what was wrong with himself. His family would be the first to say this wasn't like him—at least, not the low spirits—but after spending half an hour hammering out an acceptable fall schedule with his major professor all he wanted to do was go home, make cookie dough and eat it. What was it about this process that was bothering him so much? And how ironic was it to be a xenopsychology student and not understand the inside of his own head?

The door opened on the smell of something burning, of

popping sap. He peered inside, unbuckling his saddlebags. "Hello? Jahir?"

"Here." His new roommate entered from the hall, holding a data tablet. "There's a pot of hot chocolate if you're so inclined."

"It's not cookie dough, but it'll do," Vasiht'h said ruefully. "Let me just put my bags down." After doing so, he said, "Where'd the fire come from?"

"If you're concerned that I might have been chopping wood so soon after my fall," the Eldritch said, "have no fear. I bought the wood on the way back to the apartment. I had no idea such things were sold here."

"Well, there are fireplaces," Vasiht'h said. "Though honestly I think they're more for nostalgia than anything else. This place is plenty warm in winter." He sat near the hearth, watching the fire twirl and sizzle. "Though it is sort of mesmerizing, isn't it?"

"Quite," Jahir said, pouring a demitasse of the chocolate and setting it on the small table beside him. "I fear I wasn't up to cooking an entire meal yet."

"No problem," Vasiht'h murmured. "I'll do it later. And cookies." He shook himself, rubbed his forehead. "How was your day? Did you go to the clinic?"

"I did," Jahir said. "The visit was quite illuminating."

Vasiht'h squinted at the other male. Jahir never seemed to say everything that was on his mind. Usually Vasiht'h would have enjoyed puzzling out the subtext, but right now he didn't want to work that hard, so he asked outright. "So . . . no more fainting spells?"

"No more," Jahir agreed. "And you? You seem peaked, if I may so observe."

"I *am* peaked," Vasiht'h said, flicking his ears back and sighing. When the Eldritch didn't fill the silence, he said, "I'm a little adrift lately, and my mentor's been trying to set me back on track."

"Which . . . is not going so well?" Jahir guessed.

"Something like that," Vasiht'h said with a grimace. He took a sip of the chocolate. "So, what about you? Have your schedule yet?"

"The graduate advisor kindly helped me with it during Orientation," Jahir said. "I have five classes, most of which appear to be foundational health and science topics."

"Not surprising," Vasiht'h said. "You won't get into specific behavioral issues until after you finish the basics. Some of those courses are heavy on biology, though, so I hope you're up to date with it."

"I suppose I'll see," Jahir said. "I've attached the textbooks to my account and have been examining them. They don't seem insurmountable."

"They never do when you're skimming them," Vasiht'h said, amused. "It's only when you've got five separate professors assigning you two chapters a week that it starts to get overwhelming."

"I suppose I shall take it as it comes," Jahir said.

"Only way to do it," Vasiht'h agreed. Something about the smell of the firewood mingling with the chocolate, and the presence of the alien, and the mundane conversation . . . the combination had lifted his mood. He stretched. "I should start on dinner."

"If you need anything washed or chopped . . . ?"

"No, I'm fine," Vasiht'h said, standing. "You keep off your feet. Although . . . have you ever eaten cookie dough?"

"I have not," Jahir said, sounding surprised.

"Well, you can help with that part," Vasiht'h said, grinning. "Later."

And he did, and seemed as bemused by it as Vasiht'h had expected, and that cheered him immensely. There was something deeply satisfying in predicting someone's response and being right about it, especially when it involved a lordly alien frowning at a spoon of chocolate-studded dough and asking if the point was not that they should be baked.

Maybe he was in the right major after all.

CHAPTER 5

"ARE YOU BUSY TODAY?" Jahir asked the following morning. "No?" Vasiht'h said. "I don't really have any plans until classes start next week." The Glaseah was in the kitchen, overseeing the cooking of an omelet large enough to share. The whole process of making food fascinated Jahir, in part because he'd been sure the Alliance would be beyond such things. "Do you have something in mind?"

"I thought we might go visit the children before the semester starts," Jahir said, looking for plates. His shorter roommate commonly used a stepstool to reach some of the higher cabinets, so he thought he'd put his greater height to use.

"Hah," Vasiht'h said, and nodded. "Yes. That's a good plan. We can go early, that will give me time to finish my latest letter to my family."

Jahir set out the plates. "Tell me about them?"

"Would you tell me about yours in return?" Vasiht'h asked, glancing at him with a quirked brow.

Chagrined, Jahir paused.

"Oh, it's okay," the Glaseahn said with a laugh. "You'll end up hearing about mine anyway. I love them all, though I'm glad to be gone from home. There are seven sisters and four brothers, and my aunt and my grandparents live with us, and the clan is a bit overlarge if you like your breathing space."

"Seven sisters and four brothers!" Jahir exclaimed, stunned.

"My mother and father took populocampi seriously," Vasiht'h said. "Very seriously."

"And that is . . ." Jahir said, pouring glasses of water for them both.

"Some of the Pelted aren't as mad about reproducing as others," Vasiht'h said. "For a while, some of us have been under the replacement rate. "Populocampi" was the word someone coined as a joke to represent an initiative to have as many children as possible. Except it stuck, and it really is necessary. Or at least, some people think so."

Jahir said, "If every family ends up with twelve children, I can't imagine there being a problem."

"Ah, but most families have only one child, or two, or none. My parents decided to have a big family . . . Glaseah tend to pair off for life, but as a species we aren't very enthusiastic about breeding. It was some side effect from decreasing the hormonal load when we were engineered." Vasiht'h ran a spatula down the center of the omelet and than plated the halves, pushing one over to him. "Whatever the case, the situation's getting better. It's just not as good as some specialists would like."

Jahir wondered what those specialists would make of the Eldritch, where babies died so regularly his brother had been considered a miracle birth and all children of roughly the same generation called each other 'sib' just for the novelty. He, Amber and Sediryl had been the only children of an age among the northern Galares, and had spent many a happy afternoon exploring the nearby forests. They'd grown up and gone their ways: Jahir to learn management at his parents' summer estate, Amber to dream of the buildings that would later lead him to an offworld school of architecture, and Sediryl to an Alliance starbase of all places, after which her family had disowned her.

"Cloud-spinning?" Vasiht'h asked.

Jahir shook himself. "Pardon?"

"Your mind was wandering. A fin for a travelogue?"

The reference puzzled him until he remembered that the Alliance called their money fin. Then Jahir laughed. "Just trying to imagine living with siblings. Tell me about yours."

The run-down on Vasiht'h's many relations took them through breakfast and part of the way out of the apartment, into a chill autumn morning with another of those damp breezes beneath a low gray sky. The walk to the hospital was uncomfortable, but more because of the weather than the pace, which Jahir noticed his roommate kept rather leisurely. He made a note to buy warmer clothes.

The children's hospital, seen from the front rather than the parking lot, was faced with sculptured gardens not unlike one of the country manors at home. Together they passed through the glass doors and into the lobby. As Vasiht'h approached the front desk, Jahir stayed in the center of the tall room, sampling the emotional climate of the room the way an uncertain swimmer does the water. The faces around him were clinical in their detachment or their haste, and though the cleanliness and broad spaces of the architecture suggested the Alliance's enviable luxury with technology, the people looked not unlike the pitiably few doctors among the Eldritch: carefully controlled.

The lobby itself had been painted with a soothing aquamarine mural with sea turtles, bright fish and other streamlined creatures. The smiles on their faces did not seem to marry well with the smell of antiseptic.

"I'm fairly sure the kids we met yesterday are on the second floor," Vasiht'h said, joining him and offering him a visitor's pass sticker. "We'll take the stairs."

Jahir carefully received the pass and pressed it to his chest, before following the Glaseah. His every nerve was alert for the faintest brush of another person, but most people gave him and Vasiht'h a wide berth. The stairs ended up being broader than the Eldritch expected, the stairwell itself sun-spangled with light from the window wall. When they reached the second floor, the elevator slid open, revealing a compartment filled with people, standing elbow-to-elbow.

Jahir reflected that Vasiht'h was altogether too good at anticipating Eldritch problems.

Turning a corner brought them to doors leading to long term care. Vasiht'h touched the chime and waited for entrance.

A man with amazingly orange hair opened the door. His brown eyes seemed clouded with distraction. "Yes?"

"We're visitors, here to see some of the children," Vasiht'h said. "We're students in the psych program."

The man's brow furrowed. "Students? We don't allow students here, unless they're interning. And which children? Are you related? We don't have any Glaseah or . . ." He eyed Jahir. "Christ on a bicycle. Certainly none of you."

"We spoke with Healer-assist Berquist at the beginning of the week about a visit," Jahir said, waiting for the man to begin to look uncertain before adding, "We promised the children we'd come by. We don't want to disappoint." He spread his hands. "They found us entertaining, apparently."

"Well, if Jill said it was all right," the man said. He squinted at their stickers. "Computer hasn't kicked you out, anyway."

. . . which it certainly hadn't, because the Veil allowed the rare Eldritch visitors to Pelted worlds a great deal of license in where they went. "Please," Jahir said. "We'll stay quiet."

"Fine," he said. He pulled open the door. "If you're looking for Jill's wards they're next to the window on the right. If you're going to come often, you should talk to her about getting a permanent pass. It'll let you in this door and save me the trouble of staring at you."

"Thank you," Jahir said. "We'll do that."

"That worked out well," Vasiht'h whispered as they walked down the quiet hall. In the rooms they passed Jahir glimpsed people crouching over beds that seemed miniaturized, unreal. "I don't know if he would have let me in alone."

"You just have to know how to talk to them," Jahir said absently.

"This must be the place," Vasiht'h said, peeking into the

window next to the final door. Jahir could just glimpse the edge of a brown pigtail through the glass. The Glaseah opened the door, gathering the gazes of all six children. Three were seated at a short table in the middle of the room. One of them was on the window-seat in the sun, cradling a book. The other two were in their beds, trapped there by metal arches that partially extended over their bodies.

"Hey, Manylegs came back!" crowed a girl at the table. "Along with the Dragon Prince!"

"Dragon Prince!" Jahir said, startled.

"Well, we were trying to decide what your life was like," one of the girls said, "And we decided that you must have a dragon after all, you just didn't want to tell us about it."

"We figured it was probably engineered," said another of the girls. "You know, like some of us."

"Yeah, dragons can't be much harder than people," the third girl at the table said.

"Ladies!" Jahir said. "One thing at a time, please. Names? I'll start: I'm Jahir Seni Galare at your service. You must call me Jahir, for I fear I am no prince at all."

"And I'm Vasiht'h," the Glaseah said, his amusement richening his voice.

The girls at the table were Kayla and Meekie, two Tam-illee with oversized ears and tiny brush-like tails, and Amaranth, the human with the pigtails and bright sparrow eyes. The bald girl on the window-seat Jahir also remembered, with her limp but pointed ears: she was Nieve. In bed were another human, Persy, and a Seersa girl, Kuriel.

"Now that we're done with that," Vasiht'h said, settling himself at the table with eyes that sparkled far too much for Jahir's comfort, "why don't you continue on with the story of Jahir's life? I want to hear more about this dragon."

Only too eager to oblige, the children spun a tale about Jahir's magical dragon, which he rode daily from a palace of such proportions that Jahir reflected legendary Queen Jerisa's court would have been lost in it. The dragon conveyed him from palace

to treasure hoard, a vast cave containing all the gold and silver
and jewels the girls could imagine, which, they assured them,
was quite a lot.

"What about food?" Vasiht'h asked.

"Oh, he obviously doesn't eat much," Meekie said. "Otherwise how could he be so thin?"

"We don't think Eldritch eat," Kayla agreed.

"I think they eat," said Persy from her bed. She was peeking
past the arch that forced her to lie flat. "Salad. Flowers. You know,
no animals."

"They do *not* eat flowers," Kayla said, her large ears flipping
backward.

"Oh yeah? Then what do they eat?"

"I think they drink moonlight," Nieve said from the window,
resting her cheek on her knees. "And eat pollen-dusty rays of
sunlight."

Jahir glanced at her, surprised.

"That doesn't sound very appetizing," Meekie muttered.

"It's romantic, though," Amaranth said. "I think it goes with
the dragon." She peered at Jahir. "There is a dragon, isn't there?"

Jahir looked at the six pairs of eyes gazing hopefully at him,
then smiled and leaned forward. "There's no dragon," he said.
"But there is a unicorn." He took off his ring and set it on the
table in front of Kayla.

"Oooh! It's beautiful! Is it from your treasure hoard?"

"Just so," Jahir said. "From the family treasure, the jewels of
House Galare. That is the unicorn that succored our family, and
since then the unicorn has been on all our jewels. It is his purity
that guides us, you see."

Nieve slid off the window-seat to join the other three girls
at the table. They passed his ring to one another, admiring the
delicately carved unicorn inlaid on the face of the oval gem. The
stone spanned Jahir's finger nearly from knuckle to the first
joint, and it dwarfed the hands of the girls who handled it.

"I wanna see!" Persy said, and the girls hastened to bring it to
the bedsides of the other two.

"A unicorn is even better than a dragon," Amaranth said happily.

"Are not," Persy said, and added at Amaranth's scowl, "but they're almost as good."

"This is wonderful treasure!" Kuriel said, staring at the ring. "Is there more?"

"There's more," Jahir said. "But you wouldn't find someone like me wearing it. It's . . . well, rather noticeable."

"I bet!" Amaranth exclaimed. "Look at the size of this one ring! You have crowns?"

"The Queen has one, yes," Jahir said. "You'll note I am no queen."

"No, you're a prince, we've already decided that," Amaranth said. She offered the ring to Jahir, which prompted Vasiht'h to speak.

"He's Eldritch, Amaranth . . . you shouldn't touch him."

Amaranth's mouth opened into a little round 'o'. Hastily she placed the ring on the table for Jahir to retrieve before continuing, "You look like a prince, after all."

"Perhaps. But many people would have to—" Jahir paused, glancing at the complex-looking displays above the beds, "—choose not to be the next ruler of the world before I could even be considered a minor prince, ladies."

"So it could happen!" Amaranth crowed. "I knew it. What's it like to be a prince?"

Jahir hesitated, unwilling still to break the Veil. And yet they were all so eager, and Nieve . . . Nieve with her large eyes, nearly the lilac of a young Eldritch lady's, so intent . . . he sighed and said, "It involves a great deal of allowing people to help you dress, bathe and move from room to room. And horses."

"Horses!" A nearly simultaneous squeal. He could see the horse portion of his story was going to be popular.

Halfway through his account of the prince going to the fields outside Ontine to symbolically bless the land so it would be fruitful, the door into their small room opened for the nurse that had shepherded the children away yesterday. She waited until Jahir finished off his last sentence before saying, "All right, girls . . . that's enough excitement for the day. It's time for the rest of you to get on the bed."

Cries of disappointment followed.

"We haven't found out how the blessing ceremony ends!" Amaranth complained.

"We'll come back," Jahir promised. "The story will keep."

"Just what he said," the nurse said. "Into bed with all of you. When I come back in this room I want you all ready for your naps." She opened the door and eyed Jahir and Vasiht'h significantly.

"We'll see you again soon, ariisen," Vasiht'h said before slipping out.

The nurse closed the door behind her. She eyed them. "I'm not sure how you got my name—"

Jahir didn't glance at the woman's name tag.

"—but you haven't done any harm, and I think the rascals like you. Any light in their lives is good in my book," she finished with a sigh. "You might as well tell me who you are and whether you really are planning to come back."

Vasiht'h said, "Truly we are. I'm Vasiht'h and this is Jahir. We're xenopsych students."

"Planning to make this your internship?" the woman asked with interest. "We have a slot open once a year. It's an organizational psych rotation for the clinical track, seeing to the staff."

"We're not sure what we'll be doing," Jahir said. "It's rather early for us both to be making internship decisions. They just seemed to derive such pleasure from our presence that we thought we'd return."

"Between a Glaseah jumping rope and an Eldritch—an Eldritch of all things!—telling them stories, I can't imagine why they might have been enjoying themselves," the woman said with a laugh. "My name's Jill Berquist. I share the care of that tuplet with a couple of other people, but I'm their primary care-taker. The computer let you in? It does background checks . . . I'll put you on the visitor list, then, save Patrick some grief at the door. Mornings are best, so you came at the right time . . . but they do have scheduled doctor and family visits. If you like, I'll keep you informed."

"Please," Jahir said. He paused, then said, "If I may ask . . . what's wrong with them?"

"And the prognoses?" Vasiht'h added quietly.

Berquist paused, then chuckled, tired. She rubbed her face with one hand. "Back home, I couldn't tell you, but the Pelted are fine with sharing information that would make humans want to sue you. They have a social thing, with silence being worse than speech—"

"—because of their history on Earth," Vasiht'h said. "With their designers forcing them to stay quiet."

"Which isolated them, yes," Berquist said. "It's hard for me to get used to after working on Earth where they value privacy over that sense of solidarity. Anyway, Meekie and Kayla should be okay. They have very virulent cases of Auregh-Rosen Syndrome, which typically doesn't kill. Amaranth and Persy both have a kind of cancer. We're having trouble keeping it at bay. Cancers have become more pernicious in humans since they've become space-farers, and no one's sure why. Kuriel has cerrmoniah; we keep re-building her nerve endings, but we're having trouble keeping her body from destroying them again. And Nieve . . . well, her cells keep apoptosing and no one knows why. No one's seen anything quite like it." The woman looked away and let out a long breath. "Anyway, we're doing all we can to make them comfortable."

Which didn't sound at all encouraging. "We'll look forward to the schedule," Jahir said quietly. "If you can indicate to us any particularly good or bad time, we can attempt to arrange our own activities accordingly."

"Thanks," she said, and let herself back into their room.

Outside the hospital, Vasiht'h broke the silence to ask, "So how much of that was true? The dragon prince, blessing the fields, the horses."

"Does it matter?" Jahir asked. "As far as they were concerned, it was all true."

Vasiht'h smiled a little. After a moment, he said, "Are we

going back, then?"

"Was there ever any question?" Jahir asked.

Vasiht'h said nothing for a moment. "No. No, there really wasn't."

CHAPTER 6

THE FOLLOWING WEEK SAW the semester's start. Jahir had spent a day locating all his classrooms to spare himself the anxiety of doing so on the first day of school, and that was well: it also allowed him to arrive early enough to pick the one furthest seat from everyone else. He'd been very careful about dressing, leaving almost none of his skin exposed below the neck, and had worn gloves thin enough to write with. But even taking precautions he wanted to minimize the amount of accidental contact between himself and his classmates.

The back of the room also suited him because it prevented people from staring at him, or trying to engage him. He found it uncomfortable, being the focus of attention . . . he would have thought that the urbane, multicultural Alliance with its dozens of species would have found yet another alien unworthy of note. The opposite, in fact, seemed to obtain: the people here were *more* curious about him, as if living among so many different aliens had only whetted their appetite for the investigation of additional species.

Fortunately, he did not have much time to devote to worry, because Vasiht'h had been prophetic: keeping up with all five classes needed all his attention, and then some, for his preparation for the degree had been incomplete. He often found himself researching additional reading material, more basic in nature, and studying that before returning to the subject matters at hand: for this semester, the basic biology of the body and how it affected the mind in the varied species, engineered and natural, of the Alliance. It was maddeningly complex and often incredibly difficult work, the learning.

It was also fascinating.

"How can there be so many of you, so different, and yet so alike?" he said one evening to Vasiht'h, who was sharing the great room with him.

"Pardon?" Vasiht'h said, looking up from his own data tablet.

"The engineered races," Jahir said. "It beggars the imagination that you were all made from common stock, and yet you're often so utterly different."

"Not so different as all that," Vasiht'h said. "Most of the Pelted can interbreed."

Jahir shook his head, the minute motion of his own kind, a twitch of the chin. "Not that way. I meant . . . in the mind. Even in body chemistry."

"Ahhhh," Vasiht'h said, and mantled the wings on his lower back. "Well, there you get into the issue of culture. How culture influences the mind, and the chemical constituents of it."

"Or vice versa?" Jahir said. "The body influencing the culture, creating the mind?"

"That too," Vasiht'h said. "That's one of the things I like about psychology, actually. It's not this or that. It's . . . a loop. Everything affects everything else. You can point at something and call it a cause, but it's really a matter of perspective. Change where you're standing and it looks like an effect."

"And yet you must begin somewhere, if you wish to affect change," Jahir said.

Vasiht'h grinned. "Affecting change is for third year students. First year students have to settle for observing effects."

Jahir laughed, quiet. "And second year students?"

"All the worst parts of being a first year, and none of the good parts of being a third," Vasiht'h said. "You'll find it positively frustrating when you get here yourself."

"And if I am to do so . . ." Jahir trailed off and resumed reading. He could sense his roommate's gaze lingering for a moment, and then Vasiht'h returned to his own studies.

—∞∞—

"So Professor Palland took a stripe out of you," Sehvi said from her room several sectors away.

"Not just him, but Dami too," Vasiht'h said ruefully. "She's convinced I'm not taking my education seriously."

Sehvi wrinkled her nose. "You do not want her having that idea. Ever."

"I know!" Vasiht'h said. "I know. And I'm applying myself now, I really am. Palland wrote my schedule for me this semester. I'm being good."

Sehvi leaned forward, peering at him. "And hating it, I see." At his expression, she said, "I can tell when you've been making too many cookies, it makes your hands twitchy. It's the sugar."

Vasiht'h sighed. "I haven't been eating them. Baking just calms me down."

"You're worse than a pregnant woman, ariihir," she said, amused. "With all the cravings. Someone should keep an eye on that for you. What about that roommate of yours? Is that working out well?"

"Strangely . . . yes," Vasiht'h said. "He's a quiet type, but he likes to study out in the suite, not in his room."

"Ohhhh," Sehvi said. "You like that, at least."

"Yes. It's not as noisy as home, but it's better than having no company. And we've sort of talked our way into helping out at the children's hospital."

His sister frowned. "How's that even possible? You're not qualified. They don't let so much as a therapy animal into places like that without certification. At least, they don't here."

"I don't know?" Vasiht'h admitted. "The computer didn't flag us, I guess. Besides, Jahir just . . . made it sound like we belonged there, and they believed him."

"Oh, did they," she said, brows lifting.

"I know it sounds crazy," Vasiht'h said. "But you have to live with an Eldritch to see it. They're very convincing. They have a lordly manner." He thought of Jahir frowning at the cookie dough spoon and grinned. "Even when doing mundane things. It's fun to watch."

Sehvi studied him, then said, "Maybe you should spend more time introducing him to mundane things, then. It seems to help."

"Help him? He needs it," Vasiht'h said. "I'm not sure he'd seen a shower before he came here."

"Not help *him*," Sehvi said, rolling her eyes. "Help *you*. And it would be a lot cheaper than buying expensive chocolate and nuts all the time. Especially if you don't end up eating any of the stuff you bake."

"Hard to argue that," Vasiht'h said. "I wonder if he's ever had ice cream?"

"Less food," Sehvi said. "More culture. Or social stuff. You're good at that. See if he wants to go along?"

"I don't think he likes crowds," Vasiht'h said, thinking out loud. "So . . . I'll start small."

She grinned. "That's the spirit. Now, ask me about me, so I can tell you all about my woes this semester. It's all the messy stuff that we're not supposed to be dealing with."

"Like?"

"Like gynecology and obstetrics," Sehvi said, grimacing. "I'm going into reproductive genetics so I can stay *out* of delivery rooms!"

"Poor little sister," Vasiht'h, and then laughed ruefully. "Poor us. Not quite where we want to be."

"Yet."

"Yet," he allowed.

"So, this is a common occurrence?" Jahir asked, following Vasiht'h out the apartment's back door.

"It's why all of the buildings face inward like this," Vasiht'h agreed. "So in good weather, or bad, even, we can all talk with the neighbors." They were heading for a little octagonal building Jahir had taken for some sort of gazebo, but it was entirely enclosed with glass windows and metal fretwork, decorative and weathered. The interior was as small as it looked, a single room with a shared high table and kitchenette. "Looks like we're the first ones here."

"But not by much," Luci said from behind them. "Brett and I are right behind you." She set a basket on the table and bent down to hug Vasiht'h. "Thanks for starting these up again. It's nice to get a break."

"You're welcome," Vasiht'h said. "Jahir, you remember Lucrezia? And this is her roommate, Brett, also a healer student."

Brett was another of the ubiquitous Seersa, a silver-coated male with curious green eyes. He was carrying a bottle of wine under one arm. "Well met, quadmates. So you're the new guy?" He looked up at Jahir. "Tall, aren't you?"

"I . . . yes," Jahir said, amused. "Yes, I appear to be."

Brett grinned. "After a few glasses of this, neither of us will be sure about it, I promise."

"Is anyone else coming?" Luci asked, pulling a stool up to the center table and starting to unpack her basket.

"Just Merashiinal," Vasiht'h said.

Luci laughed. "That's enough for our first night back, definitely."

"What's enough?" asked a voice from the door.

"There, see," Brett said. "Someone taller than you."

Jahir looked toward the door in time to see an entirely unlikely figure duck through it. Another centauroid, but unlike Vasiht'h, this one was over a head taller than Jahir himself, who was often a head taller than the tallest humans. This creature had the tail and lower body of a long-legged and powerful cat, the torso of a man and a foxish face, complete with delicately pointed muzzle . . . all covered with a tawny pelt dappled with ragged spots and stripes.

"And here is Brett with wine," this new addition said. "But did he bring enough to intoxicate me?"

"Not even," Brett said with a laugh. "Come drape yourself over here, Mera, and meet the new neighbor."

"What is this?" Merashiinal said, leaning forward to study Jahir. "I have not seen your like before."

"I assure you, the sentiment is mutual," Jahir said, bending back a little. "You are—"

"Merashiinal," the creature said, grinning with a gaped mouth. "One of the Ciracaana. The civilized part of the planet, so have no fears. I will not invite you to tribal rituals involving the painting of your snowy hide."

"That's an Eldritch, Mera," Luci said, setting out the food. "Don't touch him, he's a contact esper."

"Ah!" Mera said. "Much sorry I am if I breathed too much on you."

"Fortunately I can divine very little of you from being breathed on," Jahir said.

"Oh?" Vasiht'h asked. "You can pick out anything at all? Like what?"

"That he's been chewing on parsley," Jahir said.

Merashiinal laughed. "Yes! For good breath." He tapped a fang. "I am the polite barbarian. And also, a hungry one." He dropped onto his haunches and wrapped a long tail over his feet. "So tell me what we are feasting on, and then someone can start with the complaining."

When Vasiht'h had insisted on bringing him to this gathering, Jahir hadn't been sure what to expect, or that he'd enjoy it. Even at home, he'd preferred to distance himself from intimate gatherings. That he had to spend so much time at his studies only exacerbated his instinct for solitude now that he was on Seersana. But he'd thought it would be unnecessarily cruel to reject his roommate's offer, so he'd helped bake the ubiquitous cookies. And surprisingly, he found himself enjoying the evening. Luci had brought a plate of raw vegetables and fruits with slices of thin, sharp cheese, and though he abstained from Brett's wine, the Ciracaana had brought a dark, robust tea. He'd also brought candles, delightfully: Jahir had not expected the Alliance to have anything so anachronistic, and it had reminded him of home.

They spoke of their studies, their teachers, their problems. Merashiinal was a student of natural and environmental sciences, a study he hoped to bring back to Ciracaa and apply to the preservation of his own world, still mostly unsettled. Brett and Luci, both in the healing program, were full of absurd and gruesome stories about their latest anatomy class, which Jahir tried not to find quite so fascinating. They lingered over the tea until almost midnight, in fact, until at last Brett took his leave, and then the Ciracaana. Luci began packing her basket as Jahir swept the floor and Vasiht'h collected plates.

"So," Vasiht'h said. "Not sleeping much?"

She eyed him. "That obvious?"

"I've known you two years," Vasiht'h said as Jahir listened with interest. "So is it for a good reason or . . ."

She made a face, lips pulling back from her teeth, which were pointed. "I'm just tired, Vasiht'h. You know? I do a lot of swimming against the tide."

"I do know," Vasiht'h said. "Want to talk about it?"

She snorted, closing the basket. "You trying to use your degree on me without a license?"

"Less that than maybe a friend wanting to help," Vasiht'h said. "You know if you need to talk, we're right across from you."

Luci glanced at him, then across the room, meeting Jahir's eyes. "I know. And thanks." She smiled. "One week, up and down."

"One week," Vasiht'h agreed, and she left.

"Some problem there?" Jahir asked.

"Eh, I don't know," Vasiht'h said. "She keeps things close, which is strange in itself. Harat-Shar don't tend to. She's from one of the colonies, though, sometimes the societies are very different." He glanced at Jahir and smiled. "Like what we were talking about, ah?"

"Biology and culture," Jahir agreed, setting the broom aside. "It is late."

"It is," Vasiht'h said, taking his plate.

"But I am glad we did this," Jahir finished, opening the door for the Glaseah.

Vasiht'h glanced up at him, then smiled and walked under his arm. Jahir followed.

———⊗⊗⊗———

"First, tell me how the regimen's going. Any odd side effects?" KindlesFlame said over their table at the restaurant on the top floor of the medical student center.

"None that I can discern," Jahir said. "A touch of fatigue, perhaps. And nausea."

"The nausea's hunger," KindlesFlame said. "You need to eat more. We'll start now, ah? Order something." As they looked over the menu, he added, "So how are you liking it?"

"School?" Jahir said. "I find it stimulating."

"Yes . . . it is that," KindlesFlame said, satisfied. He tapped his fingers on the table, pursed his lips. "First year, xenopsychology . . . all neuroscience, isn't it?"

"Very much so," Jahir said, and something in his expression must have divulged more than he'd intended, for the Tam-illee laughed.

"More work than you'd been anticipating?"

"I like the science," Jahir said. "I am simply . . . nonplussed . . . at how inadequate my education in biology and chemistry was up to this point."

"Don't let it distress you," the Tam-illee said. "You aren't the first student to go into the postgraduate psychology program expecting it to be softer on the science. It's always been a bit of an orphan child, psychology."

"How so?" Jahir asked.

"Traditionally it wasn't treated as medicine," KindlesFlame said. "But no one would argue that the practice of psychology doesn't have medical implications. We folded the program into our healing college because we felt that's where it belongs, but even we don't give healer titles to people who graduate with licenses to practice psychology in a clinical setting. When you leave here, you'll still be Lord Seni Galare."

"Not Doctor Seni Galare," Jahir guessed.

The other man held up a hand. "Healer, not doctor. Graduates from human-administrated colleges produce doctors of medicine. From Pelted colleges, we get healers. Same with nurses and healers-assist. It's not a distinction most laymen know, but within the field you'll get funny looks if you don't observe it."

"Because humanity and the Pelted do things so differently?" Jahir wondered.

"Because humanity and the Pelted aren't sure if they share fundamental values, and both have their reasons for formalizing the separation," KindlesFlame said dryly.

"Ah!" Jahir said. And quieter, "Ah."

Watching him, KindlesFlame said, "You are just where you belong, alet."

"Ah?" Jahir said, looking up.

"You're wondering at the separation, and the feelings and thoughts that fostered it," KindlesFlame said with a chuckle. "Already a psychologist, and not yet graduated. You'll do fine, if you can get through the chemistry."

"I like the chemistry," Jahir said. "It's the history that I'm having to ride hard to catch. I have not had the benefit of a citizen, to have grown up with the Alliance's historical context."

"Maybe not," KindlesFlame said, "but you're in the thick of it now. It won't take you long if you just keep watching."

CHAPTER 7

SETTLING INTO THE ROUTINE of lectures and studies took so long that a month passed before they could arrange to visit the hospital again.

"You're late," Berquist said when they arrived.

"I . . . we're . . . we had no idea how much time had passed," Vasiht'h said, ears flicking back.

The healer-assist laughed. "I'm just tweaking you. I didn't expect you to come back, to be honest. Since you have, I'll finalize those passes for you while you're in the room with them."

"We'd appreciate that," Jahir said.

"Go on in," she said. "They have an hour before napping."

The children were clustered at the table, sharing a stack of pages with simple line drawings on them: sea creatures, like the ones painted in the lobby. They were diligently at work coloring these with various wax crayons, markers and stubby brushes. The door opening on their arrival caused a great deal of squealing, and it was disarming to Jahir, how obviously they were anticipated and welcomed.

"We didn't get to hear the end of the story!" Amaranth reminded him, earnest in her eagerness.

"Well, now you shall," Jahir said, and pulled up one of the

small chairs at their table, much to their delight. Vasiht'h sat behind him on his haunches, like an honor guard, and this the girls would not allow when they noticed it . . . there was nothing for it but to crowd him in around the table too. That put them so close that the girls couldn't help but brush against Jahir's sides, and yet he couldn't warn them off. As they settled Vasiht'h, he closed his eyes and sorted through the clear sunlight and suffering of their minds, so bright to be so sick.

"So, the prince goes out into the fields," Kayla said once they had positioned Vasiht'h to their satisfaction.

"To bless the fields," Jahir said, taking up the narration again. If the story he told them was a little on the fantastical side, well . . . they would never know how much of it was embroidery. He even threw in a unicorn sighting, which caused them all to sigh.

"Are there really unicorns?" Meekie wondered.

"Why not?" Kuriel said. "They're probably engineered, like us."

Meekie scowled. "I want them to be realer than that."

"Being engineered wouldn't make them less real or less special," Amaranth, one of the two humans, said. "You're engineered, Meekie, and you and Kayla and Kuriel and Nieve are my very bestest friends. I wouldn't like you any better if you were human."

"But would it make us more special?" Meekie asked. "If we weren't engineered, I mean."

"Evolving sounds like hard work to me," Kayla said.

"The hard way isn't always the best way," Nieve offered.

Nieve, Jahir thought, was the girl with the touch of poesy in her. He glanced at her, saw the fatigue lines beneath her eyes just as she turned them to him. "Isn't that right?"

"It is not wise to mistake great effort for productive effort," Jahir said somberly. "As my companion will tell you himself, having witnessed my poor attempts at studying."

"He does work *hard*," Vasiht'h said. "I'm not too sure about *well*, though."

The Glaseah's timing on the comment had been perfect . . .

they had all the girls giggling.

"I can't imagine you not being wonderful at everything!" Amaranth said. "Is studying really so hard?"

"We study," Persy offered. "School things. They give us material to work on when we're feeling okay."

"Even writing," Kayla said, wrinkling her nose.

"What's wrong with writing?" Vasiht'h asked, amused.

"Why do we have to learn it when we can just talk to computers and have them do what we tell them to?" Kayla asked. "I mean, reading, of course, everyone has to read. But how come with the writing? With pens?"

"You like doing this," Jahir observed, picking up one of the coloring sheets.

"Coloring is fun," Persy said.

"Writing can be fun," Jahir said, borrowing one of the crayons. "Writing can even be art. Tell me how your name is spelled, Kayla-alet."

She did so, blushing at the very grown-up title—children were inevitably called kara, the Seersan word for child, long before they earned the formal and informal words for friend, alet and arii. Jahir waited until she'd spelled the whole thing for him, then wrote it for her on the back of one of the coloring sheets. His penmanship in Universal was not quite as assured as it was in his own language, but unlike the Pelted, the Eldritch had little access to computers and were confined to paper if they wanted to trade messages or keep notes. Poor handwriting was not to be countenanced. "There, see?"

All of the girls crowded close to look, making appreciative sounds.

"You know calligraphy?" Vasiht'h asked him, ears splayed.

"No," Jahir said. "I have merely had a great deal of practice writing." With pens that needed dipping in ink wells, but he kept that part to himself.

After that, the girls were determined to learn, and there was nothing for it but to try to teach them the principles of penmanship. It kept them quiet and seated, though, and when Berquist opened the door he caught sight of the relief in her eyes, and the gratitude, before she schooled her face. That it was a gratitude not aimed at either him or Vasiht'h did not escape him, and affected him more than he'd anticipated. What must it be like to be warden to patients this young?

"All right, scamps," the nurse said. "Time for your nap."

"Do we have to?" Kuriel said, ears sagging.

"Yes, you have to," Berquist said. "And these two need to go back to their own studies, I'm sure."

Vasiht'h leaned toward them over the table and said in a stage-whisper, "He needs to work on his studying."

"Maybe he needs to study it," Kayla said with a giggle.

Jahir contrived his most long-suffering expression, which made all of them laugh, and then Berquist herded them away from the table. "Go on. When I come back in I want to see you all on your beds."

"You'll come back?" Amaranth asked as he and Vasiht'h rose.

"We'll come back," Jahir promised, because he could do nothing else when their faces turned toward him and his companion.

"Come back sooner!" Persy added from her bed.

"If he's good and studies hard," Vasiht'h said, and left them giggling.

Outside, Berquist handed Vasiht'h the hospital passes. "Here . . . clip these on yourselves somewhere when you come in. You're already on the system's pass list, which will get you through the doors in this area, but having the physical IDs will keep the staff and security people happy. They prefer to double-check the computer."

"Thanks," Vasiht'h said. "We'll remember to wear them."

"Is this time good?" Jahir added. "If so, we might make this our scheduled time."

"Every month?" Berquist asked, her expression guarded.

"Every week," Jahir said, and glanced at Vasiht'h. "Do I have that right? The weeks here are strange. Two weeks to a month?"

"That's right," Vasiht'h said.

Surprised, the nurse said, "You'd do that? You have the time?"

Vasiht'h said, "We can make the time."

"All right," she said, still taken aback. "I'll keep a lookout for you."

"Thank you," Jahir said.

Once they were outside, Vasiht'h said, "Every week? You're sure about that?"

"Absolutely," Jahir said, and added, "I apologize if I spoke for you. I didn't think—"

Vasiht'h held up his hands. "No, I'm fine with it. I'm surprised you are, that's all."

Jahir glanced down at him. "Because . . . ?"

"Because . . . I don't know. I didn't expect you to be comfortable with children. Much less sick children."

Jahir stopped walking. Was he angry? Conflicted? Distressed? Some combination of those things. Why did it matter what this alien thought of him? And yet the thought that he might be considered unmoved by the plight of the less fortunate, particularly children! It could not be supported.

"I'm sorry," Vasiht'h said, wide-eyed. "It's not that I didn't think you'd care. It's just . . . kits don't often watch their bodies as well as adults do. They're more likely to bump into people. I saw them earlier, they were touching you at the table. And when they're sick, it's worse. To have those feelings in your head. I know, all right? I have eleven siblings! I've lived through a lot of dragging people back to their beds when they've thrown up or collapsed or . . . Goddess, that one time with Hatti and her fever—agh!" He trailed off. "I'm rambling, aren't I. I just . . . I'm trying to be considerate of your situation."

"My situation is far less dire than theirs," Jahir said slowly.

"That doesn't mean yours isn't important," Vasiht'h said, voice firm.

"I know," Jahir said. He drew in a deep breath, centering himself. "But they have so little time—"

"—they might survive," Vasih'th protested.

"Even if they do, even if they live out their lifespans," Jahir said, his voice low. "It's so little time. For me not to find some to spare for them while they have it . . . they were so glad to see us."

"I can't imagine why," Vasiht'h said, his smile a little on the forced side. "Alien princes doing calligraphy for them!"

Jahir snorted and resumed walking. "Thus speaks the alien comedian with the metronomic timing."

Vasiht'h grinned, a more natural expression this time. "I did deliver some good lines, didn't I."

Jahir smiled at him.

Vasiht'h thought about that conversation much later, fluffing his pillows to prepare for bed. It was strange to realize he'd hurt his roommate's feelings. Not that he didn't think Jahir had them to be hurt, just . . . he'd thought the Eldritch sufficiently alien to not really be capable of any connection with his shorter-lived companions. Or even to want connections like that.

How long did Eldritch live, anyway? All he knew was that it was a long time. Measured in the centuries, when most of the Pelted died in their early hundreds, like their human makers. Medicine had come far, but attempts at engineering longevity had created a lot of the cancers and genetic errors, including many of the ones plaguing the kits they were visiting in the hospital. So far breeding for longer lifespans seemed a matter of luck, and no one knew quite how to do it without collateral damage.

No, Jahir was obviously capable of caring for the rest of them. Vasiht'h wondered uneasily if that wasn't asking for trouble.

CHAPTER 8

"**Y**OU'VE BEEN DECORATING," Vasiht'h said, coming to a halt just inside the door.

"I thought it would help," Jahir mumbled from where he was slumped over the table.

Vasiht'h padded into the great room and squinted at the wall beside the fireplace. There were pages stuck there, and each page had a sketch of one of the first generation races of the Alliance, along with notes about their biochemistry, their hormonal balances, their origins and their closest biological 'kin' among the other Pelted. The sketches were endearing . . . cartoonish, but rendered in the flawless hand Vasiht'h had come to expect from Jahir's writing, so that they looked far more serious than they were.

After studying them at length, he took one down and put it in a different place.

"What did I get wrong?" Jahir said, sounding plaintive.

"You've got the Hinichi hanging out in the middle," Vasiht'h said. "But the Hinichi technically share a lot of DNA with the other dog-like races."

"The dog-like races," Jahir repeated, lifting his head. "You don't mean the Tam-illee and the Seersa?"

"Exactly."

Jahir narrowed his eyes. "I thought they were vulpine, not canine."

"It's all sort of doggish to me," Vasiht'h said, and grinned. "Don't tell them I said so, though." He patted the papers. "There, now you've got it in the right order. Karaka'A, Asanii, Harat-Shar on one side . . . that's Team Cat . . . and Seersa, Tam-illee, Hinichi on the other."

"Team Dog," Jahir said.

"Team Dog," Vasiht'h agreed. "Why do you have the Platies over there with the Naysha?"

"They both swim," Jahir said, and held up a hand. "I know, I know. The Platies are true-alien and the Naysha are engineered Pelted. But they both swim." He rubbed his forehead. "The Alliance . . . is like an immensely complex family, is it not. What with the engineering, and the engineered folk engineering other folk, and everyone being somewhat related, except for the people who aren't but who have married into the family."

"And who are now perplexed by the behavior of their in-laws?" Vasiht'h said and chuckled. "The analogy works. You, though, have been at this too long. You need a break."

"What sort of break?" Jahir asked wearily.

"Have you ever had ice cream?"

"Ice cream," Jahir repeated. "It sounds . . . cold?"

"Oh, it's very cold," Vasiht'h said.

"Is it not cold outside?" Jahir said, sounding so confused Vasiht'h couldn't help but laugh.

"Come on, alet. Get your coat. It's never too cold for ice cream."

"I confess I find myself skeptical, but—"

"But you need the break, and you know it," Vasiht'h said. "Let's go."

It was in fact cool outside—Vasiht'h wouldn't have called it cold, but he had fur, and throwing a scarf around his neck was sufficient. Autumn still had a month and a half of life in it yet, but winter came early to this part of the continent. The trees were losing their leaves, but the wind was too damp for them to rustle much; they walked together on pavement scattered with wet leaves in lurid reds and oranges, bright against the pale gray.

"It's usually a long walk," Vasiht'h said. "The gelato place is next to the arts college. I don't mind the exercise, but we're going to cheat on account of your issues with the gravity."

"And cheating entails?" Jahir asked, looking up at the wan gray sky.

"A Pad station," Vasiht'h said, turning them down the path toward it. At Jahir's expression, he said, "What? Surprised there are Pads on campus?"

"A touch, yes," Jahir said. "I would have thought their use discouraged."

"They are," Vasiht'h said. "Most people prefer the walking." He grinned. "There's a significant fee to use them, so you don't see a lot of students going through them unless they have classes on opposite sides of the university. But they're useful for emergencies. That's how the response team got to our apartment so quickly."

"A fee," Jahir said. "Very clever."

"Isn't it?" Vasiht'h said. "Psychology again—oh, Goddess. Do you have money? I never thought to ask . . . "

"I'm fine," Jahir said. "Unless the fee is exorbitant!"

"It's not that bad, as long as you're not doing it often," Vasiht'h said, and led him into the station, a beautiful, small structure much decorated with windows and climbing vines, now all wet brown thorns. They exited into a building standing shoulder to shoulder with others along a lane filled with people streaming past in the dim autumn afternoon. The smell of bread and pastries and crumpled leaves . . . Vasiht'h inhaled it and then held up a hand. "Hang on, there's a crowd. I'll tell you when there's a space big enough for us."

"Of course," Jahir said, looking over his shoulder. "It is like . . . a street fair?"

"It's next to the arts complex," Vasiht'h said with a laugh. "Of course it is. Come on."

Four doors down, they found the gelateria, which smelled of espresso and sugar. Vasiht'h watched his companion surreptitiously and hid his glee at the puzzled expression on the Eldritch's face. He stepped up next to him. "Most of the flavors are nut or fruit-based. You can ask for samples before deciding which you want."

"And this is ice cream," Jahir said.

"This is the best ice cream on campus!" the Asanii behind the counter said, leaning over it to grin at them from her mouth up to the bright brown eyes set in a calico-patched face. "Gelato is a human thing, but we Asanii made it even better."

"I can't argue with her," Vasiht'h said sagely, shaking his head.

"I have no notion what flavor I would like," Jahir said, sounding bemused.

Vasiht'h said to the Asanii, "He's never had ice cream."

"Never had . . . " she said, stunned, eyes widening. Then she straightened her shoulders. "Well then! You'll have to try all of them!"

And that, to Vasiht'h's delight, was exactly what they proceeded to do; the Asanii insisted. The first sample spoon she passed to Jahir was vanilla, and he eyed it skeptically before trying it . . . and then stopped at the taste. And closed his eyes. Vasiht'h thought he'd never seen a look of sensual bliss so acute on anyone's face; that it was so understated mattered very little, because Jahir's face was usually so composed that even the smallest expressions were magnified.

The Asanii saw it too. She actually bounced on her feet and clapped her hands in glee. "You like it!"

"Madam," Jahir said, grave. "I love it."

"All the flavors!" the Asanii crowed. "Next, almond!"

There were twenty-four flavors, and Jahir tried them all, and by the time they were done he was shivering a little.

"You're cold," Vasiht'h said, surprised.

"I did say," Jahir said.

"Get him an espresso, please?" Vasiht'h said. "And whatever

ice cream he wants. What flavor do you want, anyway?"

"I like them all," Jahir said, meek.

Vasiht'h laughed. "Well, choose one and we'll come back another day for the others."

"Vanilla, then," he said. "I am charmed by a flavor made from the fruit of a rare orchid."

Vasiht'h had a cup of the roasted chestnut, and the two of them took a table on the patio. "If you're sure, being outside," Vasiht'h said. "We'd probably be safer from people bumping into us in the store?"

"Outside is fine," Jahir said, setting his saucer on the table. "This coffee is new to me."

"It's strong," Vasiht'h said as the Eldritch lifted it to his lips. "Most people sweeten it—"

Jahir paused, mid-sip, and sighed. "Wonderful."

Watching him, Vasiht'h thought they had to do this more often. A lot more often.

———— ∞ ————

"You like him!" Sehvi said.

Vasiht'h rubbed his face. "Ugh, Sehvi."

"I mean that," she said, leaning forward so that her nose seemed to be poking him through the display. "You do!"

"He's a good roommate," Vasiht'h said. "By that I mean he's a roommate in the real sense of the word. He lives here with me, rather than just using his bedroom to sleep in. The room-mates I had before . . . it's like they were trying to keep out of my way. They would come in, say hello if I was in front of them, and scamper into their rooms and close the door. You know that hall has a little windowseat? And a space for books? They would study there. Well, Cadia used to study there. Juliesh . . . I only knew she was living here because her bed was rumpled. She was out all the time."

"And your Eldritch doesn't do that," she said, putting her cheek in her palm. The merry glint in her eye exasperated him, but he continued anyway.

"No. He studies in the great room. He asks me about my day and listens to the answer. He brings me his questions when he gets stuck on something. And he tries to help me keep house. Cleaning, tidying . . . he does my laundry!"

"You don't wear clothes most of the time," Sehvi said, perplexed. "What does he wash?"

"My blankets," Vasiht'h said, ears sagging. He laughed. "He even tries to cook."

"Tries?" Sehvi repeated, brows lifting.

"It's like he's never seen a stove before," Vasiht'h said. "And I don't mean that in the typical Pelted 'we don't know how to cook because we get our food from genies or restaurants' way. I mean that in a 'doesn't even have the first notion how food is prepared' way. I caught him trying to slice bread with a meat knife."

Sehvi giggled. "Poor thing. Maybe Eldritch princes have servants or something."

"I wouldn't be surprised," Vasiht'h said. "But you know, I give him another month or so and he'll be as capable as I am. He's really focused on learning how to live here. He'll go hunting recipes in the u-banks and pull them up in the kitchen, and follow the viseo instructions step-by-step until he gets them. He even comes with me to the market and lets the vendors there teach him how to pick produce. Says since he wakes up earlier than I do, it only makes sense for him to do the shopping."

"Ah . . . no wonder you like him," Sehvi says. "He tries."

"He really does." Vasiht'h fluffed up a pillow and leaned forward on it, resting. "More than a lot of the other students here."

"Maybe being an Eldritch means he takes fewer things for granted," Sehvi said.

"Maybe? But I expected him to be a lot more distant," Vasiht'h said. "And he's very formal in mannerism, but . . . in every other way, he's committed to being here, fully, right now. More than anyone I've met. I guess it just took me off guard. I would have thought someone who lived longer than the rest of us would have less of that . . . in-the-momentness. Care less about the passing of time."

Sehvi studied him, and her voice was softer this time. "You really *do* like him." When he lifted his head to frown at her, she shook her head. "No, don't give me any mouth about it, big brother. You make friends easily, but you've never had a really *good* friend."

"I have you," Vasiht'h objected.

"Sure, you have me. I mean outside the family," Sehvi said. "Maybe that's it, really . . . we have such a big family that you've never needed to look outside it for a real friend. But now you're out on your own and—"

"Lonely?" Vasiht'h said, and made a face. "Who's the one studying to be a psychologist here?"

"Everyone's a psychologist, a little, who has to deal with people," Sehvi said. "But I'm right, aren't I?"

"I guess," Vasiht'h said. "I guess I never thought about it. Family makes the best friends, because they never go away. They'll always be your family."

"So you pick the first alien who'll never go away," Sehvi said. "An Eldritch. Because they live forever, right?"

"Ugh, Sehvi," Vasiht'h said, covering his eyes. "Your psycho-analysis has the subtlety of a hammer."

She laughed. "All right, maybe I'm reaching. Am I?"

"Yes!" Vasiht'h said. "No! I don't know! I really didn't plan it. And if he'd been an obnoxious Eldritch, I wouldn't have picked him."

"No, of course not. But he's not obnoxious. He's mysterious and gallant and he tries hard, and he's just the right combination of humble and perfect," Sehvi said with a grin. "We should give thanks that we're born vacuumed of hormones. Can you imagine what our parents would say if you'd fallen in love with him?"

"Noooo, I don't want to think it," Vasiht'h said. "Guh. You make the worst nightmares, ariishir."

"I know, it's a talent," she said, pleased. "So when are you going to bring him home to meet us?"

"Sehvi!"

She snickered.

⸺⊷∞⊶⸺

It was, Jahir thought, an exceedingly busy life, to be so satis-fying. He had classes and studying to do every day. Once a week, he had lunch with the director of the clinic, dinner during the evening gatherings with the apartment's quadmates, and an hour or so of playtime with the children at the hospital. He shopped for groceries in the morning, did laundry in the evening, and breathed, ate and slept biology, chemistry, and basic psychol-ogy principles. And all around him moved the bright, quick lives of the Alliance's many species. As autumn grew colder and the skies grayer, the vibrancy of the people only heightened, until to be among them was to be struck painfully by the vivid scarlet scarves, the bottle green coats and lush brown capes.

"I wish we could go outside," Persy said, perched on the win-dow-seat and peering out it.

"It looks cold out there," Kayla said uncertainly.

"It *is* cold out there," Vasiht'h said. "I don't recommend it."

"Unless you have the density of fur of my companion," Jahir agreed. "You have seen how I come in."

They had—his coat was folded over one of the adult-sized seats in their room. He hadn't brought his winter garb from home, so he'd bought some from one of the campus stores . . . and a very interesting experience that had been. He'd been mea-sured, selected a style and color, and they'd put a coat in his arms ten minutes later. Remarkable.

"I miss playing, though," Persy said. "I mean, running around."

Meekie said, "When we have the energy, you mean."

All the girls looked at her.

"What?" she said. "It's true." She looked at Jahir. "You know it, don't you? Eldritch princes live forever, but we're not going to."

"I fear to tell you, Meekie," Jahir said, "but I am not immortal either."

"I can't imagine you dying," Amaranth said from the bed where she was resting. She was almost entirely covered in blankets, only her eyes and one of her ragged pigtails visible.

"Ah, but I will," Jahir said. "In fact, Eldritch histories are replete with rather alarming deaths. Shall I tell you some of the more outrageous ones?"

"You mean like knights being spitted by dragon claws?" Persy said eagerly.

"Just like," Jahir said somberly.

"You sure that's not too gruesome?" Vasiht'h said with a grimace.

"NO!" all the girls cried.

"Come then, and let me tell you tales of evil mind-mages!" Jahir said. "And the women who saved them with the power of love."

They dropped the books and markers and came eagerly to listen. Jahir pulled his chair closer to the beds and waited until the girls had arranged themselves, then began his storytelling. He would not ordinarily consider the tale of Corel killing off an entire army suitable material for children, but he had a sense of these six by now, and they were very aware of their own mortality. Epic stories where love redeemed the fallen both pleased their sense of drama and lulled their own fears by being safely mythical.

Indeed, as he told the story, he sensed them relaxing . . . so much so that he felt a pressure against his leg, and the hazy sense of someone's drowsing thoughts: Nieve, falling asleep against him. He didn't even think twice—he reached down and pulled her into his lap. How thin she was, and how light! Her mind barely impinged on his, something he found deeply distressing. Was she so weak she could barely project? He met Vasiht'h's eyes over the heads of the girls, and saw his roommate's concern. Whether it was for him or the children, he had no notion.

"And so, to this day," he said, "the castle at Rose Point lies abandoned. Its garden has grown riotous with winter thornroses, climbing up the gates to the garden where the lady lies sleeping beneath the ground. She waits, like the castle, for a new tenant, and a new era to revive her story."

"That's so wonderful," Amaranth said with a sigh. "All your stories are like fairy tales."

"They need more dragons, though," Persy said.

"Or unicorns," Amaranth said.

"Unicorns next time," Jahir promised. "For now, I see your keeper in the door."

"Aw, do you have to go?" Kuriel said. "We need a story about the Glaseah now!"

"Next time," Vasiht'h promised. "For now, will a ride on a Glaseah's back to your bed be enough fun?"

That, the girls agreed, was absolutely enough fun, so much so that the two girls already in bed protested that they'd been cheated and were mollified only when Vasiht'h promised them a ride the following week.

Jahir carried Nieve to her bed and tucked her in. How thin her shoulder was when he arranged the blanket over it. His skin tingled from the memory of her slight weight and cool body—she had a pained look on her face, and he rested the backs of his naked fingers against her cheek. *Sleep gently,* he willed her. *Dream of pollen-dusted sunlight and unicorns.*

"Me next!" Amaranth whispered from the next bed over, and he could not but obey. Touching her brought him her thoughts, accelerated by exhaustion, a confusion of images of brave ladies and dark mages and the sense of what it was like to perch on Vasiht'h's back: furry and warm and a little precarious. He obliged Kayla also, and found his roommate had arranged the others.

"Rest well, ariisen," Vasiht'h said, and they left to the chorus of their sleepy promises.

Outside, Berquist was handing off a data tablet to another harried looking nurse. She looked up at their arrival and said, "Did they—"

"They're already in their beds," Vasiht'h said.

"You put them to bed?" she said. "No, wait . . . you *got* them in bed? How??"

"My colleague offered them rides," Jahir said.

"You what?" Berquist said, staring at Vasiht'h. And then she slumped onto a chair and started laughing. "Oh, you two. You're golden. Thank you."

"It's our pleasure, really," Vasiht'h said.

"As long as you're working miracles, maybe you can see why Amaranth's so bound and determined to fight me about her treatments?" Berquist said. "She knows they're required, and she knows they don't hurt, but she always gives us trouble."

"We'll see what we can do," Vasiht'h said.

"Thanks," she said. "I mean that."

⁂

Since it was obvious that the Eldritch was reticent to discuss his thoughts, his family or his world with anyone, Vasiht'h did his best to respect his roommate's privacy. He reminded himself that being content with what one had was one of the Goddess's first commandments, and sat on his curiosity as much as possible. When Jahir detoured to one of the benches outside the hospital, he followed to be companionable, and also with a hint of worry that maybe his roommate had overtaxed himself physically, or mentally from holding the girl. He waited until Jahir sat before settling beside the bench on his haunches, mantling his wings and refolding them over his second back. And there he did his best to cling to his decision to respect Jahir's silence even as the Eldritch leaned back and closed his eyes, and gave every evidence of discomfort.

After a moment, Jahir said, "You observe she is beginning to rely on us."

"The healer-assist?" Vasiht'h said. "Well . . . yes, I'm not surprised." He studied his roommate's face. "Is that a bad thing?"

"No," Jahir said, and sighed. He rolled his shoulders and said, "That poor child, Vasiht'h. Too tired to think through her skin."

"I know," Vasiht'h murmured. "I know. Sick children are the worst." He sighed. "Can I tell you something?"

Jahir glanced at him.

"Some days, I wonder if this is a good idea," Vasiht'h said cautiously, hoping he wasn't about to offend his roommate with this bit of selfishness. "For us."

The Eldritch smiled a little. "I don't blame you for the thought."

"You don't?" The relief at hearing it was so powerful Vasiht'h flushed.

"No," Jahir said. "No, not at all. We are doing a difficult thing." He pushed himself off the bench. "But we will survive it."

. . . and the children might not, is how that ended, Vasiht'h thought. He fell into step alongside the taller male, his paws hushed on the pavement compared to Jahir's boots. And at some point, he said, "You learned to say my name right. You didn't when we first met."

"It is your name," Jahir said. "To fumble it is inconsiderate."

"Did you practice?" Vasiht'h said, and Jahir glanced at him but didn't answer.

All the way home, Vasiht'h struggled with the image of the Eldritch training himself to get the last curt sound and huff of air right, just to be polite. And grumbled. If Sehvi could hear his thoughts, she'd be crowing.

CHAPTER 9

*T*AHIR HAD KNOWN THERE WOULD BE consequences to his decision to touch minds with others. He'd been expecting nightmares, perhaps. Had even prepared for them: done as his mother had done for him as a boy, made himself a hot tisane and practiced his breath control, resting on his bed with his hands light on his knees.

But he had had no nightmares, nothing he could have defended himself against. Instead, he dreamed. Of transfusions and gloved hands and the smell of antiseptic. Of weakness so profound it made even lying in bed and dreaming exhausting. Of longing for sunlight on his face. Of the horror of touching his head and finding hair loose in his palm.

He dreamed of losing the acuity of his hearing, and knew that the dreams were blending his memories with the children's because the pain of losing music was so intense he was surprised he didn't break from sleep.

When he did finally wake, it was with dried tears on his cheeks, and the sense that he hadn't rested at all. He thought as durances went it was mild, but he did not fool himself into thinking it wasn't affecting him.

—⊶⊷⊶—

"So you've made a decision," KindlesFlame said over their coffee.

"I am closer to one, we'll say," Jahir said and studied the Tamillee's face. "And you have misgivings. Am I correct?"

" 'Misgivings' is a strong word," KindlesFlame said, refreshing his cup from the pot they were sharing and adding honey. "The medical psychology program is . . . rigorous."

"Rigorous," Jahir repeated.

"The residencies are killers," KindlesFlame said bluntly. "Most healers-assist have a rough internship. But there's a kind of shield in not being entirely responsible for someone's suffering." He paused and frowned, stirring, then set the spoon on his saucer. "They're responsible for someone's injury or disease or physical maintenance, you understand. That's not suffering. Suffering is up here." He tapped his temple.

"And the psychiatric healers-assist are called upon to deal with suffering," Jahir said.

"More distinctly," KindlesFlame said, "you are called upon to deal with the worst suffering. A good bedside manner will take care of a lot of problems. You only want a psychologist-nurse for the extraordinary cases. The chronically ill. The dying. Those deranged by pain or medication or trauma. Parents who've lost their babies in childbirth. The elderly who've been abandoned." He looked up at Jahir. "It's not like clinical practice, where for every harrowing case you'll get a handful of people who have existential anxieties, are upset about some temporary loss, or need a little help getting their life sorted out. The medical psychology program turns out the people who deal with the equivalent of psychiatric trauma care."

"And yet, individuals are needed for those roles," Jahir said, turning his cup on its saucer.

"They are," KindlesFlame said. "But I would caution you against romanticizing it too much. Trauma-care can sound— and be—very heroic. But the mundane, everyday sort of cases need handling too, and there are a lot more of them." He smiled. "I'm the head of the student clinic. I see a lot of flus, sprains and anxious stomachs. On the surface it doesn't seem very exciting. But a life like that keeps you grounded in reality, so that when the trauma does come, you see it in context."

"Does that not make it hurt more?" Jahir asked.

KindlesFlame looked at him for several heartbeats. Then said, "If you can ask questions like that, you should consider your course carefully. You're still in your first semester, alet. Don't make any premature decisions."

"This is the story of how the Glaseah got their black and white coats," Vasiht'h said to the girls grouped around them. He had Meekie in the curl of his forepaws, and Kayla's head on one of them, and the others were in a loose semicircle in front of him. Jahir was sitting cross-legged behind Amaranth, hands resting on his knees and expression as attentive as the children's. It made Vasiht'h smile, though he ducked his head to hide it. He lifted his hands and began the story.

"Long ago, when we were fresh from the thoughts of the Mother Goddess's head, She asked us what gifts we would like . . . because, you see, we were unformed at that time, just little bits of fluff and maybe-flesh that She hadn't yet shaped to completion."

"Did you have four legs already?" Meekie interrupted.

"That's probably too much form," Persy said.

"But if you have maybe-flesh . . ."

"Patience," Vasiht'h said, once he had schooled his expression. "You'll see as I go along." Once he had their attention again, he continued. "Yuvreth't, the first of our race, told the Mother that he would like for us to be great thinkers, like Her, and to be able to create as She did. So She separated us into male and female, so we could make babies—" This elicited a giggle. "—and gave us the ability to think." He tapped his forehead, between the eyes. "Like Her, which means She made us espers."

"What's it like?" Amaranth interrupted. "Being able to read

people's thoughts?"

"It's like being able to talk to people, but easier and across longer distances," Vasiht'h said with a chuckle. "Now. Yuvreth't, being clever, asked for wings that we might fly, and long legs to swiftly flee those who preyed on us, and keen noses for smelling their coming, and large ears for hearing them, and farseeing eyes that we might spot them before they spotted us—and, that not being enough, he also asked that we be as colorful as the flowers so that we might have better camouflage in the jungle, and he also wanted hands so we could make tools . . ."

"What *didn't* he wish for?" Kuriel asked.

"That is exactly how the Goddess reacted," Vasiht'h said, nodding. "She said 'These are too many gifts. If I give them all to you, I'll have none left for anything else I might make. You must choose two, and I advise you to retire and consider those choices carefully before making them!' So Yuvreth't went back to his rock and joined his new mate, Slesvra, whom you recall had just been made for him. He asked her, 'What should we give up? All these gifts are important.'

"Slesvra considered at length, then said, 'I think we should keep the gift of the mind, for if we can think, then we will find ways around our physical limitations . . . and the hands, so that we can make what we conceive.'"

"Ooh, she was smart," Persy said, eyes wide.

"She was!" Vasiht'h agreed. "So the following day, Juvreth't returned to the Great Mother and said, 'O Goddess, let us keep the mind so that we might think our way out of danger, and our hands, that we might make the tools we conceive.' And Aksivaht'h took away the wings, the long legs, the extraordinary senses of smell, hearing and sight, and the colored coat." Vasiht'h held out his hands. "Well! Juvreth't returned to his mate very upset! 'Look at us, Slesvra! We have hands and we are smart, but we are ugly!'"

The girls giggled and he waited, grinning, before continuing. " 'What good is this, my mate?' And Slesvra said, 'We will make do,' but Juvreth't didn't think it was any good at all, and he wasn't interested in making do."

"Oh, no, he's going to be baaaaad," Meekie said, bouncing a little.

"That's exactly what he was," Vasiht'h said. "While Aksivaht'h the Mother Goddess was dreaming—for that's how She makes new things—he sneaked into Her trove of gifts and stole the wings, the long legs, the colored coats and all the heightened senses! He brought them home to his mate and paraded in them for her. 'This is how we were meant to be!' he said. But Slesvra was not convinced. What do you think she did?"

"She tattled!" Kayla cried.

"She did!" Vasiht'h said. "She woke the Mother from her making-dreams and said, 'My mate has stolen the gifts!'" He leaned forward. "It may surprise you to learn that Aksivaht'h was not displeased."

"What?" Kuriel asked. "How come?"

"My mother would have been," Kayla added darkly.

"Well, she wasn't," Vasiht'h said. "Because Juvreth't was trying to do the best for his race, and believed that having all the gifts would keep them safer. It was hard for Her to punish him for this. She brought him forth and said, 'Your keen smell you may keep as your reward for boldness. And your keen sight you will keep as a reward for your cleverness. Since wings and legs you wanted, you will have them . . . though not in the way you wanted, as a reminder that you do not always receive what you wish for in the way you might wish it. You will, no doubt, find some way to profit by it anyway, and that lesson is a valuable one. However, your keen hearing I will take, and take twice—you will be deficient now in it—for there must always be a balance.' And then She sent him down to the world, him and his mate, and they were shaped as you see me now."

"But what about the coat?" Nieve asked softly.

"Ah, you were listening carefully!" Vasiht'h said, smiling. "Aksivaht'h had forgotten about the colored coat . . . She had been in the middle of a very productive dreaming, and wanted to return to it. So She sent the two down, but paid little attention to how fast they were falling, and they were falling too fast! So together they aimed for the stars to brake their fall. The night sky blackened them as they fell, but the stars they used skidded off their backs and breasts and burned them to a clean white. And that is what became of the colored coat . . . it's under here. Somewhere."

"We should check!" Kayla said, and Meekie turned a little to spread the fur on Vasiht'h's foreleg.

"It looks black all the way down," she reported.

"It was a very dark night, and a very long fall," Vasiht'h said somberly. And twitched. "That tickles, arii!"

There was nothing for it but to be tickled then, because three of them tackled him, and he obligingly laughed until his side ached before waving them off. When they turned speculative looks on the Eldritch, Jahir held up his hands and said, "Ladies, did you tickle me, I might faint."

"It's that Eldritch constitution of his," Vasiht'h agreed.

"That was a good story," Persy said. "Did they have other adventures?"

"Yuvreth't and Slesvra? Oh yes. I'll tell you more of them next time," Vasiht'h said. "There's even one where they briefly get their colored coats back."

"They're so lucky," Amaranth said. "I'd love to have my hair back the way it was."

"What was your hair like before?" Nieve asked. Vasiht'h flicked his ears forward to catch the answer.

"It was a pretty cinnamony brown color," Amaranth said, and sighed. "Now it falls out all the time."

"Especially after treatments?" Jahir asked, voice quiet, and Vasiht'h marveled at how much empathy he could put in such an understated tone.

"Yeah," Amaranth said. "Sometimes I think I'll never have my hair back." And then she blanched. "Oh, Nieve, I'm sorry! I didn't mean—"

Nieve laughed and touched her bald head. "It's okay. I don't mind."

"You don't?" Amaranth asked, surprised. "Did you have hair before?"

"Sure," Nieve said. "A light gray color. It was down to here," she touched her collarbone. "About. My gran, she used to tell me it looked like a dove's wing, but I've never seen a dove." Nieve shrugged. "But I lost it pretty soon after I got sick, and that was a while ago."

"You don't feel . . . well . . . ugly?"

"I did in the beginning," Nieve said. "But then I saw an old lady in the hospital, and she had no hair either. And she had a tattoo of an open sky with swirling birds and leaves on her scalp, and it was the most beautiful thing . . . and I thought, well, maybe hair isn't the only beautiful thing you can have on your head." She thought. "I'd like a hat, maybe. Lots of hats."

"Or crowns," Jahir offered, with what Vasiht'h thought was a perfectly straight face, one he maintained when the girls demanded he describe all the jewels of the Eldritch treasury for them.

As had become custom, the two of them shepherded the children into their beds before making their exit. Berquist—who had become Jill to Vasiht'h by this time—was sitting outside, cradling a cup of coffee on her knees. Their arrival surprised her, for Vasiht'h caught a hint of her exhaustion in her face before she put it away. "Rascals in bed?"

"And dreaming of crowns and tiaras," Vasiht'h said, and glanced at Jahir before saying, "I don't think you'll have trouble with Amaranth from now on, either."

"Oh? What magic did you work there?" she asked, incredulous.

"We didn't do anything," Jahir said. "We listened while they solved their own problem." At her glance, he finished, "Amaranth regrets the condition of her hair."

"The condition of her—oh . . ." Jill sighed. "Yes. I can understand that." She smiled, wry. "I should have asked."

"You cannot be mother, therapist and healer-assist to six children and expect perfection," Jahir said.

"Of course I can," she answered. She snorted. "I'm a nurse.

It's what we do." She set her coffee cup aside. "But you've made my job easier, and I'm grateful. If there's anything I can do, tell me."

"There is something," Jahir said, and Vasiht'h glanced at him, wondering what he was up to.

"That being?"

"When we first met the children they were outside. Kayla tells us when the weather is clement and their health allows, they can go to the hospital park, which is how they escaped."

"That's true," Jill said. "Being outside is good for them."

"Could we take them on an outing?" Jahir asked.

Vasiht'h wasn't entirely certain, but he thought there was a touch of wistfulness in the Eldritch's voice. Perhaps Jill heard it too, because she studied Jahir as she said, "What sort of outing?"

"There is a place that serves ice cream," Jahir said. "It is four doors down from a Pad station . . ."

"Ice cream!" Jill said. "I don't even know if they can eat ice cream. We have a nutritionist to create their meal plans."

"You could ask," Vasiht'h offered.

"I could, but . . . ice cream? In fall?" she said. "The weather . . ."

"If the weather's bad, we don't have to do it," Vasiht'h said. "We could bring them the ice cream instead. Make a party of it."

"But if they could go themselves . . . ," Jahir said, trailing off.

"They talk a lot about how much they miss going outside," Vasiht'h said.

She looked from one of them to the other and sighed. "Fine, I'll talk to everyone that needs talking to. But no guarantees."

"That's all we ask," Jahir said with a bow that left her staring at him.

Vasiht'h was silent as he paced his roommate to the hospital entrance, where he paused so Jahir could dress for the weather: midnight-blue scarf, black gloves, gray coat. The Glaseah even remained virtuously quiet for part of the walk home, feeling the cool damp air like a blanket on his second back and feeling a touch of pity that the Eldritch had to wear so many layers. He was in the middle of wondering what Jahir would do when it got cold enough to snow when the Eldritch finally spoke.

"They have so little."

"I know," Vasiht'h said. "It was a generous thought. It's why I jumped in on it."

"And I thank you for that," Jahir said, tucking his scarf closer to his throat and then hiding his gloved hands in his pockets. "Perhaps she was right, however. It is rather cold for sick children to be out."

"If it is, the staff won't let them, don't fear on that account," Vasiht'h said. "You've put the notion in their heads that an outing would be nice, and something will come of it."

"One hopes," Jahir murmured. "Vasiht'h? The creation myth . . . you hold to it, though the Glaseah were engineered by the Pelted?"

"I guess that depends on what you mean by 'hold to it,'" Vasiht'h said. "We know it's not literally true. But what creation myth is? And does it matter if we made it up after or before we figured out how we were made?"

"I would think it would matter a great deal, in the same place where such myths ring true," Jahir said.

Vasiht'h looked up at him, saw only the edge of his jaw and the mound of the scarf against it. "The one part that matters is true, though. The Mother Goddess did make us. She dreamed us, and the Pelted scientists smiled in their sleep, and when they woke, it was to design us, just as She'd suggested." Vasiht'h turned his face to the sky. "Juvreth't and Slesvra fell from the sky, Juvreth't and Slesvra fell from a dropper into a petri dish, it's all the same in the end. There are a lot of ways for genetic engineering to fail. The ways that the Glaseah could have failed in particular are even more numerous, given how strange a combination of things they made us out of. But we didn't fail. And that's enough miracle to prove a deity to me."

They walked up the lane to the library apartments and were almost at the door when Jahir said, "Some would say that needing proof of one's deity is a flaw in one's faith."

Vasiht'h grinned. "Those people don't know Aksivaht'h. I challenge them to go tell the Goddess who thought the universe into existence not to use their own brains."

"A fascinating goddess, I should think, your Aksivaht'h."

"She'd like you," Vasiht'h said with a chuckle. When Jahir glanced at him quizzically, Vasiht'h passed through the door and said over his back, "She likes mysteries."

Jahir laughed and followed him in.

CHAPTER 10

IT WAS NOT YET THE WEEK FOR Sehvi's call, but the wall was displaying a priority-family tag. Vasiht'h looked up from his data tablet and frowned, then padded to the door to check the great room. Jahir wasn't back yet, but he should be soon . . . it was already late afternoon.

He closed the door and sat in front of the wall. "Accept the call."

And there, in glorious dark gray and white with a bright red sash wrapped diagonally over her teal vest, was his mother, looking perky and curious. "And here is my son! Hello, lovey. Have I interrupted anything?"

"Just a review," Vasiht'h said, showing her the data tablet and struggling with sudden worry at the unexpected call. "Is there anything wrong, Dami?"

"No, no," she said, waving a hand. "At least, nothing terribly serious. Your grandmother had a bit of a heart problem yesterday and went through surgery. She's fine today, prognosis is excellent. She's already giving the staff a piece of her mind about the blandness of the hospital food."

Vasiht'h blew out his breath in a rush. "Oh, thank the Goddess."

"It's nothing to be worried about," she said. "Your grandparents are just old. Bodies get cranky as you age." She grinned. "Ask me how I know this bit of wisdom."

"Let me guess," Vasiht'h said, trying his best innocent expression. "You researched it."

She laughed. "I wish. But no, I wanted to tell you that she might appreciate a note from you for when she's out of the hospital . . . and to find out how you're doing." Apparently his expression was eloquent, because she grinned. "And no, your sister hasn't been telling tales."

"I didn't think she had," Vasiht'h said. "I'm guessing mother's intuition."

"One of Aksivaht'h's uncatalogued gifts," his mother agreed. "Passed on from Great Mother to mothers everywhere. So? I assume you're not quite settled yet."

Vasiht'h winced. "And if I said . . . no?"

"Then I'd say I wasn't surprised," she said, startling him. She laughed, more kindly. "Oh, lovey. Don't you think I know what it's like growing up in our family? I raised you all, you know. And I'm aware that not quite knowing what you wanted out of life when all around you your brothers and sisters were striking out like arrows to a target must have been difficult. I was hoping, in fact, that getting away from us would help you clear your head a bit. Maybe hear that voice inside yourself more distinctly."

"Really?" Vasiht'h said, staring at her.

"Really," she agreed.

"But why . . . didn't you tell me that when I left?" Vasiht'h asked, mystified.

She laughed. "Would you have believed me? Or would you have been offended? Or resentful?"

Vasiht'h made a face. "Why do you know everything?"

"I don't," she said, smiling. "But what I do know, I know fairly well. You take my meaning, then."

"Yes," Vasiht'h admitted. "I would have been angry. I would have believed that you thought I was too weak to know my own mind unless I was out from under the influence of other people.

But . . . that's . . . what you said. Right now. Isn't it?"

"Yes," she said serenely. At his expression, she lifted her brows and prompted, "But you're not angry because . . ."

"Because it's true," Vasiht'h said, "and I've been out here long enough to be relieved to have the opportunity, and to know that it wasn't necessarily a reflection on me as a person, but on me as I was then, and the situation I was in?"

"I can see you are taking to your studies very well," she said, satisfied.

"I guess people aren't always ready to hear something," Vasiht'h said. "You can tell them the exact same thing at different times, and if you tell them too early, they don't really hear you. They hear something on the inside of their heads." He nodded. "I understand."

"Good," she said. "And now you can tell me all about how that's going for you." She put her chin in her hands in a mannerism she'd bequeathed to most of her children.

Vasiht'h grinned. "All right. As long as you're fine with the uncertainty."

"If you're still uncertain in five years . . . then I'll be concerned," she said. "For now, you're just making your way, lovey. Trust the process."

———⚬⚬⚬———

"So, midterms are coming up," Vasiht'h said. "How do you feel?"

They were sitting at the gelateria patio, watching the pedestrian traffic pass by. The cold was sufficient that Jahir almost wished for cider—a reminder of winters at home, and a warmth more than physical—but the calico behind the counter had talked him into adding hot water to his espresso and given him a bigger cup to drink it from so he could warm his gloved fingers on its walls. This he was doing while making slow progress through a scoop of mint gelato, and he was not insensible to the irony of having chosen a flavor that made his mouth feel colder when he was already chilled. "About my prospects for passing the examinations?"

"Yes?" the other said. "Are you nervous?"

Jahir considered. "I fear I am too tired to be nervous."

Vasiht'h laughed. "Well, that's one good thing about being busy, I guess. I'll have to remember that when I'm seeing patients. 'When in doubt, tire them out and their problems will seem less urgent.'"

"It does seem to work that way sometimes," Jahir said.

"Are you sleeping enough?" his roommate asked, eyeing him. "You seem more than normally tired. Is it the gravity again?"

"I assume not, or Healer KindlesFlame would have noticed," Jahir said, though he was surprised—and disarmed—that the effects of his not-quite-nightmares were obvious to the Glaseah. "He believes I am overexerting myself in my studies, but seems to think this is normal for first year graduate students."

Vasiht'h's brows rose. "Is there some reason Healer Kindles-Flame would know you well enough to be able to tell when you're not well-rested?"

"I have lunch with him every week," Jahir said. "We made the agreement subsequent to my first and only visit to the clinic . . . he wanted to watch me for issues." He tilted his head. "Is there some reason you know him?"

"Know him!" Vasiht'h laughed. "He was the last dean of the medical college!"

Jahir paused. "He never said. I knew he taught classes, but nothing else."

"Ha!" Vasiht'h said. "Tricky of him. But maybe it's not the sort of thing that comes up in conversation. 'Hi, nice to meet you, by the way here's my curriculum vitae.'"

"I fancy not," Jahir said, idly tapping his fingers on the mug in an absent piano exercise. "He is very fond of his work at the clinic, so I imagine he stepped down from the role."

"All the deans serve for limited periods," Vasiht'h said. "He had a good run, but you're right . . . he was glad to go back to the clinical setting. Though as you noticed he still teaches."

"I suppose it's comforting," Jahir said. "Knowing that no

matter what decision one makes, one can correct it."

The other fanned his ears forward. "Wondering which program track to choose?"

"More wondering what life will look like after school," Jahir said. He studied his companion, curious. "Do you know what you'll do when you're done here?"

"Not the slightest idea," Vasiht'h admitted.

"And yet you have been in school at this university for five years," Jahir said.

"I know," the other said, rueful. "My mother tells me not to worry unless I'm here for another five . . . but by that time, the program director will have kicked me out of the university, with or without a degree." He sculpted the top of his gelato with the tip of his spoon. "Really, there are only two choices . . . become a professor, or become a therapist."

"I observe that Healer KindlesFlame does both," Jahir said, sipping his coffee. He could feel his roommate's sudden regard and wondered if his continued contact with the children was eroding what little shield he had against other people's emotions. God and Lady help him.

"You are . . ." Vasiht'h trailed off, then huffed a soft laugh. "You are right. But doing both would require a lot more planning than I'm currently doing now . . . !"

"If you are truly passionate about both, then perhaps the planning is worth doing?" Jahir suggested.

"If I was truly passionate about both, I'd be doing it already," Vasiht'h said, and sighed. "The truth is I don't think I'm really passionate about anything. There are things I'm interested in. But grand passion? That's not something Glaseah are built for. We don't get swept up in rushes like species with more excitable hormone profiles."

Jahir glanced at him then, curious. "You never have passions? At all?"

"I suppose there are Glaseah that have," Vasiht'h said, flicking his ears back. "But there's a reason we have to be reminded to breed as a social duty. It's not something we feel. We're a very thinky bunch. Not very feely."

"And yet, you are a species of espers," Jahir said. "You do not feel each other's emotions?"

"Oh, of course we do," Vasiht'h said. "They're just not . . . not overwhelming, the way they are for other races. I've felt the way people of other races flood with passion about things. It's fascinating, but we don't feel things that way. That's why I don't really mind the contact. I can observe other people's feelings if I try hard enough, but I don't feel them—" Vasiht'h thumped his chest. "Not here, where it can make my heart race and my muscles squeeze."

"No wonder you have such equanimity surrounded by so many people," Jahir murmured, trying to imagine it. To touch without being bombarded by the emotions of others . . . to be able to sense their feelings without being moved by them . . . to be able to walk among other people without hiding his skin and armoring his body against their presences . . . it must be very . . . convenient. But he was not sure he would trade his sensitivity for that convenience. To be without passion . . .

"It has its good sides, and its bad sides," Vasiht'h said. "But I can't regret how I'm made." He paused, then laughed. "I mean, I literally can't feel it, I don't think."

"Perhaps you merely haven't run into the right stimulus," Jahir said.

"I doubt it," Vasiht'h said. "Two and a half decades isn't long to live, but that's got to be long enough to have developed some passionate feeling." He shook his head. "No . . . the artist who painted that mural on the wall across from us. That's passion. I can understand it, but I don't feel it."

Jahir followed a spoon of the mint ice cream with a sip of the coffee and marveled at how the temperature extremes canceled one another out on his tongue. Perhaps something similar happened in the blood chemistries of the Glaseah. But he couldn't help a touch of disbelief and was mulling the thought of what stimulus might actually invoke passion in a passionless people when he heard what he thought was a familiar sound through the noise of the late afternoon crowd on the street. "Is that . . . ?"

And it was: a violin, coming closer, the high notes piercing in their poignancy. He scanned the crowd for the player and found her in the shape of an Asanii, a feline the color of gray smoke with brown eyes. She was playing as she walked, and the crowd opened up around her, stilling to listen. A slow piece, a melody that led over and over again to an arpeggio, which she drew out and allowed to soften. The fourth time she did so, three other violinists erupted from the crowd, answering her invitation, and the arpeggio dashed on into a lively reel. It didn't take long for the street to devolve into dancing.

It had been so long since he'd heard music that he was stunned by the impact, of being close enough to watch the street-lights flash on the strings of the first player, to see the sun gilding the edges of her furred cheek. Every note seemed to vibrate through him, until he became clear as water and all the strain of the past weeks poured out through his skin.

When the song ended, he became aware of his roommate's stare and composed himself. "Pardon. I have a fondness for music."

"You can listen to it at home, you know," Vasiht'h said.

"I have listened to music through a computer before," Jahir said, thinking of the old console he'd used at home to access his study materials. "It was uninspiring."

"Maybe the sound system wasn't set up correctly," Vasiht'h said. "The one in the apartment is really nice. Even I can tell, and I don't have good hearing, not compared to the Pelted."

Jahir glanced at him.

"If it's good enough for a cat's ears, it's got to be good enough for yours," Vasiht'h said.

"I don't know," Jahir murmured, but the thought of being able to listen to music regularly was painfully enticing.

"Do you like string quartets like this?" Vasiht'h said. "I can find you some samples, maybe."

"I like anything with a melody," Jahir said.

Vasiht'h chuckled, soft. "I think that's the first revealing thing you've said about yourself, on purpose." He nodded at the players. "They're taking requests. Would you like to make one?"

"If they play again, they will have fulfilled it entirely," Jahir said. And they did play again. He settled in his chair with his fingers laced on his stomach and closed his eyes. The wind was uncomfortably chilling, but it had nothing to do with the goose-flesh that ran up his neck and over his arms as he listened, and grew warm all over.

The players didn't end their impromptu concert for over an hour. Vasiht'h enjoyed it—he liked music as much as anyone—but he was far more fascinated by his roommate's reaction to it than he was by the music. The Eldritch had a well-schooled face and self-contained mannerisms, so much so that his body was a cypher even for people trained in humanoid body language. For him to be showing this much enjoyment of something . . . the last time Vasiht'h could remember something similar was when he'd tried the gelato, and that was a brief, sensual delight, a flicker over his features. This . . . this was the bliss that Vasiht'h associated with temple visits, and seeing it made his fur fluff. Knowing that he could maybe produce that look on his roommate's face with the sound system in the apartment . . .

He'd introduced Jahir to many of the Alliance's conveniences and pleasures, but he could tell this one was going to top them all.

The rest of the conversation had also been intriguing. He had never had an opportunity to talk with an esper from a different species: outside the Glaseah, the talent was rare among the Pelted. He'd wondered why the Eldritch had developed their touch-aversion, but knowing that they experienced the feelings of others so viscerally made sense of it. But he couldn't imagine growing up without touching his family, without the tumbling-wrestling play of his brothers, and the warm drowsy naps curled up with his sisters. Embraces from his parents, so precious, particularly from his absent-minded father, and soothing touches when he was hurt or frightened . . . what was it like to grow up without that?

Jahir probably thought his passionless life a cause for regret. Vasiht'h thought a life without physical contact was just as bad.

"Magnificent," Jahir said at last, some time after the players had put away their instruments and vanished into the crowd. His sigh was just loud enough for Vasiht'h to hear it over the murmur of the students in the street. "Truly."

"Let's go back to the apartment," Vasiht'h said. "I'll find you a few violin concertos." He glanced at the sky and squinted. "Soon, before the sun completely sets."

"And then . . . ?"

"And then the students tired of studying come out to do whatever it is artists do in their market street," Vasiht'h said with a chuckle. "I've been here. It's a party, and it gets crowded." He stood, shaking the stiffness out of his paws—the pavement had been cold—and waited for his roommate to pick up his dishes. They returned them to the Asanii and headed back.

Once home, Vasiht'h undid his scarf and said, "Sit in the chair by the fire. That should be a good place."

"In the middle of the room?" Jahir said, shedding his coat and hanging it.

"In the middle of the room," Vasiht'h said firmly. "I wouldn't know, not having great ears, but I've been told that you want space all the way around you. Luci says it cramps the sound otherwise."

"Does it," Jahir murmured, bemused. But he sat on the chair and crossed his legs, hands resting on his knee. He didn't look like a man who expected to be experiencing an epiphany, Vasiht'h thought. It was going to be fun seeing how fast that changed. He gave the computer the task of finding chamber music that had been well-received and had been recorded at the highest fidelity. It gave him a list of selections, and he chose one at random, then padded over to the edge of the room and sat, expectant.

Jahir waited, chin propped on one hand with the forefinger extended up the cheek, patient and curious.

That pose, Vasiht'h noted, lasted about one heartbeat into the recording.

Strangely, the smug satisfaction he'd been anticipating—been looking forward to!—didn't rise at the sight of his roommate's breathless attention. He felt embarrassed instead, as if he was witnessing something too intimate for company, and a little bit humbled, because he couldn't think of a time he'd ever felt so strongly about anything as Jahir obviously did about listening to music. His family, maybe. But that was love, a comfortable and familiar sort of feeling. Not at all something he might worship with his posture, with the angle of his spine and his hands clenched on his knees, and his eyes closed and flickering. And perhaps—no, he was certain, that was a gleam in the folds beneath his closed eyes.

Vasiht'h had wept a few times in his life, in response to physical pain. To cry because of a feeling, because he was moved . . . he couldn't imagine it. He very much wanted to get up and leave Jahir to the privacy he deserved, but he was afraid of making noise, even to rise and sneak away.

So he stayed until the piece ended, some fifteen minutes later, and he felt every movement like a penance until his shoulders hunched and his ears flattened, and he could look at nothing except his hands folded together over his lower body's chest.

After the last notes died away, Vasiht'h thought to leave, but Jahir was so still . . . he almost feared breaking the silence more than the music.

But at last, Jahir said, "Ah, Vasiht'h. Such a gift."

It was not the sort of comment that wanted a cavalier response. Not said so quietly, so heartfelt. He flushed and said, "I had no idea, or I would have told you earlier."

"And I wouldn't have known to ask," Jahir said. "That recorded music could sound so real . . . !"

"I could teach you to use the library," Vasiht'h said, tentative. "And the compensation system . . ."

"Yes! Please," Jahir said. "Only . . . may I do it in my room? I would hate to disturb you."

"I don't mind it," Vasiht'h said. "I really don't. Anytime you want, you can use the great room for music. But yes, you can play it in your room too. I'll show you."

And this he did, an act that didn't take long, and then Vasiht'h thought to make his escape and leave the Eldritch to his communion. But as he gained the door leading back to the great room, Jahir said, "Vasiht'h? There is music here by Glaseah, I imagine? Do you have favorites? I'd like to hear your music."

"I don't always listen to music by Glaseah," Vasiht'h admitted. "But I do like some of the earlier composers . . ."

"Would you give me a tour?" Jahir said, and the brightness of his eyes seen past the floating display . . . Vasiht'h couldn't deny them, was secretly delighted to be asked, to be allowed to share this, no matter how poorly he was capable, with his far more intense friend.

He didn't even think of it until hours later, finally tumbling onto his nest of pillows and blankets, that Sehvi was right. At some point, Jahir had become more than a roommate. A friend. Strange and wondrous thought.

CHAPTER 11

"I WANT TO WARN YOU BEFORE you go in," Jill said as they joined her before the door into the room. "Persy's in intensive care for now."

"Is she—" Vasiht'h began, flicking his ears back.

"It's been a difficult few days," Jill said. "I can send you a message if something changes before you come back next week."

"Please," Jahir said.

"In the meantime, I think your visit is going to be a very welcome distraction," she said. "They miss her. And they're scared."

"Then we'll do our best to cheer them up," Vasiht'h said, glancing up at his roommate.

"Absolutely," Jahir said, in that voice Vasiht'h had come to expect from him: so calm to be so resolved. It settled him; he found he needed it. He knew the children were sick, of course. Intellectually. Opening the door and seeing one of them missing made it real in a way he found discomfiting. Their half-hearted greetings only made it worse.

"Come," Jahir said, waving them over to the floor by the window-seat, where they'd made themselves a corner nest with a soft colorful mat and pillows. They followed him as if he was calling magic to his fingertips, and he sat first with his back against the corner, before holding out a hand to the nearest, Amaranth. She went in his lap and Meekie curled up against his side. Vasiht'h sat facing his roommate and made a couch of his lower body, and Nieve and Kayla and Kuriel used it as a back-rest. He found the warm weight of their bodies grounding, even if their thoughts drooped like parched flowers.

"Not a good few days," Jahir said, surprising Vasiht'h, who hadn't thought broaching the topic directly a good idea.

"No," Kuriel said, picking at the toes of one of her paw-like feet. Her fur was thin there, probably from whatever treatment she was undergoing. "They had to take Persy away."

"She couldn't get up," Kayla said, subdued. "She didn't even try when Miss Jill asked. It was like she couldn't hear anyone. Her eyes weren't staring at anything, either."

"And they won't tell us anything," Kuriel said, slicking her ears back. She looked up, frightened but defiant. "Like we're too young to know. But she's our friend, and we're all sick. We know what they're doing. We know she might die. Do they think we don't?"

"I don't think they think that at all," Vasiht'h said. "I think they don't want to worry you, that's all."

"We worry more not knowing," Amaranth said in a small voice, and Vasiht'h remembered that she and Persy had the same diagnosis . . . some virulent cancer.

"Did they tell you about it?" Meekie asked, glancing up at Jahir.

"Alas, no more than they told you," Jahir said. "That she needed an intervention." At Meekie's frown, he said, "Help. Special help, to change something that was going on in her body."

"So you don't know when she'll be back either," Meekie said.

"Or if," Kuriel muttered.

Kayla said, "We made a card for her. Miss Jill suggested it. But she probably can't look at it, if she's sick enough to be somewhere else."

A brief silence as the girls contemplated this. Meekie broke it, plaintively, to say, "I wish I had chocolate."

"Me too," Kayla said.

"I'd like flowers," Nieve murmured.

"Oooh, yes," Meekie said. "Bright ones. Yellow and pink and white."

"Maybe a red one too," Kuriel said, drawn out of her glower. "Red flowers can be really happy-looking."

"What do you want?" Nieve asked Vasiht'h, twisting against his back to look at him.

"A cup of kerinne?" Vasiht'h said, since his real answer, 'for all of you to get better again,' seemed cruel. "Or, you know, my mother used to bake these ugly-shaped festival breads . . ."

"Ugly-shaped?" Kuriel asked, ears flicking forward with interest.

"Oh yes," Vasiht'h said. "My mother was a professor, and always very busy between all of us kids and her work. She didn't really have much time to be a good cook, but she refused to buy the festival breads; she said it was against the spirit of the Creator Goddess's holiday to get someone else to make something for you. So every year she would shake out the instructions and painstakingly make the bread, from bowl full of yeast to knotting it to baking it. And every year, it was hideous, lumpy and strange." Vasiht'h smiled, eyes lowered. Then shook his head. "But delicious. It was always delicious."

"It wouldn't have been the same if it was pretty," Kayla said. "Because then it wouldn't have been your mom's bread."

"Yes," Vasiht'h said. "She kept trying, because she wanted to do something special for us."

"What about you?" Meekie asked Jahir. "What do you want right now?"

Ordinarily Vasiht'h would have been very interested in this answer. Looking at his roommate, though, he saw strain lines around Jahir's eyes and mouth. It made him wish the Eldritch hadn't been so adamant about allowing the girls to touch him.

He was so busy being worried that Jahir's answer caught him completely off-guard and left him laughing with everyone else.

"I want," Jahir said. "A *pony*."

———∝∞∝———

The pony answer had been in earnest, apparently, because Jahir told the girls a story about learning to ride on a pony, and his adventures with the pony, and it was better than any storybook as far as they were concerned. Vasiht'h was so relieved to see the children smiling that he was disturbed . . . his anxiety at their distress was a far more acute feeling than he was accustomed to. It was on his mind all the way back home, and he was still mulling it over when Jahir set a bowl on the counter and said, "You must make cookies."

"What?" Vasiht'h asked, startled, looking up at him.

"I would guess that if I asked, you would tell me that Glaseah do not brood," Jahir said. "Despite your giving every indication of doing so. Whatever it is that has furrowed your brow, though, it will be removed by baking . . . and we have a quad meeting tomorrow night, so the results won't go to waste." He took down a spatula from the tools hanging against the wall and set it with great deliberation on the bowl. "So. Come and bake. I will measure the ingredients for you if it pleases you, or if you prefer it, you may do so yourself."

Vasiht'h stared up at his roommate, wide-eyed. "I . . . don't know what to say."

"Say 'Jahir, I would like a cup of tea while I am working on this, would you make it for me, please?'"

"That sounds nice?" Vasiht'h said weakly. And added, "What kind of cookies am I making?"

"Your nut butter cookies are very popular at the meetings," Jahir said, bringing the kettle to the sink. "We have ingredients for it."

"Which you know because . . ."

"I did the shopping," Jahir finished. "And I have learned to put aside materials for baking against your occasional upsets."

"I don't have upsets," Vasiht'h protested, though not as aggressively as he felt he should.

"Then against the times when you have issues to work out," Jahir said. He began heating the tea. "Come, take up the spatula. I'll leave you to think, if you wish."

"No," Vasiht'h said, and sighed out, a deep sigh that seemed to come all the way from his lower lungs. "No, I'd like it if we talked." He padded into the kitchen, careful not to bump into his taller roommate.

"It's about the children, I imagine," Jahir said, spooning some of the tea leaves into a wire strainer.

"I guess that part was obvious," Vasiht'h said. "It's just . . . I know they're seriously sick. I don't want them to get sicker. I want them to get better."

"Of course," Jahir said, and glanced at him.

"You are looking at me like you can't believe I noticed it? Hadn't noticed it before?" Vasiht'h started going through the cabinets for supplies. "We're out of vanilla extract."

"I had not known we had it," Jahir said. "I suppose we could pay for the genie fee?"

"No," Vasiht'h said with a wrinkled nose. "I don't really want to use up our energy budget on baking supplies. I'll just improvise, I guess." He hunted through the extracts he had left. Lemon? With nut butter? No. "You haven't agreed with me. Or disagreed."

"Should I have an opinion?" the Eldritch said, a little more delicately than Vasiht'h expected. He looked up over his shoulder at his roommate. "It is a matter you might find offensive. Or troubling."

"That you think I might be distressed that children could die?" Vasiht'h said.

"That *you* think you might *not* be distressed that children could die."

Vasiht'h froze, tub of sugar in his arms. He was aware of his own heart racing.

"Vasiht'h?"

"I . . . of course I . . ." He put the tub down and rubbed his forehead. "It hurts, thinking about it."

"It would be abnormal for it not to," Jahir said.

"That's the problem," Vasiht'h said. "I don't want to feel those things. It's not overwhelming, you know, more like . . . like an anxiety. But I'm not sure why I'm feeling it. Am I gratified it's not as intense an emotion as I imagine you would feel? Am I disturbed that I felt anything at all? Am I disturbed that I didn't feel it more deeply? One of the reasons I decided on psychology was because I like people, Jahir . . . but also that I feel like I can survive hearing about their problems and helping them with their grief, because I don't have that deep an empathy. What if I'm wrong? What if the first really hard case I tackle demonstrates to me that I'm not going to be able to handle it?"

Jahir was silent, setting the lid on the teapot and fetching two cups and placing them on two saucers. He brought out spoons and honey, and only when he'd set everything on a towel did he say, "Maybe you won't. Would it be so bad to have empathy?"

"It would if it prevented me from doing my work!" Vasiht'h exclaimed.

"Were you decided then, on the clinical track? I thought you were also considering the research concentration."

"I was, sure, but . . ." Vasiht'h trailed off. "I wasn't sure if I wanted clinical. Now that I think I might not be able to do it, I'm upset. Does that mean it's what I wanted in the first place? Or is it just that I'm unhappy that I no longer have any choices?"

"Perhaps that is what you must contemplate while baking," Jahir said. He took his cup of tea. "Make your batter, alet. I'll build us a fire."

"All right," Vasiht'h said, feeling out-of-proportion comforted by the domesticity of it all. He sighed and went through the cupboard. Nut butter with nut extract? For extra nuttiness? He had Selnoran more-almond, which he'd bought on a whim when he'd had too much spare fin. He should have saved it, but he couldn't pass up a gourmet import. He set out all his ingredients and tools and went to work, and at the edge of his vision he could see Jahir moving to and fro, bringing wood, stacking it with expert hands, and coaxing the fire to life. The Glaseah was completely sure that no one had ever used the fireplace since the apartments had been built, and if they had, he couldn't imagine they'd been as good at making them as Jahir. There seemed to be a trick to it, or at least, a system.

But he made the cookies, and the routine calmed him. He'd done this for as long as he could remember, first with his older sisters, then by himself, then teaching his younger sisters. Not just baking, but cooking too. The creation myth had mentioned nothing about whether the Goddess had given Glaseah discerning palates, but Vasiht'h loved the smell and taste of fresh food, and more than that, loved the meditative process of making it.

He put in a tray to bake—three cookies, two for him and one for Jahir—and stored the remainder of the dough for tomorrow so the results would be fresh for the gathering. Then he took his cup of tea, still warm from the teardrop-sized heater in the saucer, and brought it with him to the hearth, where the fire was hissing and snapping.

"I don't know what to think," he said once he'd settled. "But I'm a little calmer about the uncertainty."

"A great wisdom, that," Jahir said, "given how little in life is certain."

"Yes," Vasiht'h murmured. "I guess that's the point."

CHAPTER 12

WHEN JAHIR HAD FIRST STARTED classes, he'd found the material daunting: not just dense, but wall-like, insurmountably complex. There were so many species in the Alliance, to be so varied and yet to have come from the same fount. Humans had engineered a batch of ur-Pelted; those Pelted had developed, via segregation during their exodus from Earth and some tinkering by Pelted scientists, into the core species of the Alliance: Team Cat and Team Dog, as Vasiht'h had put it. But there were others: the inscrutable Naysha, created by humans as the same time as the Pelted, meant to function as mermaids— mercats? Merotters? God and Lady knew—but in practice far more alien than ever any mermaid of myth. As well as the Aera and the Malarai: extreme human experiments the Pelted had rescued just barely from genetic self-destruction. And then the Pelted had engineered new species of their own, in what Jahir suspected had been an attempt to come to terms with their own identity as made-people . . . and that had given rise to the Glaseah, the Ciracaana, the Phoenix. And then there were the true aliens, the Platies and Flitzbe, with whom few people could truly communicate and almost no one saw, and the Akubi, with whom there could be communication, often more meaningful than the conversations that could be sustained with the ostensibly less alien Phoenix.

It was a truly boggling amount of information to absorb, and Jahir had lacked any of the cultural context that might have helped, context someone like Vasiht'h would have had growing up as one of the members of the Alliance. The Eldritch were not technically members, but allies, like humanity; unlike humanity, however, the Eldritch had embraced their xenophobia and chosen not to foster any stronger tie with their neighbor than was necessary to ensure they were left alone.

When he first started the classes, he'd been behind. He'd worked hard to catch up to his classmates, and he was certain he hadn't. Not really. The chemistry, the basics of the biology, that he could grasp, did grasp easily, in fact. But he often couldn't remember how many Pelted races there were, or their names, and recalling information specific to their brain chemistry without the framework for something as fundamental as knowing all of them by heart . . .

He'd been very frustrated.

But at some point, all that confusion had . . . vanished. A scaffold had appeared in his mind, become populated with scent, sound, sight and memory. Some of those memories were his own: sitting on a bench, watching other students pass by; taking notes in the back corner of a room, listening to one of his classmates ask a question; pouring tea for one of the quadmates at the weekly evening gatherings.

But most of those memories weren't his.

They were the girls'.

He'd begun absorbing the Alliance culture through the skins of the children when he held them or touched them. When he tucked them into their beds, they gave him their fatigue and their fear, and also their worlds. He'd had no idea it was happening until he'd spread his books and data tablet on the desk in his room so he could begin his studies for the midterm examinations. Staring at the diagrams in one of the books as he opened it, seeing the information on the page, so bald without context, brought it into abrupt focus.

He sat, very hard.

The dreams grew more powerful with each visit they paid the children. They remained free of overt menace; for the most part they were things of pale grief. But they were completely involving, and it didn't matter that the children did not have a sense for how much they would miss if they died, could not invest those dreams with regret. Jahir had already lived over ten times their lifetimes so far, and he did know what they would miss if they died, and it hurt him horribly to know.

But he had found somewhere to go, to keep himself from feeling just how unbearable that sorrow was . . . and it was to his roommate.

Vasiht'h took him to ice cream, to galleries, to the quiet parties every week in the center of the quad. Vasiht'h sat near him, studying in their great room, sharing the fire and the busy, contented quiet. Vasiht'h cooked while he did laundry; made him laugh even when he didn't let those laughs reach his lips; steadied him when they went to the hospital. Perhaps four feet made it easier to stay grounded . . . the thought made him smile. But he was deeply grateful for having met the Glaseah.

Nevertheless, it troubled him that he'd taken so much from the children. The Eldritch ethical philosophy on the use of esper abilities was quite straightforward: don't. The nuances of how one dealt with the children's accidental gifts were not described in a normal Eldritch universe. Waking up melancholic from the dreams of their plight didn't seem enough compensation, particularly when he realized that Kuriel had taken care of his problem with Seersana's calendar. As might be expected of a race that had created all the major languages of the Alliance for the genetically-engineered Pelted, including Universal, the Seersa had a deep and broad tongue of their own, one that included every known phoneme that could be created by a humanoid mouth and throat. Their calendar had sixteen months in four seasons, and all of them had names that Jahir could not, for the life of him, remember . . . until he could. Kuriel, the only Seersa in the group, native to the world and the language, had somehow passed it to him through her skin.

———— ✣ ————

"You seem preoccupied," KindlesFlame said. "This is mid-terms week, isn't it? Worried about that?"

"No," Jahir said truthfully. The waiter, a Seersa male with tiger stripes on a brown pelt, set down their cups, black coffee for the Tam-illee and black tea for him. The plate between them held a selection of what were locally called chat-snacks, small, bite-sized samples of the foods these coffeehouses served.

"So, if not that, then what?" KindlesFlame said, plucking up a square of cheese decorated with a curled slice of sweet pepper.

Jahir debated the merits of maintaining his silence. He valued his privacy and felt bound to keep the Eldritch Veil. Nor was KindlesFlame an esper himself, to give him advice specific to his conundrum. But the Tam-illee was a healer, educated in what constituted professional behavior in a clinical setting, and he had broad experience as an administrator of both a school and a clinic, tasks that had no doubt involved counseling juniors on similar problems. Jahir glanced up, found the man studying him with a frank expression, curious without veering into unseemly interest.

"You are aware, somewhat, of how my abilities work?" he said at last.

"You're a contact-esper, yes?" KindlesFlame said. "I assume that when you touch people, you get some sense of their surface thoughts and emotions."

"Their emotional state I can sometimes sense without touch-ing, if it's intense enough," Jahir said. "But touching, yes. Skin to skin particularly. Often more than their surface thoughts, and a great deal more than their surface emotions, depending on the length of the contact. Clothing blunts it somewhat." He paused, then said, "This being my experience. Every Eldritch is different."

"Naturally," KindlesFlame said. "Go on, then."

"The children at the hospital . . . I have been allowing that sort of contact." Jahir looked at the plate and moved one of the small caramels with a fork, but did not take it. "It seems mean to refuse them when they want to be held."

"I couldn't imagine doing it," KindlesFlame agreed. "So. You've been reading them. Where's the ethical problem?"

"I think . . . it's helping me with my studies," Jahir said. "I now have a better sense for the cultures of the varied Pelted species. And I seem to have finally fixed the Seersan calendar in mind."

"And this concerns you because you feel you've taken something from the minds of these children without their permission," KindlesFlame said. He tapped the caramel with the side of his fork. "If you're going to play with that, at least put it on your plate. Better yet, eat it."

Jahir obliged and halved it with his fork while KindlesFlame considered. It made him feel better, that the Tam-illee had divined the source of his discomfort so quickly, and did not minimize it with an easy response. He let the other man think while attending to his plate. The caramel was salted and had some spice in it. Living with Vasiht'h had given him enough of an education in them to guess at it. Cardamom, perhaps? Nutmeg? Something with a touch of a citrus. It married well with the tea.

"These thoughts you get from them," KindlesFlame said. "Private things, I imagine?"

"Were they my thoughts I wouldn't discuss them with anyone," Jahir said, and because KindlesFlame had asked—a healer, a professor, and the former Dean of a medical college— he analyzed the thoughts he could remember receiving and said, "Though not in the sense that they contain personal information. More . . . thoughts in response to being ill. As one might imagine from their situation."

"Of course," KindlesFlame said. "Have you discussed those thoughts with anyone?"

"No," Jahir said. "I would never. I have not asked permission."

"And I assume these children don't know that you've gotten something from this exchange," KindlesFlame said.

"They knew they were not supposed to touch me because

it meant I would know their thoughts," Jahir said. "Vasiht'h explained it to them when first we met. But that was some time ago, and such things slip from the minds of children unless reinforced. Particularly in the face of a deeper acculturation toward touch as a source of comfort."

KindlesFlame chuckled softly. "You're getting the language right . . . good for you." He wedged his fork under one of the other caramels and lifted it onto his plate. "I'm guessing that's the real source of your unease. You haven't discussed it with them. Have you considered telling them what's going on and asking them if it bothers them?"

"No," Jahir said, surprised.

"I would recommend that," KindlesFlame said. "Explain to them the cost of touching you, see if they're comfortable with paying it. If they say it's fine, then your ethical problem disappears. If they say it's not, then you tell them you can no longer hug them. Part of autonomy, alet, is patients accepting they have responsibilities to fulfill in the healer/patient relationship."

"They're children," Jahir said. "How much autonomy can you expect them to have? They are still wards of their parents."

"I think it's even more important with children," KindlesFlame said. He warmed his hands on his cup. "You're right in that they aren't allowed to make decisions as to their care; that's the responsibility of their guardians and the patient advocates assigned to them. So little remains in their control. Letting them make any decision at all helps immensely."

"Then I must," Jahir murmured. "And I thank you for helping me to settle the matter."

"Of course, this doesn't answer your broader question," KindlesFlame said, "which involves the ethical use of your abilities in a clinical setting . . . and that's not something we have guidelines on. We don't have enough espers to justify a class on psychic ethics for medical personnel, and even if we did, we don't have any materials made up for it. There's probably a book on it somewhere, though." He frowned, thoughtful. "You might check in the library, see what you find. But I suspect it's something you're going to have to work out for yourself if you go the clinical or medical routes. The latter particularly." Jahir glanced at him, and he finished, "When you're seeing patients in an office, the likelihood of your touching them by accident is very low. When you're seeing them in a trauma unit and they're flailing on a bed . . ."

Jahir said, "Yes . . . I see."

"You know there's a bulletin on you out," KindlesFlame added casually.

"Ah?"

"The Dean of the Medical College and the head of the children's hospital are both friends of mine," the Tam-illee said. "They sent a note to their staff and faculty about your care and feeding." He stirred his caramel-sticky spoon in his coffee and sipped. "Apparently, your arrival was a first for the entire university, not just my clinic."

"I imagine so," Jahir said.

"They're quite concerned with keeping you happy," Kindles-Flame said. "The dean tells me the word is that you're withdrawn in your classes. She's worried this is a sign that you're displeased. Is it?"

"Displeased!" Jahir said. "No. I'm just staying out of the way."

"Preventing entanglements?" KindlesFlame said with an arched brow.

Surprised, Jahir said, "Ah—yes."

The Tam-illee said, "Tell me, alet. What would you say to someone studying a subject that is bound to put them in constant contact with other people, who also holds himself apart from them to prevent entanglements?"

"That he should perhaps avoid too-perspicacious Tam-illee professor-healers," Jahir said.

KindlesFlame snorted and said no more, but then, he didn't have to. Jahir had received the message quite clearly.

⸺◦∞◦⸺

"You've done well," Palland said, setting his data tablet aside.

"I have all your tests back and you've gotten great scores on all of them."

"That's good news," Vasiht'h said, dropping onto the pillows across from his major professor's desk.

"But you've always done well on your tests," Palland said, "so that's nothing new. And you've been avoiding me, Vasiht'h."

"I know," Vasiht'h said. "I've been studying more than I anticipated. This semester's been . . . different."

"Different," Palland repeated, lifting one furry brow.

"Different," Vasiht'h said. "I . . . I think I might be going research."

The other brow rose to meet its twin. "Exactly what is this difference? It must be an extreme one to have caused you to make a decision. I admit to suspicion."

"I'm just not sure I'd be suited to a clinical environment," Vasiht'h said, rubbing one paw on the other.

"If you were happy about that decision, you wouldn't be fidgeting while telling me about it," Palland said, and came around his desk. He drew up one of the chairs and sat on it, leaning forward with hands clasped between his knees. "All right, alet. Talk to me."

"I'm just not sure I'll be able to maintain emotional distance from my clients," Vasihth said, looking down at his feet.

Palland's eyes narrowed. "Let's back up a bit and start at the beginning. Why haven't you been haunting my office the way you usually do?"

"I really have been busy," Vasiht'h said. "Studying. And . . . I have a roommate, we've been doing a lot of things together."

"Including volunteering at All Children's, yes?"

Vasiht'h looked up, startled. "You know about that?"

Palland snorted. "Alet, everyone knows about it. There's only one Eldritch on campus and you're at his side half the time."

"More than half, if you count the time we spend at the apartment," Vasiht'h said, and sighed. "Anyway, it's not about him. It's about the volunteering. It's made me realize . . . maybe I'm never going to be a good therapist."

"You realize this is a little like a surgeon taking on a completely shattered body as his first patient and determining from his imperfect performance that he'll never be any good at surgery," Palland said.

"I know," Vasiht'h said. "I'm aware that dying children are a worst-case scenario when you're talking about therapy. But if I can't handle the worst cases, sir, should I even be bothering with the easier ones? What's the guarantee I won't fail on those too?"

"You may be overreacting," Palland said, gently.

"I may be," Vasiht'h agreed. "But I'd still like to have next semester's schedule center on research courses."

"All right," Palland said. "Have you chosen a research topic? You'll need one by the end of spring term if you're going that way."

"I . . . I haven't," Vasiht'h said, flattening his ears. "But I'm sure I'll come up with something."

"Give it some thought," Palland said.

—∞∞∞—

When Vasiht'h arrived, Jahir was setting out the cookie trays. He'd found the dough Vasiht'h had moved from the freezer compartment to the refrigerated and thought to save him some work. "Good after—did something happen, alet?"

"What? No," Vasiht'h said. He shook himself and drew his messenger bag from his shoulder. "No, I'm just distracted, that's all. Things are fine, I passed all my exams. You?"

"I did as well," Jahir said, satisfied. "And we have a message from Hea Berquist: Persy is out of danger and back with the other children."

"She is?" Vasiht'h said, looking up sharply. "Oh, that's . . . that's wonderful. That's great!"

"So I have hazarded the guess that I might be able to finish the cookies for tonight's gathering."

"Because I won't need to?" Vasiht'h laughed. "Okay, yes. Go ahead." He went into his room; Jahir heard the thump of the bag hitting the floor next to Vasiht'h's desk. The Glaseah's voice came through the open door. "So how are you feeling about things? Being halfway through the term and all."

Jahir considered, then resumed setting little scoops of dough on the trays. "Satisfied. I may in fact survive this degree."

Vasiht'h laughed from the door to his room, padded over to the kitchen. "Want something? Coffee? I'm making kerinne for myself."

"Coffee sounds fine," Jahir said. "So what has you distracted?"

The Glaseah eyed him. "Do you always listen to everything so carefully?"

Amused, Jahir said, "Should I not be paying attention to you when you speak?"

Vasiht'h snorted and got out the pot, setting it on one of the burners. "I was just thinking about a research topic."

"Ah . . . so you've made a choice?" Jahir asked, careful of his tone.

"I think so," Vasiht'h said, and glanced over at him. "You don't approve."

"I hardly think it my place to approve or disapprove," Jahir said. "But I do question how someone who managed to derive any emotional content from my last statement would not be wasted in a laboratory."

Vasiht'h laughed. "Just make the cookies."

"I hear and obey," Jahir said, to make the Glaseah laugh again, and counted himself well-pleased when it worked. He sipped the coffee when it appeared at his elbow and put the cookies in to bake. He did not have his roommate's touch with food, but he was at least comfortable in the kitchen now; he could cook and bake most things, so long as they weren't too complicated, and he could prepare any number of warm drinks without burning himself or scalding them. His cuisine would not have passed muster with the head of the kitchen at home, but it was often quite edible. All in all, he was satisfied with his progress, given that he'd never seen a modern appliance before moving here.

"So," he said, as he cleaned and the scent of nut butter and sugar slowly began to fill the air. "A research topic? Have you any thoughts on the matter?"

"None," Vasiht'h said, sounding resigned. "I'm hoping to get some ideas tonight. You know, by not thinking about it."

"I've heard it often works that way," Jahir said.

Vasiht'h craned his head past the chair to look at him, but Jahir kept his face smooth and his eyes strictly on the tray he was rinsing for the party.

"You have a wicked sense of timing," Vasiht'h said at last. "With that dry humor of yours."

"I have no idea where I might have learned it, either," Jahir said, and ducked when Vasiht'h pantomimed throwing a pillow at him. But he grinned as he dried the tray. His relief at passing his examinations and having a course of action to pursue in regards to the children had lightened his spirits considerably.

They were not the first ones to the meet in the center of the apartment courtyard. Brett was already there, sitting on a stool with his paws hooked on one of the rungs. He looked up when they entered and held up his wine glass, already in use. "To hellish midterms. Speaker-Singer damn and praise them, for toughening us up."

"Failed something?" Vasiht'h asked.

"No, but it was a near thing with histology," Brett said. "Bring me one of those cookies, I need to stimulate my brain chemistry."

From the door, Luci said, "That didn't even make sense, Brett."

"I'm telling you, the neurons are fried," Brett said. "It's the pre-exam cramming."

"Or the post-exam wining," Luci said dryly and set her insulated pitcher of cider alongside the bottle. "Where's Merashiinal?"

"Merashiinal is here, with roommate, and food," the Ciracaana said, ducking into the room with a bag in his arms. The aroma was mouth-watering, whatever it was. "Did not have energy to cook, so I have hunted for you instead. At the wild, wild restaurant."

The Ciracaana's roommate was another female Seersa with a black and white pelt, often too busy to attend, which Jahir found

a pity because she sang when tipsy, and she had a fine mezzoso-
prano that made him miss the choral work at home. Leina said,
"The wild, wild human restaurant, even."

"Ooh," Brett said. "Yes. Bring it here. Let's have some vintage
food, something ancient enough for our DNA to recognize."

"How about it, Merashiinal?" Vasiht'h asked. "Is it raw meat?
That should satisfy Brett's craving."

"Sadly, not raw," the Ciracaana said. "But curry!" To Jahir, he
added, "You will like it, tall stalk."

"If it tastes anything like it smells, I know I shall."

Leina held up a small hand. "Wait." Everyone looked at her.
"Did we pass?"

A chorus of 'yes's answered her.

"Good!" she said. "Because along with whatever it is that
Vasiht'h has baked, and it smells amazing, I brought ice cream."

"Alet," Jahir said, "you are my new favorite person."

She laughed. "Your new favorite Seersa, anyway. We already
know who your favorite person is."

Jahir glanced at Vasiht'h and lifted a brow. Vasiht'h shrugged
and leaned just a little toward him. "Don't mind them. They're
jealous."

It was a festive gathering, and they ate all the curry—which
was in fact, just as delicious as it smelled—and the others drank
wine and Jahir had cider and all of them had cookies and ice
cream and stayed up far too late debating which of them had
had a harder time with midterms, until at last the meet began
to disperse.

"So, Brett-arii," Vasiht'h said when only he, Jahir and the
Seersa remained, "what's going on with Luci?"

"You noticed, did you," Brett said.

"It's kind of hard not to notice," Vasiht'h said. "She was the
first to leave, and that almost never happens. And she was more
snappish than usual, and talked a lot less. Is something wrong?
Do you know?"

"Yes and no," Brett said. "Respectively. She hasn't talked to
me about it, and I haven't heard anything through the walls, so

to speak."

"A school matter perhaps?" Jahir offered, curious.

"I doubt it," Brett said. "Luci's so good at this that she arrived already on the Dean's List, practically, and she hasn't left it since. People joke about her staking the territory out."

"Personal then, maybe?" Vasiht'h asked.

"It's a better guess," the Seersa said with a sigh. "But a guess is all it is." He slipped off the stool and whuffed. "Well. I have drunk enough to float a starbase. I'd better waddle home before my kidneys regain consciousness and start punching my spine."

"Now there's an image," Vasiht'h said, one ear sagging.

Brett grinned. "You know how it is with the healers. Macabre humor. Night, you two."

Vasiht'h folded his arms, frowning at the door, then turned and said, "You noticed it too, didn't you?"

"Of course," Jahir said. And then, because the imp was in him, added, "So has a research topic sprung fully-formed into your head?"

"Don't make me hit you with the tray," Vasiht'h said.

Jahir hid his smile and opened the door for them both.

CHAPTER 13

HE FIRST THING VASIHT'H DID when they saw Persy was hug her. He did it quickly so she wouldn't see his expression at the sight of her, so thin and wan. She'd been so small already . . . her time in intensive care seemed to have wicked her away. "We missed you!" he said.

"I missed you too!" she said.

When Vasiht'h released her, she looked up at Jahir, and he went to one knee and gravely offered her his hand. She shyly set hers in it and then stepped into his arms: little head, ragged blonde hair in a tail with a purple-and-pink flower clip, pressed against a broad shoulder, with one of the Eldritch's pale hands resting on her narrow back . . .

Vasiht'h lost his breath and couldn't say why. Just that he thought he'd remember the sight forever: a little girl who was paying too much to stay alive, and a man who was paying too much to love her.

When Jahir leaned back, he studied Persy's face and then kissed her brow. "You're back now," he said.

"We told her it wasn't the same without her," Amaranth said.

"No one speaks up for the dragons," Kayla agreed.

Jahir chuckled. "Well, now the dragons have their advocate

once again. Shall we speak, ariisen? For there is something I must ask you."

And what was this about? Vasiht'h wondered, and sat in the pillowed story corner with as much curiosity as the rest of them. Jahir sat and rested his hands on his knees, studying the faces lifted to his.

"When we first met," he said, "in the parking lot, jumping rope. Do you remember Vasiht'h's explanation of why you must not touch me?"

"Because you feel our feelings," Kayla said. "That's what he said."

"That's right," Jahir said. "But we have been touching recently, and I am concerned that you have not remembered what that means."

The girls glanced at one another. Kuriel said, "It means you're reading our minds, I guess."

"It does," Jahir said. "And I wasn't certain that was something you wished to allow."

"Well . . . why not?" Kuriel asked. "I mean, what does it hurt?"

That gave Jahir pause, so Vasiht'h filled it. "Sometimes we have thoughts and feelings we don't want other people to know about."

"Like what?" Meekie asked, more curious, Vasiht'h thought, about this hypothetical person's potentially interesting thoughts than about any application to her own situation. He suppressed his chuckle and said, "For instance, maybe you have a friend who tells you that she gets to go to a big party that you didn't get invited to. And you want to be nice to her and be happy for her, but you're really upset that you can't go. Would you want her to know that you were upset? Or would you rather she believed you when you said you were happy for her?"

That gave them pause. Then Amaranth said, "I think most of the time I just say 'aw, I wish I could go' . . . ?"

"Yeah, and then the other girl understands, because she'd want to go if she couldn't," Kayla agreed.

Kuriel added, "As long as you weren't too mean about it. You say the 'aw' part once and then you don't keep thinking about it."

"And then the girl tells you she'll save you a piece of cake and try to bring you back a balloon!" Meekie added.

"And if she can't, she can at least bring you back all her memories of it, and spend a wonderful afternoon telling you every detail," Nieve said, wistful.

The pause this time belonged to the adults. Looking at them, Nieve said, "I think you mean different kinds of thoughts, right? Like if our parents could feel it when we hurt inside."

"Yes," Jahir said. "Like that."

"And you know those things," Nieve said.

"When you touch me, you tell me. Not on purpose, though you could so direct your thoughts if you wished. But yes."

Nieve glanced at Persy, who nodded.

"But then someone knows," Persy said. "Someone who won't hurt as much as our families would. But at least someone understands."

Vasiht'h said, "What about your friends here? Don't they understand?"

Persy glanced at the other girls, and in their gazes there was an accord. "Well, they do too. But not completely."

"Even I can't know what you feel completely," Jahir said, his voice gone suspiciously husky.

"But it's pretty close, isn't it?" Persy said. "When you hugged me, I could tell you were taking it in. You were, weren't you."

"Yes," Jahir said.

"Then it's someplace safe," Persy said. "Nieve's right."

"The question is, does it hurt you?" Nieve asked.

Jahir cleared his throat and said, "Hurt is a strong word."

It was, and Vasiht'h wondered suddenly just how well his roommate was handling all this. They slept on opposite sides of the apartment, separated by several walls. Would he know if Jahir was suffering?

"But if it's the right word . . . ," Amaranth said.

"Say rather that it can be uncomfortable. The way it can be when you hug someone and their elbow is in your stomach,"

Jahir said, with such a straight face that Vasiht'h didn't catch why the girls were giggling until he replayed the words in his head. "So, am I hearing then that you do not mind my knowing your thoughts."

"No!" Amaranth said, and was the first to hug him, and then all the rest did too . . . at the same time, and sitting across from the Eldritch, Vasiht'h couldn't decide if the expression on his face was pain or happiness. Maybe it was both? He almost reached out to intervene, but no matter what Jahir said about allowing children to touch him, adults were a different matter.

"You also teach me things," Jahir said when the flood had receded and he remained with only Nieve in his lap. Persy migrated over to nestle against Vasiht'h's bulk, and the others arranged themselves in between.

"Like what?" Amaranth wondered.

"Kuriel has apparently taught me how to count days and months in Seersan," Jahir said. "A matter I believe I would never have mastered without her subconscious aid."

Another chorus of giggles. "Well, it is hard for non-Seersa," Kuriel said, earnest. "But most of them get it after a few years."

"I have, but don't ask me to pronounce them without an accent!" Vasiht'h said.

"What else have we taught you?" Kayla wondered.

"I can now remember the differences between all the Pelted," Jahir said. "Something I was also having trouble with . . . there are rather a lot of you, and I come from a world with only one sentient species."

"That's a good one to know," Persy said. "Because there really are a lot of Pelted."

"You have given me so much, in fact, that I feel the scales are uneven," Jahir said. "I wish I might give you something in return."

"Oh, but you do!" Meekie exclaimed. "You give good dreams!"

"I . . . what?"

The other girls were nodding. "When you tuck us in. We dream about nice things. Unicorns and music and summer."

"All of you?" Jahir asked, bewildered.

They glanced at one another. Kayla said, "Well, it's strongest the day you tuck us in."

"But I still have dreams with summer mornings a few days after," Meekie offered. "They're just not as strong."

The other girls nodded.

Jahir looked at Vasiht'h, wide-eyed. "This is perhaps something you are doing?"

Vasiht'h shook his head. "Not intentionally. And if it were coming from me, it wouldn't be unicorns and music and summer. It would be the sorts of things my sibs and mother used to lull me to sleep with. The evening sky and the stars dancing and the Mother Goddess breathing through the wind chimes." He cocked his head. "Have you been trying to give them good dreams?"

"I . . . I do wish them to have pleasant dreams," Jahir said. "And I admit to the unicorns." He glanced at the girls and said, "They being protectors—"

"Like on your ring!" Amaranth crowed.

"We remember," Kayla agreed.

"Then it's probably you, yes," Vasiht'h said.

"I . . . I never intended!"

"But we like it!" Kuriel protested. "They're nice dreams."

"And I wake up feeling better," Meekie said with a nod.

"Does it make you feel better?" Kuriel asked. "Knowing you're trading instead of just taking things?"

"I admit I would feel far better if I'd known I was doing it," Jahir said helplessly.

"We didn't know we were giving you our useful thoughts either," Kayla pointed out. "So it was like that for us too."

"Maybe we should just stop trying to understand it and be happy about it," Persy said.

"That sounds like reasonable advice to me," Vasiht'h said. "How about a board game?"

That plan met with approval from the girls, and had the secondary effect of focusing their thoughts on a single thing, and strongly. Vasiht'h glanced at his roommate once or twice during the game and was pleased to see the lines of tension around his eyes easing. The Eldritch might be older than all these children's grandparents, but when he didn't seem older than time, he came across as a young man, curious, thoughtful, still trying to understand his place in the universe. Too young, Vasiht'h thought, to have lines like that framing his eyes. It was good to make them vanish.

⸻ ∞∞∞ ⸻

There was nothing about that session with the children that did not overwhelm Jahir, from the generosity of their hearts to the innocence of their gifts, from the sensation of their open embraces to the realization that he had in fact granted them something in return for what they'd shared. It seemed utterly unbelievable to him. When it was time for their naps, Vasiht'h glanced at him and said, "Maybe I should try it myself, yes?"

"Ooh, yes!" Kuriel piped up. "I want a manylegs dream of windchimes and stars."

"Me too!" Meekie said.

"And me!" Kayla said.

Vasiht'h chuckled. "That leaves the other half for the summer, and the warmth of day, ah?"

"Yes," Jahir said, humbled. And helped the others onto their beds. This time, he paid attention to the gift, made it more distinct, tried to find some happy memory of a warm breeze sifting his hair, of the look of sunlight through leaves. *Rest*, he thought to Amaranth as he tucked her in, and she sighed, contented. He touched Persy's cheek. *Rest*, he told her. *And welcome back. Rest, the crisis is over for now.*

He came to Nieve last, Nieve with her great lavender eyes. She wiggled one hand out from under her blankets, just enough to beckon with a thin finger. He leaned close, and she whispered, "It's okay to be sadder for us than we are for ourselves."

For a moment he couldn't speak. Then, gravely, he said, "I will keep that in mind."

Satisfied, she closed her eyes. He arranged the blanket

around her shoulder and leaned close until he could sense the shape of her ear. And then without speaking into it, he said, *Rest also, thou.*

They withdrew, then, and Jahir could not move.

"Hey, you two—" Berquist stopped and stood. "Did something go wrong? There's nothing on the monitors—"

"Nothing like that," Vasiht'h said. "It's just . . . the situation gets to you sometimes. You know."

"I do," she said with a sigh, and Jahir thought that she looked at him, but he couldn't tell . . . he was too busy sorting through the inside of his own head still.

"Can we ask you something?" Vasiht'h continued.

"Sure?"

"Do the girls sleep better lately?"

Berquist's voice became more thoughtful. "Yes, actually. It's something we've been tracking. We don't know exactly what's going on with it, but if we can keep it going . . . good sleep is vital." She chuckled a little. "Maybe they just prefer the princess treatment from nice-looking princes. But speaking of princess treatment . . . we've got approval for the outing."

That focused Jahir's thoughts admirably. "We do?"

"Next week," she said. "There's supposed to be a warm front. We've got the okay from their parents—most of them are coming, so you'll finally get to meet them—and Patrick and I volunteered to keep an eye on them. I'll send you the details." She glanced up at Jahir. "You are coming, aren't you?"

"Madam, we wouldn't miss it," Jahir said.

"Good," she said. "Very good." She smiled. "Next week, then."

Jahir didn't know how he knew that Vasiht'h would say something . . . and not just that he would, but almost to the moment when he would finally choose to break his silence. Had he come to know an alien so well, then, to be capable of such predictions? He found it comforting, and meditated on that comfort as he waited for the inevitable opener. Vasiht'h delivered it exactly on time, a little over a third of the way home.

It was not, however, the question he was expecting.

"Are you all right?"

"Pardon?" Jahir said, glancing down at him.

Vasiht'h continued padding along at his side, two quick foot-falls for every one of the Eldritch's. "It takes a lot out of you, being touched like that. Are you all right?"

"Is it so obvious?" Jahir asked, surprised.

"It is to me," Vasiht'h said. And then, muttered. "At least, I think. Your face changes. The skin around your eyes." He looked up, and Jahir could see the reflection of the autumn sky on brown irises, dark pupils. "So . . . are you?"

"I believe so," Jahir said after a moment.

"And you would tell me if you weren't. Because . . . I can't help you if you don't. And because I don't like the idea of you just . . . suffering, quietly."

"I'm not suffering," Jahir said, quiet, because the baldness of Vasiht'h's answer required more than he usually gave. "I have discomfort. But it is only a slightly more acute version of what I expected on coming here, to the Alliance." The Glaseah looked at him, so he finished, "You all die too young."

"I guess that's not something you're used to," Vasiht'h said, though it had taken him long enough to answer that Jahir guessed he'd been distressed.

"Death?" He thought of how many Eldritch died, and so easily. If they were not injured, if they were not expecting children, if they were not children and so vulnerable to disease and mishap, the members of his race could expect to live almost fifteen hundred years. But they did not have the Alliance's medi-cine . . . not even close. "No," he said. "I know death better than I like. But it's a different thing, seeing it here."

"I can't even imagine," Vasiht'h said.

"It's not something I recommend." Jahir folded his hands behind his back. "Did you really give them dreams of windchimes?"

"Oh, yes," Vasiht'h said. "We had some outside our windows. It's a way for us to manifest the evidence of the Goddess: She breathes, and Her breath moves the chimes. It's common to put chimes outside children's rooms, and places someone makes things, or works on creating something new." He glanced at Jahir. "And you? Unicorns and sunbeams?"

"I like warmth," Jahir said. "The unicorns seemed like something they'd like." He flexed his fingers through a piano exercise, feeling the weight of the House ring on the fourth. "In truth, Vasiht'h, I am not sure I have my arms around the entirety of what I've learned today."

"Then let it sit," Vasiht'h said. "Better yet, sleep on it. Sleep makes sense of patterns . . . brings wisdom."

Thinking of his sad dreams of failed blooms, of waking up with the taste of saltwater on his mouth, Jahir said, "Sometimes."

Sehvi's image leaned close enough that had they been sending on a solidigraphic stream he could have felt her looming over his shoulder. "You look worn out, big brother. Carrying some load I don't know about yet?"

Vasiht'h covered his face with one hand and didn't bother to lift his head. "I need a research topic, Sehvi . . . preferably before the end of the semester, or Doctor Palland's going to think that I'm just running from clinical."

"And are you?" Sehvi said. "Running from clinical?"

"Argh, Sehvi!"

She held up her hands. "Think of it as practice defending your reasons."

He moved his hand just enough to glare at her from the eye not covered by his forelock.

She frowned. "Wow, this is serious, isn't it."

"It will be if I don't come up with a topic!" Vasiht'h said. "I thought it would be easy! Instead I just stare at a blank data tablet and nothing happens."

"You know, usually people who want to do research have some notion of what they're interested in researching," Sehvi said. "That's why they go into it."

"Not always," Vasiht'h said, grouchy. "Sometimes they just want to get tenure and this is the quickest way there."

"So that's your goal then? The classroom, not the lab?"

"Yes," Vasiht'h said firmly. He was firm because he really wanted it. That's what he was telling himself. "It's family tradition."

Sehvi snorted. "When your family has three aunts and two uncles and three times that number of cousins, I don't think you can claim there is a tradition just because our parents and grandparents sort of did similar things."

"You're not helping," Vasiht'h mumbled.

"Fine," she said. "Fine. I take it you did okay on midterms."

Vasiht'h lifted his head and frowned at her. "You don't have to sound so grumpy about it."

"I am grumpy about it," Sehvi said. "I think you're making a mistake."

"Look, ariishir, I just . . ." He trailed off, and looked at her, his favorite of his siblings, and his closest. He sighed. "I don't know if I can handle it. All right?"

"No, it's not all right," she said, surprising him with her vehemence. "You should be in practice, Vasiht'h. We both know it. I don't know what has you running scared of it, but you're going to regret it."

"But I don't know!" Vasiht'h exclaimed. "I don't know that I should be in practice, and I don't know how you do!"

"Aksivhaht'h save me," his sister said, ears flattening. "Vasiht'h! You do nothing but take care of people! For as long as I've known you, I've watched you do it. You want to make sure everyone's okay. That they feel good, that they're not hurt, that they're content and settled in whatever they're doing. You can't relax unless you're taking care of someone else. You were doing it to your classmates . . . you tried to do it to your former roommates and they wouldn't let you and it made you unhappy. This is what you *do*! And you want to go teach in a classroom? Classrooms are where people go to get away from taking care of people!" She paused, then added, "Don't tell Dami I said that."

"I won't," Vasiht'h said, fighting a laugh that was a little too close to pain.

"You're making a mistake," his sister finished firmly. Her firm sounded a lot more definitive than his had.

"Maybe I am," Vasiht'h said, thinking of his conversation with Jahir. "And if I ever agree with you I'll go back and fix it." He smiled a little, resigned. "Maybe you can have this chat with my roommate, while you're at it. I think he's going to go the wrong track too."

"Oh?"

He nodded. "Unless I miss my guess, he's going to take the medical concentration. But I'm not sure it will be healthy for him. He really feels things."

"So would you stuff him in the research track too?" Sehvi asked. "You know, keep him safe in a glass box with you?"

"Well, when you put it that way," Vasiht'h said, making a face. When he looked up, his sister was staring at him with lifted brows. "What?"

"You see?" she said. "You're doing it now."

"What?" he said, wary.

"Taking care of other people," she said. "You think he's making a mistake. It bothers you. You want him to be well."

"I want him to be well because I like him!" Vasiht'h said.

"You want everyone to be well, ariihir, you just won't admit it," she said. "So Tall, Bright, and Mysterious is careering toward a cliff, is he? Have you told him yet?"

"N-o-ooooo," Vasiht'h said. "He hasn't made a decision yet. Maybe he'll change his mind."

"You should discuss it with him. Maybe you'll talk some sense into each other," Sehvi said. She grinned. "You could give up your wrongful concentrations and go into practice with each other. Wouldn't that be something? Glaseah and Eldritch, esper therapists at large!"

"Don't be silly," Vasiht'h said, but the idea clung to him like a dandelion seed.

CHAPTER 14

*L*ADY MOTHER,

I hope this message finds you well, and the Seni also. It should be the fullness of spring by now, something I envy; the cold here is wetter than I expected. I have bought a coat. I know you will ask.

My studies are fascinating, and the Alliance is . . . much as I expect you know it is. I am learning a great deal, and only a part of it involves what I am being formally taught. I suspect this is why you did not object to my leaving. If it is not too uncouth to ask . . . am I right?

I am still receiving your stipend, for which I thank you. It is, however, overmuch, and could more profitably be kept back to use on our lands. My needs here are few and I fulfill most of them myself in a way I suspect would scandalize the household.

With tender regards,
Your son
Jahir

The day of the outing dawned warm, as promised. In the morning, then, while the children still had energy, they arrived at the hospital and were directed to the Pad room to wait. Vasiht'h flexed his toes and asked his roommate, "Are you nervous?"

"About something befalling them?" Jahir asked.

The fur along Vasiht'h's back fluffed up. "Ugh, that too. But I was thinking more about meeting their guardians finally."

"I admit that part had not occurred to me as something worthy of anxiety," Jahir said. "I suggest a trade. You worry about the parents, I worry about the children."

Vasiht'h found himself grinning. "Then who's going to worry about the nurses?" And at the Eldritch's expression, laughed. "Hah, got you."

"We'll have to split them between the two of us," Jahir said as the first people spilled into the room. The children first, gleeful, wrapped up in long coats—even a warm day in winter was more comfortable in layers—and then their many guardians. Vasiht'h did not have time to dwell on his anxieties, because from that point on there was a stream of introductions: each girl wanted to tell the adults attached to her all about the Eldritch prince and the dancing manylegs Glaseah. It became a blur: "Glad to meet you, yes I volunteer here, oh you've heard about me," but soon enough Jill was wading into it calling for everyone's attention . . . and then they were filing across the Pad and into the cool bright morning. A quiet one: it was morning in the middle of up-week, just after midterms, and many of the street's usual pedestrians were in their classes or studios.

What a sight they must be, Vasiht'h thought, padding alongside Amaranth and her mother and father. This procession of six girls, to have spawned a trail of almost twenty adults, all hovering around them protectively. And yet . . . it was worth it.

"It's such a pretty day out!" Amaranth said to him. "And the air smells good. And a little like—"

"ICE CREAM!" Meekie squealed.

"Did Hea Jill not tell you where we were going?" Vasiht'h asked.

"No!" Amaranth exclaimed, bouncing once on her feet. "No! Oh wow, ice cream!"

With a swiftness that belied their illnesses, the girls were in the gelateria, small hands spread on the glass as they stared into the case at the twenty-four flavors. Their expressions were so enrapt it hurt, in a way that was both good and bad, and completely confusing. He edged back toward the wall and found Jahir there, with Jill. Surprised, he looked up at his roommate. "I thought you would be up there with them. It was your idea."

Jahir's smile was absent, his eyes on the crowd around the case. "Perhaps. But this was not a gift for me, alet."

Vasiht'h followed his roommate's gaze and saw it lighting, not on the children, but on the guardians. "Ah. Yes, I see." He watched for a while, then said, "But you will get ice cream, won't you?"

Jahir laughed, one of his low, quiet laughs. "Vasiht'h. I am in a gelateria. What do you think?"

Vasiht'h grinned. "Forget I asked."

After the children and their families had their scoops and were scattered to the tables at the warm edges of the shop to eat them, Jahir went to order his own.

Jill said, "He really likes . . . ice cream?"

Vasiht'h laughed. "I don't know anyone who likes it as much as he does."

She frowned. "It wasn't something I imagined him eating." Vasiht'h raised his brows at her and she said, "It just seems so . . . mundane."

Vasiht'h grinned. "You should see him with cookie dough."

The expression on her face . . . Vasiht'h laughed and followed Jahir to the counter.

Today seemed a fine day for something pale, since the last time he'd had gelato he'd had chocolate. He ordered coconut and a cup of espresso and brought it to one of the last remaining tables, where he ate slowly, savoring not just the delicacy of the flavor, but the contentment in the store, so palpable he could feel it like a mantle on his shoulders, one that could warm him. He was barely into the bowl when an older woman rose and walked to him, sat across from him. He didn't know how to judge her age, but from the deliberation of her movements and the sag of her skin, she was very near the end of her span. A Tam-illee, with felt-short fur the fine, bright gray of a fog in spring. He recognized her from her eyes. "You are Nieve's grandmother, perhaps?"

"That I am," she said. "She's spoken a great deal of you, young prince."

"I'm not—" The look on her face, patient, indulgent, amused . . . he stopped and laughed. "As you will, Matron."

"Mmm," she said. "Nieve mentioned your courtesies. You have fine manners and a light hand. I can see its evidence in my girl."

"And is it yours I see in her love of poetry?" Jahir asked.

"And her father's as well," the woman said, nodding. "I just wanted to have a look at you, and thank you for her fine dreams and good memories. She'll be traveling light when she goes, and everything she packs counts."

Jahir felt something in him become very still. He met her eyes and said, "You speak of her dying with great equanimity, madam."

"Would you have me speak of it with wailings and weepings? Or worse, not at all?" she said, and snorted. "How would that give her comfort?" She shook her head. "I'm old, young prince. From this side of a life, you speak of many things with great equanimity, no matter how much they pain you."

"Yes," Jahir murmured. "I imagine that must be so."

"So then," she said, tapping the table with a thin finger. "Pay attention now. For I don't give advice often, seeing as how the young rarely listen to the old when they're convinced they're right."

"I am listening, Matron," Jahir said.

"Some distance, young prince," she said. "Find a way to hold some to you."

"How—" Jahir stopped. Of course. Nieve, with her too-wise eyes. "I see some things run strongly in your family, madam."

"When I was young," she said, contemplative, "I felt everything like a river, like a wide, wide river running, and I was a twig in it. The problem with that is that a twig is powerless against a river. A life deeply-felt is not so useful to other people as a life spent doing something about those feelings."

"Is the point of life then to be useful to others?" Jahir wondered.

She smiled and arched one brow, a thin thread of dark gray against light. "What other point is there?" And then she turned and said, "And here is my little girl, trying to sneak up on me."

"No, gran," Nieve said, climbing up on the chair beside her. "I was just trying not to disturb you, that's all." She slipped her arms around the older woman's waist and beamed at Jahir. "You eat ice cream!"

"I love ice cream," Jahir admitted.

"Miss Jill said this was your idea," she said. "If it was . . . thank you. This has been the best day. I can't even remember a day this nice."

God and Lady, how it hurt to hear such things and know that she was comparing them to weeks spent under the supervision of a hospital staff. But he answered, simply, "You're welcome." Seeing them together, the crone and the maid, and both of them younger than him, he suddenly wondered how living in the Alliance could be made bearable, because at the moment he could not imagine how it could be managed.

~∞∞∞~

The ice cream outing had interrupted their usual schedules, so after seeing the girls back to the hospital and taking leave of their assorted guardians, the two of them returned to class. Vasiht'h stopped by his professor's office to pick up material for the lecture he'd missed—he could have requested it through the network, but found the faculty reacted better to flesh-and-blood visits—and then he went to his afternoon session. He was having trouble concentrating on the subject, though. It didn't help that it was the already dry Cognitive Roles in Perception class.

By the time he staggered to the apartment, he was tired and

couldn't tell why, but he strongly suspected it was depression. He started the bath, an indulgence he didn't usually bother with, and then sat next to the tub while it filled, measuring bath salts into a cup and prodding at his own mood.

The girls had had a wonderful time. He would have thought that seeing them in a normal setting, doing normal things, would have cheered him. Instead, it made him think of all the experiences they were missing. He sighed and rubbed his face.

Part of Glaseahn religion involved trusting the Goddess, and another part understanding that everything in it was Her dream, Her interwoven thoughts. If he went to a siv't and asked the priests, they would tell him that people didn't die because the Goddess never forgot them. That was part of having a Goddess's mind: unlike the mortals who worshipped Her, She could hold an infinite number of thoughts in Her mind. If Her attention was sometimes more focused on one aspect or another of reality, well . . . that was to be expected. But the dead were merely separated from the living by the same thin wall that separated dreams from reality. Vasiht'h had once heard it said that if they could learn to bridge that wall, they would also know how Aksivaht'h's dreams made the worlds.

It had been a long time since Vasiht'h had made the trip to one of the on-campus shrines. The university maintained several for the major religions of the student body. The one for the Glaseah didn't have a priest, but the important functions of Aksivaht'h's clergy weren't services Vasiht'h could imagine asking for while on campus anyway, so it didn't bother him. Maybe, he thought as he carefully walked down the shallow ramp into the tub, he should go back. Light a candle, try to find some calm.

Maybe, he thought, this was what Sehvi was trying to tell him about needing real world experience. He had been very fortunate in his life, not to experience much suffering. And he thought he could help other people deal with their own?

He sighed and settled in the water with his torso draped over the edge and his head in his folded arms. "This," he muttered, "is the part they don't mention about college. That all the real learning takes place outside of class."

But the water was soft and fragrant—a musk-and-green-scent combination he liked from home—and he was mindful of the fact that the Goddess needed quiet minds to work Her will. So he drifted, letting the heat relax him, and only left the water when he thought he might fall asleep in it. By that time it was late enough in the evening that he wondered at his roommate's absence. He peeked down the hall and didn't see Jahir in his room and was just beginning to worry when his message queue chimed. He went to the wall in the great room and spread his box on its large display: "Am fine, just walking. Home later. –J."

Vasiht'h let out a sigh and then smiled, rueful. "And now," he said to the imaginary Sehvi in his head, "we are well enough acquainted that we know we'd worry without telling one another when we'll be late." He looked up at the ceiling and said, "I blame you for this!"

Imaginary Sehvi snickered, and to prove that he wasn't being influenced by her he made a late dinner and set aside the leftovers in the stasis box. The note he left was a physical one, because Jahir seemed inclined toward them. 'Food is in the box.'

And then, because the day had seemed uncommonly long, he went back to his nest, plumped the pillows and paused to smell his freshly laundered blankets. He smiled and pulled them up over himself and read for a while before he could no longer keep his eyes open, and then he slept. He woke only a little when he heard the front door hiss open, and the quiet footfalls of his roommate; but then Jahir moved out of easy hearing range, and comforted by this evidence that he had indeed returned, Vasiht'h turned over on his pillows and went back to sleep.

After afternoon class, Jahir left the building and started walking. He didn't stop until he felt lightheaded and tired, at which point he found a convenient bench and sat on it. Since his first faint he had been scrupulous about taking his adaptation medicine and minding the warning signs of over-exertion; his goal was not to earn himself another clinic visit. But when he had his wind back, he rose and resumed walking until once again he needed to pause. He kept his pace slow, and rested at need, but at home it had been his habit to take long rides when he needed to clear his mind. Absent a stable and a convenient place to ride, then, he improvised.

But it didn't help. Everywhere he went, he was surrounded by the wonders of the Alliance. By the tall, clean buildings with their enormous windows and the sweeping beauty of their landscaping; even in winter, gone stripped and frost-burnt, the grounds were striking. And the architecture was only a backdrop, a crown for the true jewels that shone with a fierce and glittering beauty: the people. So many people. He knew them by sight now: Tam-illee passing him, fox-points on their conical ears and long brush-tails, a Karaka'An and Hinichi sitting together on a bench, bent together, clots of Seersa, somewhat more ubiquitous than the rest for this being their world . . .

He knew their reputations also. The Pelted had all sprung from the same small source, and segregated themselves into different races, and yet one could sense they were once all one species, one family with different personalities. Thus the linguist Seersa and the engineer Tam-illee and the scientist Glaseah and the hedonist Harat-Shar. . . .

What did that make the Eldritch? he wondered. The Alliance's token elder race, fading into irrelevance.

He veered from that thought and kept walking.

His late afternoon snack was a cup of buttersquash soup from Tea and Cinnamon, along with a pastry made with flour ground from seeds that had a bright, piquant flavor. He ate and watched the jewels of the Alliance crown, set all around him. So healthy, the people passing in and out of his field of vision. And even so, they would die too soon. He had his data tablet with him from class, and he brought up the statistics while finishing his strong black tea. The averages for most of the bipedal Pelted were in the low one hundreds: on average, around one-hundred-twenty, perhaps. The Phoenix lived a little longer, at the upper range of

two hundred. But for the most part, every single person around
him, the slim gray male who'd served his soup, the eager, focused
students who'd shared his lecture during the afternoon, the professor teaching it, the counselor who'd helped him select his first
courses, Vasiht'h, KindlesFlame, Luci and the quadmates, and all
the children not just in the hospital but all over the city . . . they
would all live, grow old and die in less than a tenth of his lifespan.

He could go home, of course. Pack now and go back. But
the only thing waiting for him at home was stasis: eight or
nine hundred years of managing one of the Seni Galare's minor
properties while waiting to inherit. He could probably fill some
of that time: exploring and mapping, breeding horses, playing
music, learning one—or two—or three—professions. He could
allow his mother to find him a bride and make an early attempt
at heirs.

But the Queen had already had a survey done of the planet,
though she told few people about it. And he'd already bred horses
through several generations. He had his whole life to play music,
and the reason he was here was to learn a profession. And he very
much did not want a wife yet, particularly given how high the
mortality rate was for pregnant Eldritch women.

The alternative to going home, though, was staying here:
a visitor to an eternal garden of beautiful, short-lived flowers,
and he fated to remember them long after their own grand- and
great-grandchildren did not. The only way he could imagine surviving that heartache was not to care . . . but his life had prepared
him to dismiss people he'd already disliked, for the Eldritch dedicated themselves to holding each other apart and were masters
of cutting remarks and petty cruelties.

Nothing he had lived through had taught him how to cut off
people he could be fond of. Rather the opposite, given how rare
it was to find an open heart.

He was sitting on a bench halfway to the School of Languages
when he realized how late it was. His roommate would worry, he
thought, and left a quick note. He was putting the data tablet
back in his bag when he realized if he wasn't careful, it would be

too late for him to go. The relationships he was building would become too strong for abandonment. And then he would be committed to seeing this experiment to its finish, and learning how he fared.

The only question was, how much time did he have left, before he could no longer leave?

His walk did not resolve any of his questions. It had served only to crystallize them. He returned to the apartment heavy-hearted, to find Vasiht'h had cooked for them both. He ran his fingers lightly over the edge of the paper note—such a delightful anachronism, and he had a hunch as to why Vasiht'h had chosen it. He wondered if it was too late for some of the people around him, and what harm he would cause by amputating the relationships to save himself.

He ate dinner standing up in the kitchen, in its silence, and by the dim glow of its night-light. And then, resigned, he washed up and went to sleep.

Vasiht'h had been hoping for the dreams of the Goddess, something inspiring, something to help dispel his anxieties. Barring that, he would have settled for some pastoral thing like the dreams he'd tried to give the children, of the breath of the Goddess in windchimes, and the smell of Anseahla drifting in through his open window at home.

Naturally, he had none of those things, and woke up solely because he'd cramped his foreleg badly enough to cut off circulation in it. He couldn't feel the paw even. He sighed and forced himself to his feet. He was used to giving himself a numb limb now and then; arranging a centauroid body for sleep was an awkward exercise even with practice and a lot of bolsters. The only thing for it was to walk until the feeling returned. He'd make himself a tisane; that would help him fall back asleep once he could wiggle his toes and feel them. Vasiht'h limped to the kitchen and hunted in the near-dark for one of the herbal tea bags.

He was pouring hot water into his cup when he heard a noise he never wanted to hear again in his life. He'd been told that people moaned in pleasure and had yet to experience it, though he imagined it must be a pleasant sound. He'd heard that people also moaned in pain, and had failed to imagine what it must sound like, and had not really tried.

It sounded like distress made manifest, as if the Goddess had taken anguish and made it palpable, made it more real than pain like that ever should be. He dropped the kettle and jumped back from the resulting splash, then turned on a paw and ran for the sound. He couldn't imagine what horror had inspired it, but he expected . . . blood, sickness, something. To dash into his roommate's room and find him sleeping—

—but sleeping with tears on his cheeks—

He didn't stop to question the rectitude of it, or whether Jahir would have permitted it, or what his ethics professor would have said. He reached with his mind and almost his hands, desperate to make the grief stop, and said, *Rest.*

And: *Softly. Softly.*

And: *Hear the wind through the chimes. Smell the night-blooming irises. The Goddess is passing through your dreams.*

He could feel his words sinking into that dreaming mind and stilling whatever sorrow was moving through the Eldritch. When he opened his eyes and withdrew, he felt the bad dream reasserting itself, so he sank to his feet, belly to the ground, and concentrated. Not just on his own offering, but on memories of Jahir's descriptions of the gifts he'd made the children. Sunlight too, then. Music, since Jahir loved it so: lullabies and harp-song from the concerto they'd been listening to last. The sense of lengthening days that turned into beautiful blue nights.

It was hard work, but he became aware of a great sense of peace while doing it. He smoothed out his roommate's troubled aura and blew soft breath into it—serenity—and carefully held himself away from whatever thoughts and images were inspiring the nightmare, not just to observe his roommate's privacy, but to prevent those things from bleeding into what he was making.

And at some point, he fell asleep, and his subconscious mind kept that link alive and shared his calmer dreams with Jahir.

───── ∞∞∞ ─────

It was a noise that woke Jahir, one that didn't belong in his room, a slow scrape that he couldn't place. And then his eyes didn't want to open . . . his lashes were matted. He frowned, feeling beset and aching in every joint and not remembering what he'd done to earn such opprobrium. But he managed to look, though the will to lift his head was not yet in him, and found his roommate's shoulder sliding in slow jerks down his wall.

Was he still sleeping? No, he thought not. Vasiht'h was in his room. And come to that, his dreams had been strange: a true nightmare this time, of serving as gardener in a place where the lush soil bore flowers that were already rotting as they pushed their way through the ground, and him powerless to change that, or to save them. And then a breeze had blown through that dream, and carried the sound of metal chimes and wooden clicking. Night had fallen and brought with it peace, along with a renewal of his sense of wonder and curiosity, the same traits that had brought him forth from his world in the first place.

He could only surmise his roommate had divined his predicament and applied to him the same treatment they'd given the girls.

Did that bother him, he wondered? He stretched his fingers, felt no memories that did not belong to him, excepting the dream-hazed impression of an alien night, and that one, like Vasiht'h's presence, was unobtrusive and easily held apart from his own mind. Had the Glaseah touched him? Would he remember, given how understated Vasiht'h's mental aura seemed to be?

More importantly, what would he have done had he heard his roommate in extremis? And if his answer was 'do something to help,' then he could hardly fault Vasiht'h for the impulse. Particularly when he had succeeded, and so gently.

This, he thought, was the Alliance, summarized in one bedroom: its mysteries, its temptations, its promise of loss. Jahir sighed, breath rippling the mounded sheet next to his face, and thought that he was not ready to give it up yet. He did not look forward to a repetition of the nightmare, though he thought it would not be the first until ultimately he came to a decision: to make his peace with what staying meant, or to turn his back on it.

But in the mean, he had a savior to care for. He debated waking his roommate, but was not sure he could navigate the conversation that might ensue if he did. Instead, he rose and sat on the edge of the bed until he was sure his limbs were of an accord with him, and then he ghosted past Vasiht'h. He returned with pillows and the blanket from the Glaseah's room and made him comfortable—carefully, but even so he brushed once or twice against the sleeping alien's body. And again, he felt only the faintest of responses, as he had when they'd first met on the parking lot. What a wonder, he thought. To touch without punishment. He could grow accustomed to it, if he wasn't careful.

After settling the blanket over Vasiht'h's back, Jahir returned to his own bed, and was only too glad to lie down. Whether his subconscious had decided it had delivered itself of its message, or whether the Glaseah's presence deterred any more painful dreams, Jahir slept uneventfully, and was glad of it.

On waking, Vasiht'h found a pillow under one of his forelegs, which was helpful, as were the ones bolstering his back. But he'd fallen asleep against the wall of Jahir's room and that had kinked his spine badly. He grimaced and struggled upright, found a blanket draped over his lower body as well. He was not surprised to find the bed vacated, given the hours his roommate kept. But the sign that Jahir had also taken care of him . . .

He pulled the blanket to his face and sighed into it, grateful that he had not given unpardonable offense. Then he squared his shoulders and went to look for his roommate, and face . . . whatever it was that had happened overnight.

Finding Jahir sitting in the great room chair by the fire,

sipping a cup of tea, didn't surprise him. But having the Eldritch
set the cup down and rise the moment he appeared did: almost
as if he was someone important who needed formal greeting. He
approached, hesitant, and stopped when Jahir went to one knee.
His expression must have been eloquent, because his roommate
smiled and said, "To put our heads on the level."

"Oh," Vasiht'h said, weakly. "Right."

With his hands resting easily on his knee, Jahir said, quiet.
"Thank you."

How could two words sound like a hundred? Maybe that's
how poets worked. Maybe they could all imply an entire night of
unplanned intimacies with a handful of words. Bearing witness
to someone's nightmare and soothing it—that was intimacy,
wasn't it? It felt like it. Vasiht'h flipped his ears back and said,
"I didn't mean to push in on you like that, but you were . . . you
made a noise. It was . . . you sounded like you were in trouble."

"I was, in my own way, and you helped," Jahir said. He leaned
back and fetched a second cup off the table and offered it. "The
mint tisane you like. I hope I didn't make it too strong."

Vasiht'h stared at the saucer, where he could see the edge of
Jahir's thumb—no glove there. He flattened his ears entirely and
looked up at his roommate.

"Go on," Jahir said.

"I'm a lot clumsier than you are," Vasiht'h said. "What if I . . ."

"Go on," Jahir said, more gently.

Biting his lip, Vasiht'h took the saucer, keeping his hand on
the opposite side. He managed not to touch the Eldritch, but his
hand was shaking badly enough that some of the tea sloshed
over the side. Chagrined, he said, "Sorry."

"For that?" Jahir said. And then quieter, "For any of it? You
should not be. I am telling you truly. Vasiht'h? Look at me?"

Because he hadn't been, he'd been looking very fixedly at the
tea (which, if he judged the color correctly, was neither too strong
nor too weak, but very close to exactly how he liked it). But he
looked up, as asked, and found Jahir waiting there, patient.
Eternal. He thought of Sehvi's observation about him choosing

to befriend someone who'd never leave and felt renewed chagrin . . . at that, and at the fact that he was trying to find some word to compare his roommate's eyes to, and rather than something poetic, like a gemstone or . . . or a flower, or something else, he kept thinking of orange blossom honey. A clear, bright yellow, like . . . well, yes. Like honey.

"What is it that you fear?" Jahir asked.

"I barged into your room and inflicted myself on your dreaming mind without asking permission," Vasiht'h said. "And then I fell asleep in your room with you, also without asking permission. Probably right in your path out, too, so you could trip on me . . ." He tried not to fidget. "I did a lot of imposing. I don't want that to make things . . . less comfortable between us."

"Does this seem less comfortable to you?" Jahir asked, brows lifting. He sounded amused, but in a nice way.

"You're *kneeling* in front of me!" Vasiht'h exclaimed.

Jahir did laugh then. "No, no. Kneeling is both knees. I have cause to know. Will it please you better if I sat again?"

"Yes?" Vasiht'h said weakly.

"Then I shall do so," Jahir said. "But I meant what I said. I am grateful for your succor."

Vasiht'h had never heard that word outside of old books, and almost didn't recognize it. He fidgeted with his tea while his roommate sat back down, then finally sipped and said, "This is perfect."

"Good," Jahir said. "I had hoped. Breakfast, though, I did not touch, as I wasn't sure when you'd wake and . . ." He trailed off and sighed before finishing with a quirk of a smile, "I had forgotten until just this moment that food can be held in stasis here indefinitely."

Vasiht'h blew out a breath, and all his awkwardness flew away with it. "Oh good. You've left me something to do."

"You do have a better hand with it," Jahir said. "Though I hope I am at least a passable cook by now."

"You are, you are," Vasiht'h said. "But it's nice to know you're not perfect at everything!"

"Hardly," the Eldritch said, shaking his head with that little motion that barely swayed his hair around his throat. "Hardly, alet. So, are we well?"

"Yes," Vasiht'h said. "If you're sure."

"Not only am I sure, but I will tell you that, do you feel the necessity again in the future, you are more than welcome to do something about my nightmares," Jahir said. "And perhaps, if you're comfortable, you might grant me the same permission?"

"Anytime," Vasiht'h said, feeling better. "And now, I will make breakfast. Or we'll be late for lecture."

CHAPTER 15

THE LETTER FROM HOME ARRIVED electronically, which did not surprise Jahir given what it cost to send packages across the Alliance, and even more what it would take for something to come from the otherwise unknown location of his homeworld. It was strange to see his mother's handwriting floating above his desk, though, for all the world as if she'd written the missive on paper and then had it transferred. The juxtaposition of the technological with the archaic felt like too obvious a symbol of his dilemma.

To My Beloved Son, Greetings:

I am pleased to hear that you are settling well, and that you find your studies engaging. As you noted, there is a great deal to be learned from our allies, and by all means you must stay until you have had your fill. There is no pressing need to draw you back, and if there is, I shall be sure to tell you.

Your thoughts on your stipend are generous and appropriate. I would follow your wishes if the money were my own, but it is not: rather what you have is a gift from the Queen, who would not have you lack for the funds to embark on any experience you might wish to have while outworld. You may attempt to return it to her, but I do not recommend it! Or if you find no use for it, keep it, and bring it home with you when you are ready to return.

Matters here are very much the same as when you left. You will be glad to hear that Bright the Moon has delivered herself of a healthy foal, and he looks just like his dam. I know you had a special fondness for her and would want to know.

With Much Love,
Your Mother,
J

Jahir narrowed his eyes as he sat back in his chair. The Queen was nominally the head of his House: Seni was part of the Galare, and well thought of by the Queen but not, as far as he knew, one of her intimates . . . if Liolesa could be said to have any, other than her true-cousin, the head of House Jisiensire. That he should be receiving money directly from her made him a touch nervous, implying as it did that she was interested in his progress off-world.

He sighed and closed the letter, opened his books. God and Lady knew what that would come to, if it came to anything. At some point, when his mother passed him the mantle, he would swear allegiance to Liolesa as one of the family heads within her House, but he had not expected to be of any note to her until then. Certainly he did not want power, or to invite trouble, as inevitably one might when closely linked to the throne and the woman who ruled from it despite those who would prefer otherwise. It would please a great many people to see Liolesa deposed, and to see her pro-Alliance notions gone with her.

Blessings, he thought, and curses. And hopefully neither come to roost any time soon. He bent to his studies.

—— ⚬⚬⚬ ——

"I'm ready for midwinter break," Brett said that evening.

"Two months," Leina said. "We can last two months, right?"

The five of them contemplated this over hot cider, pasties stuffed with meat and diced vegetables, and a cake. Vasiht'h wanted to call the latter a case of ambition, but he feared it was more an admission that the things he had to work through were now requiring several hours of effort rather than the half hour a batch of cookies would have warranted. "I'll believe it when we get there," he said. He refilled his cup. "Luci out tonight?"

"Yeah," Brett said. "She's usually gone for some Harat-Shariin thing once a week, and said this week it happened to fall today."

"Some Harat-Shariin thing," Jahir murmured.

"Probably involves drunken orgies," Leina said.

Merashiinal huffed. "Too cold out for drunken orgies. For me, anyway. I miss a good strong sun on my backs."

"Speaking of which," Brett said, "Are you going home for the break?"

"Eh," the Ciracaana said, stretching one of his hind legs. Vasiht'h envied him the height, but only until Mera bumped the wall with his paw. Very few cozy spaces were large enough for one of his species. "Too far to go for such a short visit. Instead I am going to the summer side of the world. Spend some time roaming the Spindle Tree National Park. With the wild animals and such." He bared his teeth and added, "Rar, I am most dangerous."

Brett laughed. "You probably are. What about you, Leina?"

"Oh, my parents will skin me if I don't show up for the holidays," Leina said, nibbling at the edge of her pasty. "We have a big to-do for Rispa's Day, and we have friends over for the Order of the Universe too."

"There are two holidays at the end of the term?" Jahir asked.

"There are a thousand holidays at the end of the term," Brett said.

Vasiht'h poked the Seersa with a spoon and said, "All the Pelted have their own winter celebrations, plus there's the Order of the Universe, which is the Alliance-wide holiday."

"Yes, but . . . I imagine these are . . . not all celebrated at once? Or on this world?" Jahir asked, and then stopped, touching his brow with his fingers. "I think I have given myself a headache attempting to contemplate the logistics of a multi-world holiday system."

"You and everybody else," Brett said with a guffaw. "No, no. On Seersana, winter's weird because the end of winter is also the end of the calendar year. On some worlds it's not. So here you get Rispa's Day, which is the end of winter, and then New Year's Day right after. And then because of the students here, a lot of them will celebrate their particular end-of-winter holidays during Seersana's end-of-winter, rather than trying to figure out what time of year it is at home and celebrating it here off-season."

"I believe I understood that, God and Lady help me," Jahir said. "And then . . . the Order of the Universe?"

"Is the Alliance celebration of the end of the year and of all its member species," Vasiht'h said. "It's a list of all the major holidays of the Pelted. Every world finds their day and then schedules the other days in front of and behind it in the order given. So here, Rispa's Day is the fulcrum, and then the rest of the holidays are strung out before and behind it. On worlds with homogeneous populations, the other holidays are basically just excuses to send letters or packages to friends. In places like this, where there are lots of other Pelted, the Order can feel like two weeks of solid parties."

"You should see the ones on Selnor," Leina added, licking her fingers. "No one parties like the capital world. Plus, all the ships and starbases run on their schedule, so you can imagine the entire Fleet celebrating at the same time. . . ."

Jahir looked at Vasiht'h. "I beseech you to draw up some sort of schedule so I remember to wish the proper people the proper greeting on the proper day."

Vasiht'h laughed. "I'll remind you. Really the only ones you have to observe are your own! And if you want, buy presents for everyone and give them to them when you see them."

"Most holidays involve presents," Leina agreed.

"Or cake," Mera said, cutting himself a slice.

"Or cake," his roommate agreed, amused. "Or breads. Or cookies. Or pastries. Or feasts! Are we going to have another this year, Vasiht'h?"

"Feast?" Vasiht'h said, and made a face. "I don't know. I think this semester has chewed me up pretty well. But I could probably manage a bread."

"Like one of your mother's," Jahir said, surprising him.

"Yes," Vasiht'h said. And laughed. "You remembered that story?"

"It was a good story," Jahir said.

"What story?" Brett asked. "Tell!"

"It was nothing," Vasiht'h said, smiling. "My mother's attempts at feast bread, that's all. Hopefully mine will be less lumpy." He poked Brett. "Smaller slice, or it'll fall apart over the edge of the serving knife."

"Ouch! What's with the poking tonight?" Brett asked.

"I just like poking you," Vasiht'h said, and tried the cake himself. It was vanilla, with a more-almond cream between the layers, and a meringue frosting . . . he thought he'd done rather well. From the looks on everyone else's faces, they thought so too. So well that they wheedled about the feast, and he actually said 'yes,' though Goddess knew where he'd find the energy.

As usual, he and Jahir were the last to leave the meeting house; he boxed the remains of the cake and Jahir cleaned.

"That was properly convivial," Jahir said. "I cannot imagine what more celebration we would need for a holiday. Will you advise me, if there are customs I should know?"

"Really the gift-giving is the only one that needs mentioning," Vasiht'h said. "Mostly little things though, unless you're on intimate terms with someone." He took the box and said, "Ready?"

"Let us," Jahir said. "I find myself wanting a cup of coffee after your excellent dessert."

Vasiht'h licked his lips then said, "You know, that sounds perfect. I wonder what a coffee-flavored frosting would be like with the more-almond?"

"Ah!" Jahir said, laughing. "You wish to reduce me to a sweet-laced torpor."

"Is that what you're doing when you're stretched out in front of the fire?" Vasiht'h asked, grinning. "Looking all languid?"

"It is hardly my fault if your cooking is so sublime it requires contemplation," Jahir said.

This was, Vasiht'h thought, Eldritch teasing. It made the fur on his shoulders stand on end in pleasure, to know that he'd earned it. He padded into the kitchen from the back door . . . and froze.

"You said I could come and talk any time," Luci said from where she was curled up on their floor with her back against the wall. She wiped her eyes with the side of her hand and said, "Well, here I am."

"Luci!" Vasiht'h said, and crouched next to her.

She waved him off. "I can get up." She pushed herself to her feet, tail flicking beside her ankles. "That frosting was good by the way. I licked it off the spatula while I was cleaning up the dishes in the sink."

"You didn't have to do that," Vasiht'h said.

"It gave me something to occupy myself," she answered. "Though there was no cake anywhere . . ."

"I'll cut you a slice," Jahir said, and gently took the box from Vasiht'h's hands, somehow without brushing against him. "Won't you sit down by the fireplace? I'll build a fire in it in a moment."

"It's cozy," Vasiht'h agreed. "Come on." He led her to the great room and let her pick a seat, watching her. She was on the surface the same Lucrezia, but her fur was matted around her bloodshot eyes, and she was bent with hunched shoulders that somehow didn't communicate exhaustion, but defeat. He fretted a little, brought her an afghan. She took it without comment and curled up on the couch's far end, leaning on its arm. She didn't say anything when Jahir returned and set a plate on the table beside her, and a teapot with three cups. He poured before going to the hearth to do whatever magical Eldritch thing he did to make the fire start and last for several hours. Vasiht'h waited for him to finish, and for the warmth and light of the fire to make the room feel friendlier and closer, and then he said, "What's going on?

We've all been worried."

"We have, have we?" she said, eyeing him. When he didn't flinch, she sighed and took her cup, warming her palms against it as the steam coiled up to her face. "I guess Brett's said something."

"He was not the only one to notice," Jahir said, sitting in the chair across from her and taking his own cup.

She rubbed her face again with her palm. "You don't know much about me, tall and pretty. I don't know much about you. But somehow I don't mind talking in front of you. How does that work?"

"He's an Eldritch," Vasiht'h said. "There's something about them."

"Yeah," she said, glancing at Jahir, tired. "I guess." She drew in a long breath and said, "Well. You know I'm colony-world Harat-Shariin."

"I remember," Vasiht'h said.

"And . . . I'm really colony-world bred," she said. "I wasn't raised with Harat-Sharii's culture. I know what we're supposed to be like . . . we're supposed to be enthusiastic and passionate, people whose love for life spills over into sex." She caressed her cup with her fingertips. "I don't have that. I mean, I have the passion, but I don't want it to spread all over indiscriminately, like some kind of virus. I want one person. One man, preferably, so we can have kits the old-fashioned way."

"Nothing wrong with that," Vasiht'h said when she stopped.

"No," she agreed. "I know there's not. I mean, I went from a colony world with a mixed population to Seersana. I know there are other ways to do it, and what I want isn't unreasonable. But I . . . fell in love with someone. Someone homeworld-bred. We've been together for six months now, and . . ." Her breath this time was ragged, too much for her to go on.

Vasiht'h stared at her, heart aching for her, and yet he had not the slightest notion what to say.

"And you love him desperately," Jahir said quietly, "and yet you cannot make it work."

"Yes!" she said, and shuddered. "He loves other people too.

He loves me, but other people too. And I don't want other people. I want him. And I can't share him. I'm going to have to give him up and I can't bear it." She straightened her shoulders and said, "He told me if only I was homeworld-bred, none of this would matter, and couldn't I just . . . try to embrace what I was."

"That was cruel," Vasiht'h said, finding the words. "You already are what you are, Luci, and what you are is fine."

"I know," she said. "I know. But . . . I tried. I've been trying. It just doesn't work."

"Have you considered asking him to do for you what he would have you do for him?" Jahir asked. At her sharp glance, he said, "To try and be a colony-world Harat-Shar."

"I . . . I haven't, no," she said, looking away. "I'm afraid he'll say no."

Gently, Jahir said, "Lucrezia, you have nothing to lose. It is already not working now. If he says no, then how will things change?"

"Things will change because I'll have no excuse to keep him in my life," she said, putting her tea cup on the table and sliding her arms around herself. "At least now, I can pretend there's a future."

"Oh, Luci," Vasiht'h said, gently, and rested a hand on her foot.

"It's ridiculous, isn't it?" she said, sniffling. "I'm the girl who has it all together, and I'm falling apart over a man because I won't sleep with his lovers."

"You *can't* sleep with his lovers," Jahir said. "There is a difference."

"And you aren't ridiculous," Vasiht'h said fiercely. "You're wonderful, and you do have it together. This isn't about you. It's about a culture problem. You're just . . ." He sighed. "You're on the wrong sides of it. Both of you are."

She rubbed her nose. "You know what the worst part is? He really loves me. He wants me to be the first wife in his train, he wants my children, everything. It's just that he wants his other lovers too. He says . . . he can't choose between us, that it would be like asking a parent which of their children they love more. But I don't want to be one of his lovers, loved equally but differently. I want to be his *one* love. And I feel selfish, even though I know that it can work that way. It worked that way for my parents. They had one another. They had me and my brother. And we were *happy*. That's what I want for myself."

"There is nothing wrong in that," Vasiht'h said firmly.

She sighed and slumped. At last she seemed to see her tea and took a half-hearted sip of it before looking at the fire. "It is soothing, isn't it. So many colors. Who would have thought a fire would look like that when you're used to candles."

"I had no idea until Jahir introduced me to it," Vasiht'h said.

She lowered her face. "Thank you. Thank you both."

"For what?" Vasiht'h said. "We've hardly done anything—"

"You've listened," she said. "And you haven't tried to make me do one thing or another. Everyone I go to wants me to do what they think is wisest, or what they think is best for me. I know they're telling me those things because they care about me and don't want to see me hurting, but . . . it just makes it worse. The two of you just . . . listened." She shuddered. "I know it'll be time to do something about it soon, whether I like it or not. I just . . . I just wanted to talk about it without having to defend myself."

"You can always do that here," Vasiht'h said firmly. "In fact, if you want to stay, you can. We'll make up the couch for you."

She glanced up at him, eyes widening.

"So you don't have to be alone, or with people who don't know what's going on," Vasiht'h said. "If you want."

"I . . . I think I do," she said, ears flipping back. She glanced at Jahir. "Is that all right with you too?"

"If our hearth gives you comfort, alet," Jahir said. "Then absolutely, you are welcome."

"Then . . . thanks," she said, wiping her eyes. "I'd like that."

Jahir brought the blankets, then, having recently done the laundry, and Vasiht'h donated some of his pillows. She curled up on their couch with her knees tucked against her chest, watched the fire, and made no conversation; they let her rest.

Some half an hour later, Jahir stopped at the entrance to Vasiht'h's room and said, "She sleeps."

"Already?" Vasiht'h said, looking up from his Health Perspectives reading.

"Already," Jahir said, "Would you like warm cider? I made some for myself."

"You did?" Vasiht'h said, confused. And then, "Actually, that sounds nice. Come in?"

The Eldritch entered, bringing the tray with him. He set Vasiht'h's mug on the desk and settled on one of the larger floor pillows.

"I'm sorry," Vasiht'h said, chagrined. "I don't have any furniture in here for bipedals . . . you could bring something in from the other room?"

"I'm fine," Jahir said, and there was a silence then, one that would have been comfortable had not Vasiht'h felt uneasy in his own skin.

"Thank you," he said finally. "For knowing what to say to her."

Jahir shook his head, just a little. "Knowing what to say to her, alet, was the least of what she needed. And what she needed, you gave her."

"That being a place to sleep?" Vasiht'h asked.

Jahir snorted. "You are not so oblivious, Vasiht'h. She herself told you. You listened. Without judgment, without advice, without pushing. That's the substance of what we are studying, isn't it?"

"Part of therapy is doing something about a patient's problems," Vasiht'h said, uncomfortable.

"Part of therapy is supporting a patient who is struggling to find an answer for their problems," Jahir said. "And making suggestions when they seem at a loss."

"Like Luci is now?"

"Lucrezia knows her path," Jahir said. "Her grief is about walking it."

"And what do I have to offer someone like her?" Vasiht'h

asked, rubbing his toes on the floor. "I've never been in love. I've never felt that strongly about anyone, to cry over losing them. How can I help someone with something I can't imagine?"

"Like you can't imagine your desperate desire to make Meekie's disease go away? And Amaranth's? Like you can't imagine your fear when you heard they'd taken Persy away?"

Stunned, Vasiht'h looked at his roommate, who was sitting with one knee up and the other stretched before him, incongruously relaxed for the intensity of his eyes.

"That . . . that's . . ." And then he stopped and looked away.

"That's unfair?" Jahir offered.

"No, that's true, and I hadn't thought about it, and . . . you're right," Vasiht'h said. "The fact that those girls are sick does hurt, and that I can't fix it . . . it's like something's bleeding where I can't reach to heal it."

"Then you have everything you need to understand someone like Lucrezia right now," Jahir said. And held up a hand. "You are about to tell me it's not the same. And the causes for your suffering are, indeed, different. But the feeling of helplessness and sorrow, the wish that things could be elsewise . . ." He tapped his chest. "That is the same for us all."

Vasiht'h frowned. "I didn't think of it that way."

"You are too accustomed to thinking of yourself as passionless," Jahir observed. "But being without storms of emotion does not make you unfeeling, alet. And you listen to people, and care for their welfare, and you can do that without losing yourself in them. I think you underestimate the value of what you offer those who seek you in their need."

"It was so obvious to you," Vasiht'h said. "That I was troubled."

"You did say," Jahir said. "When we were speaking of your doubt, the one that made you choose to go the research path."

"And you think it's a bad idea." Vasiht'h set his cup back on the desk. "You still think, because you've been telling me so in your understated way for a while now, haven't you."

"I think you underestimate your talents," Jahir said again. "And I wanted to tell you that what you did for Lucrezia was a kindness, and she needed it, and you knew exactly what to do when you saw her. You didn't flinch. You didn't flounder. You went to her and you listened, and you gave her a safe place to recover." He stood, cup in hand. "You might ponder that instinct, perhaps."

Vasiht'h wanted to laugh it off, but found he couldn't. Instead, he said, "Thank you."

Jahir smiled. "Good night, alet." And left Vasiht'h to stare after him and wonder if he was flushed from the praise, from embarrassment, or from the uncomfortable feeling that he was making a mistake.

———— ✦ ————

Jahir had gone to bed that night with little thought other than his fatigue and a sense of regret over the grief of aliens. Despite the events of the evening, he did not dream, but slept so heavily that when he woke abruptly in the middle of the night he didn't know why. And then he felt it, a wrongness so deep that he was off the bed and grabbing his nightrobe before he could guess at the cause. He ran for the great room and found Lucrezia whimpering in her sleep, and as Vasiht'h stumbled out of his own door, the Eldritch went to her . . . and so did the Glaseah.

They arrived together, and they reached for her together, and Jahir felt the brush of a warm, solid side, as if he was touching Vasiht'h with his hands rather than sensing him pass in mind. He felt the ghostly hands of his roommate steadying Lucrezia's sleeping thoughts, and Jahir blew the remembered breath of an alien goddess through her nightmare, and gently cleared it away. The weft of Vasiht'h's presence, twining with his, felt far too easy; made soothing the Harat-Shar a simple matter. Beneath them, she sighed out and turned on her side, relaxing.

Jahir leaned back, shaking. Between himself and his room-mate he sensed for the briefest of moments a golden line, glimmering as if lit by the fire that had died to embers on the hearth. And then slowly it faded and took his sense of Vasiht'h with it, and the anchor of that steadying presence.

Vasiht'h looked at him over Lucrezia's head, eyes so wide they were rimmed in white. He whispered, "I'm sorry—"

Jahir put a finger to his lips and shook his head. "She sleeps," he answered, very low. "That is all that matters." And then, because he had to know, he framed the words as a thought and offered it. *Can you hear me thus?*

Of course, Vasiht'h said, and with that thought came fretfulness, something Jahir felt as the scratch of new wool against skin before it ebbed with the fading line. And then, covering his face, the Glaseah said, "Goddess, I'm sorry, I didn't mean to—"

Jahir held his hand out, just close enough to draw the Glaseah's eye. He whispered, "An accident. There was no harm." And then, *Hush.*

Vasiht'h quieted and glanced at Lucrezia, who was sleeping. He drew in a breath and whispered, "Think she's fine for the night. You want to keep watch?"

"We'll know if she needs us," Jahir said. And gently, "Good night, alet."

Vasiht'h bit his lip, then nodded and padded back to his room, pausing to look over his shoulder once. Jahir met his gaze and tried to imbue it with all his goodwill, and the Glaseah sighed and vanished into the dark.

Jahir went also, sat on his bed and found his hands shaking. Had he just willingly touched minds with an alien? Two aliens? Several times? He had rearranged Lucrezia's nightmare with the help of his roommate, had *felt* Vasiht'h at his side, in the shared space of her mind. And there had been no . . . no horror. No whelming of his own thoughts. Nothing but a comfortable presence, a welcome feeling of being in good company, doing good and gentle work. And the direct touch of the thoughts afterward . . . he had had such congress with Eldritch before, while training, and found it distasteful, but touches from his own kind had always come dense with disgust and heavy enough to scatter all his thoughts. No Eldritch had ever had the light touch his roommate had shown, nor the finesse to give such an intriguing sense of the feelings behind it.

And yet he'd touched other aliens before, by accident, and they had been worse than any Eldritch, so loud he'd not only lost his own thoughts but briefly gained memories of theirs. He remembered the muscle memory the medical technicians had endowed him with, so powerfully he'd been confused as to his own identity. Was it because the Glaseah were an esper species, that they knew how to interact with others without harming them? Was Vasiht'h a special case? Was it somewhat of both?

Jahir lay back down and pulled the sheets over his shoulder, and slept fitfully, trying not to look too closely at his own feelings on the matter, for fear he would find less of the discomfort that would have been respectable in an Eldritch . . . and more curiosity than he knew how to fight.

CHAPTER 16

ASITH'H WOKE AN HOUR later than usual. A bleary Luci was making coffee in his kitchen, and when he approached she handed him a note. In Jahir's impeccable hand: "There is part of an omelet in stasis. –J"

The omelet part was three times the size Vasiht'h expected, and he shared it with Luci over her coffee. As she hugged him on her way out, she said, "Thank you for everything, and especially for letting me stay. For the first time in months, I slept well." She smiled, lopsided, and though she looked worn out, there was a calm in her that surprised Vasiht'h. "I even had dreams . . . about the wind in my hair, and a feeling that no matter how hopeless things seem, that . . . they change. They will change, even if you can't imagine it now."

That stayed with him all day, distracting him from lectures he really should have been taking notes for. By the time he got home, his restlessness had graduated to full-fledged agitation, one that exploded when he accepted Sehvi's call; without waiting for her greeting, he said, "I feel like I'm getting everything wrong!"

She held up her hands, wide-eyed. "Slow down, ariihir. Start from the beginning? Sit!"

"I can't sit," Vasiht'h said, pacing in front of her worried image. "I'm having feelings I don't know what to do with. And I don't know where any of it is coming from! There are children in trouble, and I keep pushing my roommate and Goddess knows when I'll push too hard and then he'll probably go away, and I have no research topic and I'm completely sure I'm not suited for practice now but if that's true why can't I think of anything to research?" He grabbed his head. "Goddess."

"If you say that a third time She might manifest just to see what all the fuss is about," Sehvi said. "I knew about the children and the research problem. What's going on with the roommate? Did something happen?"

"Yes!" Vasiht'h said, and then dropped onto his haunches, sighing. "I touched his mind."

"Yes?" she said.

"And you don't *do* that with Eldritch!" he exclaimed. "And I've done it three times!"

"Was he offended?" she wondered.

"He said he's not," Vasiht'h said. "But what if he's just trying to be polite?"

"Well, does it seem like he is?" she asked. "Is he avoiding you?"

"No," he said slowly. "At least . . . I don't think so?" He dragged his hands over his face and said, "Sehvi? I thought I saw . . . I thought . . ." He took a deep breath. "For a moment, I thought I felt a mindline."

She sat back. Then, after a moment: "Are you sure?"

"No!" he said. "I'm not! That's part of the problem!"

"I think it would be more of a problem if you were sure." She frowned. "Mindlines . . . they're supposed to be raveled on purpose. It's rare for them to form on their own. Usually it's only between suitable people."

"I know!"

"Are you sure?" she said again. "I mean . . . that's like love at first sight. We don't do love at first sight."

"Sehviiiii!" Vasiht'h said, putting his head down on his desk. Muffled, "Would I joke about something like that?"

"Does he know?" she asked. "Do Eldritch have mindlines?"

"How should I know!" he exclaimed. "I haven't exactly asked. 'Say, do you people have the rare habit of bonding mentally to people either by accident because it's your destiny, or on purpose to serve some grand ideal, thought to thought, heart to heart, forever until death?' Ugh!" He covered his face and sighed. "I doubt it anyway. They don't seem to hold with using their abilities at all. They find it distasteful."

"So he probably doesn't know about it," she said. "No harm done, then, right? If you saw it, it dissipated. A mindline might show in response to something, ariihir, but it doesn't stick unless you consciously support it."

"I know," Vasiht'h said, pained. "But if it was trying to . . . what am I missing, Sehvi? What if . . . what if there's something there? Something worth exploring?"

"I don't know. What if there is?"

"But it's ridiculous," Vasiht'h said. "I'm Glaseah and he's Eldritch, and he's going to go become some sort of healer-assist and I'm going to end up in a classroom, and where would it ever go? Nowhere."

"Right," she said.

"And even if it did, how ridiculous would it be, for him to be yoked to someone who'll die probably before he's middle-aged?"

"Right."

"And with someone whose people don't even use their abilities—"

"Mm-hmm—"

"Even if he was the one who initiated the touch the last time, after we fixed Luci's dream problem—" He stopped and looked up at her. "Stop that!"

"What?" she said.

"Stop being so . . . so . . ." He threw up his hands. "Smug!"

"I'm not being smug," she said. "I'm indulging your hysterics, because I'm a good sister and I love you. Now tell me more about this dream problem? You fixed someone's dreams?"

"Oh," Vasiht'h said. "Yes. We discovered at the hospital that if we wish good dreams on the children, they sleep better. And I calmed one of Jahir's nightmares with my mental touch—that was the first time I overstepped myself—and Luci came by the other day and was having trouble, and the two of us together, we smoothed her nightmare away. She told me today she felt much better." He frowned. "She looked much better too."

"Hmm." Sehvi tapped her fingers on her cheek, thinking. "I've never heard of an esper using mental touch to fix dreams like that. I mean, not on purpose, or formally. Do you suppose it helps them with other things, like their mental state?"

"I . . . don't know . . ." Vasiht'h said. "Huh."

"Not a bad research topic?" she offered brightly.

"You're being smug again," he said.

"You're welcome."

"It's nice being inside now," Amaranth said, peering out the window.

"But we could be making snow angels!" Persy said with a sigh from her bed, where she was confined by a halo-arch that occasionally chirped.

"Not in that snow, I fear," Jahir said. "It is wet and soggy, and not at all a proper snow for enjoying."

"It's more mud than snow," Vasiht'h agreed. "It's been a warm winter. More gray and brown than white."

"I guess I don't miss wet snow, then," Persy said.

Meekie and Kayla were sitting at the table, drawing; Nieve was on the window-seat again, looking out with Amaranth. Kuriel, like Persy, was on her bed by healer-assist's orders, and Jahir was sitting between them. Too aware, perhaps, of their exhaustion and their drawn faces, and that several of Kuriel's toes and fingers were again wrapped against the cuts she accidentally gave herself when she couldn't feel them. But they were glad of him, that he could tell too. And sitting across from him at the table, Vasiht'h's presence was warm and steadying, and he wondered now that he had the sense of it how he hadn't realized that his roommate was projecting an aura. It was simply so gentle a projection that he'd taken it for . . . what? His imagination?

"At least the holidays are coming soon," Meekie said. "Maybe we'll have cookies, like last year."

"Cookies sound good," Vasiht'h said.

"And presents!" Kayla added. She glanced at Vasiht'h. "I know Glaseah give presents. What about you, Prince Jahir?"

He had long since stopped fighting the sobriquet, since it was such a durable pleasure for them to use it. "Our customs are very different, perhaps. I have heard that there is a grand holiday for the entire Alliance, and that we shall be celebrating it, and that of course we have the Seersa's end of winter observance . . . but I don't know the human or Tam-illee customs. Or, come to that, the Glaseahn ones." He glanced at his roommate with lifted brow.

"Oh, well," Vasiht'h said, with embarrassment Jahir could read despite the fur on his cheeks hiding any blush. "We do, but only at the end of the year. At home we don't have winter like this. We have two dry seasons instead, and a wet season in the middle." At the evidence of the children's curiosity, he said, "Most of the Pelted celebrate midwinter, because winter is cold and harsh, and because the days get shorter and the dark lasts longer. So at the solstice, the shortest day of the year, they celebrate that from then on, winter's on its way out. But since we have no cold like this, we never came up with any holiday to celebrate it. So we wait until the new year, and then have a big party then, and it's the Maker's Day. Every new year is something newly made, you see? So we 'make' the new year during the Maker's Day, and then on the first day of the new year we have a feast. Because we're all tired, having done all that making."

"But there are presents, right?" Kayla said. "I heard that."

"Oh yes," Vasiht'h said. "On the Maker's Day, we give presents to people, symbols of what we'd like them to have in the new year. And we receive them as symbols that those people want to be part of our lives for the year." He grinned. "A lot of people get engaged on Maker's Day. It's considered very romantic, to pledge to make a new life together on the day when everyone's making their lives for the year."

"Wow," Persy said, eyes wide. "That sounds like a lot more fun than just giving people things you think they'd like! That's how we do it." She pursed her lips. "At least, for Christmas, which is what my family celebrates, and we had it before the Hinichi did."

Kayla said, "And we have solstice parties, and a big, big dinner on New Year's Day. Or we did, anyway. It's quieter now that my parents moved here. All our family's back on Tam-ley."

"But Miss Jill has a party for us here," Meekie hastened to add. "And it's a really nice party."

"With cookies," Jahir murmured.

"With cookies," Meekie agreed. "I don't think there's anything better than a warm cookie."

"Now I want to draw cookies," Kayla said.

"Ooh, me too," Amaranth said, and abandoned the window to Nieve. The latter looked out of it a little while longer and then carefully slid off it, pausing to seek her balance. As the other children reminded each other of the variety of cookies they'd had last year, Jahir went to her side and asked, voice low, "Shall I carry you?"

She looked up at him, then back out the window. Then she smiled at him. "That would be nice."

She was so thin in his arms, and not warm enough. He placed her on her bed and drew the blanket up around her shoulders. "You have been at the window too long, and allowed the cold to leech from it into you, Nieve-arii. You are no winter maiden to withstand such things."

"A winter maiden," she said with a sigh. "That sounds like a story. Will you tell me?"

There was nothing for it but to pull his chair over so that she could hear better, and to tell her one of the stories of the winter maidens, so popular among his kind . . . because the winters were long, and tragedies far too common among the Eldritch. If he omitted the genesis of the winter maidens—who were formed by dying untimely—they made pleasing tales, if the children's reactions were any indication. And it settled them, and kept them from fretting at their enforced bed-rest.

After he and Vasiht'h had seen them to their naps, Berquist stopped them outside and said, "We've got the end of year coming up soon. You're welcome to come to the party . . . I'm sure they've told you all about it, the scamps."

"They have, and we'd be glad to," Jahir said. "Hea Berquist— Kuriel's hands . . ."

"The cerrmoniah's having a bad flare-up," she said. "But we're on top of it. It's not unexpected, they all get a little worse when it gets damp out."

"I see," Jahir said. "We'll hope for better, then."

"As long as it's not colder-better," Berquist said, and smiled at them. "I'll send you the party invitation. It'll come in the mail . . . the girls like to make them."

"We look forward to it," Jahir said.

Outside it was still and gray, with a damp wind blowing cold on his face and his throat above the scarf he tucked into his coat. He hid his gloved hands in his pockets and walked alongside Vasiht'h, glad of the Glaseah's radiant warmth and unable to sense whether it was physical or mental. He was quite involved with his own thoughts, but his roommate's question scattered them handily.

"Jahir? Do your people ever willingly touch minds?"

"Ah?" he said, startled. And then, shaking his clinging hair from his face, "No. There are stories of people whose minds have touched by accident, and become entwined, but they are . . ." He looked for a good word. "They're like myths. Fairy tales, maybe you would say?"

"Humans would, anyway, and we're all human-descended no matter how odd we look," Vasiht'h said. "So you spend your lives . . . locked in your own minds, even though you could reach past them."

"Of course," Jahir said. "We all are born with abilities we choose not to exercise, for one reason or another."

"Because the mindtouch is always unpleasant," Vasiht'h said.

Jahir glanced down at him, and the Glaseah didn't meet his

gaze. After a moment, he said, "You're concerned still that you have trespassed on me."

Vasiht'h grimaced. "No—well. Yes."

"Though I have told you it was no cause for offense?"

"I just don't want to make you uncomfortable," Vasiht'h said, lowering his head, shoulders hunching.

"You have not!" Jahir said. "I will not blame you for not being Eldritch, Vasiht'h. And I'm rather glad you aren't, at that."

Startled, Vasiht'h looked up at him. "You mean that."

"Of course," Jahir answered, drawing in a slow breath. Too quick, and the cold seemed to burn down to his bones. "Would I be here if I did not want congress with aliens?"

"There's congress, and then there's *congress*," Vasiht'h said, and Jahir could taste his chagrin like something peppery. It stayed with him, lingering in his mouth like something real.

"I assure you," Jahir said, "I am not at all offended, and I still stand on my request that you come to my aid do you believe I need it. And I hope I am still permitted to come to yours."

"Of course!" Vasiht'h said. "I . . . yes. Of course."

"Vasiht'h," Jahir said. "Truly, I am not distressed." He clicked his tongue against the roof of his mouth, baffled at the pepper echo. "Though now I want ice cream. Shall we ruin our supper? I have the oddest impression of having tasted something spiced. It wants vanilla. Or chocolate."

The look Vasiht'h gave him was far more intense than Jahir was expecting, but the Glaseah finally looked away and said, "Let's have your ice cream, and then eat dinner." He grinned. "You only live once."

"Vasiht'h!" Palland said, and subsided, so stunned his ears were pointing straight up, and trembling. Vasiht'h had never seen him quite so excited about something . . . at least, not something he was responsible for. "You're saying that you believe espers can effect a positive change in the state of someone's mind by changing their dreams?"

"That's my premise," Vasiht'h said. "I've never changed any-one's normal dreams once they were already asleep, just their nightmares, but that seemed to have a good effect. I thought that since dreams are one of the ways we process things, being able to see someone's and maybe nudge them might be an interesting way of conducting therapy? I haven't tried it, though."

"What an astonishing idea," Palland said, tapping his cheek with a finger. "Of course, we have very few espers come through the program . . . it's almost as if being able to read people's minds easily makes people not really want to." He chuckled. "Well. You've certainly surprised me. I didn't think you'd have a topic so soon."

"Why?" Vasiht'h said. "Because you think I'm not suited for it?"

Palland glanced at him over his stack of books. "And now are you fishing, alet?"

"No," Vasiht'h said. "I honestly want to know."

"Then . . . yes," Palland said. "I think you'll find the lab sti-fling. But if you go on to prove me wrong, I'll be pleased to eat my words."

Vasiht'h watched his professor unbury his data tablet, frown-ing. There was something to the way the Seersa had said that. "But you don't think you'll have to."

Palland cocked his head, setting his data tablet down on top of his desk. Then he said, "Tell me, alet. You do this research. You discover it works. Then what?"

"Then . . . I don't know," Vasiht'h said, startled. "I guess people can use it."

"What people?" Palland asked. "As I said, we don't get many espers through here. I can't remember the last one, in fact. So you go and pioneer a therapeutic method that can only be used by espers, and then don't use it? When you're one of the few people who's able to do so?"

"You think I'll be more interested in using the method than researching it," Vasiht'h said.

"Won't you be?" Palland said.

Vasiht'h frowned, looking away.

"Here is my guess," Palland said—not without kindness, given he was predicting that Vasiht'h was going to be gloriously wrong in all his intentions—"you will embark onto the research track with this brilliant topic. You'll prove that it works. And then you'll leave research to go into practice using it."

"That seems like a very ambitious course," Vasiht'h said.

"Who said Glaseah can't have ambition?" Palland said, discomfiting him anew. "Now. If you're serious about this, and you are . . . ?" He trailed off, and Vasiht'h nodded emphatically. "All right. Then let's talk about the permissions you'll have to get to run a trial on people, and get you into some directed study hours next term."

—————ഇരോ—————

"So how are you feeling?" KindlesFlame said, putting his sensor and data tablet away and clearing their table for their drinks. "If I'm to take my readings here at face value, I'd say the regimen's worked. Any more bouts of fatigue?"

"No physical ones, at least," Jahir said. "I'm not fond of cold, however, and I am so deeply involved with my studies that I'm surprised by such novelties as food and sunlight."

KindlesFlame chuckled. "Well, another two weeks and you'll be done with it, and you can rest between terms. How are you feeling about the material now?"

"Fairly confident," Jahir said. "Though God and Lady know I may be deluded as to my competence on the matter. The subject remains alien to me—if you'll pardon the expression."

"It's apt," KindlesFlame said. He leaned back in his chair, hands resting on his knee and his cider cup steaming between them on the table. "And it'll get easier, the deeper you go into it."

"That's encouraging," Jahir began.

"Unless it doesn't, and then you'll drown," the Tam-illee finished, and laughed at his expression. "Oh, rest easy, alet. I'm teasing. Once you get to be my age you've seen so many mournful faces near finals that they all blur together and you stop being able to take any of them seriously. 'This too shall pass.' "

"Yes," Jahir said, thinking of all too many things here that would. He glanced up. "Do you know, Healer, that I still have not a notion what to do with what I'm learning?"

"Is this about the decision on what track to take?"

"Only inasmuch as my lack of imagination gives me no guidance," Jahir said. He cupped his gloved hands on the walls of the mug. "I have to imagine, though, that one does not enter into a degree at this level without some idea of how to employ it."

"You'd be surprised," KindlesFlame said dryly. "But here now. Let's assume that you came here for a psychology degree so that you could use it in some way. Is there something you could do at home with it?"

The thought was risible. A license to practice therapy among people who were riddled with secrets and vicious fears. He would never be done with the work, were he allowed to begin it at all, and he wouldn't. No one would talk to an heir to a seat in the royal House, unless they wanted to manipulate the situation somehow. "I'm afraid not."

"So that limits you to practice here, in the Alliance," KindlesFlame said. "If 'limit' is the right word with all the known worlds available to you, and all the starbases and ships linking them besides." He tapped his finger on the desk, as he was wont to do while thinking. "Have you any interest at all in the research track?"

"I think not," Jahir said. "At very least, it has not drawn my attention at all."

"So your choices are medical or clinical."

"Just so," Jahir said. "And I find the clinical route attractive, in a pastoral way; it's something I could imagine sustaining save that I wonder if I would not become overmuch involved."

"That's always a concern, of course," KindlesFlame said. "But I'm not sure how you'd avoid it in the medical track either. If anything, it's more extreme there: acute cases tend to incite acute feelings."

"Mmm." Jahir looked away. "I suppose. But at least those

cases are severed from you decisively."

"Maybe," KindlesFlame said. "But I think you'd find the clinical setting a better fit for your personality. And I think you'd have an advantage there, being Eldritch, one that would work against you in an acute care setting."

"Ah?" Jahir asked. "How so?"

The Tam-illee grinned. "Everyone's going to want to tell you their problems."

Jahir frowned at him. "If that is more teasing, Healer—"

"No, not at all. I laugh at it because it's true." He took up his cup and sipped from it before saying, "There's something about you that inspires confidence. I think part of it is that people are aware how many secrets Eldritch keep, and assume that their own secrets will be just as safe. They'll also think . . . 'he's lived so long, he'll have seen everything already, so my personal shame won't be so shocking.' There's a psychology, you see, to a therapist's appearance: species, presentation, dress. Some part of that you can control, and some part of it you don't. And you just . . . have it. That thing that makes people want to talk."

"Are you serious?" Jahir asked, startled.

"Oh yes," KindlesFlame said. "You listen well." He smiled. "Probably to keep from talking too much. Yes?"

"Perhaps," Jahir said, and the Tam-illee chuckled. "But surely these things don't make up for my being able to read their thoughts. Would that not distress patients?"

KindlesFlame snorted. "With you gloved and keeping your distance all the time? Not at all. No, I think you'd be a very successful therapist, if you committed yourself to it. Not to say you wouldn't excel at the medical application, if that's really where your heart lies . . . ?"

"I don't know," Jahir admitted. "I find chemistry easy, at least. Probably the easiest part of my studies."

"That's handy, particularly if you want to specialize in pharmacology." KindlesFlame nodded. "That's not a bad thing for a practicing therapist, as well. In fact, if it interests you, you can always take the pharma courses as an adjunct to the clinical track. It'll make a little extra work for you, but you'll use it."

Jahir shook his head minutely. "You aren't making the choice any easier, Healer."

"It's not my job to make the choice easy. It's my job to make the potential choices clearer, so you know which one you want." KindlesFlame stirred his cider, inhaled the steam. "You still have a little time to decide, anyway."

Jahir attended to his own drink, watching the students pass on the sidewalks below their perch on the glassed-in balcony. Their posture had changed as the weeks had worn on, and now with finals approaching he thought he could read their nervousness, their late nights, and their focus in their body language and the speed of their gait. "If an Eldritch therapist inspires confidences, what of a Glaseah? I don't see many of them."

"In the medical campus?" KindlesFlame shook his head. "You'll catch some of them in the research labs, but for the most part they don't often practice any form of medicine. You'll find the exceptions, but the culture tends to turn out scientists and teachers. Which is a pity, because they're a friendly species . . . they put people to ease. And they're hard to faze, emotionally."

"I see," Jahir murmured. At KindlesFlame's inquisitive look, he said, "My roommate is a Glaseah, and two years into his psychology degree."

"Ah! Well." KindlesFlame grinned. "There's a gem. I bet he'll never want for work. If he's going clinical. Is he?"

"He's not sure," Jahir said.

"I hope he does go into practice," KindlesFlame said. At Jahir's glance, he said, "Like I said earlier, once you get to be my age, you've seen so many students that the patterns become obvious. I like to see a student break the mold. They're usually the ones that go the farthest."

That thought stayed with him after lunch, dogging him through the afternoon lecture in neuropsychology. The pattern-breakers going the farthest. Was it so? It made him wonder . . . was that what had the Queen so interested in the Eldritch willing to leave the world? He knew very well the troubles their people faced, and the opposition the Queen had to getting them to change, even to save themselves. For a small investment of her time and money, she could cast some seeds on the wind and bring them home, and perhaps with them, some hope of change.

Which reminded him that he had money, and it was now growing close to the holidays. He could buy presents. It seemed an excellent notion, particularly after KindlesFlame's pass on his health. He could go into the city and explore, now that he was more confident of the world.

The Pad station that normally took him to the gelateria with Vasiht'h sent him to a central hub in Seersana's capital city, in which the university was set like a gem in a crown. From there he selected an esteemed shopping district and stepped over the Pad, and on to adventure. It was the first time he'd chosen to go out into an Alliance city: his trip to Seersana had involved the Queen's courier service ship ferrying him to a station in orbit, and from there, via shuttle and Pad, to the campus. His impression of the Alliance thus far was of bustle, and broad, high, clean spaces: great terminals with windows taller than a cathedral wall looking out onto orbital space busy with transports and interstellar vessels.

It was late afternoon when he walked out among the crowd of Pelted strolling down a pedestrian walkway bordered in shops: shops with real shingles hanging from their eaves, painted in pastel colors and shrouded with small flowering trees. Lamps with lace-like ironwork hung from short posts, glowing in the red light of a setting sun. It smelled like flowers he didn't recognize . . . and flowers he did, as when he caught a sudden, startling draft perfumed with roses. And it was busy and bright and it felt *healthy*: like a society in its prime, rather than the declining world he'd left.

Even surrounded by the Pelted, all of whom did not brush against him—not on purpose anyway—he could not help but love it. Breathe it in and feel it as a promise of a good life.

He could go back home, and he would . . . eventually, for the Seni would need him. But until now he'd been uncertain that he would find the world outside the university setting appealing enough to risk the losses he would inevitably endure living among the short-lived races of the Alliance.

But for this?

For this, he could imagine staying. For the size of the Alliance, for its wide spaces, for its many and fascinating people, none of whom he could predict.

Jahir drew in a long, slow breath of the winter air and went to find his gifts.

———— ∞ ————

He returned, triumphant if a little shaken by the effects of dealing with so many people so close by . . . but he assuaged his jangled nerves by walking the long way home from the Pad station. By the time he stepped through the apartment door he felt powerfully alive and very content, and his arrival brought Vasiht'h up short. Perhaps something of his epiphany remained visible in his face, because the Glaseah put down the knife he was using to chop mushrooms and said, "Something's changed. Something good. You've decided something."

"You can tell?" Jahir said, putting his bags beside the hall to his room and unwinding his scarf.

"Yes," Vasiht'h said, padding out of the kitchen. "Can I help with those?"

"No, no, it's fine," Jahir said, and shrugged out of his coat. "I was about to ask you the same. What are we eating?"

"Winter soup," Vasiht'h said. "It seems a good night for it. Mushrooms, spinach, a lot of broth. It's mostly done though, you can relax."

"I'll lay in the fire, then," Jahir said and suited action to words. As he stacked the wood, he said, "Vasiht'h? What prompted you to choose the psychology program?"

He had startled his roommate, if Vasiht'h's pause was any indication. He thought the emotion had a sharp bite, like a knife slipping against the finger—no, that was real? The Glaseah had his finger to his mouth and was frowning.

"Is it so surprising a question?" he asked.

"It is a little out of nowhere," Vasiht'h said. "I guess . . . I chose it because I like people. I like understanding them. I like helping them. When I do that, it makes the world around me seem a calmer, safer, happier place. Less entropic." He glanced at Jahir. "Why do you ask?"

"I don't see many Glaseah in this part of the university," Jahir said. "And Healer KindlesFlame tells me that is more typical than for them to be here. He tells me Glaseah are more like to become scientists and teachers? You are apparently an anomaly, alet."

"Well, therapy is a way of making too," Vasiht'h said. "It's just a people-and-community sort of making, not an ideas-and-science making."

"That is a fine way of thinking of it," Jahir said, and gently blew the fire to life, thinking of the breath of an alien goddess. When he had done, he looked over his shoulder to find Vasiht'h staring at him. So he said, "I'm staying. I know not what I'll do when I am done here, alet. But I will stay, and see what more the Alliance has to teach me."

Saying it made it real and he savored it, like a dark red wine, so strong he could smell the bouquet. He would pay the cost, he knew. But he had a sense now what he was buying with it, and he was eager to meet it.

———✼———

That night before bed, Vasiht'h rested his head in his arms on his desk, the rest of his body crouched on the floor, reflecting his tensions. In his mind he had the picture of his roommate as he'd returned from whatever errand had taken him off-campus: cheeks flushed and his eyes . . . like sunshine through honey. He imagined his silent conversation with Sehvi: "He's picking up things he shouldn't, ariishir. Once in a while, he tastes my thoughts, as if he's still reaching for them. And he's staying . . . he's going to stay, in the Alliance, once he's done with school."

"And I want to be there, where he is."

With a noise somewhere between a moan, a sigh, a laugh, Vasiht'h covered his eyes with his arm.

CHAPTER 17

THE WEEK OF FINAL EXAMINATIONS seemed to arrive precipitously, and with it a gray sky and weather that alternated between sullen rain and slush: no clean white snow here, merely endless repetitions of cold, wet days that made Jahir wonder if he would take a catarrh. But perhaps the nights spent studying indoors had protected him; no doubt it helped that those nights were spent in an apartment already warm enough without the fire he and his roommate had come to enjoy for pleasure more than physical comfort.

He was deeply gratified to pass all his classes, though he could read his struggles in neuroscience in the grades. His touch with chemistry saved him in physiological psychology, at least, and the grounding the children had given him in the Pelted had most certainly solved at least one weakness in his education.

There was, he thought, much cause for celebration, and he was glad that the term was over, and could now indulge himself in one.

"And here are your visitors," Berquist said, opening the door for them. "Come early!"

The girls were in the midst of decorating their room, threading strings through silver and gold paper stars and smoothing a red paper cloth over their play table. At their healer-assist's comment, they one and all looked up and exclaimed. Jahir had set aside his finery when coming here, having researched the customs of the Alliance. But he thought, for once, he might come dressed for the occasion, if only to delight them, and from their expressions it had worked. Surcoats were out of fashion at home, having given way to the longer court coats, but the Pelted wore many variations of them. He normally wore plain ones here, finding them suitable.

"Oh look at the silver thread!" Amaranth exclaimed. "You look like a prince!"

"Are they snowflakes?" Kayla said. "They are!"

"It is winter," Jahir said, putting his bags on the table. Vasiht'h padded in behind him, grinning, and the girls squealed again.

"Hat! Hat!"

"Hat!" Vasiht'h agreed, ducking so Kuriel and Meekie could bat the pompom at the end of it. "Hello, ariisen. Happy holidays."

"Have you passed the week well?" Jahir said. "And are you meaning to hang those stars from the ceiling? I might be of some aid to you there."

"Here," Kayla said, handing him one of them. "It should stick, if you can touch the string up on the ceiling. Miss Jill said it was all right."

Jahir took it from her and affixed it so that it hung down on its string. He took the next too.

"We're having cookies today!" Meekie said. "So everything's already great."

"How about you?" Amaranth asked. "You had tests this week, right?"

"We both did fine," Vasiht'h said. "Though we're glad it's over!"

"And we are both at liberty, and so we thought to come early for your party," Jahir said. "Particularly after receiving such beautiful invitations."

"So are we scattering glitter on the table now that it has the cloth on it?" Vasiht'h asked, looking at the abandoned packets.

The girls were eager to give them direction. For once, all of them were off their beds, though Kuriel and Persy sat often to rest. But the excitement of the holiday was imperishable, and Jahir was glad to be spending some part of it with them.

When they'd finished the decoration, he said, "I see we have some time yet before the guests arrive. Perhaps it is a good time . . . for presents?"

"You brought us things?" Persy said, eyes wide.

"We both did," Jahir said, and Vasiht'h nodded.

"It is a holiday," the Glaseah said, and grinned. He reached into one of the bags they'd brought. "Unless you want to wait?"

A chorus of 'no's answered, and Jahir sat on one of the small chairs, watching Vasiht'h distribute the gifts. Berquist had examined them and declared them suitable, and they were for the most part trinkets, so as not to overwhelm them. But he'd found several stores selling children's gifts and had been unable to resist . . . a little curving pillow shaped like a dragon for Persy, and one like a unicorn for Amaranth; a set of new pencils for Kayla, who had taken to penmanship despite prior complaints, and a set of paints for Meekie, who much preferred to draw while the others attempted their calligraphies . . . and for Nieve:

"A hat!" Nieve exclaimed. And then started laughing. "It's a sleeping cap!"

"Since I seem only to see you when I am putting you to your nap," Jahir said.

She lifted it for the others to see: it was pale purple and silver, elegant despite the soft knobby yarn from which it had been made. Its end was long enough to trail onto her chest, reaching just past where she'd indicated her hair had once rested, and there it ended in a soft puff of yarn. "It's wonderful!" she said, placing it on her head. And then she giggled. "It has holes for my ears? It does!" She adjusted the cap to let them poke through and then hugged him, and it was a wind out of spring, warm and new and bright. He felt the crush of her head against his chest and his heart fluttered.

Yes, he could love the Alliance.

Vasiht'h's gifts were clever: puzzles and board games and paper dolls, and other things they could occupy their hands and minds with together. And since they had some time before the children's guardians arrived, they broke open one of the puzzles and began it, while overhead the paper stars glinted.

It was a very successful party, particularly the cookies, which were frosted and sprinkled with sugar and cinnamon. They stayed until it ended and the children's parents left, and then they helped Berquist shepherd her charges back to their beds, overdue for their naps but glowing with happiness. He whispered his dream-wishes to them as they drifted off, soft with snow-outside but warmth-within, and thought he sensed Vasiht'h doing the same.

"There," Berquist said, as they slipped out. "That was a perfect day for them." She smiled at them. "Thanks. The two of you are gold."

"Do you need help cleaning up the decorations?" Vasiht'h asked, folding the bags they'd brought and pausing at the last one.

"No, leave them," she said. "They enjoy having them up for a while. I'll take them down after New Year's."

Jahir said to Vasiht'h, "That last box is for her."

"For me?" Berquist said, surprised.

Vasiht'h glanced in the bag, then offered it to her. She glanced at Jahir before unwrapping the gift and laughing. "You bought me coffee."

"I'm told it is a very particular and high quality kind," Jahir said. "And they permitted me a sample and it was sublime. You're always with a cup in your hand when we come out of their room ... I thought you might enjoy it."

"That's very thoughtful," she said, looking down. Her fingers stroked the ribbon twice, a quick gesture, and then she closed the box and said, "Happy holidays, ariisen."

"And to you," Jahir answered.

On their way home, Vasiht'h said, "You know she finds you

attractive."

"Does she?" Jahir asked, startled.

"You didn't realize?" Vasiht'h said. "I thought, since you bought her a gift . . ."

"It was the furthest thing from my mind." Jahir glanced at his roommate. "Have I unintentionally initiated a courtship?"

"No," Vasiht'h said. "At least, nothing that formal, not with a bag of coffee beans! But you might have given her hopes."

Jahir shook his head. "I hope not. She seems a sensible woman; hopefully she won't take it for more than it was."

"I hate to tell you this," Vasiht'h said. "But there's almost nothing sensible about love."

That made him laugh, and that he could despite the experiences that informed his opinions on the matter was something of a triumph. Jahir smiled up at the gray sky and said, "And here I thought you had no idea on the matter."

Vasiht'h muttered something, but he didn't press.

"Come," he said instead. "The day is good and not yet sped. Let's go shopping for the new year feast. Mera will be sore disappointed if we don't mull enough wine to inebriate him."

"I don't think we have enough money to buy that much wine," Vasiht'h said. And then paused. "Wait, we're mulling wine? I don't even know what mulled wine is!"

"Then," Jahir said, amused, "I shall teach you."

⌖

Vasiht'h slept in the morning of Maker's Day. No doubt his mother would have been scandalized, but after the pummeling finals had given him he felt he was entitled to some sloth. Not much, but some. In fact, he'd been planning to sleep until well past breakfast, but the smell of something baking lifted his chin from his mound of pillows. He wrinkled his nose and then pushed himself reluctantly upright before padding into the great room.

There was a fire on the hearth, hissing and popping. On the table there was a coffee pot and two saucers, but only one cup; the missing cup was in the kitchen at Jahir's elbow. The Eldritch was bent over a data tablet, leaning past a bowl where he had both hands mired in something.

"What on Her worlds are you doing?" Vasiht'h asked, joining him.

"I," Jahir said, "am making the feast bread. You did not tell me it involved sticky toppings." He looked down at the bowl. "I tried a spatula, but it seemed faster to mix it by hand."

"And now you've got butter all over your fingers, where it's melted because of the warmth of your skin," Vasiht'h said with a laugh, but he was having trouble breathing. His roommate was making him breakfast? His holiday breakfast, at that?

"Alas," Jahir said. "I fear my festival bread is destined to the same questionable state as your mother's."

"It will still taste good," Vasiht'h said. "Let me get it out of the oven so you can spread the topping on. You'll see, by the time it's done melting in there you won't be able to tell it was messy."

"It's not the topping I'm worried about, so much as my hands!"

Vasiht'h grinned. "Just lick them. That's what we used to do."

Jahir wrinkled his nose, and if there was anything as ridiculous as an Eldritch prince in his kitchen, in an apron too short for him, fingers deep in sugar . . . Vasiht'h hid a laugh and got the bread out.

The bread wasn't the only thing Jahir had managed . . . somewhere he'd found a proper nut butter, an imported one from Anseahla, and sweet citrus wedges. The coffee was oily and black, and cut through the honeyed sweetness. That his roommate had bothered to research the morning customs for the holiday—he hadn't had to. It made Vasiht'h wish he could have done the same, but of course there was no information about Eldritch holidays available and Jahir had deflected the question any time anyone had asked. If the children hadn't been able to get an answer out of him, Vasiht'h knew better than to try. That he'd at least been warned they gave gifts was enough.

The gifts came after breakfast. Jahir brought him his and set it on the table, with a touch of hopefulness in his eyes . . . Vasiht'h took it and eyed him. "You didn't have to buy me something."

"It is the custom, though," Jahir said.

And it was. But the custom for Glaseah was about crafting the shape of the year in front of them, and Vasiht'h wasn't sure how he felt about receiving one. Part of him hoped Jahir didn't understand, because it gave him space to breathe past his own conflicted feelings: about his life after school, about his fondness for the Eldritch, about the unlikelihood of any of it coming out the way he hoped.

The other part of him knew better. Jahir was far too good at listening.

He set the gift on his lap and unwrapped it, slowly, making it last . . . half afraid of what he would find. And what he found puzzled him. "It's . . . a kit?"

"Open it?" Jahir said.

He did and found thread and needle, and a jar of something that he opened and sniffed—something buttery? And a selection of . . . patches? In tan leather?

"It's a repair kit," Jahir said. "For your bags. I noticed some of them are fraying." He threaded his fingers together. "The shoulder bag particularly seems old, almost to the point of needing replacement . . . but I thought you must like it to keep it, thus the kit."

Startled, Vasiht'h said, "I . . . I don't even know how to sew!"

"I can teach you," Jahir said. "And to maintain the leather also, so it lasts longer."

"I'd like that." He looked again at the kit and no longer wondered if Jahir had understood the spirit of Glaseahn gifts. Maintenance of things one intends to keep, along with the tools and teaching to make it possible . . . the Goddess Herself would have approved of it, and the commitment they implied. Friendships, too, needed maintenance. He drew in a deep breath. "I have something for you too. Wait here."

He returned with an envelope and set it on the table between them. As Jahir reached for it, he sat and tried not to fidget. He had a good guess at the reaction he was going to get, but like

Jahir's gift, it implied his own involvement, and he never liked to intrude on the Eldritch's privacy.

But the expression on Jahir's face when he read the slip inside the envelope blew all those worries away. His roommate looked up, wide-eyed. "You have bought concert tickets?"

"I have bought season passes to the student concert series," Vasiht'h said, trying not to twitch his tail. "We can go to any of their performances. Or all of them. They have everything from chamber music to full-on orchestras, and choral groups . . . everything the music college does, they offer."

"Oh, Vasiht'h!" Jahir said. So quietly to be so heartfelt. "I wonder when the next performance is?"

"Next week!" Vasiht'h said. "But today there's an outdoor choral concert if you're interested. They're doing holiday carols. It's not for a few hours, and we'll have plenty of time to be back to start baking for tomorrow . . ."

"Oh yes, we must!" Jahir said. And laughed. "It's perfect. Thank you, alet. It is . . . it's perfect."

"And maybe while the cake's in the oven, you can start teaching me to sew," Vasiht'h said. "I can't believe you noticed that my bag's coming apart, but you're right. And I'd hate to lose it."

"I would be delighted."

—————∞∞∞—————

And that was what they ended up doing. Vasiht'h wondered how he'd learn to sew when they only had one needle between them, but Jahir had a similar kit: older, definitely, and larger, with materials for cloth as well as leather; when Vasiht'h asked, he said, "Some clothing needs to be sewn closed," and that struck him as so bizarre that he didn't ask. It wasn't until much later that he looked it up on the u-banks and found out that yes, there were outfits that were fastened onto people by sewing a few stitches here and there in lieu of something more reasonable, like stick-strips or zippers or even buttons.

Clothing baffled him, but he was grateful to learn the mending, and sitting with Jahir over the practice squares he felt a frisson of contentment so intense it was almost painful.

After that, they walked to the center of campus. The concert was taking place in the grand plaza in front of the university administration building, and five tiers of bleachers had been set up for the chorus, which was over a hundred members strong: not only Pelted and humans, but some of the aliens as well. Vasiht'h saw the Phoenix and Akubi sections standing in the back and hid his grin, anticipating his roommate's surprise.

The first time the Phoenix section lifted their voices, fluting far above the range of any humanoid throat, he felt Jahir shudder next to him. And the Akubi, birds as tall as a room and with chests broader than Vasiht'h's barrel, could sing both higher and lower than any of their Pelted companions, and their basso crooning made even his fur stand on end. He could only imagine how it sounded to his roommate, with his so-much-better ears. Like Heaven, maybe, if his expression of bliss was any indication.

He waited as they began the walk back for the inevitable conversation; realized that he *was* waiting for it, and how much pleasure it gave him anticipating it.

"I could do that every day," Jahir said at last with a sigh.

"Well, now we can do it every week," Vasiht'h said.

"But then when will have time for ice cream?" Jahir said wistfully.

Vasiht'h laughed. "Obviously we'll go to the concerts, and then go out for ice cream. Problem solved."

"Yes," Jahir said, and grinned at him. "I suppose it is."

Cooking for a feast, even of only six people, was far more work than Jahir had imagined. It made him wonder how the servants managed at home. So much he didn't know, even about his own world; he had to believe he'd return far more prepared for whatever responsibilities would come to him. Vasiht'h made a good guide in this as in all things, and set him to preparing in advance for the dishes that would need to cook or rest overnight. He set to it with a good will.

In the morning he did not rise immediately, but let himself enjoy the sensation of ease, the strangeness of a new year on a new world. At home it was already summer, and his mother would be preparing for attendance on the Queen for the summer court. He might have gone with her this time; it was not required of the heirs to join their matriarchs for the courts, but many of them went anyway, to meet the men or women to whom they would eventually be betrothed—if they hadn't already been, in the childhood ceremony. Jahir hadn't been, and though his mother had made no mention of it he knew there was talk already. He probably would have been dutiful and gone, and would right now have been overseeing the packing of his trunks.

Instead he was here: free and with the promise of all the known worlds before him, a celestial diadem to shame the Queen's, and with the beautiful uncertainty of a life amid alien confederates, all of them unpredictable, and all their learning available to him. He set his head back down on the pillow and allowed himself the luxury of remaining abed until he heard the clatter of bowls in the kitchen. Then, smiling, he drew on a robe and went to help.

In the early afternoon their quadmates arrived, bearing their own gifts: Brett had brought some outrageously alcoholic eggnog, something Jahir had never had until the Seersa plied him with it. "This goes to Vasiht'h," he said with a laugh, because its richness reminded him of kerinne. Merashiinal came with arms full of pine boughs and packs of candles to decorate the table. His roommate Leina brought a delicate flan, quivering on the plate, and Luci brought up the rear with a plate of bright purple potato wedges, arranged in a circle around a bowl of some creamy yellow dip.

In short order they had the feast assembled: a roasted goose and a caramelized ham, a salad dressed in a light sauce, a great dish of greens that had been steamed and then sauteed to flavorful perfection, purple potatoes and yellow—served mashed and candied with pureed nuts a darker swirl in them—mushrooms stuffed with spiced crab . . . and the wine, mulled to Jahir's satisfaction, though he was not a great drinker and had not the exact spices for it. Plus cider and water and then coffee and eggnog and strong black tea to go with the flan and the honey cake, and the marzipan balls and peppermint brittles Vasiht'h had overseen cooking down on the stove with all the ferocity of a hawk.

It was good to see Luci laughing. Jahir could see the shadows in her eyes, but she seemed better, and when he asked Brett later, the Seersa said, "Oh yes. She's been much more here, if you know what I mean."

"I do," Jahir said. He was cleaning dishes, something that involved sliding them beneath what appeared to be a magic wand mounted alongside the refrigerator, which left them spotless. "And I'm relieved to hear it."

Brett set another stack of plates beside him and said, "So can I ask you something?"

Jahir glanced at him.

"How do you do it? The volunteering." He rubbed his hands on his sides. "I know I'm going to have to do a pediatric round at some point, and . . . I don't know how I'll be able to do it. Sick adults I have no trouble with. Sick kids . . ." He shook his head.

"I suppose it's done the way one does anything else," Jahir said. "By bowing one's head and moving through it."

"Do you have any?" Brett asked.

"Children?" Jahir said, startled. "No."

"Want them?"

Such a question. It could only be asked by aliens, who either had children easily, or had access to technologies that could make them possible. "Yes," he said. And at Brett's glance, added, smiling, "Not yet, however."

"No, me neither," Brett said with a chuckle. "But I do want them, you know? And I know when I go into that round, I'll be looking into those faces and thinking 'what if this was my baby?'" He shuddered. "I have nightmares about it."

"It seems a strange thing to have nightmares about when you have none of your own," Jahir ventured.

"Is it?" Brett said. "I guess you'd know." He sighed. "Well, I'm borrowing trouble, and on New Year's Day, too. Vasiht'h would poke me and tell me to take care what shape I'm forcing the year into."

"Do I hear you talking about me poking you?" Vasiht'h asked, padding into the kitchen to refresh the coffee pot.

"You do," Brett said. "And I'm all for that fat chair over there, which is too far from you to be poked." He grinned at Jahir and ambled off.

"What was that about?" Vasiht'h asked.

"I'm not sure." Jahir finished with the last of the plates and looked after Brett. He thought of KindlesFlame's observation, and wondered.

They spent the rest of the evening playing board games while making desultory attempts to reduce the remainder of dessert to crumbs. Merashiinal had gone through enough of the mulled wine to declare himself pleasantly inebriated, and a tipsy Ciracaana was wholly beyond Jahir's experience: the male could sing, and did, and often interrupted himself to make some witty remark that had them all dissolved into laughter made more painful by far too full stomachs. He was sad to see them go.

Luci was the last to take her leave, and she hugged Vasiht'h at the back door.

"Everything bearable?" the Glaseah said.

"It hurts, but . . . yeah. Bearable." She rested her head against Vasiht'h's. "Thanks for not asking if things were okay."

"I didn't think they would be," Vasiht'h answered. "I just wanted to know how you were."

"You're a gem," she said. "Both of you. And thanks for the party."

"Any time," Vasiht'h said, and closed the door behind her, looking satisfied.

"Well, then, alet," Jahir said. "Have we made a good shape for the new year?"

"I don't think the Goddess could complain," Vasiht'h answered, and dropped onto the carpet in front of the fire. "Though I think if I eat one more thing, I'll pop." He draped his upper body on one of the chairs and said, "We still have a few days left of vacation. What do you think you'll do?"

Jahir savored the notion for several moments, settling on the chair before the fire's last embers. "I think," he said at last, "I will gorge myself on sleep and leftover goose. And dream of music."

"Funny you should say that," his roommate said. "Do you know, last night I heard that chorus in my sleep?"

Jahir smiled and let his head rest against the back of the chair. "So did I."

He thought nothing of the coincidence: the music had been glorious. He also had the feeling Vasiht'h was staring at him, but when he opened his eyes, his roommate was watching the fire.

CHAPTER 18

"A QUESTION," JILL REPEATED when Vasiht'h approached her about it. Jahir was still inside, whispering the last of his dream-offerings to the girls, so it seemed a good time.

"Yes," he said. "I wanted to ask your advice on something. I'm starting research for my thesis, and it's on the effect of dream interventions on mental health."

The woman's eyes lost focus a moment, then she looked at him with lifted brows. "I've heard some pretty wild topics around here, but I think that might be the least expected of any I've run into. This is . . . what, an exploration of your esper abilities on people as psychiatric patients?"

"More or less," Vasiht'h said. "I was wondering if I could do it here. Before I talked to the hospital board, I wanted an insider perspective on whether it's a good idea. What do you think?"

Jill frowned, her arms folded and her fingers drumming a beat on her forearm. "Mm. If you want my advice . . . I'd ask if you could do it on the staff, not the patients. There are a lot more hoops to jump through if you want to run studies on patients. We staffers, on the other hand, are used to being abused." She grinned, and then added, rueful, "And we could use any help we can get. A medical study that involves us sleeping sounds divine.

I'd sign up in a heartbeat."

"That's a good idea!" Vasiht'h said. "Thank you, Jill-alet."

"My pleasure," she said. As Jahir stepped out of the room and closed the door gently behind him, she said, "It really has improved their health . . . being able to sleep well once a week."

"Do you think?" Vasiht'h asked.

"Oh, absolutely. No question." She smiled. "It won't cure them, but every little bit."

"Yes," Vasiht'h said. "Thanks again for the advice."

"No problem." As they left, she called, "And I was serious! Sign me up!"

Glancing over his shoulder, Jahir said, "What is Healer-assist Berquist wanting to sign up for?"

"I thought I'd base my research project in the hospital, since we already volunteer there," Vasiht'h said, waiting for his roommate to don his coat and gloves before they headed outside. According to the calendar the first week of the Seersan year was also the first week of spring, but in practice it was usually soggy and cold and not much different from the last week of winter.

"And you have a topic, then?" Jahir asked, once they'd gotten outside and on their way to the apartment.

"Oh, yes. You'd be interested, actually. On whether active manipulation of dreams can have a positive psychiatric effect."

Jahir glanced down at him. "This being on your mind since Lucrezia's stay, I am guessing?"

"And what we do with the kids," Vasiht'h agreed. "My major professor was over the moon. He thought it was a promising topic."

"I should certainly like to know the results," Jahir said.

"Me too. Jill suggested running the tests on the staff, since it's easier to do that than get permission to work on patients," Vasiht'h said, working it out in his head as they walked. "I think that's a good idea. The staff's probably underserved anyway; there's psychological support for the patients everywhere, but I'm betting the staff forgets to take care of themselves."

"So, you will spend time on this project as part of the curriculum this semester," Jahir said. "Is that right?"

"Yes," Vasiht'h said. "We take directed studies, that's basically just an excuse for me to get together with my major professor and work on this." He glanced up at the Eldritch. "Did you decide yet?"

"On a track?" Jahir shook his head, something that looked less like a negation and more like . . . some kind of animal shying. "I asked my advisor to suggest classes relevant to either medical or clinical concentrations, and took half from each. Perhaps more direct experience with the subject matters will help me choose."

Vasiht'h grinned. "So did they put you in Patient Assessment in the Clinical Setting?"

"Yes?"

He laughed at the Eldritch's expression, which he could read as surprise and concern despite how little his face changed: something about his eyes. "You'll like it. It's a lot of information and you'll have to learn it quickly to keep from falling behind, but it's fantastic. A big favorite."

"I look forward to it," Jahir said. "I also have Clinical Management of Acute Care Cases, which is part of the medical track, Pharmacology, an Abnormal Psychology Overview, and Mental Diseases of the Exodus."

Vasiht'h wrinkled his nose. "The Exodus class is harsh. Actually the whole thing sounds like a heavy load. Are you sure about taking it all at once? The drug class is going to be a lot of chemistry."

"That should be the easiest part," Jahir said. "I am more concerned about the practical work. But if it's too much, best to know now." He folded his arms behind his back and said, "Your thesis does interest me. How do you plan to study it?"

"I don't know yet," Vasiht'h said. "I'm writing a few drafts on how to go at it, and hopefully Doctor Palland will have some advice." He sighed. "It feels sort of fuzzy, to be honest. My mother and father are always doing research projects, but hard science seems a lot easier to test than people's reactions. You figure a molecule's only got so many ways to react to things. But people?"

"That's what makes people so endlessly engaging," Jahir said. "One never knows."

Which made Vasiht'h wonder, suddenly, whether he ever would, and if not, why he was bothering.

———⊶⊷———

He asked Sehvi about it later. She snorted and said, "You're the one who decided you were destined for psychology research."

"Not for research," Vasiht'h said. "*Teaching*. Research is just what you have to do to get to a teaching position."

"Uh-huh," Sehvi said. "You're going to have to do six more years of research if you want to end up in front of a college classroom. What are you going to study when you're done figuring out if dreams help people work out their problems faster?"

"Hopefully by then I'll have come up with another topic," Vasiht'h said. At his sister's arch look, he said, "I'm committed to this. I'm going to do it."

"You are running," she said.

"I am not running from clinical," Vasiht'h answered, flicking his ears back.

"No, you're running from your roommate *and* from clinical," she said. "Basically, away from everything that's making you realize that you can be troubled by your own feelings. Where do I send my psychologist brother to get psychologized?"

"That's not even a word," Vasiht'h growled.

Sehvi huffed. "You need therapy, ariihir."

"What I need is support!" Vasiht'h said. "And that's what I'm not getting! Even my major professor thinks I'm going to end up in practice. How can I give my heart to something that no one will take seriously?"

"Maybe it's because we don't think you're taking it seriously," she said. "But I won't harangue you about it anymore. Tell me instead if the mindline's still trying to manifest."

"Ungh," Vasiht'h said, and dropped his head into his arms. "As if I didn't have enough problems."

"I guess that's a yes?"

"We both dreamed about singing a few nights ago," Vasiht'h said, shoulders drooping. "Which ordinarily I wouldn't think anything of, but I'm beginning to question whether my being able to read his body language so easily is me just being used to Eldritch minimalism, or if I'm reading his aura without trying to."

"And he's still getting something off you," she said.

"Little bits here and there," Vasiht'h said. "At least he doesn't seem to have realized that's what's happening."

"So when are you going to tell him?"

"Tell him!" He looked up at her, aghast. "Why would I ever tell him?"

"So that maybe he can decide whether he likes the idea?" she asked, folding her arms.

"No, no, no, never," Vasiht'h said, shaking his head. "Never. He's Eldritch, and they hate the mental touch of other people, and even if he doesn't mind it from me in emergencies it's not something they'd do. He told me himself it's something out of crazy mythical stories with grand and tragic and doomed relationships. Did I mention they're tragic?"

"It is sort of implied by the doomed part," she said. "Don't you owe it to him to explain why he's tasting your feelings?"

"If it becomes obtrusive, maybe," Vasiht'h said. "But for now?" He shuddered. "No. I like things the way they are, Sehvi. I don't want them to change." He flushed, grateful that his fur hid it. "He's teaching me to sew. Because he noticed that my bags are coming apart, so he bought me a repair kit for the new year."

Her brows shot up. "He bought you a year-gift! Did he understand?"

"I . . . think so. As much as an alien can, anyway."

"And you got him something too, I bet," she said, and grinned at his look. "You did! What did you give him?"

"Concert tickets for the season," Vasiht'h muttered. "For both of us."

She shook her head. "Oh, ariihir. I don't know why you're still fighting this. You've already lost."

————∞∞∞————

Jahir wasn't sure what to expect from the Clinical Management class. He'd read the précis, but he'd been imagining more
study; certainly he'd been assigned a textbook. But the first
day of class, their instructor—Lasareissa Kandara, a short gray
Seersa with pale eyes—had given them an overview and then
led them from the classroom to a large empty hall, their foot-
steps echoing. She barked a command, and the emptiness was
replaced, instantly, with the frenetic bustle of an acute care ward.
Jahir had fleeting impressions of people racing by with floating
beds, and a cacophony of noises: the warble of machinery, the
groaning of people in distress. It was so real that he froze, his
skin pebbling beneath his clothes at the breezes he imagined
he felt each time someone ran past him. And then he realized
the breezes were real, and the projections were solid when one
brushed him on the way past.

"When we're done with this semester," Kandara was saying,
"you won't be standing here staring at this like people petri-
fied by an oncoming train. You'll be in the thick of it, managing
your particular patients. I'll give you reading, and once a month
we'll get together to discuss it. But our classes will take place in
this lab. Those of you here for nursing will go on to do two more
semesters of this class. If you're here for medical psychiatry,
you'll get this one class, but we'll have specialized scenarios for
you." She looked around, meeting their faces as around her the
activity swirled. "This simulation is solidigraphic and it's been
built from data taken from actual acute care facilities all over the
Alliance. You won't find a better preparation for the real thing. "

Falling in behind the woman on the way back to their classroom, Jahir fought his unease. He wanted, very much, to believe
her, but he feared that the only thing the class would prepare him
for was a false confidence in his ability to handle the environment. The solidigraphic nurse who'd brushed past him had had
weight, volume, even a smell.

But no emotional presence at all.

He'd been hoping that Patient Assessment would be better; he'd glanced through the text before class and found it all intriguing. Who would have thought the position of someone's feet could tell you so much? But he was alarmed when the Seersan professor declared, with amusement and a fine sense of dramatics, that they'd be practicing their skills as they acquired them . . . on each other. This excited everyone but Jahir, who had not entered into the psychology program to be analyzed, and had a responsibility to maintain the Veil of Secrecy that had been part of Eldritch culture since its founding besides.

"You have to have known it would come up," KindlesFlame said. It was their first lunch of the new year; there were hints of buds on the trees, but no flowers yet, and it was still cold enough to make hot coffee as much a matter of warming his hands as enjoying the flavor.

"That we would become our own test subjects?" he said.

"That you would be subject to the curiosity of your classmates," KindlesFlame answered, breaking off a piece of his millberry scone. "It's a psychology program, and you're a rare alien."

"I am a rare alien who would prefer not to be studied," Jahir said. And sighed. "I suppose there is no delicate way to have myself removed from the process."

"Without becoming the object of even more intense curiosity?" KindlesFlame snorted. "Not likely." He stirred his coffee and said, "You could always disturb them by reading their minds. I doubt you'll find many willing partners after doing that one too many times."

"I would never," Jahir said.

"Never?" KindlesFlame lifted his brows. "Now there's an intriguing comment. You plan never to use your abilities on other people?"

"They are not something to be used," Jahir replied, finding even the process of putting it into words distasteful. "And certainly not on people, without consent."

"But with consent?" KindlesFlame pressed.

"Even with consent, it is not so light a matter." Jahir flexed his fingers on his cup. "And not a comfortable one for me."

"We often have to do uncomfortable things in the course of our duties."

"That's different," Jahir said.

"Is it?" KindlesFlame's mien had turned decidedly professorial. "If your abilities can help save someone, what then?"

"Surely that is a hypothetical, and not likely to happen," Jahir said. "How many esper therapists can there be in the Alliance? And if their abilities were so powerfully useful, then would not all therapists be espers, or at least a greater percentage of them?"

"Ah-ah." The Tam-illee wagged a finger. "No wiggling out of it. What I'm doing now is no different from your Clinical Management professor's doing with her simulations. We are simulating a patient whose mental state can be healed with the intervention of your mind. Would you?"

"If there was any other way—"

"And if there's not?"

Jahir looked away.

"Let me phrase it a different way," KindlesFlame said after a moment, his voice gentler. "You have abilities that your peers don't have. Doesn't it behoove you to use your unique talents? Why were they given to you, except to be used to add to the positive energy of the universe?"

"This is straying onto rather philosophical ground," Jahir said.

"Of course it is. If you have no philosophical ground for your work, you have no place to stand from which to make decisions. Ethical ones, moral ones. You won't know the boundaries of your duty, and what you owe your gods—assuming you have any— the world, and your fellow men and women."

"And if you, Healer KindlesFlame, had a touch so sensitive that trailing it over fabric gave you friction burns, would you go about touching everything?" Jahir asked, looking up at him.

"No," KindlesFlame said. "But I also wouldn't throw myself

into a profession that required sewing." He lifted a brow. "You're going into a field of the mind, with an ability to touch minds that very few people share. Doesn't that suggest something to you? A lost opportunity, perhaps?"

Jahir grimaced. "If it was so simple . . ."

"If it was so simple, the rewards probably wouldn't be worth the effort," KindlesFlame said, and sipped from his cup. "You're going to have to suffer some discomfort to grow into your new role, alet. You can choose to do so in a way that minimizes that discomfort . . . or you can in a way that maximizes the growth. But you can't have both."

CHAPTER 19

HE FIRST CONCERT OF THE spring term was in fact a comic opera, and Vasiht'h wasn't sure if his roommate would want to go given the subject. But Jahir vanished into the bathroom to dress the moment he returned from the afternoon lecture, and exited it in one of his more formal outfits, cinnamon tunic over white shirt and brown trousers and boots. Heartened, though he still couldn't imagine an Eldritch at a comedy, Vasiht'h went and found one of his few short vests, the red one with the fringed tassels. When he appeared in it, Jahir said, "And I had no idea. You do wear clothes?"

"Sometimes," Vasiht'h said. "For decoration mostly. Or if the weather's severe. Female Glaseah usually wear clothes out of courtesy to the Pelted. Most of them have nudity taboos."

"I admit it hadn't occurred to me they might not," Jahir said, reaching for his coat and gloves.

"Oh, some of them don't; the Aera and the Harat-Shar would wander around nearly naked if you let them, and the Phoenix don't care either. But the Pelted were originally designed as companions for humans, which meant, in effect, that they were used for sex." Vasiht'h saw the pause that interrupted Jahir's sliding the coat on, so short it was like a hiccup. "You'll get into that in the Exodus course. A lot of the circumstances surrounding the design and flight of the Pelted still affect us all, though it's been hundreds of years."

"Yes," Jahir said, subdued. "I imagine it might."

"Anyway. I have a few of these for semi-formal occasions," Vasiht'h said. "And a sari for the nice ones. Maybe if we end up going to one of the concerts with visiting musicians . . . those tend to be more formal."

"I should like to see it," Jahir said, pleased, and opened the door for his roommate, and they went.

The opera was in the larger of the student concert halls, with several projections set up behind the stage, high enough to be seen by everyone in the audience. The cast was all Seersa, save for a few brave Tam-illee, and the comedic aspect involved the fact that operas were traditionally sung in languages that the audience couldn't understand. The protagonist of the opera was trying to set up a tryst with a lover who was committed to someone else, and they'd agreed to meet at a masquerade, but the protagonists' unfortunate accomplices were all very, very bad at their jobs, and there were constant eavesdroppers hoping to spoil the protagonist's plans.

But the true humor involved the cast constantly hopping off stage into the audience and dragging up a member of it, and the protagonist hurriedly switching languages, improvising the lyrics in the new one to make it incomprehensible to them. The projection behind him kept a running translation, with often hilarious effects—the music had been written for the Seersan language, and the improvisations were often very low art. At one point, someone scrabbled nearly to the back of the audience and started pulling at the wing of an Akubi, which suffered itself to be led with a gaping grin up to the stage.

The protagonist stared at it and lost three or four of his lines to laughing—the Akubi were infamous mimics, and finding a language that could confound them would have taken a Seersan specialist. He finally managed a few hoots and whistles, figuring the only language an avian mimic wouldn't understand as a language would be . . . fake bird noises. Even the orchestra had to stop until they could catch their breath, the woodwinds faltering while the strings labored creakily on until the other sections could compose themselves. The Akubi preened, obviously pleased, and flew off stage to return to its seat.

Vasiht'h surprised himself by laughing all the way through it, to the point of having to wipe his eyes, and if Jahir was more restrained he could feel the Eldritch's delight radiating off him like summer sunlight. His skin kept the memory of it as they walked to the gelateria afterward, a short trip from the music hall.

"Are all Seersa thus?" Jahir asked. "So easy with language?"

"Oh yes," Vasiht'h said. "Though that man they had playing the lead was amazing. But definitely a production that could only have come out of the brain of a Seersa. They grow up learning languages, making them, preserving them. They even have to add at least one word to the dictionary before they grow up. It's part of their coming-of-age."

"Is there no Seersa that has no talent for it?"

Vasiht'h glanced at him, curious. "Oh, I'm sure there are some that are better than others. But I think it's a little like a Glaseah or an Eldritch without the esper profile."

"Surely not," Jahir said. "I would imagine the language predilection is culturally fostered, not biological?"

"Well, sure," Vasiht'h said. "But at what point is culture so unavoidable that you just soak into it? If you're born hearing a dozen languages spoken, you're going to grow up differently than someone hearing one." He looked at the Pelted passing them. "The Seersa were given the task of language preservation and creation during the Exodus. They made and maintain Universal. They keep records of Meredan, the secret language the Pelted developed among themselves on Earth and that was spoken on shipboard after they fled. They made the languages whole-cloth for the Pelted who wanted them . . . the Harat-Shar, the Hinichi, the Tam-illee, all us third-generation engineered. Language is part of their identity. Even if you're not so good at it, you can't help but be a part of it."

"And is it your duty, then, to use that ability?" Jahir wondered.

Vasiht'h looked at him sharply, then passed under his arm as he held the door to the gelateria open for him. He ordered the mascarpone and watched Jahir waffle over the flavors before deciding on pistachio and espresso to go with it. They sat outside to watch people go by, and once they'd settled, Vasiht'h . . . waited, wondering if he would be rewarded, if he was reading his roommate right.

And he was. "Does your religion have aught to say on the subject?"

"On your duty to use an ability?" Vasiht'h said. He mantled his wings. "The Goddess is not fond of idleness."

"No one is," Jahir said, lifting a hand in what looked like a dismissive gesture, one Vasiht'h hadn't seen yet. "It is the matter of special talents that I wonder at. If you are born with an unusual ability, does that obligate you to use it?"

"Why would She have given it to you if She didn't intend you to do something with it?" Vasiht'h said. "Anything else would be a waste, wouldn't it?" He tilted his head. "What's this about, anyway? I can tell it's something."

Jahir grimaced over his coffee. "I do not know how you divined that—"

"You're too intent on it," Vasiht'h said. "Come on, tell me. If not me, then who, right?" And then held his breath, realizing that he didn't want to know the answer if there was someone else.

"No, it's a matter you might have opinions on yourself," Jahir said after a moment. "Healer KindlesFlame has suggested to me that to practice therapy without the use of our abilities may not be . . . ethical? Moral? That it comprises a lost opportunity." He glanced at Vasiht'h. "Do the Glaseah have counselors amongst themselves, and do they use their abilities?"

"I guess they must?" Vasiht'h said. "Since we talk mind-to-mind as often as mouth-to-mouth. We were always a little lax about language; the Seersa made us one but we mostly abandoned it, and switch from Universal to telepathy when it suits us. But I've never been to a counselor, so I don't know." He glanced at his roommate. "But you know, my research is based on accidents that we stumbled on, using our abilities to treat people. Even if it was just their dreams, and even if it was just to help them sleep better . . . we could have just woken them up. Or sung them a lullaby until they calmed down. But we didn't, did we? We used the tool to hand, the one that came to us by nature."

Jahir frowned, resting the brim of the cup against his lips but not drinking, his eyes distant. Finally, he said, "Some would suggest that the use of a power that a patient can't defend against is immoral."

"Well, a patient can't defend themselves against a surgeon's scalpel," Vasiht'h said. "And they certainly don't know how to use one themselves."

"They could be trained—"

"I don't think it matters." Vasiht'h shook his head. "Without the training it's as inaccessible to a layman as our abilities are to people born without them. And who's going to train to be a doctor just so they can argue their own treatment with a surgeon? Time and opportunity are just as big a barrier as biology."

"Are they?" Jahir grimaced. "It doesn't seem plausible."

Vasiht'h snorted. "You want to sign up for a fifteen-year-schooling to be a doctor? Toss your responsibilities, upset your family, maybe go hungry, just on a whim, or against chance? Who can afford that kind of detour?"

Jahir looked at him suddenly, face set, and Vasiht'h blanched under his fur. "All right," he said. "Maybe you could. But I'm sure even you would think twice about it, if you were involved in something that needed you every day."

The Eldritch looked away, and Vasiht'h felt it like a bandage ripped off a small wound: a pain, quick and intense and gone. Not his, he knew, but Jahir's, and he was still reading him after all. He smoothed the fur down on his arm surreptitiously.

"This research you've embarked on," Jahir said finally. "It will result in a methodology that will be available to very few practitioners, given its requirements. Do you feel that you are in some way obligated to employ it, because you are one of the few?"

"I don't even know if it works—" At Jahir's skeptical look, and how did he do that by barely moving his brow? he said, "All right. I know it works on seven people. But seven people don't make a repeatable clinical study."

"What does?" Jahir asked. "If you get some forty or fifty people at the hospital, will that be sufficient to prove it?"

"Maybe as a potential," Vasiht'h said, staring at his ice cream and fighting the slow sink of his gut as he worked it out. "After that, I'd have to expand it, try to get a thousand people, maybe."

"A thousand people."

"Yes," Vasiht'h said, trying to imagine managing all that data.

"A thousand people, whom you would have to personally test yourself," Jahir said, "given the lack of other esper psychologists to aid you."

"I'll find someone," Vasiht'h said.

"And if you do? That only leaves five hundred to each of you apiece." Jahir glanced at him.

"We'll manage."

"And if you do, how will you know that the study is measuring the effects of dream intervention, and not the effects of *your* dream intervention? If you are the only one giving the cure?"

Vasiht'h stabbed his ice cream and drew in a shaky, determined breath. "The problems," he said, "are surmountable." Because if they weren't, he finished to himself, he would tear his own fur out.

—⦅∞⦆—

Jahir's first session of the Pharmacology class startled him: he'd grown accustomed to classes of under twenty people, so to end up in a lecture hall among a hundred was unexpected. It was so large, in fact, that the professor had four assistants. The one assigned to his section was a young Tam-illee male in the loose, unisex garments that seemed to make up the uniform for those in the medical profession. After the general lecture, he drew them aside and said, "I'm Jander, and I'll be your teaching assistant for the semester. Professor Aredi's available for your questions, but you'll get quicker answers from me. My job's to grade your work, and to help you figure out how to remember it, because it's a lot. Twenty percent of you are going to have to retake this class." He looked at them. "But anything I can do to help you prevent that, I'm going to do. We've got several different mnemonic systems, and they're as old as this school. They've helped generations of students fix all this stuff in mind, and they'll help you."

"I don't know why we have to learn them, when it's all in the u-banks," someone said.

"Because if someone's dying in front of you, your first instinct won't be to consult a computer," Jander said. "Sometimes seconds matter. When you have the leisure to double-check your memory, you should. But when it counts, you should know. I've used all these mnemonics myself, though some of them work better for me than others. I'll teach you all of them, and you can keep the one that helps you."

Jahir was writing notes as he started the list, and stopped abruptly when the Tam-illee said 'music.' They went over the visual techniques first, and started on the linguistic, and didn't get to the rest; so after the class was dismissed, Jahir stopped near the Tam-illee and waited for him to look up. Which he did, and started. "Iley bless, I didn't see you. And . . . wow." He straightened his shoulders. "Ah, so, how can I help you—"

"Jahir," he supplied. "You said something about music?"

"Oh!" Yes." Jander chuckled. "Music's how I did it, actually. It's something of a tradition in medical schools, to come up with songs to remember things—it started with a Karaka'An way back forever ago who made up the ditty for the Exodus diseases." He canted his head. "For the pharma stuff there are a bunch of different songs, using different taxonomies. Some start with the species and organize the drugs into verses based on which affects which and how. Others start with drug class and then name the drug and then talk about the different species and how they're affected by it; that one's clever, actually, because it uses a different scale for each species—" He broke off. "I'm not boring you?"

"I don't suppose there's sheet music?" Jahir asked, hopeful.

"Oh is there!" he laughed. "I'll send you a note. There's a publishing press that does nothing but put out books of the teaching music."

Jahir said, "Jander-alet, I believe you have assured my grade in this class."

The Tam-illee grinned. "We'll see, we'll see."

That went entirely better than Patient Assessment, which with each passing session grew more uncomfortable. The material itself was fascinating, and when the professor demonstrated body language or behaviors, or when he played them solidigraphs, it was deeply engaging, and Jahir could see how Vasiht'h had called it a college favorite. But the practices with other students were painful. He dutifully made the observations and was often correct, but they never seemed to know what to make of him. The exercises always had the same pattern: his partner would be eager and intrigued, and then increasingly frustrated or discouraged, until at last they stopped trying.

He'd thought this was going unnoticed; the class had some forty people in it, and the professor couldn't listen in on all the exercises.

But he'd been wrong.

"Mister Seni Galare, if you would come up here with me a moment?" Professor Sheldan called.

Startled, Jahir froze. Then, reluctantly, he set his materials aside and went to join the older male at the front of the classroom.

"You'll indulge me a moment, please?" the Seersa asked him, and what could he do but agree? Sheldan nodded, then said, "Very good. How are you finding the subject?"

"Fine, thank you?" Jahir answered, perplexed.

"No trouble incorporating the tails and ears on the Pelted? You don't have them."

"No, not at all." He kept his growing discomfort tightly reined, wondering what the point of this exercise was.

"Very good," the Seersa said. "Could you bring me your textbook? I've forgotten mine."

This from someone who could call up the text at any point and project it for the class seemed utterly nonsensical, but he retrieved his book anyway and set it on the podium. Sheldan said, "Thank you," and picked it up, leafing through it. "Now then. Can you tell me, Mister Seni Galare, what it signifies when the crest of a Phoenix flexes?"

"I fear I have not read so far in the text," Jahir said.

"Nothing about the nictating membranes of the Naysha either, then," the Seersa said. "You were assigned that last class."

They manifestly had not, but Jahir said, "I'm afraid not, sir."

Sheldan nodded and slammed the book shut with a noise so abrupt several students in the front row jumped. Jahir flinched but didn't move.

"Superb!" Sheldan said, and his demeanor went from remote to gleeful in a heartbeat's time. He addressed the class now. "What you have here is the result of deliberate training to minimize tells. Most of you have had a chance to have Mister Seni Galare here as a partner, and have been puzzled as to why you can't read him. You won't be able to without a great deal of experience, because he's had deportment classes. This isn't a failing in yourselves or your nascent ability, but an example of something beyond your skill level at this time." He grinned at Jahir, and his body language suggested something unpleasant, a superiority that suffused his satisfaction. "We would save something like this for a second or third class. But you'll observe that even when made uncomfortable by pressure or lied to or even scared, we saw almost no change in body language, yes?"

A murmur of agreement, as Jahir fought not to flush.

"You'll see variations of control over body functions all the time," Sheldan said. "But rarely something this extreme." He nodded to Jahir. "You may sit." He went, grateful to go and fighting his embarrassment. Behind him, the Seersa finished, "For now, we'll excuse you all from practicing on him."

At the end of the lecture, Jahir stayed at his desk while his classmates walked past him, many with speculative looks. When they'd all exited, he gathered his books and stood, and looked at his professor.

"Yes?" the Seersa asked, and from his casual air of waiting, Jahir thought grimly, he'd been waiting for this.

"That was uncalled for, sir."

"Tell me, Mister Seni Galare," Sheldan asked. "Are you a sociopath, a military operative, or an abuse victim?"

Speechless, Jahir stared at him.

"None of the above?" the professor said, gathering his materials. "Probably trained in a culture where everyone moves the way you do, yes? Let me tell you something, alet. How you present yourself will see you judged, whether you want to be or not. Your body language is so closed off that it comes across as a flat rejection of everyone around you. People's curiosity about Eldritch will carry a lot of them past that barrier—at least super-ficially—but you're turning a lot of people away at the door. If that's intentional, that's your business. If it's not, you might try using some of what you're learning to your benefit."

Jahir stared at him, trembling with anger and mortification. He forced himself to calm and said, "Sir, you had no cause to call me up before the entire class and use me that way. Without even asking my consent to the experiment."

"Is that how you really feel about it?" Sheldan said. "Because most people would have been delighted to be singled out as special."

"To be singled out as special is one matter," Jahir said. "To be called out as, essentially, a freak in comparison to 'normal' people. . . ."

"I did no such thing," the Seersa said. "I told people the truth: that you're a special case because you've been trained to lie with your body."

That was so shocking an accusation that he could not move, nor draw breath to defend himself.

"That's what it is," the Seersa said in response to his silence. "You feel something and you hide it from us all."

"That is the barest courtesy due to others," Jahir said. "To keep from discomfiting them with histrionics."

Sheldan snorted. "It's not histrionics to be surprised by loud noises, or to frown when you're accused of not keeping up with your schoolwork." He shook his head. "You can frame it however you want. People are going to read it as you hiding things from them . . . or lying. If you haven't learned that yet, consider yourself warned." He lifted his brows. "Is that all?"

"That," Jahir said, "is quite enough. Yes. Thank you."

The professor nodded and left him in the empty room. It was a long time before he could compose himself to leave, and even then he could feel his heart racing, so violently it could be felt all the way down in the veins of his wrists.

⚬⚭⚬

For someone who'd been trained to lie with his body—he thought the words bitterly—Jahir reflected he could not use the same techniques to lie very well to himself. He barely made it through his afternoon lecture; certainly he remembered very little of it, and when he left he found himself trembling so much that he had to find a bench and rest for a while until he could gather himself to go back to the apartment. He arrived to find Vasiht'h already there, making use of the morning's produce to make dinner. The sounds were soothing, even if he felt raw from nape to heel, and he drew his bag off slowly, and his gloves more slowly yet before allowing himself to sit on one of the chairs.

He did not expect Vasiht'h to miss his agitation. For someone with such supremely trained comportment, he seemed very easy to read to his roommate. And . . . he found he was in some part waiting for the sound of paws approaching, and for the warmth of that now familiar voice. When it came, he let out a shuddering breath, glad. If Vasiht'h could read him, and wanted to, he was surely not so completely closed.

"Alet? What happened? You look. . . ."

"I look what?" Jahir lifted his head, wanting to know if Vasiht'h could tell.

"Shattered," Vasiht'h said, eyes widening. He hurried in front of Jahir and sat, leaning a little toward him; Jahir could tell the Glaseah would have been touching him if he'd been allowed. "What happened?"

Jahir said, low, "Professor Sheldan decided to exhibit me to the class as an example of that rare animal, someone trained not to reveal themselves through body language. Which he did by calling me to the front and attempting to unsettle me while everyone watched."

"He did what?!"

"He says such body language is typical of sociopaths and spies," Jahir said.

The Glaseah were so strangely put together, with the short centauroid half and the odd ears and the wings. They came across as harmless and affable, particularly since they were endowed with such phlegmatic personalities.

But Vasiht'h put his ears back to his skull and his lips wrinkled back from teeth Jahir abruptly noted had fangs. The great soft paws apparently had retractable claws, yellowed things with wicked points that sank into the rug and caught the fibers. And his eyes, usually so friendly a brown, became almost incandescent. "He did not," Vasiht'h hissed. "He did NOT do that to you. And he did, didn't he?" He reared back and turned. "I'll tell Doctor Palland. That's absolutely inexcusable!"

"I cannot see as to how any of his fellows would do a thing about it," Jahir said. "He saw something of value to teach the class, and he used me to do so. He told me himself that if I had nothing to hide, I would not have been distressed—would in fact have been honored to be so exhibited."

"Aksivaht'h forget that!" Vasiht'h snarled. "That was wrong!"

This blazing rage—that it should have kindled on his behalf—Jahir could not decide whether to be astonished or dismayed. "Vasiht'h—"

"No," his roommate said. "It was wrong, Jahir. To humiliate

you in front of the class? My mother's a professor! I know how they're supposed to act! We'll tell Doctor Palland and he can take us to the dean—"

"Vasiht'h!" Jahir exclaimed. "Please! It is enough!"

The Glaseah paused, eyes narrowing.

"There is no profit in it," Jahir said, his conversation with KindlesFlame looming suddenly large. "To reprimand him, and for what? They will not take his class from him. And then I must continue in it, if I wish to take it, for there is no other professor to do it, is there?"

Vasiht'h bared his teeth, but said, "No . . . that's his class."

"So I must take it to have the degree, and if I speak against him, then I will have that to deal with for the remainder of the term—no, I can't countenance it. We all must learn to deal with some unpleasantness in pursuing our courses. Is that not our duty?"

"It is not your duty to be abused by someone with more power than you," Vasiht'h snarled.

"Then tell me how I am to do this, without prejudicing the man against me."

"If he gives you a false grade because you got him in trouble—" Vasiht'h began.

"And how would I prove it?" Jahir asked. This at last penetrated his roommate's anger, but not as he'd hoped, with understanding. Instead, Vasiht'h looked horrified.

"Do you really think that's how it works?" the Glaseah said. "That the university would let a professor bully a student and then fail him? That you'd be punished for defending yourself?"

How wonderful it would be to believe that the Alliance was without such sins . . . but where there were men and women, there were all the darker motivations of their hearts: their fears and jealousies, their attachments to power, their complacencies and rivalries. If it was not so foul here as it was at home, still Jahir could not believe such things wholly absent. "Please, Vasiht'h. I am . . . I am very much moved by your affront. But I would ask you not to bring this to anyone."

Now the Glaseah was trembling: no doubt outraged at being asked to hide the affair, and Jahir had no idea how he knew it, but he did.

"Please," he said again.

Vasiht'h looked away, and Jahir saw how quick his breathing was, and how the fur on his shoulders bristled. But he calmed himself, somehow, enough to say, "All right. But I think you're making a mistake."

"Perhaps," Jahir allowed.

"And if he does any other thing against you, you *will* tell me, and you will tell someone else."

"Yes," Jahir said, feeling more confident of that promise—he did not think Sheldan malicious, only thoughtless, in the way of someone too accustomed to his own prestige. And still Vasiht'h's fur had not come flat, and it filled him with wonder, to see it. Softly, he said, "You have not shied from me at all."

Vasiht'h looked at him with a frown, and to quell his angry question, Jahir said, "The professor said my body speech is a rejection, and that only those superficially interested in me for the glamour of my species would ever be interested at all in courting my attention. But you have stood by me since you met me. Did you not feel that rejection?"

"I . . ." Vasiht'h deflated, his frown now consideration and not anger. He shook himself. "Of course you're not forthcoming. You're Eldritch. Expecting you to be otherwise is unreasonable."

"You accept that I give little away," Jahir said.

"But you do!" Vasiht'h said. "If anyone bothers to pay attention. They're just so used to Harat-Shar throwing themselves on them, and Aera waving those huge ears around, and all these obvious signals . . . they miss the subtle things. They forget even to look for them."

"But why did you pay attention at all?"

"Because . . . maybe . . . I don't know." Vasiht'h sat back on his haunches. "I met you in that parking lot, and you were so kind to the girls. You didn't back away from them. You didn't hold yourself apart from them. So I know it's in you."

"In essence, then, you kept to me because luck showed you there was something worth the pursuit," Jahir said, low.

"No!" Vasiht'h said. And hissed, rubbing his face. "I am making mud out of this, and it's important. Part of what makes the Alliance what it is, and wonderful, is that it's full of different people. But you saw what happened with Luci. She grew up one way, because she could, and she loves being that way . . . but being around people who are very different, there's more misunderstanding, and more ways to be hurt, and more ways to assume that someone is going to be one way because you are, when they really aren't." He sucked in a breath and blew it out sharply. "I think because the Pelted all came from the same place, sometimes they think . . . like a clan. And you aren't part of that clan, and they don't understand you. They want to treat you like a human because you look a little like one. But you're not. And it's hard to blame them for that when most of them have never met an Eldritch and probably won't ever again."

Jahir listened to this, hoping it would make him feel better, and all it did was make him feel further alienated. He looked down at his hands, and the House ring he still wore there.

"Jahir," Vasiht'h said, his voice urgent for all its quiet. "Even if I hadn't met you with those kids, I would have known you for what you were. You might not advertise every one of your feelings, but your eyes . . . there's nothing mean in your eyes."

He looked up, heart tight in his chest. And said, after a moment, "You mean that."

"Every word," Vasiht'h said. "That idiot might not see it, but he's also not looking for it. And your classmates only see someone they can't reach because they don't know what it's like to have someone's thoughts in your head. If they knew, they'd give you the space you needed to feel safe." He reached out and pulled his hand back, rueful. "You see, even I know and I can't help it, sometimes. Acculturation."

Jahir glanced at the hand, thought to the few times he had touched the Glaseah in passing, and how unexpected and gentle those touches had been.

So he extended a hand and rested his fingers briefly on his roommate's wrist . . . and took into himself all the aftermath of Vasiht'h's adrenalized anger, his fear, his . . . yes, his passion. And even feeling it, he knew it for his roommate's and not his own and knew not how Vasiht'h managed it, but he was glad and grateful and overwhelmed that he could.

The fur beneath his fingers was softer than he expected, like felt over the inside of the wrist. And, cold and sudden through it, lanced his roommate's shock at the touch, and his happiness.

Jahir let his fingers slip away and said, only, "Thank you."

Vasiht'h stared at him, quivering, and said, "I . . . you . . ." And trailed off, before managing, "I'll make us tea."

"Tea sounds very good," Jahir said, and let his roommate escape to the kitchen while he sagged back in the chair and breathed through his own reaction. The felt-soft memory lingered on his fingertips.

CHAPTER 20

"THERE'S NO WAY AROUND IT," Palland said, shaking his head. "You're going to have to personally administer the treatments, Vasiht'h, and that's going to limit the size of the study. At least while you're in school; you're not going to be able to oversee anything larger while still attending classes. And the study design is going to be necessarily inexact. When you're working with people self-reporting their mental state, you introduce a lot more error into your results."

"I guess I'll just have to make do, then, if you think the study is still worth writing up," Vasiht'h said uncertainly, looking at the amendments Palland had made to his original research method.

"Oh, if for no other reason than that it's provocative, absolutely," the Seersa said. "This is a fascinating new approach. If all it does is prompt discussion, that's still worth the effort."

"All right," Vasiht'h said. "I've already talked to the hospital board and they were willing. I just have to write up the call for volunteers and get their consent forms and I can get started."

"Good," Palland said. "You're not finding it too much of a burden on top of your classes?"

"No," Vasiht'h said. "Though I wouldn't want to be doing this without the directed study hours." He glanced at his professor, vacillating. Then, "Sir? Hypothetically . . . if a student were to get you in trouble for something you did wrong, would you fail them?"

Palland's brows shot up. "Pardon me?"

"I mean . . . would you take it out on a student who got you reprimanded," Vasiht'h said.

"Hypothetically," Palland said, voice dry.

"Hypothetically," Vasiht'h agreed.

"Well, hypothetical-me probably shouldn't be doing things that get him reprimanded," Palland said, leaning back in his chair. "But presuming he did, it would be bad form for me to punish the student who turned me in. Hypothetical Evil Me would certainly be examined by the administration if I were to go and fail someone who had a history with me."

Vasiht'h breathed out. "That's what I thought."

"That's not to say it hasn't happened," Palland continued, and Vasiht'h looked up at him, wide-eyed. The Seersa sighed. "We're all fallible, alet. Your masters here no less than you students." His smile was decidedly crooked. "It doesn't happen often, but yes. Sometimes a troubled history keeps making trouble."

"Oh," Vasiht'h said, almost inaudibly.

"Now, is there something you want to tell me about this hypothetical situation?"

More than anything he regretted his promise not to talk about it. But he had given his word, so he said, "No . . . no, it's not for me to say anything."

"Mmm-hmm," Palland said. "A word of advice, then." Vasiht'h looked up and the Seersa finished, "It's a lot easier to hang someone out to dry if they're already isolated. You students think you have no power, but when you close ranks around one another, we notice. It's the same with people as with animals, alet. One deer by itself is easy prey. A herd of deer with all their horns turned out at you . . . that's a different matter."

"I see," Vasiht'h said, frowning.

"I think you do," Palland said.

It wasn't too hard to make the arrangements, once Vasiht'h decided what to do; more a matter of remembering two schedules instead of one. And if he occasionally missed the rendezvous, he still figured showing up most of the time was better than not trying at all. So that afternoon, he packed quickly from his last lecture and trotted to the nursing hall, where the pharmacology class was held. He arrived just in time to be waiting for Jahir when the Eldritch appeared in the door.

Surprised, Jahir said, "Alet?"

"It occurred to me that your class is on the way home from mine," Vasiht'h said firmly. "I thought we could walk together."

"That would be pleasant," Jahir said, still bemused. But Vasiht'h could see the students glancing at them on their way past and tamped down his satisfaction before it could leak. He had no idea if Jahir was still getting emotional data from him, but he didn't want to give his roommate any reason to feel uncomfortable. Particularly since he wasn't planning on changing his mind about doing it.

So he padded home at Jahir's side, and made sure everyone saw him doing it, and felt a little better. A few weeks of that, he thought, would do some serious damage to Professor Sheldan's assertion that the Eldritch was rejecting everyone around him.

"Meekie and Kayla aren't here," Berquist said. "But it's not any emergency. There's a specialist visiting from Tam-ley and he wanted to see them."

"No worries, then," Vasiht'h said.

"And even perhaps some hope?" Jahir added.

"Maybe," Berquist said. "But I wouldn't bet on anything. Go on, the others are waiting. And you can tell them if they're interested today they can go outside in the hospital garden, it's warm enough finally. We can get a chair for Amaranth."

And that idea was met with great enthusiasm, so with Berquist's aid they all went down to the first floor, where the hospital kept extensive gardens near the chapel for both patients and visitors. The girls were allowed to ramble for as long as they had energy, and they were so inclined, until at last they stopped in a small round area adjoining a fish pond. There in the warmth of a spring sun, they took seats on the grass, or lay on their bellies to watch the fish, and Vasiht'h settled himself with his paws before him like a sphinx. Jahir sat beside him, and thought the heat was too wan but a great improvement on the wet, cold weather of the previous weeks. Berquist was with them also, though she was sitting on a nearby bench, updating reports.

"Do you think they'll cure Meekie and Kayla?" Amaranth said, wistful.

"I doubt it," Persy said, lying on her back with her eyes closed. "But they might not come back."

"Persy? What do you mean?" Vasiht'h asked.

"I was in a group with some other girls before," Persy said. "And there was a special doctor who came, and one of the girls, her parents decided to send her along with him. So she left. I don't know what happened to her."

"Maybe she got better," Nieve said, quiet.

"Or maybe she died," Kuriel muttered.

"Look at this fish!" Amaranth exclaimed. "It's got orange patches!"

Much oohing and aahing. As the three by the pond peered into it, Nieve stood and padded over to Jahir, pausing in front of him. Wordlessly, he offered her his hand, and she took it, sitting in his lap with her back to his chest. Her thoughts ran through him, faint as veils: her pleasure at the warmth, her resignation over Kuriel's pessimism, her awe at the color of the sunlight through leaves. Jahir lifted his head to look at it himself, and let her thoughts teach him their beauty.

Wordlessly, Vasiht'h edged closer until they were almost touching, and then all three of them considered the light. Jahir wondered that he didn't think it at all strange, that his roommate should know instinctively what they were contemplating.

It would have been unimaginable to him before: that closeness like this could inspire serenity and contentment instead of discomfort or pain.

It came to him very slowly, the realization that the body resting against his was just a touch less frail. "You seem stronger," he said, surprised.

"I am stronger," she said, meeting his gaze before looking up at the leaves again. "I sleep better. It makes things easier."

Astonished, Jahir glanced at Vasiht'h, who lifted his brows.

"I used to know a poem about leaves," Nieve said. "But I don't remember it anymore."

"Spring has given rise to a great deal of poetry," Jahir said. "If you can't remember it, there are surely more."

"Do you know any?" she asked, glancing up at him.

"I do, yes, but not in Universal," Jahir answered, but Vasiht'h was already reaching for his saddlebag. He took out a data tablet and said, "Lyrical poetry?"

"Oh yes!" Nieve said. "Will you read it to us?"

"I'll let my roommate do that," Vasiht'h said, and handed over the tablet. "There. You have the better voice for it. Being the Eldritch prince."

Jahir sighed, and then laughed a little. "Very well. If it would please you, alet."

"Yes," Nieve said, and cuddled up against him, startling him as much for the sudden visceral memory of her grandmother reading to her, holding her in a rocking chair, as for the way his heart cramped at the ease of her affection. How could Sheldan have been right, if these children had no issues with him at all? Or was it because he permitted them the touch? But surely not, for the other students were not necessarily free with it either. Perhaps it was as Vasiht'h said, and a matter of culture, his presence creating a conundrum for those who could not stretch to allow him to be uniquely himself.

And yet, if he stayed here, how Eldritch would he remain?

But oh, he could not really miss it, if it meant this. Careful as much of himself as of Nieve's frailty, he curled an arm around her shoulders and paged through the poetry collection Vasiht'h had found him before settling on a poem with an innocent ending. He read for her, finding the rhythm of the words, and as he did the other girls padded closer to listen, and even Berquist lifted her head and closed her eyes.

The spent a good part of their time together that way, Nieve's thoughts narrowing to an echo of his own voice in her head, no burden to him at all. He read until he found himself clearing his throat, and Vasiht'h said, "You should drink something."

"I should at that," Jahir said, and handed him the data tablet.

"That was good," Nieve said with a sigh. "I could listen to poetry all the time."

"It is pretty," Persy agreed. "I liked the one about the dryads by the creek, with their moss shawls. That's good enough to dream to."

"And speaking of dreaming," Berquist said, her shadow falling over their bodies, "it's time to go back."

The children protested, but allowed themselves to be herded back to their rooms. Vasiht'h settled Kuriel and Amaranth, leaving Persy and Nieve to Jahir. He asked the former, "Shall I give you the dryads for your dreaming?"

"I think they'll come no matter what!" Persy said drowsily, and cuddled into her blanket. Jahir smiled and wished her no more than a deep sleep, and a happy one, before seeing to Nieve.

"It must be a wonderful thing, to be a poet," she said to him.

"I think it must be," Jahir said, bringing the blanket up to her shoulders.

"You're not one?" she wondered. "You act like a poet."

"I fear such things are beyond me," Jahir said, and then added because he could not deny her, "But music, that I know."

"Oh!" She shivered. "Music is even nicer. You are so lucky!"

"Close your eyes," he said gently. "And I will share my luck with you."

She did, quickly, and he bent close. The Veil prevented him from divulging anything of his world and culture to outsiders, but she was young and frail, and not likely to remember the dream he sang to her in the privacy of her own mind: a lullaby his mother had sung him, remembered because it had been her voice and not his nursemaid's, and carried with it the memory of safety, of growing beneath her heart.

"That was a good session," Berquist said when they'd joined her outside the room. "I never thought to read them poetry. Books, yes, but not poems." She glanced at him. "You read well."

"You flatter me," he said, polite. "But it is not my first language, and I am sure I made any number of errors."

"No, she's right," Vasiht'h said, joining them. "There's a knack to it."

A knack he had acquired because reading aloud was one of the few entertainments a group might have in a long winter, trapped indoors, he thought. But he said only, "Thank you."

Once they were outside, Vasiht'h looked up at the sky and sighed. "It's good to have sun on my back again." He grinned up at Jahir. "And you look much happier out of that coat."

"I *am* happier outside the coat," Jahir agreed, and did not question that Vasiht'h knew it. Perhaps that was what allowed him to accept the next comment so easily.

"Almost as happy as when you have a child in your lap." Vasiht'h mantled the wings on his lower back. "If I didn't know Eldritch didn't touch, I would wonder if it wasn't something you'd done before."

"It is hard to resist children," Jahir said. "You have a soft touch with them yourself. Will you have some of your own?"

"A personal question!" Vasiht'h chuckled. "You must be trying very hard to keep me from asking more of my own." Before Jahir could start at this observation, the Glaseah said, "I definitely want a family."

"You . . . have someone with whom to begin one, perhaps?" Jahir wondered. He had little notion of his roommate's customs, or even his relative age.

"No, I'm not planning to marry," Vasiht'h said. "I mean, I suppose it might happen, but . . . it's not something I was ever interested in."

They walked for some time while Jahir considered this from every conceivable angle, and found no purchase. When he glanced down at Vasiht'h he found the Glaseah looking up at him with a grin. "You left that unexplained just to perplex me."

"Yes," Vasiht'h said, laughing. "I'm sorry. You remember I told you we didn't fall in love, not really, and that we mate only to make families?"

"Populocampi," Jahir said, remembering the strange word.

"Yes. Well, since we don't really have attractions like that, it can be hard for us to form attachments. Since we're still obligated to help keep the species above replacement rate, we have priests and priestesses who provide us with children."

"Not orphans, I suppose," Jahir said, struggling with the notion. "Their own get, maybe? Offered to you to raise?"

"No, no." Vasiht'h shook his head. "They mate with you, and then you keep the children. So I would go to a priestess, and she'd carry my children until they were born, and then I would take them to raise."

"I . . . cannot imagine it," Jahir said. "And all this because it is . . . easier? And the children are raised without one of their natural parents?"

"Better one parent than none," Vasiht'h said. And added, "I don't think you really feel it in your bones. If we didn't force ourselves to have children, Jahir, we wouldn't, and there would be no Glaseah. We don't *feel* those things. The priests and priestesses are trained in ways to help us perform, even, because otherwise we might not even manage that." He shrugged, a strange motion of both shoulders and withers that reminded Jahir of a horse twitching away a fly. "I can love people. But I don't want to have sex with them. And though I love my parents and I know they love me, they're not in love with one another and you can tell. It's comfortable, but the bonds are different."

"And you do not want that for yourself," Jahir said.

"You say that as if it's something special to have," Vasiht'h answered. "It's not. It's a friendship that happens to have involved making children, and at that point why make a good friendship awkward with sex?" He shrugged again. "But children, yes. I want at some point." He glanced up. "And now we'll get to the question you deflected, and I'll ask: will you?"

Jahir thought it unlikely that he would have a choice, and contemplating the marriage that would be arranged for him, particularly given the state of his heart, was painful. "I cannot imagine otherwise," he said in all candor.

"Mmm. I can tell that's not a comfortable topic," Vasiht'h said. "Tell me instead how you're doing in Patient Assessment."

Jahir looked down the path; they were approaching the small bridge, and there were ducks in the pond, with ducklings following in ragged rows. "Professor Sheldan has not called me out again."

"I guess that's all you can hope for," Vasiht'h muttered.

"Indeed, that is all that I do."

⸎

His comment to Vasiht'h was not a lie, strictly speaking: Sheldan had left him alone since that day. But the professor's decision to exclude him from the practical exercises meant he no longer had the opportunity to practice on his classmates, and he suspected that in someone of lesser will that might have resulted in failure. But he refused to accept the disadvantage, and used the time the other students spent in their practical exercises studying them as they studied one another. It lacked the feedback the one-on-one sessions would have afforded him, but being alone also allowed him to consider the others at length, without their self-consciousness.

He did not confine his attention to them alone. He also watched the professor, and attempted to put the Seersa's own principles to use in studying him. Only he couldn't be sure he wasn't projecting a sense of pomposity and self-inflation onto Sheldan as justification for his own feelings about the man. That his fellow students now thought him a pariah was clear enough; Vasiht'h acting as guard to him had kept them from showing their unease or contempt more obviously, but it was there, and

Sheldan did not diffuse it.

That Vasiht'h *was* acting as a guard was unquestionable, and that he didn't want it spoken of. Perhaps because he thought Jahir would object? But after three hours of the emotional pollution of his classmates' feelings toward him, he needed his roommate's steadying presence.

Nor was that his only trouble: the Clinical Management class was hectic. That it was intended that way didn't assuage his outraged nerves. The lecture portion of the class was brief, and then they were thrown into the simulation, each to rush for his assigned section to deal with whatever it was that awaited them. As Jahir had noted the first day, the simulations had no emotional presence; they cried out in pain, they had weight and volume, the medicines and antiseptics used on them had smells, they were in every other way convincing simulacra; but they weren't real and he knew it, and he couldn't help being affected by that knowledge.

His complacency left him wide open for the inevitable moment one of his classmates ran into him, bounced back and grasped his arm to apologize before running on—

—frustration, fear, anger, pride—

It overrode him so completely that he could no longer make sense of his limbs: they were on someone else's body, sprinting in another direction. He fell, and couldn't remember deciding to fall, and hit the ground and even that felt surreal, as if he were split between bodies.

And then there was yelling, and that made the confusion worse. The world started splitting into unrecognizable pieces. Someone touched his arm and he became another mask, blurring the two he'd been holding—

"Stop that! You'll . . ."

. . . and then the words evanesced, and he lost his hold on everything.

───❦───

When Jahir woke next he was on one of the simulated beds;

no, this was a real one. Kandara, his nursing instructor, was peering over the halo-arch at him, and when he opened his eyes, she made a noise and tapped a call button on the wall. He was still marveling that he could understand the shape of her face when KindlesFlame hove into view overhead. "Well, you've given the staff quite a scare."

Could he speak? He could, and with his own voice. "Healer KindlesFlame. It's good of you to come."

Kandara guffawed. "Speaker-Singer. Not awake half a minute and going to offer you tea."

KindlesFlame snorted, then sat on a stool. "How are you feeling?"

He considered himself, then said, "Vague."

"Do you know what happened?" Kandara asked. "I saw Bonard bump into you, but it didn't look hard enough to knock you out."

"An accident, I'm sure," KindlesFlame said when Jahir didn't answer. "Lasa, will you excuse us a moment?"

"Sure," she said, warily. "But if there's some health problem I need to know about—"

"We'll be sure to tell you," KindlesFlame said, and waited for her to go before turning his gaze on Jahir and lifting a brow. "So?"

"You were right," Jahir said. "It was an accident."

"Someone touched you, I'm guessing."

"It's not . . . just touch," Jahir said. "There is more to it. There are people I can touch." He ignored the sight of the Tam-illee's other brow going up. "There is some variable I don't know yet."

"But apparently in some people, just bumping you can knock you unconscious."

"I would have gotten my bearings had someone else not compounded the error," Jahir said, trying not to be frustrated. "But two personalities in one skull are hard enough to manage. A third is asking a bit much."

"I don't need to tell you what a liability this could prove to be," the Tam-illee said at last. "If you can't figure out what exactly it is that's giving you problems, and how to work around it."

"Healer," Jahir said, feeling put-upon, "I am in class to discover these things. Pray give me the opportunity to learn before you put me to the test."

"I would gladly give you all the time you need," KindlesFlame said. "But I'm not the one in charge of giving you the test, and you may not have the luxury of learning before you get hurt." He held up a finger. "No, don't argue. This really hurt you. You had concussion symptoms without organic head trauma. We can tell Nurse Kandara that you smacked your head on the ground harder than it actually did, but between the two of us, no lies. Your body reflects it when someone disorders your mind with their touch. Iley knows what will happen if recurrent mental trauma can have cumulative effects, and I end up treating you for a coma."

Jahir flinched, despite himself.

"What you need to do is find yourself an esper doctor, or failing that, another esper to give you advice," KindlesFlame said. "You told me you have a Glaseahn roommate? Start with him."

"All right," Jahir said, subdued.

"Good." The Tam-illee tapped the halo-arch, which withdrew, leaving him free to sit up.

"I feel better now."

"You feel better now but you were out for forty minutes," KindlesFlame said, and Jahir could see the worry in his eyes, just past the anger. "So don't push it."

"As you say." He inclined his head. "May I go?"

"Yes, and Lasa's waiting for you outside. I'd tell her the truth, but if you can't, then she'll accept the lie that you fell wrong."

Research, Vasiht'h decided, was awkward. Or at least it was in studies that required his personal attention. Having received and examined over seventy forms from volunteers, he'd narrowed the initial study to twenty people; it had seemed too small a pool to him, but Palland assured him it would be sufficient as a proof of concept. Plus, it would be manageable for him while also working his normal course load.

Patients were not the only ones with mandatory naptimes at the hospital; apparently staff working shifts of over eight hours were required to sleep at least forty-five minutes in one of the rooms designed for that purpose. Those rooms were hidden behind the visitor centers, operating theaters and patient care rooms, one every two floors, and just walking into one made Vasiht'h's fur smooth down. Low light, the trickle of water—real water, he discovered, from a fountain in the back that doubled as a drinking fountain—and within small sculpted cubbies, one bunk just large enough for the typical Pelted. There were nests in the back as well, and a few cubbies that were collections of pillows on a floor elevated in a shape he thought he'd love to nap on himself. The air was cool and dry and smelled faintly of lavender.

When he'd imagined doing this study, he'd thought of a room full of subjects, sleeping on beds, and he would go from one to the other either affecting their dreams or leaving them to act as controls. But thanks to the erratic schedules kept by the staff, his own limited time, and his need to act on each of them personally, he had to show up and do two or three of his subjects, then leave and come back the following day to do the next few, and so on until he'd managed them all.

Vasiht'h was grateful that the room they used for their naps was so relaxing. He didn't want to imagine what he'd inflict on his subjects while suffering from an anxious mental state, and anxious he certainly was from trying to keep such an erratic schedule.

His latest subject, Kievan, was a perpetually tired Tam-illee whose coworkers had confided to Vasiht'h was 'probably depressed.' Having met him, Vasiht'h thought he was certainly depressed, and there was no 'probably' about it. The healer-assist was always glad to lie down, so much so that Vasiht'h felt bad for forcing him to undergo the study at all, except that he'd volunteered.

The Tam-illee settled in the cubby while Vasiht'h waited at its edge, checking his data tablet.

"I'm ready."

"All right, Hea First," Vasiht'h said. "Just relax, then."

"I don't think that's my name anymore," the Tam-illee said, and sighing, set his head on the pillow.

Vasiht'h peeked in. "Hea?"

"First," Kievan said from the dark. "My FoundName. I chose it after the first ethical oath healers ever swore, and it says 'First, do no harm.' But I do. No matter how hard I try, how hard we all do. We fail, and we're failing on the most vulnerable people imaginable."

Vasiht'h set the tablet down and stepped into the cubby, sitting with his tail curled over his paws. "That sounds serious, alet."

"It is!" he said. "It is." He rubbed his eyes with the side of his forearm without lifting his head from the pillow. "I keep thinking . . . I should change my FoundName to something more accurate. But I can't find anything." He made a noise that might have been a strangled chuckle. "Kievan BurntOut, maybe. Kievan GaveItUpForGardening."

"Do you garden?" Vasiht'h asked, guided by the Tam-illee's willingness to find some humor in it.

"No, actually," Kievan said, and looked at him wryly: two glints in the dark, the low light reflecting off his eyes. "But . . . I'm so tired. I signed up for your study because . . . because I was grasping for straws. I don't want to give up my work. But I'm so tired of watching people suffer. Little children suffer."

It had to be harsh, Vasiht'h thought: a Tam-illee doing work in a children's hospital, given how difficult it was for Tam-illee to conceive. Of all the Pelted left, they remained the most raddled with reproductive issues; it was why Sehvi was studying on Tamley, because the cutting edge of technology on reproduction was there, where it was most needed. "You came here because you love children," he said. "And you wanted to help them."

"Helping them doesn't always save them," Kievan mumbled.

"Sometimes it does," Vasiht'h said.

The Tam-illee was quiet for a long moment. Then he said,

"Sometimes it does. But what if that's not enough for me? What if I can't bounce back from this?"

"What if you don't?" Vasiht'h asked. "Would that be the end of the world?"

Again, quiet, but a more considering quiet. When the Tam-illee spoke, he sounded puzzled. "You know, I never let myself wonder. I just assumed . . . you know, you assume things. That if I turned my back on nursing, I was . . . I don't know. A failure. Not good enough. And that I was failing the children, most of all. But that makes me a lot more important than I am, isn't it? To think that the world stops turning if I make a different choice."

"People make mistakes," Vasiht'h said, remembering Sehvi and Palland's skeptical looks over his own decisions. "But that doesn't mean they can't correct them, and make better choices later."

"And that's not the end of the world," the Tam-illee muttered.

"Not doing something, and maybe burning yourself out because of it sounds a lot worse, honestly," Vasiht'h said.

"There's something to that," Kievan said. And pulled the covers up over his shoulder with a faint frown and a distracted look before glancing at Vasiht'h with more animation than he'd ever shown before. "Thank you, alet. You've given me a lot to think about."

"Good, I hope?" Vasiht'h asked.

"I think so. At very least . . . different from what I was already thinking." The Tam-illee settled down, closed his eyes.

"I'm glad I could help," Vasiht'h said softly, as his subject passed out of consciousness. And then he backed out of the cubby. The Tam-illee was one of his controls, so he was supposed to be leaving his dreams alone. And yet he wondered if he'd be able to use the results at all, because for better or worse, that had seemed very much like an intervention.

He thought he'd be frustrated at the loss of the time and work he'd already invested in Kievan First. On the way back from the hospital, what he mostly felt was contented . . . like lifting his head up to the sun and feeling grateful to be alive. That he had done a little good for someone that day, no matter how minor.

He also resolved not to tell Sehvi about that feeling. Goddess knew what she'd say about it.

—⊷∞⊷—

Vasiht'h got home to a quiet apartment: not a surprise, since today was one of Jahir's medical track classes, one he'd thought it safe to leave him at. So he was very upset to be wrong when his roommate arrived looking wan and slow. How he sensed it, he wasn't sure, but he knew that Jahir had had an unusually poor day though not, he thought, as bad as the one with Sheldan. The memory made his lips peel back from his teeth and he shook himself. He took the pot of chocolate he'd had simmering on the heat and poured it into two cups before joining the Eldritch in the common room.

"Thank you," Jahir said, vaguely, when the cup had been set at his elbow. And then he seemed to notice the smell and looked at it with more attention. "Oh? Chocolate? This is a treat."

"I felt like one," Vasiht'h said. "It's imported chocolate, too, from Earth. They have to ship the whole thing in stasis. Won't even put it through Pads, the company says it does something to the flavor."

"How fascinating," Jahir said, and sipped. And closed his eyes, cup still at his mouth, smelling. "It has a bouquet? Like wine. How extraordinary."

"I thought you'd appreciate it," Vasiht'h said, satisfied. "Now. Tell me what has you looking so worn out."

"Do I really look it?" Jahir asked, chagrined. And sighed. "No, I must. And you read me better than anyone on this world." He set the cup on the saucer, the motions very deliberate. "There was an incident during class. Involving a classmate who ran into me."

"Oh, no," Vasiht'h said, quiet, feeling that there was more.

"And another, who decided to help me up once I'd fallen—"

"Oh, no," Vasiht'h said again, with feeling, and closed his eyes. He shook his head and said, wry, "I'm betting that went well."

"I ended up under a halo-arch," Jahir said. "With no less than Healer KindlesFlame in attendance. And he not very pleased with the situation, as you can imagine."

"I can," Vasiht'h said.

"He suggested," Jahir said after a moment, "that I discuss the matter with another esper, and mentioned you in particular. When I had no good answer as to why I might bear the touch of children, and you, but not random encounters with others."

"Have you and I ever had a random encounter?" Vasiht'h asked.

"I touched you, now and then, by accident when we first met, jumping rope."

"That's not really accidental," Vasiht'h said. "We were both doing the same thing. Focused on the same thing."

"And this student was focused on doing the work of the class, which I was also," Jahir said. "I cannot find the pattern in it, alet."

Vasiht'h wrinkled his nose. "I admit, I was never very interested in telepathic theory either . . . but I'm due to call Sehvi tonight. She might know. She's kept company with doctors since she was a kit."

"Sehvi . . . your sister?" Jahir asked.

"One of them."

Jahir seemed to consider, for long enough that Vasiht'h wondered if he would agree. It must be difficult enough to reveal his problems to people he thought he knew fairly well; but to a stranger? But Vasiht'h hoped, and thought he caught a faint hiss, like the tide receding from the shore: resignation. And a glimmer on the waves that suggested hope. "Yes. Yes, I think that would be helpful, if you're willing. Thank you, alet."

"My pleasure," Vasiht'h said, and tried not to smooth his fur down. To have the mindtouch recur—in all he'd heard about it, he'd never been told that it would feel nice. Comfortable and easy and good. That of course he should feel the feelings of his roommate, who would probably find the idea distasteful if not repellant. He sipped the chocolate to settle his agitation, and went to make the call.

———∞∞∞———

"Sehvi," Vasiht'h said, sitting on his glee. "This is my room-mate, Jahir."

On the other side of the screen, Sehvi's eyes were wide. She'd believed him about having an Eldritch roommate, of course, but he was sure some part of her hadn't been able to imagine it until she saw Jahir sitting on the pillow just in view, one knee up to his chest and his arms loosely looped around it.

"Alet," Jahir said. "I am pleased to make your acquaintance."

"Ah, and it's good to make yours. Thank you," Sehvi said, still staring. She shook herself and said, "Ariihir? What's this about?"

"I thought I might ask you, since you paid more attention to the mental training, and knew some doctors," Vasiht'h said. "What might cause someone to have a worse reaction to some people's mental touch than others."

Sehvi sat back, gaze narrowed. Then she glanced at Jahir. "This is about you, I'm guessing?"

"You do, correctly," Jahir said. "I am concerned that there seem to be some few people whose touch I can bear—if not fre-quently, than at least without losing my own sense of self in theirs—and others who can apparently render me unconscious."

"Ohhhh," she said. "Wow. You're that sensitive?"

"I have no notion," Jahir said. "Given that I have no context for comparison!"

"But he's passed out twice," Vasiht'h added.

"Once," Jahir said.

"Twice," Vasiht'h said. "When the medical technicians got to you, you swooned when they put their hands on you."

His roommate grimaced. "Well. Perhaps a touch of discom-fort then, also." More normally, "I knew how to operate the instruments they were using for several hours afterward."

"Goddess bless," Sehvi said, shaking her head. "I don't envy you that."

"Is this sensitivity something you've heard of, then?" Vasiht'h asked. "And the pickiness of it? Why does it only work with some people?"

"Oh, it's not that it doesn't work with some people," she said. "It's more like . . . some people are a warm draft and other people are a bonfire." She considered the Eldritch with a pitying look. "Or maybe it's like . . . some people have super-sensitive taste buds, and a little pepper for us is nice, but it burns them."

"That sounds . . . dire," Jahir said.

"Oh no! It's not bad," she said. "Any more than someone with a good ear for music, or a refined sense of touch, or a super-fertile body is disadvantaged. It just means that some things are going to affect you more."

"But how can he tell which people are going to be the problems?" Vasiht'h asked.

"That I can't tell you," Sehvi said. "I'm only a level more advanced than you in the practice, ariihir. I do remember that some people are always projecting, and some people are always withdrawing, or more like there's a scale and some people are on the projecting side and others are on the withdrawing and most people are somewhere in the various middle parts. The ones that project tend to dump everything they're thinking out, and they put the push of their emotions behind it, so it's like their thoughts are a point they can turn into a spear just by heaving all the empathic content in after it. The people who pull back are the ones who draw all that in." To Jahir she added, "That can be disconcerting too, to have someone suck in your emanations. Especially if you're not much of a projector. It gets intimate quickly."

"And there's no way to tell," Vasiht'h said.

"I gather that if you get good at it, you can start making predictions," Sehvi said. "But I was never that good an esper. You know, ariihir. I can send and receive well enough to use it, but some of the fancier stuff the higher levels of practice can do . . ." She shook her head. "Not in me, that's for sure."

"So there is no way to tell," Jahir said, quiet. Considering, Vasiht'h thought. "And no way to protect against it?"

"If you're holding a barrier against those things already, and they're pushing through . . ." Sehvi shrugged.

"What about treatment?" Vasiht'h asked.

"Of what, being bruised by mental contact?" Sehvi said. "That's pretty far beyond anything I've heard. Even having hung around doctors most of my life. I gather the important thing is to separate yourself from the overpowering presence and do things that remind you of who you are. You know, centering yourself."

"I see," Jahir murmured.

"Can you think of anything else?" Vasiht'h asked her.

She shook her head. "No. Other than it helps to have calm and safe influences around you. That part you know—" to him, not to his roommate. "It's just common sense. Home should be a place you can use as a refuge. It makes a big difference."

"It does," Jahir agreed. "And I do have such a refuge. Thank you, very much, alet."

"Any time," she said, her eyes lifting as the Eldritch rose and bowed to her before taking his leave. Vasiht'h watched the door close behind him, then rested his folded hands in his lap and waited.

Sehvi looked at him and said, "Wow."

He started laughing.

"So that's him? No wonder you want to keep him. He's adorable!"

"That . . . wasn't exactly the word I would have used to describe him," Vasiht'h said. "But I understand the impulse."

"The impulse!" she said, and shook her head. "No, he's wonderful. You look at him and you can't decide if you admire him or you want to protect him. Is half the campus following him around with moon eyes?"

"Not that I know of," Vasiht'h said. "Though the healer-assist at the hospital has a crush on him. She hasn't said anything, thankfully. I warned him about it, but I can't imagine what he'd tell her if he found out for certain."

"Probably something courtly that would make her feel horribly embarrassed," Sehvi said, grinning. "That accent! Too fun. Are you still getting mindtouches?"

"Yessss," Vasiht'h said slowly. "And I think he is too. I'm not encouraging it."

"You have more willpower than me!" Sehvi said. "I'd probably be trying." She grinned. "You sure about that? Maybe you can talk him into the mindline? You'd make perfect partners. You've even got matching coloring!"

Vasiht'h looked down at his white chest and then eyed her.

"Well, white and black and white and white still matches," she said. "Very striking!"

"You sound worse than a Harat-Shar," Vasiht'h said. "Are you hanging out with too many?"

"No, but let me tell you, ariihir, the Tam-illee are just as bad. The moment they spot you they start matchmaking." She laughed. "It's just they want you to have kids, while the Harat-Shar want you to have a harem." She tilted her head. "You really think he'll be okay?"

"I hope so," Vasiht'h said. "But I'll keep an eye on him anyway."

There was only one thing for it, Jahir decided. If he wanted to survive his intended course, he would have to treat it as a matter of life or death, and act accordingly. He had been taught dueling, a necessary evil not just because he was male, but because he was the heir to the Seni, and he had hated it. His one experience with it could creditably be called by his textbooks traumatizing. But the adrenaline-fueled quickness of fighting, and the expansion of his situational awareness . . . yes. If he employed those things, he might be able to work in a crowded ward.

He put the concept to the test the following week, spending a few minutes before class summoning the necessary focus. When the lecture ended and their instructor set them loose, he went, and all his consciousness seemed to spread out with him, warning him whenever his classmates were too close. He called the results a success, though at the end of the session he was exhausted and nervy, like a skittish colt. Taking a walk helped settle his agitation, but it did nothing for the exhaustion except, perhaps, exacerbate it.

But it would work, he thought, so he kept at it. It helped that other than Patient Assessment, his classes were sedentary, their only stresses involving memorization of a great deal of data. At the teaching assistant's suggestion he had bought the book of study songs, and found it so delightful he'd bought the others, even for the medical subjects he was not likely to take. Paging through one of those volumes he'd found an alphabet song of Exodus diseases, which stayed with him when he went to his class on psychological disorders of the Exodus. Studying those gave him renewed respect for the Pelted. He could only imagine what it was like to live with the knowledge that one had been engineered for unsavory uses, and then been forced to flee because there had been no other path to liberty.

The Exodus had also inspired other, less predictable issues: trauma over the loss of a sense of family, resentments over the segregation of individuals that had resulted in the races of the Alliance—sometimes called species, but able to interbreed—as well as anxieties over whether the Pelted were becoming too much (or not enough) like their progenitors. Humanity's return to the galaxy had only compounded those problems, and while their instructor told them the disorders relating to current issues in the Alliance were covered in another class, still Jahir could imagine what it must be like, to live side by side with one's makers. The Eldritch themselves were an artificial creation, but it had been self-willed; a conscious decision to become separate. They had not begun from slavery and abuse.

It was on his mind while washing vegetables for the quad-mates' evening; for once, he and Vasiht'h had been detailed to bringing the savories, as Leina had a new recipe from home she wanted to try on them.

"Fin for your thoughts?" Vasiht'h asked.

"Wondering what it is, to be Pelted and have so many traumas to overcome," Jahir said. "It astonishes me that they ever welcomed humanity into the Alliance."

"Not all humans are bad," Vasiht'h said, tasting the dip before wrinkling his nose and going for the spice cabinet. "After all, a lot of them had to pull together to help the Pelted flee."

This, it turned out, was not Luci's reasoning, when he put the question to the rest of them later. "Oh, you have to feel pity for them."

"Pity?" he asked.

"Sure," she said, picking at a strand of celery trapped between her fang and the omnivore tooth alongside it. "They were it, for the longest time . . . the pinnacle of civilization in the entire galaxy, as far as they knew. They made us—made entire sentient species!—from bits of animals they thought attractive. They had space ships and space stations and even colony worlds. And then we up and turn our backs on them, and then they get into a civil war that smashes their entire solar system back to the industrial age—"

"A bit of an exaggeration there," Brett said, dry.

"Only a little," she said. "And they spend ages struggling back toward what they left behind. Then, out of nowhere, here we come. And we've been building peacefully on their technology and science ever since we abandoned them. They get to see us come over the horizon in these sleek, expensive ships that can do things they only dream about. And the people they engineered for bed-toys are now so far beyond them that the only reason they're not calling us master and mistress is that we don't care about conquering them."

"That's got to hurt," Leina said, cheek in her palm. " 'Hi, we could be holding a grudge, but you're so unimportant we don't want to bother subduing you.' "

"Harsh," Merashiinal said, shaking his head. "It is not all true. Humans were important when we met them again."

Jahir thought of his reading, and the pages comparing some of the feelings of the Pelted with those children feel for separated parents. "I imagine so."

"Maybe, but no one thinks of humans as our daddies anymore," Luci said, dipping a purple carrot and snapping the tip off with her fangs. She crunched, contemplating the flavor—and a strange sight it was, watching a leopard eat vegetables—and then said, "Well, maybe some people do, but only when they're writing angsty teenage poetry about the origin."

"Now that, I take issue with," Brett said. "There's good literature written about the relationship between humanity and the Pelted. And there really is some sense still that they're our parents. It's just that we're the grown-up children who've moved out and done better than them."

"Humanity must have its share of disorders on the matter," Jahir said.

"There's an elective for that," Vasiht'h said. "Disorders of the Rapprochement. Talks about the problems humans have integrating into the Alliance and dealing with the reality of the Pelted."

"That sounds interesting," Brett said.

"It sounds dull," Leina said, making a face. "Humans think it's all about them. Like the worlds revolve around them. If you ask me it's about time they got shaken up. Now, who's ready for my experiment?"

"What *is* the experiment?" Brett asked, willing to be distracted.

"It's an apple pie!" she said, lifting her chin.

"An apple pie!" Vasiht'h said. "I thought this was a recipe from home!"

"It is!" she said. "The only reason people think of humans when they think of pie is because they were born first."

"Sibling rivalry on top of abusive parent/child," Brett said to Jahir. "Things get convoluted around here."

The apple pie was in fact delicious, if misshapen. When they had eaten their fill and Merashiinal had put away the last of the wine, they dispersed, all save—

"Can I help you bring the trays back?" Luci asked.

"Sure," Vasiht'h said.

The Harat-Shar preceded them into the apartment, where Jahir disposed himself to cleaning the dishes. Luci pulled one of the stools out from under the counter and perched on it to watch as he and Vasiht'h tidied the kitchen.

"It didn't work out, I'm guessing," Vasiht'h said.

"We don't know," she admitted. "We've both agreed to take a step back. For a semester or two. See how we feel when we see each other again." She rubbed her chest with a thumb, grimacing. "I feel like I've ripped out part of my heart. But what else can I do?"

"Distance can sometimes give perspective," Jahir offered.

"Yeah, and you would know, wouldn't you?" she said, glancing at him. "How about it, Tall and Pretty? Have better advice for me?"

Jahir considered while putting the tray away. What could he say that could be of use to a woman with such different life experience? And on a topic that he was not exactly expert in, having made his own, unpardonable error? He rested his hands on the counter and said, "Love is not enough, without commitment."

Startled, Luci said, "Yeah, that . . . would make sense."

She glanced at Vasiht'h, and so did Jahir, wondering if his roommate would have something to add. The Glaseah was boiling water for tea, and when he looked up and saw their gazes, said, "Acts are the language of love. That's what the Goddess teaches us. Words might do for thoughts. But love needs to be communicated in actions."

Later, after she'd left, Jahir said, "The precepts of your goddess are wise."

Vasiht'h chuckled. "We like to think so. But it's not anything you don't already know."

"Ah?"

The Glaseah shook his head. "It would be a pretty bad religion if it was telling you things you didn't already understand in your heart to be true. None of us need to be told that love is powerless when it has no form, and that we are the form it takes. We know it instinctively." He looked up. "You do. You're doing it all the time. You're risking yourself to know us. Isn't that love?"

"This from the person who professes himself to be without passion?" Jahir said. "You no less than I are manifesting love through your acts."

"Maybe I am," Vasiht'h murmured.

———— ❦ ————

"That's the third subject you've lost so far," Palland said. "What are you doing to them, Vasiht'h?"

"You're assuming I'm doing something!"

"Yessss, I am," the Seersa said, folding his arms. "Because if you give a healer-assist a guilt-free excuse to sleep, by the Speaker-Singer they put their heads down on a pillow and black out like a freshman after a party binge." He pointed a finger at Vasiht'h. "That leaves you. Are you telling them to leave? Is there something about them that's making them inappropriate subjects?"

"No!" Vasiht'h exclaimed, startled. "Nothing like that. It's not their fault at all!"

Palland hesitated, then said, "And you're not covering up an error. On your part."

That made him flush. "No! Well, not of the sort you're thinking." At Palland's arched brow, he said, "I've been talking to them, when they say something. And I think I'm contaminating the study by listening to their problems."

"And offering advice," the Seersa said dryly.

"Not really advice, just . . . a sympathetic ear?" Vasiht'h said, rueful. "So I can't tell what's having the beneficial effect, me talking to them before they lie down, or me touching their dreams."

Palland covered his face with a palm and sighed. And then laughed. "You know how ridiculous this sounds, doesn't it?"

"That I'm messing up my research project by doing impromptu talk therapy with my subjects?" Vasiht'h smoothed the fur on his forelegs and said, "Yes, I know."

"And you're still sure you want to go through with it." The Seersa leaned back. "It's not too late to change tracks. You can still get in under the five-year deadline handily."

"I know," Vasiht'h said, stubborn. "But I'm going to do this."

"If you're sure . . ."

"I am."

Palland sighed. "Fine, let's see if we can fill your three slots with some of these other people you originally interviewed. If we're quick we can get it done in time for you to go play escort to your alien friend."

"You know about that?" Vasiht'h asked, surprised.

"Everyone knows about it," the Seersa replied with a huff. He tapped the data tablet. "Now. Focus. And remember—" Pointing the finger at him now. "No more fixing your subjects."

"Yes, sir," Vasiht'h muttered.

Vasiht'h kept Palland's critique in mind when he went back to the hospital, but he found it hard to not respond to comments his subjects made while preparing for their naps. Maybe he should change his research topic from the effect of dream manipulation on emotional stability to the capitalization of patient vulnerability during the period leading up to sleep? He sighed. The only way he could really see to keep from repeating his mistake was to not see the subjects at all, and that felt so . . . wrong, somehow. Like the rejection the Patient Assessment professor had accused his roommate of. He did try not to say anything for the first few sessions after his discussion with Palland, but the alienation was too painful. The separation felt artificial to him, gave him the uncomfortable sense of being the one with power in the relationship.

The research itself was as promising as Palland had thought it would be, though with such a small sample size it was hard to tell. But the people he soothed during their sleep seemed to have a more manageable stress level as the weeks went past. The ones who got both talk and the sleep soothing did noticeably better, even. But some part of him couldn't help wondering what good it was, to do research like this so someone else could use it—and who would? When in practice it only suited espers (and, some part of him whispered, himself)?

He took some comfort in taking care of his roommate, who

needed it. Not just the walks back from Patient Assessment, but the concerts, too . . . and on the days Jahir came back from his medical track classes he seemed particularly tired, so Vasiht'h did everything he could to make him comfortable. It helped, though not as much as he would have wanted to see.

He wasn't the only one to notice, either.

"How come you look so tired?" Meekie asked Jahir as the girls abandoned the corner nest to go work on their letters.

Jahir put down the tablet he'd been reading poetry from. "Do I look tired?"

"Uh-huh," she said.

"She's right," Amaranth agreed from the table where she was setting out paper. "You bend a little over when you walk, like you forget to stand straight. I do that too, when I've had a bad few days."

Jahir's wince was so slight Vasith'h would have missed it, had he not been waiting for it. "The schooling can be taxing," he said finally. "This semester has been a bit of a challenge. We have just had midterms, and they required a great deal of preparation."

"You need to rest more," Meekie said. "That's what they always tell us when we get run-down."

"And eat carefully," Kayla agreed.

"And lie down even if you don't think you're tired," Persy offered from her bed. "And can you make me one of your puppets, 'Ranth?"

"Sure," Amaranth said, reaching for the glue-strips. To Vasiht'h, she said, "Maybe you can make him rest."

"I try," Vasiht'h said, hiding his amusement at her fussing. "But when people grow up there's only so much you can do to make them do the things that are best for them."

"Is it because he's bigger than you and you can't march him into his room?" Kuriel sounded interested.

"That can't be it," Amaranth said. "Look at him, he's got four legs and a heavier body. He could just sit on him."

Vasiht'h covered his face until he was sure he wasn't smiling quite so hard. When he lifted his head he found Jahir looking at him ruefully, and that . . . that was a taste like sour yogurt, an undeniable mindtouch. He cleared his throat and spoke as if it wasn't distracting him. "It's more like . . . when you get older, you learn to respect other people's autonomy."

"I've heard that word," Kayla said. "The healers use it, sometimes."

"It means we have the right to act the way we think we should, without someone else interfering," Nieve said quietly.

"That's right," Vasiht'h said. "I respect Jahir's autonomy, which means—"

"That if he wants to make himself sick running around without resting, you'd let him?" Kuriel asked. "That doesn't seem like a very good friend thing to do."

"Maybe good friends interfere," Meekie said.

"Maybe good people interfere?" Amaranth frowned. "I don't know. I think sitting back and letting people hurt themselves is mean. If you could talk them out of it."

"Or sit on them," Kuriel said.

"Did Miss Jill tell you we're allowed to go outside every other day now?" Nieve said to Jahir, who was wearing a look of what Vasiht'h judged to be pained amusement.

"She did not," Jahir said to her, grateful for the change in topic if Vasiht'h was any judge. "And how have you found it?"

"It's wonderful," the girl said, fervent.

"Though we haven't been able to get as far away from the hospital as we did that day we jumped rope," Kayla said.

"It's hard to walk that far anymore," Persy said, resigned.

"We'll just have to wait for a day when we all feel good again at the same time," Kayla said. "Then we'll sneak out."

"Yeah." Persy sighed, smiling. "That would be perfect."

"But even if we can't run away," Nieve said to Jahir. "The sun is the most wonderful feeling in the world."

"It's so hard for them," Jahir said to him on the way home. "And so easy for us."

"Yes," Vasiht'h said, his thoughts busy and messy: the research project, his feelings about helping people, his feelings about Jahir and the mindtouches, and the stinging pain of being fond of those girls and knowing the challenges they faced. Too much, he thought, but he was glad too, and wasn't sure why yet.

"A fin for your thoughts?" Jahir said.

Surprised and tickled to have his own words turned back on him, Vasiht'h said, "Just that . . . there's a lot going on in my head, and I haven't worked any of it through yet."

"Mmm," Jahir said. He looked up at the sky, so clear and soft a blue. Then out over the shining field bordering their sidewalk, nodding with flowers. Spring had cleaned up after winter, Vasiht'h thought, very nicely, and he hadn't even noticed. When Jahir paused and looked out over the grass, Vasiht'h couldn't begrudge him the view. He stood next to his roommate and drew in a long breath: pollen and warm breezes.

Jahir checked the buckle on the bag slung from his shoulder to hip, then pushed it behind his back. "A beautiful view," he said.

"It is," Vasiht'h agreed.

"And that tree, yonder. Would be perfect for climbing."

Vasiht'h squinted: in the distance he did see a tree, surrounded in an apron of grass, with a low branch that nearly touched the ground and bright new foliage spreading over it like a veil. "I wouldn't know . . . I'm not good at climbing! But it would be nice to nap under."

"So it would," Jahir said. "And we are not due anywhere for some hours."

"That's true," Vasiht'h said, feeling a glimmer of something suggestive . . . of mischief?

"Mmm," Jahir said. And nodded. "A very good tree. And I will get there first."

"You'll what—hey!"

But the Eldritch was already sprinting over the field, leaving him behind, and who would ever have thought that something bipedal could run that fast? Startled, Vasiht'h lunged after him, worried. "You shouldn't—the gravity—what if you're not—"

His roommate didn't fall, and didn't call back to him either, and Vasiht'h ran after him and at some point he felt the spring of the grass beneath his feet and the sun warm on the fur on his back, flashing off it, and there was something glorious about just running, running for no other reason except to run. He could hear his roommate laughing even though he made no noise, and his heart pounded through every limb in his body as the mind-line raveled between them, brief and brilliant, before unwinding again when Jahir grabbed the low-hanging branch and swung himself onto it, his momentum shaking the leaves.

Panting, Jahir looked down at him and said, "A tie, perhaps?"

"You're crazy!" Vasiht'h said, laughing, and collapsed on shaded grass that was cooler than the sun-soaked field's. "I probably lost half my materials between here and the sidewalk."

"And was it worth it?" Jahir asked.

Vasith'h looked up at him; the Eldritch had his back to the trunk and was slouched in the dip of the branch, one foot up and the other hanging. He was still breathing deeply, but he looked content, his face turned just enough to catch the sun.

"Yes. Yes, it was definitely worth it," Vasiht'h said.

CHAPTER 21

"So you survived midterms," KindlesFlame said. "And how did you do?"

"Well," Jahir said, and proud of it. "You'll be gratified to hear I've had no other incidents in the Clinical Management class. Kandara congratulated me afterward the examination, even."

"Did she?" KindlesFlame said, brow up. "It's hard to get praise out of Lasa. You must have impressed her."

"I could hardly fail to, given how little cause she had to be impressed when I began," Jahir said, turning his cup on its saucer. The Tam-illee was drinking iced coffee, to go with the miniature cheese puffs they'd ordered . . . Jahir found he still preferred warm drinks, though he looked forward to summer putting paid to that when it got properly hot. "The pharmacology information was very dense, and I fear I won't remember it when I need it, but the test was easy enough."

"It'll take a while to settle, and you'll need more of it if you're serious about going medical. We get a lot of derangement from drugs," KindlesFlame said. "We try to avoid using things with severe side effects, but sometimes the only tool you have is a clumsy one, or a dangerous one, and all you can do is palliate the side effects." He leaned back in his chair, legs crossed, all ease.

"So, have you chosen yet?"

"Alas, no," Jahir said. He thought of how good it was to sit down after the Clinical Management sessions. "I find the medical work fascinating, but . . . I have concerns that it might prove physically taxing."

"You might have an easier time of it elsewhere," Kindles-Flame said. "That regimen you finished in winter will help you live here comfortably, but it doesn't change that you're bred to a less strenuous gravity. You'd probably find a station or ship far more comfortable."

"Mayhap," Jahir said. "But I have not made a decision yet as to where I will go to practice when I'm done. And I'm not entirely sure how to make that decision."

"A lot of people end up making those connections during their residencies," KindlesFlame said. "That's why the good ones get snapped up so quickly. The big hospitals on Selnor and the other populous worlds can get you a lot of exposure to people who know people who know just where you'd be welcome, and for a tidy salary."

"That sounds promising?" Jahir said. "How does one acquire such a residency position?"

"Most of the serious ones?" KindlesFlame smiled. "You need exemplary grades and recommendations from notable faculty. Like, say, me."

"Ah!" Jahir said, and laughed. "I see. So I must impress you."

"You need to convince me you can handle it," KindlesFlame said. "And . . . if you can get through Clinical Management on your feet, and with Lasa's approval, then you might have it in you. I'm still skeptical, but I've been surprised before." He tapped his finger on the table. "If you're serious about it, you might consider applying to Fleet, too."

"Ah?" Jahir said. "The military?"

"They have a medical division," said KindlesFlame. "And they need the medical-track psychologists. It's a good living, and they take care of their own."

"I have no notion how that would work, given the political situation between the Alliance and my world," Jahir said, finding the thought absurd. Fascinating, but absurd: he hated dueling, and could not imagine himself in a martial organization. Granted, Fleet had not found any wars to fight yet, but the border between the Alliance and the Chatcaavan Empire was perilous enough to inspire skirmishing now and then, and there was the perennial trouble with pirates and slavers . . . "I'm not sure what my monarch would think of it."

"Well, something to keep in mind," KindlesFlame said. "Even if you don't decide to join, you can end up as a contractor for them, especially if you're near one of the military bases. The sector starbases are all Fleet establishments . . . they rent space to civilian concerns, but it's a good place to get the hybrid practices. And you'll have the benefit of the lighter gravity, since they typically don't run them as dense as the average planet."

"I have to imagine such a place would be remote," Jahir said, frowning.

"Oh, some of them are," KindlesFlame said. "But most of them are more like miniatures of Selnor: all the capital world's diversity of population with the assurance of a Fleet presence and the excitement of a port city. The big cruise liners are run out of starbase docks, and the merchant trade does lively traffic going from starbase to starbase. They lease separate refueling stations there, but it's a good stop for most of them. You'd have any number of opportunities there . . . there are big hospitals for the acute practice, and a major civilian city to set up an office if that's what you prefer."

The picture KindlesFlame drew intrigued. Jahir knew very little about the Alliance's starbases, but he thought he would go back to the apartment and do some research. "That bears investigation, I think. I thank you for the idea."

"My job," the Tam-illee said, patting his chest once before leaning over to take one of the cheese puffs. "Giving you ideas. Now you just have to get through school to make something of them."

---⊸⊶⊷⊶⊶---

It was a fine afternoon for a card game, so Jahir taught the children how to play Queen's Gambit, which they took to with startling aptitude. Persy and Kuriel soon proved themselves the most skilled at it, winning with a cheerful bloodthirstiness that would have unmanned most of the people he'd played against at court. Even Vasiht'h gave up after a few games, saying with a laugh, "I know when I'm out of my league!"

"Then you can help us set up for a puppet show," Persy said, pleased to be out of bed for once. "Come on, manylegs."

"Yes, ma'am," Vasiht'h said, and went to set up the cardboard theater while the girls debated which of their handmade characters to use.

Nieve was still in Jahir's lap, her cards forgotten on the carpet and her mind a gentle thing breezed through with sunny dreams of unicorns and trees: Berquist had taken them out the previous day and the sensory impressions had lingered. He rested his arms around her and closed his eyes, letting her lead him through the veil of sunlight. From a distance he could hear his roommate's discussion with the girls: about this puppet needing repair before use, and that one needing a more colorful hat to indicate her role in the upcoming drama as empress-elect of the universe. He thought it would be a good play, indeed, couldn't conceive how it could be anything else with such authors, and such a fine, peaceful day to receive it.

"We're just about ready, I think," Vasiht'h was saying, when gray corruption ate through his world so abruptly Jahir felt as if he was falling through it, but he wasn't—he wasn't. It was Nieve, Nieve gone stiff in his arms, her mind collapsing in on itself beneath the sudden, catastrophic failure of her body. Vasiht'h saw the look on his face and started to lunge toward him, but the door burst open first and Berquist was there, and several more people, prying Nieve from his lap and swamping him with their panic—his mind impressed abruptly with readings plummeting on distant screens, alarms screaming—and through it all, Nieve

... Nieve just *gone*, the sweet rambling of her mind quenched and nothing left to replace it.

Her body was parted from his and rushed away, and he staggered and fell—to one knee? He couldn't remember. But there was a pressure at his wrist, pulling, not a hand, but a touch free of any personality at all, and a voice near him, "Come on, out, someone's coming to see to the girls and we need to get you out of here—"

Yes, he said, or at least he thought he said, and stumbled, trembling, in Vasiht'h's wake . . . for it was Vasiht'h, wasn't it?

When his eyes cleared, they were in the stairwell with its high, distant windows. He was sitting on a step, though he didn't remember getting there. His clothes and hair were soaked through with sweat and clung to him, and his heart was beating hard enough to disorder his breathing.

Vasiht'h was perched on the landing behind him, one paw on the step. He had a length of leather in his hand—the strap from his bag, Jahir saw, and the end of it was looped around his own wrist, no doubt how he'd been guided.

"With us?" Vasiht'h asked, voice rough.

"Yes," Jahir said, and cleared his throat. "Vasiht'h . . . Nieve . . ."

"I don't know," Vasiht'h said. "They took her away. The evening duty healer-assist is with the girls now. They were frightened. All of them, adults too."

"We should—"

"We won't," Vasiht'h said, his voice steady, though Jahir could see the grief in him and didn't know how. "We're volunteers here, Jahir. We don't have the training. We'd be in the way. And you . . . you've had a really bad moment. You look like you're going to collapse."

Jahir glanced down at the strap around his wrist.

"Yes," Vasiht'h said. "That's why I haven't undone it yet. I'm afraid if I do you'll pitch forward down the stairs."

It seemed mean of spirit to argue with what was in fact the truth. He could feel the crumbling of Nieve's mind beneath his still, and the horror of it was nauseating. He swallowed and put his head down against his knees, willing the memory away, but it wouldn't go. He thought his fingers were shaking.

The door to the stairwell opened. He began to shift to allow the person room to pass, but it was Berquist's voice that spoke, and she was not moving. "She's in surgery now. It's bad, but we don't know when we'll have more news. You both should go get some rest."

"Will you call us?" Vasiht'h asked for them both, because the news had paralyzed Jahir.

"Either way, yes," she said. As Vasiht'h rose, she added, "Thank you both. For everything you do."

"We're glad to do it," Vasiht'h said, and then she left. Jahir felt his roommate's gaze even though his eyes were closed. "Arii? Can you get up?"

"Yes," Jahir said, though the world was vague and distant. Somehow they made it downstairs, and out through the lobby, into the world, and that was worse somehow. The sunlight, the normalcy of it, the birdsong and the soughing of the breeze through new leaves. He staggered, felt the loop on his wrist catch, managed to straighten.

"Just keep walking," Vasiht'h murmured. "We'll be home soon."

"Yes," he said again, even though the nausea was redoubling. The ash-crumbled reality inside him kept trying to find a reflection in the world outside and failing. All he could remember was the vertiginous feel of everything dissolving from around him.

That he got partway home before he fell was, he thought in some distant place, astonishing.

That Vasiht'h caught him, even more so.

———⋙⋘———

Vasiht'h hadn't thought he could breathe through so much fear: for Nieve, for the girls and their families, for the staff and the doctors battling a disease they hadn't even catalogued, and overwhelmingly, for his roommate . . . who, if he was not mistaken, had just felt a child die in his arms. Walking down the sidewalk, Vasiht'h held his breath every time Jahir's foot came down, wondering if that would be the step that failed to hold him up, and once or twice it almost wasn't . . . enough so that when the moment came, he wasn't ready.

But he remembered watching Jahir fall that first day in the apartment, and the horror of being frozen. Remembered, and refused. When the Eldritch crumpled, he dove up and grabbed him before he could hit the pavement. The mindline flared open with a sizzle of sparks and gave Vasiht'h a momentary glimpse into the hole his roommate had fallen into. He threw a strand of himself down like a lifeline and made an anchor—built walls between the Eldritch and Nieve's powerful sending—and finally clarified the boundaries between them both so Jahir wouldn't get lost in him, too, with all this bodily contact. Because he was really holding him: he could feel Jahir's head heavy over his shoulder, the spill of hair tickling the bottom of Vasiht'h's second back, between the wings. For someone from a lighter world, he had a surprisingly heavy torso.

"All here?" he whispered when he felt tension begin to reanimate his roommate's body.

There was a long pause. Then: "I believe so." A shivering through the gleaming link, like water disturbed by a falling rock.

"Enough here to get back to the apartment?" Vasiht'h said.

"We must," Jahir said. And forced himself to stand, so slowly that Vasiht'h's joints ached to watch—or were those his roommate's impressions? As they parted, the mindline dissolved in glittering pieces, leaving an afterimage in Vasiht'h's mind that shone like the sun on ocean waves.

Despite the Eldritch's determination, there were several moments on the way back that made Vasiht'h's heart seize . . . but somehow, Jahir didn't fall again, and they passed over the threshold into the apartment.

"Sit," Vasiht'h said, and got no argument: his roommate settled on the couch and took the blanket brought to him, said nothing while Vasiht'h went to make them both tea. He found, while shaking out the leaves, that his hands were trembling. Vasiht'h stared at them. His own reaction to Nieve's abrupt decline? His fear over Jahir? Reaction to having managed a crisis to a point of stability? All of the above, probably. He set his mouth in a firm line and got the leaves into the strainer, put the water on to boil.

When he came back to the couch, Jahir had his feet up under himself and the blanket close, head bowed. It made his face shocking when he lifted it. Vasiht'h was used to thinking of Eldritch skin as colorless, but he saw he was wrong: healthy Eldritch skin was a white that glowed, like a polished pearl. To see it wan and gray . . . it made all the sharp angles in Jahir's face seem knife-like, unfinished.

"Tell me," Jahir said. "Tell me they'll save her."

Vasiht'h paused. And wished, very much wished he could lie. But he couldn't, not when faced with the intensity of his roommate's gaze. "They'll do everything they can. And everything in the Alliance Core is a lot. There's every reason for hope."

Jahir looked away, and Vasiht'h heard the thought that followed, tasting like bitter medicine. *Every reason, save that she was dying.*

Vasiht'h chose not to refute that. What he'd sensed through their touch made him think that Jahir was right.

There was no cooking that night; Vasiht'h knew better than to try with the memory of Jahir's nausea still strong in his throat. But his roommate did drink the tea, and so did he, and that settled them both, a little. Not much, but a little. Vasiht'h kept waiting for the message alert to chime, and knew Jahir must be anxious for it, too.

But the chime didn't come. At last Vasiht'h suggested that Jahir might shower and get ready for bed, and thankfully that suggestion met no resistance. While his roommate was busy, Vasiht'h rinsed the cups and the pot and went to his own room. He should have been working on compiling more of his research results, but when he looked at his desk he couldn't find the energy. He rubbed his arms and wondered at himself, at why he hadn't fallen apart, and why he felt so calm. Sad and anxious, yes, but . . . strangely steady. He remembered his mother saying once that it was easier to be strong for other people than to get through something on your own. Was this an example of that? He didn't feel strong. Just deeply present, and willing to be patient with his own fears.

When he stepped back into the great room, it was to find his roommate already there, lying on the couch this time. Vasiht'h stared at him, then went into the Eldritch's room and fetched out his pillow and blankets. He brought them and said, "Lift your head."

Jahir opened his eyes, then said, "You didn't have to—" And then subsided at Vasiht'h's look. He lifted his head so Vasiht'h could get the pillow under it, then submitted to the blankets being tucked around him. "Thank you," he said, voice raw.

Vasiht'h shook his head and went into his own room, returning with his blanket and some extra pillows. He arranged his own bed on the floor next to the couch. When he finished, he found Jahir watching him.

"Do you want to sleep alone tonight?" he asked the Eldritch.

"No," Jahir said.

"Me neither," Vasiht'h said, and curled up on his cushions, exhausted. He pulled the blanket up over his second back and onto his torso, rested his head down. He could hear Jahir's breathing, his shifting on the couch. Could sense him, just a little, through the mindtouches that kept wanting to recreate the mindline: a shocky gray pallor, a throbbing like a wound with a freshly ripped scab. He wanted very much to soothe away Jahir's cruel dreams, but he knew better than to try with his own mental state so low.

The following morning brought them no news, and classes could not be ignored. Neither of them had the appetite for breakfast, but Vasiht'h made one anyway and forced them both to eat at least some of it before they left. His morning lecture didn't hold his attention; he was relieved that his afternoon period was his directed study but not one of the hospital sessions. Too soon, he thought, to go back with equanimity, and certainly he couldn't imagine performing the sleep-soothing on anyone in the hospital without his thoughts being contaminated by the memory of what he'd seen there the day before. He spent the afternoon working through the study results to date instead, and returned home glad to put down his tablet and give up for the day.

Jahir was just walking through the door when the message alert chimed. They both froze.

"I'll take it," Vasiht'h said, and went into his room to do so. He waved it open and found a very short message in text, and he stared at it for several minutes while his heart raced. So few words, to be so devastating.

When he left his room, Jahir was sitting on the couch with his face in his hands. He looked up when Vasiht'h padded close, and then his shoulders tensed.

"They tried," Vasiht'h said. "But they lost her."

Jahir put a hand to his face, covering his eyes. Vasiht'h could see the wrist quivering. He didn't say anything; wasn't sure if it was his place to try, if his roommate would welcome it or find it an intrusion.

"That child," Jahir whispered. "So young."

"It happens," Vasiht'h said. "It's horrible and senseless, but it happens."

Jahir said nothing to that for so long that Vasiht'h thought he'd offended. But then the Eldritch held out a hand without looking up, without uncovering his face. Swallowing, Vasiht'h slipped his own fingers under his roommate's, trying to project his steadiness, his calm. He had the sense of being a rock off the coast of a beach, with the waves slapping its sides, washing over it, rushing past. He held fast.

Jahir threaded his fingers through Vasiht'h's and said nothing more. A little while later, he learned that his roommate was weeping by the smell of salt in the air . . . the smell, and nothing more.

———◦◦◦———

How he was to stumble through his classes, Jahir had not the slightest notion . . . but that he had to, he felt in his bones with an urgency that had neither name nor explanation. He bowed to it and bent to his studies, and tried to breathe through the grief in his heart. Little Nieve, so bright and new, with her love of poetry and her eyes like young hyacinths. He had thought himself resigned to the reality of the Alliance's many peoples dying so quickly. But to be confronted with the evidence, in a way he could not deny—

It was too much pain, and unexpected. He gave himself to his books and drowned himself in chains of drug reactions, long lists of traumatic disorders. But even so he felt parted from it, from himself, from the world and the sunlight of the advancing spring. He was so distant from it all, in fact, that he found powers in himself he hadn't thought possible, of both stamina and observation. It was the latter that occupied him in Patient Assessment, now drawing near its final sessions and the professor still ignoring him. The week following Nieve's death, Sheldan dismissed the class and Jahir found himself still in his seat. When the last of the students had departed, the Seersa glanced at him skeptically, one ear canted, and said, "Yes?"

"Your issues with humanity are not my concern, professor," Jahir said, "though by now your behavior toward the two humans in class makes it plain that you have them. I would remind you, however, that no matter how I look I am not human, and had even less cause than those students to have earned the public humiliation you put me to. That your conclusions were faulty is only an indicator of the depth of your personal trouble. I may be reserved, but I have made friends here, and not one of them thinks of my reserve as an indication of rejection. Unlike you, they have internalized the Alliance's multiculturalism, enough to both delight in what is different, and understand that it is different."

Sheldan's ears had flipped back during this speech, and his

eyes had grown wider, and by the end of it his tail had stopped its slow swish. He said nothing for so long that Jahir felt compelled to speak. "If you wish to reprimand me now for insolence, that is your prerogative. But I will not retract any of it."

"Reprimand you!" the Seersa exclaimed. "I should!" And then with an exasperated growl. "I should, except you're right."

"I beg your pardon?" Jahir said, feeling a faint surprise.

"You're right," Sheldan said, frowning, but his expression was distracted, as if he talked to himself. "Right in front of my nose, and I never looked at it. I suppose that's how things go when you want to deny them." He was silent for several minutes, then shook himself and looked at Jahir, folding his arms. "I suppose you feel I owe you an apology?"

Jahir gathered his tablet and books and put them in his bag. "I will settle for your not treating my grade prejudicially."

"Even in your favor?"

He looked up.

"Because that was a fine piece of patient assessment if I ever saw one," Sheldan said, wry.

"I suggest," Jahir said, "you seek counseling. And give me the grade I earn, whatever that might be."

"I'll do that," he said, and narrowed his eyes. "And you, young not-a-human? Something's eating you."

"You need not concern yourself with me," Jahir said. "And I am three times your age, professor. By no definition am I your young anything."

That silenced the Seersa, and Jahir left him behind, relieved that there were only a few weeks left in the semester.

———— ❧ ————

It was hard, so hard to step foot again in the hospital. Indeed, he sensed Vasiht'h's uncertainty the morning of their scheduled visitation. But he prepared for it as usual, and presented himself to the Glaseah at the door so that they might go, and he did not miss Vasiht'h's little sigh—resignation? Relief? Both, perhaps. So they went, and they passed into the lobby with its cheery sea creature murals, and the tension that leapt up his shoulders gave him a headache. The stairwell was even worse. But he put one foot behind the other and followed the sight of Vasiht'h's tail all the way to their landing, and passed through the door to the section where a very tired Berquist was sitting at her station, filling out paperwork. At the sight of them, she said, "You came."

"We came," Vasiht'h agreed. "Are they . . . ?"

"They're inside," she said. "And feeling about how you expect." She managed a smile for them. "Thank you for coming."

"We could do nothing else," Jahir said, because that was true, and then Vasiht'h opened the door for them both.

The moment the girls saw them, they hurried over for embraces and reassurance that Jahir could not deny them, even knowing now too well, far too well, the cost of those things. He rested his face against Amaranth's limp hair and smelled antiseptic and young skin and sickness, and closed his eyes against the grief, lest it spill over and alarm them.

They retreated to the corner nest, closer than usual: Vasiht'h sat at Jahir's side, close enough to touch, and spread his body in a curve in front of him, and the girls piled into the middle and leaned on them both. He felt their pain like wounds, and bent his head to keep them from seeing how hard he took it.

Vasiht'h, he thought, knew. He didn't know how he understood this, but he did. He didn't know why it comforted him, either, but it helped.

"Well," Vasiht'h said finally. "I don't know what to say. Maybe some of you can help me?"

"Miss Jill says we should talk about what happened as much as we want, and that includes not at all," Kayla said, subdued.

"Do you want to talk about it?" Vasiht'h asked her.

"Noooooo," Kayla said, slowly. "What is there to talk about?"

"We miss her," Meekie said. "And it was horrible, what happened, and not fair. But everyone seems convinced we'll be scared."

"We're not scared." Kuriel was picking at her toes again. "None of us had Nieve's problem. It's not going to happen to us that way. Though if it did, I'd go the way she did."

"How's that?" Vasiht'h asked, ears flattened.

"Suddenly, and like that. In someone's lap." Kuriel looked up at Jahir, and startled he met her eyes. "She was happy. I saw it. She died really suddenly, but the last thing she felt before she died was . . . happy."

"She was good at that," Persy observed, quiet. "Good at being happy. Even when she was hurt, even when she wanted to be outside or doing normal things, she was always better at being here than we are."

"I'm sick of being here," Kayla said, ears flattening.

Amaranth sighed. "Me too. All of us are."

"Are *you* okay?" Persy asked Jahir. "You looked awful. You still do."

"Of course he's not okay," Amaranth said. "Nieve died in his arms!"

Vasiht'h winced and opened his mouth to speak, but Jahir shook his head, just enough for his roommate to see him. He said to Persy, "It hurt me, to feel her die. She deserved better."

"My mother says we don't always get what we deserve, but that we should make the best of what we have anyway," Meekie said.

"Nieve did that," Persy said, nodding.

"She did," Jahir said. "I think she truly did."

"We should listen to some poetry," Amaranth said. "She would have liked that. Can you read? Is that okay?"

"It is," Jahir said. "Though I did not think to bring my tablet."

"I did," Vasiht'h said, low, and brought it forth from his saddlebag. Startled, Jahir took it, and felt across its surface the transmission of something fine and soft as the foam on a wave: concern, affection . . . pride. He brushed a thumb against the tablet's edge, wondering if he was touching his roommate and not aware of it, but no . . . their hands were separated by the length of the device.

"Thank you," he said, and did not know what he was thanking Vasiht'h for: remembering the tablet, taking care of him, coming here with him, being who he was. All of it, perhaps. He didn't know, but he thought the Glaseah did, because Vasiht'h lowered his head as shy as a maiden blushing.

"Now then," he said, with a deep breath. "What shall we read today?"

"Something about sunlight, and spring, and flowers," Persy said. "She would have liked that."

———⊗⊗⊗———

When they had returned to the apartment, Jahir sat in the chair in the great room and slowly began removing his boots as his roommate made tea. He was holding a flavor in his mouth: herbal and astringent, a taste like anxiety and tension held in check. Rolling it over his tongue made him feel the physical lack, and savoring it made him realize just how many such strange sensations he'd had in the previous months.

"Vasiht'h? Why does your concern have a flavor?"

He heard a long pause, and then the saucers and cups being set on the tray. "You've noticed, then."

"It is not always a taste," Jahir said. "Sometimes it is sensory. An impression of velvet, or sunlight, or the sound of something. But those things one might mistake for memories. The tastes are strange."

His roommate sighed and brought the tray, setting it on the table between them. "It's called the ahv'shev. Mindtouch."

"Mindtouch," Jahir said. "And there is a word for this."

"It's one of the few things we kept from the language the Seersa made for us," Vasiht'h said, pouring himself a cup of the tea. "For the most part, we abandoned it for Universal, or mind-speech. But the vocabulary relating to psychic phenomena, we kept."

"And this is what makes your feelings have sensory weight." The idea was improbable. That it didn't distress him was surely a sign of just how emotionally depleted he was. He'd had a hard time feeling anything, and to rouse himself to actual dismay was beyond him.

"Yes," Vasiht'h said. "It's . . . involuntary. At this stage, anyway."

"At this stage?"

His roommate was flushing under his fur, if Jahir was any judge. It was hard to tell, but the pelt thinned near his eyes, enough to see. "Yes. Being capable of receiving mindtouches is an indication that there is . . . the potential to sustain a mindline."

"This being . . ."

"A permanent psychic channel between two or more people," Vasiht'h said. "It's rare. It has to form between two compatible minds, and to be sustained it has to be . . . well, nurtured. Built up. If you do it right, it starts supporting itself, and then it never turns off." He cleared his throat. "Et'ahv. The mindline. I've never met anyone with one, it's that infrequent."

"And these mindtouches indicate a compatibility . . . between us?" Jahir asked.

Vasiht'h was looking very fixedly at his tea. "Yes."

The idea should have offended him. Instead, he found it vaguely relieving, explaining as it did the uncanny impressions he'd been receiving. That those impressions had implications was a matter for some other time, when he had more energy to devote to assessing his own feelings. Perhaps he would be distressed to know that he could be yoked to a short-lived alien. Perhaps he would be glad, because he was fond of Vasiht'h, and that too was a realization he was not ready to examine at any length.

Instead, he said, "I am guessing Glaseahn literature does not cover the topic of rare and precious mindlines forming with aliens."

Vasiht'h laughed shakily. "No. Not at all."

Jahir nodded and poured his own tea. He could feel his roommate's anxious concern like sandpaper on his skin and closed his eyes. To make it stop, he said, earnest, "I am not upset at you, arii. It is scarcely under your control, that we are able. Rest your fears aside. Please."

"All right," Vasiht'h said.

---x000x---

"Oh, ariihir. What happened?"

"Do I look that bad?" Vasiht'h asked.

"Like someone rolled you flat for pie," Sehvi said, worried. "What's wrong?"

Vasiht'h slumped and let his head rest on his arms on the table. He opened one eye just enough to make sure the door was closed before saying, "One of the girls at the hospital died. In Jahir's arms."

His sister's ears slicked back. She looked about as stunned as Vasiht'h felt, getting through these past two weeks. "Did he . . . is he okay?"

"No," Vasiht'h said, dragging his hand over his forelock to his nose. "No, he really isn't. He's gone numb. It's some kind of shock, it has to be. I can feel it between us like wadded cotton."

"Like wadded—wait, you're still getting data off him?" she asked, leaning toward the screen.

"I am. So is he." Vasiht'h grimaced. "He asked me about it yesterday."

"And you told him?"

"And I told him."

"Well, don't just leave it there!" Sehvi said, worry making her exasperation sharper. "What did he say? Did he rush off in disgust? Swear off ever talking to you again? Tell you we Glaseah are dirty mind-readers without any proper psychic manners?"

"He just . . . accepted it," Vasiht'h said, helplessly. At her ferocious scowl, he said, "I mean that. I explained it, he listened, and he accepted it, and told me he wasn't upset with me. That's it."

"I guess that's more than you could have expected, what with him traumatized," Sehvi said with a wince. "Probably not the best time for you to have broken it to him."

"He asked," Vasiht'h said. "What was I supposed to do?"

"Exactly what you did." She studied him. "And you? How are you holding up? You like these little girls yourself."

"I . . . I'm sad," Vasiht'h said. "Oh, Goddess, Sehvi. I'm sad.

But I can bear it. Does that make me callous?"

"It makes you useful, I'd think," was her reply. "If everyone fell apart at the least bit of sadness, who'd be left to pick up the pieces? You're sad, right? Should you really have to become completely nonfunctional to prove it?"

"I hope not, because I am functional," Vasiht'h said. "Honestly, I'm too busy being worried about Jahir to be too hard on myself about it. He feels everything so much."

"Not always a good thing," Sehvi said.

"But not always a bad thing, either." Vasiht'h frowned a little. "You need both."

"Sounds like he's got all the feeling and you've got all the not enough?"

"Maybe," Vasiht'h said, thinking that it might be true. "Or maybe I haven't gotten to the things that would make me feel too much, yet." He sighed. "I've got this research study to finish, and it's limping along because I keep contaminating the data. I'll probably end up invited to some sort of wake. And I've got a roommate to keep from self-destructing. I'm ready for this semester to be done, ariishir."

"My poor, big brother," Sehvi said, shaking her head. "If I could come bake cookies for you, I would."

"I know," he said with a smile.

They talked then, of other things: of her research (going much better than his), of her fellow students, of the irritations of grant-writing. It was a calming conversation, and he was glad to have it, to listen to something normal. But when his sister terminated the call and left him alone in his room, he found his head back in his arms, and his thoughts again on his roommate.

His roommate . . . who'd called him 'arii', finally. When had he gone from alet, a formal form of address, to arii, the intimate?

Did it matter? Jahir had not rejected the mindtouches, and had called him friend.

After a moment, he pushed himself up and went to make dinner, and to make sure his friend ate. He almost made it out the door, too, before the chime went off, and he stopped to check the message header. Then he frowned, spreading the message. It had been sent to him, Jahir and to several other people, and . . . it was no invitation to a wake. It was in fact a privilege he hadn't expected, not at all.

He padded out into the great room, trembling, and forced himself to start on dinner. By the time Jahir came out of his room, the meditation of chopping vegetables and starting the pots warming had calmed him down.

"Did you receive . . ."

"Yes," Vasiht'h said, setting down his knife. "Do you know how much of an honor it is?"

"I . . . no." Jahir sat on the chair facing the kitchen, so he could look that way. "There is some custom here that I haven't apprehended, I am guessing."

"We should have been invited to the wake," Vasiht'h said, going back to the vegetables, but more slowly, watching his fingers. "For Tam-illee, that's where most people end up. That's when people talk together about the deceased. The funeral . . . the funeral's for people who meant something to the person who died. We get ashes."

"Ashes," Jahir repeated.

"Some of her remains. We get anointed on the forehead with them. Usually it's for family and close friends only."

Jahir was silent for long enough that Vasiht'h feared he'd set off some terrible reflection in him. But all his roommate said was, "I pray you will educate me in the formalities, so that I do no dishonor."

"As much as I can," Vasiht'h said. "I haven't been to one myself, but I know about it from friends. We can look up the information together."

"Thank you," Jahir said.

"I'm making soup," Vasiht'h added. "It's light, it should go down easily. And you will eat it. Won't you?"

"Soup sounds very good," the Eldritch said, but he sounded distracted. Vasiht'h frowned but held his peace.

CHAPTER 22

T HE FUNERAL WAS BEING HELD in a park off campus. He and
Vasiht'h left the university via Pad and took a tram the rest
of the way. He was aware of the transport, distantly. Of how clean
it was, how functional to be so elegant: the vast windows, and
the green of spring smearing in them from the speed. No experience in his life had prepared him to gauge distances between
places without the steady gait of a horse to beat them out, or the
cadence of his own feet. He could have been a thousand miles
from the apartment or one, and he couldn't tell, and he wondered how much of that was his own lingering alienation.

It would not last, he knew. The ritual hung before him like
the point of a sword, caught in that endless now between the
initiation of a lunge and the wound it opened. But he was ready
to be done with existing in stasis, with being unwilling to truly
face the path before him.

They arrived at the park, into a day that presaged summer,
hot and dry and so bright the grass shimmered like mirrors
beneath the breeze, leaving afterimages when he blinked. The
congregants were waiting at the top of a hill, and the Tam-illee
custom of wearing white to funerals made them blaze, so that his
eyes watered.

Vasiht'h stopped beside him, looking up the hill, then over at
him. Quietly, he said, "We're here. You ready?"

"Who is ever ready?" Jahir asked. "And yet we must do our
duty, in despite."

Vasiht'h shifted his shoulders beneath the white vest,
mantled his wings. "So we must." He set off up the hill, and Jahir
followed.

Nieve's grandmother, as the oldest surviving member of the
family, was waiting with a small wooden box. The sun gilded her
pale gray fur, gave her a mandorla; her patience seemed other-
worldly. Age, then, did not confer equanimity, he thought. He
was probably her elder by a good sixty years, but he could not
accept this death with the calm she exhibited.

"We're all here," she said at last. "So let's begin." With no
fanfare, she turned to Nieve's father. "With you, Deron."

The Tam-illee dipped his head, and Nieve's grandmother
opened the box, touching her thumb to a strip on the inside and
smearing it on his brow, then putting her fingers in the ashes
and wiping them on the mark. "She once told me that one of the
things she loved about you was that you never stopped grieving
for her mother. Because it made clear how much you loved Elise,
and kept her a part of the family."

The Tam-illee closed his eyes, teeth bared from the effort
of not crying, and managed to say, "Now I will keep them both
alive."

And so it went: everyone came to be marked, was told something Nieve had said about them, and shared something in return.
The family and friends of the family first, of which there were
only seven—so few, Jahir thought, to cling to, with so much grief
to share—and then came the rest of them. A schoolteacher, the
last one Nieve had had before she'd been forced to live full-time
in the hospital. The principal surgeon who'd worked on Nieve's
case, a middle-aged Seersa whose sorrow seemed as much shock
as anything else. The most junior doctor in Nieve's surgical team,
who wept unashamedly. Berquist, who held her mask firm until
Nieve's grandmother said, "You . . . she said so many things of,

it was hard to choose one." And then she choked on a sob and covered her face, and trembled through the anointment.

Vasiht'h was second to last and stepped to it with grace, one Jahir found admirable and beautiful, torn between envy and pride and understanding the reasons for none of it.

"Nieve told me that it was a wonderful world, when you could meet a stranger over a jump-rope and have him turn into a friend," she said, brushing the ashes on. "She said it was proof that there was magic everywhere, just waiting."

Vasiht'h closed his eyes. When he opened them, his shoulders had relaxed. "Then I've done the Goddess's work, and I am grateful to have been Her instrument."

The Tam-illee nodded, and her smile was gentle, but pleased.

And then it was his turn, and he went to her. She looked up at him and beckoned him with her fingers. "You are a bit taller than the others, arii."

He dipped low then, realized belatedly that he would have to feel her touch on his bare skin, but she was already brushing him with her thumb: a chrism, and beyond the oil he felt her powerfully: her sorrow, her resignation, the length and breadth of her perspective, supported by years of living, of loss and laughter and watching life.

"She thought you a kindred spirit," she said, meeting his eyes. "And told me that it didn't matter how old you were, and how young she was, that you shared something deeper than what you both seemed on the outside."

And what came out of him was, "She was right."

The old woman nodded and smeared the ashes on his brow. Then she turned and opened the box, holding it to the wind, and gently poured it onto a breeze that bore it away with the perfume of flowers. The congregants watched, their silent goodbyes so powerful Jahir could feel it like a wave of coolth, the pain of it given away, eroded.

After that, the first few participants began to leave. Jahir looked down from the hill, wondering where Nieve would gambol now with the wind. She would have delighted in it, he thought.

To dance like some sylph of the season, bringing the scent of new blossoms to unexpected corners.

"This is what it's like for you, isn't it," Berquist said. He had not noticed her coming to stand at his side; he glanced down at her and found her looking into the distance. The wind had tousled her hair, left it loose to frame her face: one of its strands had caught on the chrism on her brow, a line of gold against gray.

"Pardon?" he asked.

"This is what you can expect," she said, and raised her face to study his. "To stand like this at the funerals of the people you let into your life."

Had her voice been accusatory or pitying, he might have flinched. But she said it with all the trained distance of a healer-assist, who dealt with suffering and death every day. "I am afraid so," he said after a moment.

She nodded and assayed a smile, faint and sad but honest. "You . . . oh, it would be so easy to fall in love with you. You're gentle and mysterious and courteous like something out of a storybook and—God, yes, gorgeous too." The sound she made would have been a laugh, had she given it more of herself. "But that's what we'll always be to you. A risk and a short road, and this waiting for you at the end. And anyone who loves you has to be okay with that. With what we'll do to you when it's over."

He stared at her, unable to speak.

"And I can't. I couldn't do that to anyone," she said. "But for the pleasure I had thinking about what it would be like . . . would it offend you if I said thank you?"

"No," he said. And then, because she had made him a gift, a great gift, he said, "If I gave you a moment's pleasure for so little cost, I am grateful."

That made her laugh, and then cry a little also. She wiped her eyes and said, "See, there you go again." Shaking her head, she said, "I'll see you next week."

"Indeed," he said. And added, "Alet?"

She paused, and he held out his hand. Startled, she looked at it, then up at him, asking permission with her eyes. He left his hand open and waited, and at last she came close enough to rest her fingers in his. He was gloved, but he felt her: deeply, her regret, her pain that death came too quickly for everyone, her commitment to barring it and her guilt that she couldn't, not often enough. He breathed through her sorrow until he could keep her hand without trembling, then brought her fingers to his lips and kissed them.

She rewarded him with a frisson of delight that pierced the gray veil over her emotions.

"Alet," he said. And then, "Jill."

She flushed and took her fingers back. And then inclined her head, resting her palm against her heart. "Lord Seni Galare."

He watched her go, a bright figure against the green lawn, the sun gilding her hair, saw her brush the back of her hand tenderly against her cheek.

"Life goes on," Nieve's grandmother observed as she joined him. When he glanced at her, she said, "Remember that, old alien, when you feel too much pain."

Because she seemed disposed to speech, because she loved poetry, and because he had no recourse to wisdom here among the short-lived Pelted save that he turned to one of them for it, he asked, "But how can it be borne?"

"The same as anything," she said with a sigh. "Day by day, and honoring them by learning what they had to teach you."

Vasiht'h approached, sat beside Jahir, attentive.

"I buried her mother before her," the Tam-illee went on. "And my sister besides. The only sense you can make of it, aletsen, is the sense you give it in your own heart. And like everything, you can choose to use those things to grow twisted or straight."

"And if there is no path to the sun but a twisted one?" Jahir asked.

"Then still, you grow toward the light," she said. She shooed them gently. "Go on now. Get back to living. None of us know the hour, so it's no use pretending otherwise."

Jahir bowed to her and headed down the hill, Vasiht'h trailing him. Once they'd reached the bottom, he glanced over his shoulder at the silhouette of the old woman in white, her face toward the sun.

"I don't know about you," Vasiht'h said, low, "but I don't think I've got a wake in me after that. What do you say we go home?"

"I think I would like that very well," Jahir said.

——⊷⊶——

After that, they had finals, and he acquitted himself well despite the weight of the material and how hard he'd had to work to acquire it. During that last week of the term he found himself taking a great many walks beneath trees grown lush and dark and over fields that had lost their spring flowers to summer's encroachment. These walks, he thought, were a gift from KindlesFlame and the Alliance's technology, which made it possible for him to ramble far from any aid without fear for what his light-gravity adapted body could bear.

It was the same technology that had failed Nieve, and would fail all the Alliance's peoples in the end.

He had attended funerals at home; they were an inevitability of a culture without advanced medicine, particularly among the young, the elderly, those attempting children. He had accepted those deaths as part of being Eldritch, as frustrating and heart-breaking as they were: the Queen would have brought technology to the world, had a xenophobic people been willing to accept it from outsiders.

Was the pain of that worse than the pain of having access to such wonders, and knowing that they failed? An Eldritch he befriended might pace him through centuries, and pass away after a thousand years of amity . . . or he might die as Jahir's father had, centuries too young from a riding accident. Nieve's grandmother would tell him—had told him—that a creature with a millennial lifespan might die at thirty, and a creature who would live only a hundred years might live all hundred, and there was no predicting either. She was right, he knew. But it was too hard to bear in his heart, where such decisions were made.

To love in the Alliance, he thought. Because inevitably there would be love.

At the end of the week he made an appointment with Khallis Mekora, his graduate advisor. When he arrived, she greeted him absently, waved him to a chair as she pulled up his record. "So, alet," she said. "What can I do for you?"

"Summer term," he said. "It seems a short one?"

"It is," she said. "Sixty days instead of ninety. Most people use it to pursue research projects, electives or minors." She glanced up at him. "You're planning to use it for something, I assume?"

"I would like to," he said. "I have chosen a concentration and I suspect I will need the summer to make up ground I might have lost on other classes this term."

"Very good," she said, shuffling through the interface. "And that concentration would be—"

"Medical," Jahir said. "And the faster I move through it, so much the better."

"Well," Palland said, studying his data tablet. "On the whole, I say it could have gone worse."

Vasiht'h flicked his ears back. "That's not exactly a glowing recommendation, sir."

"Oh, hells, alet," Palland said, tossing the tablet aside. "It's not your fault. Not the way you're thinking, anyway. You're essentially pioneering psychic therapy. I have a notion how to put the research together, but the ways it keeps getting contaminated . . . you can't really plan for that. The mind is still too complicated for any of us to deconstruct, no matter what we might know about the brain it sits in. Add the fog layer of esper abilities—which we know even less about—and it gets hairy."

Vasiht'h flexed his toes and sighed. "But it's still not much good."

"You got useful data out of seven people," Palland said. "That's a good start. You can build on that in your next study."

"My next study," Vasiht'h repeated, ignoring his sudden

dismay. He remembered his predictions for Jahir about the course of his research and feared he was about to hear every one of his suppositions confirmed.

Palland's next words did not hearten him. "Oh yes. Seven people doesn't make a useful data set. You'll be repeating this study for a few years, I'm betting. Iterating it each time to get closer to a pure result."

"A few years," Vasiht'h said, suppressing a flinch.

"Did you expect any differently?" Palland said. "This is what research is, alet. It's sifting results, tossing out the ones that can't be used because you did something wrong or didn't control for some variable you didn't realize would be important. And then it's repeating it over and over until you get something you can usefully generalize as applying to the population at large. Once you do that, then you can maybe start refining the results."

"Refining them how?" Vasiht'h asked.

"Oh, say . . . you have data here for seven people all of whom are Pelted," Palland said. "But you haven't pulled the data out and looked for distinct results within each species because you don't have enough data to do that with. You start getting hundreds of results, you can maybe start looking for trends. You didn't have a Glaseah in your study, for instance. Does this psychic therapy work better on them because they're also espers? Or is there some cancellation of the effect? That sort of thing." Palland tapped the tablet. "I'm being conservative when I say this could take a few years. To be honest, if you're really serious about this, you could make it your life's work."

"My life's work," Vasiht'h repeated. "To research the effects of dream therapy on people."

"Yes," Palland said. "It would be an amazing career, too. You'd be giving talks all over the Core, I bet." He grinned. "You like traveling? It can be fun, jetting all over the Alliance to give lectures. Pretty good pay too."

"That part doesn't sound too bad," Vasiht'h admitted.

"Well, think about it, and get me a plan for summer term," Palland said. "Summer's a good time to do this sort of work.

You can afford to take a light course load since you'll be working toward your degree with the directed studies. Now, aren't you due over at the hospital?"

"Right, I'm picking up the last of the surveys," Vasiht'h said and rose. "Thank you, sir."

"My job," Palland said, waving it off. And added, with too knowing a look, "This is the life you're signing up for, Vasiht'h. Just so you're aware."

"I know," he said, and did. Which was part of the problem. He left his professor's office, agitated. It was one thing to look forward to being a professor teaching students, and another to realize that most of his time would be devoted to doing something he found frustrating or tedious (or both!) in order to earn the right to that classroom. And while traveling the Alliance on a lecture circuit sounded like fun, he wasn't sure how he felt about making psychic therapy research his 'life's work.' Especially if it worked. *If* it worked. With seven people to go on, he could be imagining it all, no matter how rigorous his methods.

He was not in the best of moods when he passed into the hospital lobby; distracted by his own thoughts and wanting only to collect the last few surveys from his subjects so he could go home and mourn. Though what he'd be mourning, he couldn't be sure of. Increasingly he thought it was less the paucity of his study results and more his life . . . and how ridiculous was that, when this was the point where his life should be opening up, full of opportunities? Opportunities so exciting he was willing to work hard for them?

Something was wrong, and he felt it as an oppression. It was so involving that he almost bumped into Kievan First, who was waiting for him at the desk. Shaking himself, Vasiht'h said, "I'm so sorry, alet! I didn't see you. I didn't—"

"No, no, I'm fine," the Tam-illee said. "I was hoping to catch you before you finished the study."

"Ah?" Vasiht'h turned to face him more fully, frowning. "What's this about?"

"I'm having a Renaming, and I was hoping you'd attend."

"A Renaming!" Vasiht'h exclaimed. "You're choosing a new Foundname?"

"I am," Kievan said. "I thought for weeks about what you said. About how there was nothing wrong with mistakes, and changing your course if it was the wrong course. And the more I thought about it, the more I thought . . . that maybe I'm on the right course." He squared his shoulders. "I think I needed permission to leave in order to realize how much I wanted to stay. So I'm renaming myself as a rededication. And I hope you'll come, since you were the one who helped me see the path."

"I may have helped you see the path," Vasiht'h said, startled, "but you were the one who decided what it meant to you, and what to do—" He trailed off, because the Tam-illee was smiling, and it was a friendly, easy smile, and a little whimsical. It made him smile too. Grin, actually, wide and honest. "Of course I'll come. Send me the time and place and I'll be there."

"Thanks, alet," Kievan said, satisfied. "I'll do that."

All the way home, Vasiht'h floated on that encounter. When he got to the apartment, he hunted through the storage closet for a sheet of colored paper, bought for the occasional invitations and gifts. The u-banks were full of step-by-step instructions for paper folding, and using them he made a very credible image of the Goddess, with one sheet for Her upper body and forelegs and a second for the hindquarters and wings. She was bright red with gold stars and swirls—the only paper he'd had, but he thought it suited Her quite well. He put this effigy on the hearth and lit a stick of incense in front of it, then sat with his forelegs stretched before him and hindlegs neatly tucked beneath him, in conscious mimicry of Her pose. Folding his hands, he bowed his head and closed his eyes, and said a thank you. For Kievan, of course, but for all the things he'd been neglecting in the past months, having been too busy to visit the siv't. And when he was done, he left the incense burning and made cookies, feeling confused but lighter in spirit than he had for days. He left the first cookie for Her.

Jahir came home a few hours later and immediately stopped at the door. "There is a smell, like myrrh."

"And myrrh is?" Vasiht'h asked, curled up in the great room with his data tablet and a cup of kerinne.

"Ah," Jahir said, spotting the trail of smoke in the air. "Incense." He removed his boots and sat on the chair facing the hearth; Vasiht'h watched him, watched the pupils dilate in the honey-colored eyes as his friend studied the makeshift altar. That was a form of listening, he thought. To really look at something, to try to understand it. It's what would make the Eldritch good at practice. Who wouldn't be flattered by such dedicated attention?

At last, Jahir spoke. "The goddess . . . likes cookies?"

"Brains need a lot of carbohydrates to function," Vasiht'h said. "And She does nothing but think."

Jahir chuckled, a sound that was too tired for Vasiht'h's taste, but it was a laugh. He hadn't heard his roommate laugh since Nieve's death. "I cannot argue the science, having suffered through a semester of physiological psychology."

"No, you can't," Vasiht'h agreed, pleased. "And there's a cookie for you in the kitchen."

"And if I eat it, will you tell me what prompted this?" Jahir asked.

Vasiht'h wrinkled his nose. "Not fair. How'd you figure out how to manipulate me?"

"You are very dedicated to feeding me," Jahir said. And added, resigned, "And I have not been diligent about eating, and I know I have given you cause for worry. I am sorry, arii."

Vasiht'h pursed his lips. Then said, "You'll eat the cookie?"

"I'll eat the cookie," Jahir said, and rose to fetch it. He brought it back, with a very small cup of the leftover kerinne. For someone with an insatiable ice cream tooth, he was very sparing with other high-fat sweets. "So. The goddess? May I add She is very beautifully done."

"Making Goddess effigies is very popular among us," Vasiht'h said. "It's part of honoring Her mandate to make things." He set his cup down. "One of my research subjects told me today that I helped him. That was a good feeling. I wanted to show my gratitude properly."

"This was an effect of the research?" Jahir asked, sampling the cookie.

"No, he was one of the subjects I had to discard. I contaminated him by talking to him," Vasiht'h said. He glanced at the incense, still ember-red. "I remember being unhappy when I found out that I'd lost all the time and effort I'd put into him. I'm glad he showed me that I had my head in the wrong place about it."

"Have you reached some conclusion about the research, then?" Jahir asked.

"No . . ." Vasiht'h said. "No. It's not just about how I feel now, after all. It's about what I want the shape of the future to be. What I want to spend my days doing. That part, I'm still not sure of. Starting a practice isn't all blankets and cookies. It's going to involve things I don't like. The question I have to answer, then, is if the things I don't like about research are worse than the things I don't like about practice. I haven't seriously started to explore those questions yet."

"That sounds like a worthy endeavor," Jahir said. He finished his little cup of kerinne and set it aside. "I have made my own choice."

Vasiht'h looked up at him sharply, then breathed out, seeing the tension in his roommate's jaw, an emotional pain made manifest in the body. "You're going medical."

Jahir brushed at the edge of the cookie, flaking off a few crumbs. "And you will tell me that you find that choice ill-advised."

"No," Vasiht'h said. "No, I wouldn't ever tell you that. Just . . ." He grimaced. "It wears you out so much. How can you keep that up, day after day?"

"Nieve's grandmother would say 'one day at a time,'" Jahir said.

"Nieve's grandmother would probably also say not to borrow trouble," Vasiht'h said. He sighed at Jahir's look. "But no, I won't belabor it. It's your choice to make, and if it's what you want, I'll support it."

"That is . . . very kind of you," Jahir said at last, and the words felt soft and damp with dew, and had some of the anticipation of dawn in them, and the quiet of it. Vasiht'h closed his eyes to savor the feeling; when he opened them he found the Eldritch watching him, and knew that mindtouch had been shared: that Jahir was aware of it this time. He wanted to pull back from it, but couldn't.

"It is . . . a wondrous thing. Isn't it." Was that awe? He thought it was, a quiet voice that belonged in a shrine.

"Glorious," Vasiht'h said even as it faded. He sighed, then said, "Eat the cookie. It's got jam in the middle."

"Jam in the middle!" Jahir said. "I will apply myself directly."

And he did, as the incense drifted up from the stick and the Goddess watched with what he couldn't help but think was both approval . . . and mischief. Surely that boded well? He hoped.

CHAPTER 23

"I CAN'T SAY I'M SURPRISED," KindlesFlame said. "How do you feel about the decision?"

"Resolved," Jahir said. "There is a great deal to draw one to the practice of medicine in the Alliance."

"So long as you're not confusing the tools of medical practice with the practice itself," KindlesFlame said, stirring honey into his coffee. "The most effective medicine is often the least invasive."

"That comment would seem to invite elaboration?" Jahir said, glancing at him.

"You haven't heard that before?" The Tam-illee huffed. "You should get it engraved on your forehead so you can see it every day in the mirror. You'll need it where you're going." He lifted his spoon as if to underscore the point. "We've had discussions about patient autonomy before, yes?"

"Yes," Jahir said, curious.

"There is a level of autonomy that exists here," KindlesFlame tapped his brow. "The obvious one, where we negotiate the patient's treatment with the patient. But there is another level of autonomy, a cellular level. The body feels it has the right to solve its own problems, and often it will with very little intervention from us. If we respect and support the healing process, then the body will demonstrate to us its power. When we intervene in a way that disrespects that autonomy, we often do harm with the good that we do. We have to be careful how we usurp that autonomy, or we'll sabotage the healing completely." Kindlesflame pointed the spoon at him. "The lightest touch possible. That's what we aim for. In any form of medicine, psychiatric or not."

Ridiculously, Jahir's first thought was of how much more effective gentling horses was than breaking them. He was entirely sure the Tam-illee would find the metaphor bizarre, but it stuck. He said, "You would tell me then, that I am infatuated with the technology of medicine, and might forget that the goal is not to use it unless absolutely necessary?"

"I am telling you that medicine is ninety percent indigestion, lifestyle adjustments and head colds and ten percent heroic measures," KindlesFlame said. "Don't lose sight of that."

"I shan't," Jahir promised. "But I am still intent on my course."

"Then impress me with your dedication," KindlesFlame said. "And I'll help you get one of the good residencies. You've got some time, yet . . . they're awarded at the beginning of summer, so you'll have a good two years to prove yourself." He grinned. "You could even take a vacation for a term, if you work hard enough."

"The degree is four years, not five," Jahir said. "Two years of education, two years in residency. I have been in school for almost one already—"

"The degree is four years, if you hit the ground running," KindlesFlame said. "Unless you loaded up on the medical track electives last fall . . . ?"

"No, but I am planning to make up for lost time in summer," Jahir said.

The Tam-illee flicked his ears back. It was the first time he'd done so in front of Jahir; it made him think abruptly of Sheldan's diatribes about controlled body language. "You know summer's a short term. And you're not going to have any margin for error if you go all out."

"I know," Jahir said. "I'm still willing."

"Obviously you're willing," KindlesFlame said. "The question is . . . why? What's your rush? You have the time."

"I may," Jahir said. "But if I am to live in the Alliance, Healer, I must surely live at its pace."

The Tam-illee leaned back and crossed his arms, regarding him as if he were some interesting puzzle. "You remember my lecture about using the talents and advantages we were born with?"

"I do."

"Then, if you'll forgive me for being blunt—one of yours is time. Is the leisure to take things at a healthier pace. Why wouldn't you take advantage of that?"

It was a good question. Particularly since Jahir had no idea what was driving him so powerfully. An anxiety, he thought, too deep to be examined: a sense that no matter how slowly he lived, everything around him was slipping away . . . flowers that sprouted already dying, and him powerless to change them. "I may avail myself of those years, it's true, alet. But the people around me can't."

KindlesFlame looked away—to hide his eyes, Jahir thought. Then he sighed and took up his cup. "If you're going to rush it, then, at least rush it smart. Stagger the practicum with the straight lectures. People born to this gravity well and still in their prime have burnt themselves out trying to front-load the simulation classes."

"I am grateful for the advice," Jahir said. "And I'll be sure to do so. The advisor assigned to me has been very helpful, though she issued her share of warnings to me."

"Did she?" KindlesFlame said.

"Her exact words were 'if you want to eat, breathe and sleep school, that's your business. But don't expect a social life.'"

The Tam-illee snorted. "That sounds about right."

"To be truthful, Healer," Jahir said. "I look forward to it. To have a challenge . . ." He drew in a long breath, let it center him. "That is no small blessing."

"Let's see how well you like your blessing by this time next year," KindlesFlame said dryly.

—— ∞∞∞ ——

The invitation to Kievan's ceremony arrived in Vasiht'h's box the following day: it would be held at the general campus's shrine to Iley, rather than at the hospital's multipurpose chapel, on the down-week rest-day at the end of the month, in the afternoon. A response was requested: would he and guest be able to attend?

Vasiht'h hit 'yes' before he finished reading, and then sat up. And guest!

"Would you like to come with me to a Tam-illee rededication ceremony?" he asked Jahir when his roommate arrived later in the afternoon.

"I beg your pardon?" Jahir asked, pausing on the way to the great room's chair.

"I've been invited to a Renaming for one of the healers-assist at the hospital," Vasiht'h said. "And I'm allowed to bring a guest. Would you like to go? The Tam-illee have them when they change their Foundnames."

"I would be glad to," Jahir said. "I don't know the customs, though."

Vasiht'h smiled. "Me neither. I'll have to look them up before I go. Living here's gotten me used to a lot of Seersan customs, but not so much the Tam-illee ones. We'll figure it out." He padded to the kitchen to start the baking for the quadmate gathering. A crumble, he thought: the stone fruits were coming into season, and Jahir had brought home a bag of peaches that smelled divine. He started measuring out the ingredients for the batter. "You have any plans for the end of term? We've got the entire month off before summer session."

"I fear my plans involve studying for summer's classes," Jahir said. "The term is short enough that I find myself concerned over whether I'll be able to manage them."

Vasiht'h frowned. "Just how many classes are you taking?"

"Five," Jahir said. "The same as spring and winter."

"Five!" Vasiht'h put his spatula down. "Are you crazy?

Summer classes are—"

"Notoriously condensed, yes, I know," his roommate said with a sigh. "And of the catalog available I've chosen the ones least likely to be impossible when shortened thus. But I want to be done with the coursework by this time next year, arii. The good residencies are awarded at the beginning of summer."

"That's so soon," Vasiht'h said. He couldn't make himself pick the spatula back up. The crumble suddenly seemed very unimportant.

"I don't want to spend forever in school," Jahir said. "There are things to be done outside it." And then, chagrined. "Ah, I do not mean to imply that being a teacher is an unworthy goal."

"I didn't take it that way," Vasiht'h answered. "Some people aren't suited to the university life, and that's all right."

"Just so," Jahir said. "Shall I help you?"

Vasiht'h forced himself to resume mixing the batter. "I'm almost done with this part. I just need to cut the peaches."

"I can do that for you." Before Vasiht'h could object, the Eldritch joined him in the kitchen, bringing with him a mind-touch, something deeply unsettling that Vasiht'h's mind interpreted as the unexpected revelation of rot in food. And it was very much a subconscious thing: he could feel a layer floating over it, like the smell of baking bread. He wondered uneasily if this was what was driving his roommate's decisions, and if so how it could be helped, or fixed. He couldn't imagine living with that unexamined anxiety.

That he'd sensed something so layered didn't help at all. The last thing he needed was the mindtouches growing more frequent and more complex.

"I would not want you to censor yourself on my behalf," Jahir said, surprising him from his reverie. Vasiht'h glanced at his roommate, found his gaze fixed on the peach he was carefully slicing. The bright orange flesh against those white fingers, the ambrosial scent, the concentration . . . it was hard not to be struck by it, and to hate the thought of losing it to exhaustion—or success. Because if Jahir managed, he would be gone in a year, and Vasiht'h didn't want to lose his company.

"Excuse me?" Vasiht'h said.

"If you are concerned, upset, if you have things you would tell me but think I might not want to hear," Jahir said, and rested the knife on the cutting board to glance at him. "I hope you will tell them me, and not attempt to spare me. I value your opinion."

"You do?" Vasiht'h asked.

"I do," Jahir said, and resumed his work. "You keep me grounded, arii. I cherish that."

Cherish!

"Then I'll do my best to keep at it," Vasiht'h said.

⁂

Their quadmates were far less restrained when they heard Jahir's plan. Brett guffawed and said, "You trying to die young? Keep up with the rest of us?"

Leina covered her face. "Ugh, Brett, could you be any more tasteless."

"He could," Luci said. "Doesn't change that he's right." She peered at Jahir over her wine glass. "He is right, you know."

"Death by cramming," Brett said, lifting his own glass. "Self-willed academic suicides. The college is littered with them."

"For a college littered with them there aren't that many bodies lying around," Vasiht'h observed.

"They're all underground," Brett proclaimed. "Why do you think the grass is so green?" He leaned forward and waggled his brows. "Fertilized by the decayed remains of over-stimulated brain matter."

Jahir rested his cheek against his fist and lifted a brow.

"That is the most skeptical expression I've ever seen on him," Vasiht'h said to Brett. "Congratulations."

"What do I win?"

"More sangria," Leina said, pouring for him.

"What are you trying to prove?" Luci asked, ignoring the banter. "Because a plan like that's got to be hiding some psychological issue."

"That is the Vasiht'h's line," Mera said. The Ciracaana was slumped on the table, though Jahir suspected that was as much from over-indulgence as from the alcohol. He and Leina had brought more of the curry and everyone had eaten until they'd mopped their plates dry. "Yes? You, Glaseah. Trot out the therapeutic wisdom."

Vasiht'h snorted. "And practice without a license? No, thank you."

"I know the path is likely to be arduous," Jahir said, warming his hands on his coffee mug. "But I intend to walk it."

"You intend to hike it, and then collapse on it, and then crawl to the summit, is what you actually mean," Luci said with a sigh. "But I guess there are always a few who want to do things the hard way."

Brett snorted. "Spoken by the woman who always does things the easy way."

Luci stuck her tongue out at him.

The Harat-Shar followed them to their apartment after the gathering disbanded, carrying the tray with the sad remains of the peach crumble, which had been almost entirely devoured. Jahir thought the only thing that had saved it was Leina's hazelnut torte, which had been so dense Mera had accused her of hiding a neutron star in it. He opened the door for his roommate and the Harat-Shar and let them precede him before going to the kitchen to begin washing up. Vasiht'h filled a teapot and said, "So are you here to harangue my Eldritch?"

Luci smirked. "Would it make him change his mind?"

They both looked at him. He said nothing, and scraped the last servings of the crumble into a smaller bowl for storage.

"I didn't think so," Luci said, amused.

The tea steeped as the two of them bantered, and Jahir enjoyed the implied camaraderie, the safety of being here, among people he trusted.

When Vasiht'h gave the Harat-Shar a cup of tea, she brought it to her nose and sniffed the steam, had a sip. "I really just wanted to tell you that . . . I haven't spoken to him in a month."

He could not have seen or sensed Vasiht'h's pause in any normal way, and yet he felt it and shared it. He let his roommate ask for them both. "Arii? Your choice? Or his?"

"Mine," she said. "More or less, anyway." She rubbed her eye with her free hand, and then had another sip of the tea. "I love him so much it's too hard to be a little bit friends with him. It's easier not to talk to him at all. And I don't think time is going to change what we need, and can't give one another."

Vasiht'h sighed. "Oh, Luci. I'm sorry."

"Me too," she said, her voice trembling. She cleared her throat. "But . . . there's got to be someone else out there I can love who also wants what I want."

"You'll find someone," Vasiht'h said. "It's a big galaxy. And once you're done with school you'll be working somewhere with a lot of people in it. You're bound to meet someone new."

"I can hope," she said. And laughed a little. "You know, it's funny . . . half the reason I think I come here to talk about it is because you two have what I want."

Jahir had been accepting a cup of tea from Vasiht'h when she said this, and it startled them both.

"Excuse me?" Vasiht'h asked.

"I mean it," Luci said. "Look at you two. You're not just room-mates, the way Brett and I are. You keep house together. You cook together. You go out together. When you move, you don't bump into each other because you always seem to know where the other person's going to be." She rested her chin in her hand. "When I sit here and we're talking, I can feel it . . . like you're not two people, but a pair, with your backs to each other, facing out." She lifted her head. "Do you have that metaphor, or is it a Harat-Shar thing? It's part of the angel religion, the idea that on life's battlefield your partner is the person you trust enough to guard your back."

"The metaphor is self-explanatory," Jahir said, and it was, and it struck him powerfully.

"Well, that's what I want," Luci said. And added, "Except with sex. Personal preference there."

Vasiht'h laughed shakily. "Yes. At least you've got enough Harat-Shar in you for that."

"I do, don't I?" she said, and smiled. And sighed. "It still hurts. I keep waiting for the hurt to stop. But distance helps, a little. Makes it easier not to keep picking at the scab. I guess that's normal too."

"So I've heard," Vasiht'h said.

"And you agree, Tall and Pretty?" Luci asked.

Thinking of his own grief on the matter, Jahir said, "Distance makes many things bearable."

"I'll hope," she said. "For now I guess I'll go it alone. I'm used to it, even though it's not as nice as having someone to walk with." She pushed her tea cup across the counter and said, "I want to thank you for all you've done for me, listening to me complain about this. And yes, I know you're about to say it's not complaining, but let me make fun of it a little, it helps. Anyway. If there's anything I can do for either of you, tell me, please."

"We will," Jahir said, since Vasiht'h was still staring at her.

"Good," she said, and slid off the stool. "Then I'll leave you both to your cozy domesticity. Relish it for me." At the door, she paused and added, "And Pretty—you enjoy this moment right now. Because you're not going to remember any of the coming year." She pointed at him. "You let your roommate take care of you before you end up in the clinic again."

"I will so endeavor," Jahir said, and she huffed, mostly to herself, he thought. She left, closing the door behind her. He rinsed out his cup and returned it to the cupboard. "A woman of great perspicacity, Lucrezia. And introspective, as well." When Vasiht'h didn't answer, he reached over him for the teapot and refilled the Glaseah's cup. "Come now. What has she said that has shocked you so? She told us the truth she observed."

"It was . . . was . . ." Vasiht'h said and trailed off.

"Presumptuous?" Jahir guessed.

"Yes!"

He tried very hard to hide his amusement. "You did say she was Harat-Shariin enough." Vasiht'h glanced at him, wild-eyed.

"They do have a reputation for outrageousness."

Vasiht'h stared at him. Then at his cup. "You . . . refilled my tea."

"You should drink it," Jahir said.

"I think your schedule's going to kill you," Vasiht'h blurted.

"I trust you will help prevent that sorry fate." Jahir set the honey in front of his roommate. "Did not Lucrezia so adjure?"

"Uhn, there are so many bad ideas in the world," Vasiht'h muttered, rubbing his face.

"Then let us go forth and make those mistakes," Jahir said. "And learn something from them."

CHAPTER 24

Vasiht'h had been attending Seersana University since
he'd enrolled as an undergraduate, and for the life of him he
couldn't remember a single spring term that he hadn't wanted to
end sooner: to get to warmer, drier weather, to get to the holiday
before summer, to get to the shorter term with its less strenuous
expectations. But with finals looming he found he wanted everything to slow down, and nothing was obliging him.

Frustratingly, the more agitated he became, the calmer his
roommate seemed: as if, having made his decision, a great weight
had fallen from him. That little kernel of anxiety was still there,
Vasiht'h thought, but the relief of having chosen what to do
about it had given the Eldritch the peace he'd been absent since
Nieve's death.

"And what are we doing here?" Jahir asked.

Vasiht'h glanced past him as the Eldritch preceded him into
the room, then slipped in himself and shut the door. The girls
were grouped around Kuriel, who had a foot and hand in three
separate laps; the only one not participating was Meekie, who
was lying on her bed, eyes half-lidded.

"My mother said I could get my claws painted," Kuriel said.
"And Miss Jill said it might help me remember to keep an eye on

my hands and feet, stop bumping them so much."

"So we're painting them!" Kayla said. "Rainbow colors!"

"With flowers," Amaranth added.

"Or squid," Persy said, bent over Kuriel's foot and trying to hold one of her toes down for her tiny brush.

"And you approve of rainbow squid?" Vasiht'h asked her.

"Oh, rainbow squid are fine," Kuriel said. "I asked for a dragon, but Persy said my claws are too small."

"They're a lot bigger than my nails!" Amaranth said.

Kuriel wiggled the fingers of her free hand. "I want them to be super-bright so I won't hurt them anymore." She glanced over her shoulder and lifted her tail. "Look, I even got to dye it!"

The tip of the Seersa's tail was fluorescent blue. Vasiht'h sat next to the girls and said, "You are going to be the most colorful girl on the floor."

Kuriel grinned. "I asked my mom if I could get my fangs colored, too!"

"And?" Jahir said, pulling up one of the small chairs and having a seat.

"And she said 'when you start losing feeling in your gums, and not a moment before.'" Kuriel sighed and grinned. "I guess she had to say that."

"Do you paint your claws?" Amaranth asked Vasiht'h. "You have them, right? Four fingers, four toes, claws upon those?"

"I have them, yes," Vasiht'h said, and laughed at his roommate's expression. "You better tell Jahir the other half, he's never heard the rhyme."

"Five toes and five fingers, human nails linger," Amaranth said obediently, and Kayla held up her five-fingered hand in demonstration.

"See?" Kayla said. "Nails. No retracting. I think it must be great to have claws you could hide in your fingertips! The rest of us have to use scissors."

"Or swords!" Persy said, bent over Kuriel's foot.

"You have a sword, don't you?" Amaranth added.

"A knife, at least," Jahir said. "As I said, I am no great lord to wear a sword."

"Oooh, that sounds like a story!" Kayla said.

"Yeah, and Vasiht'h-alet told the story last time, about Yuvreth riding the giant dragonfly," Persy said. "It's your turn!"

"A story about famous swords?" Jahir said, with a quirk of his mouth that was charming because he didn't seem to realize how it made him look: like someone who could laugh at himself. "I think I can do that. Let me see, how to begin—"

And begin he did, and told some sort of convoluted tale of a queen and her quest for the perfect sword, none of which distracted Vasiht'h from the realization that while his roommate had been wearing that smile, he'd been feeling something incredibly complex, something that tasted like iron filings in Vasiht'h's mouth, and smelled like oil and crushed velvet, musty with age, and all of it felt like pain and honor and regret.

He knew, of course, that his roommate kept his secrets close but he'd never had such incontrovertible evidence, both of that enigmatic past and the fact that the mindtouches could give him a window into it. He would have expected to feel shut out at this proof, to resent Jahir for not talking. Instead, it gave him a feeling very nearly like glee: that such secrets existed, and that he might know a little more about them than anyone else could. He rubbed his face, weary, wondering what was going to happen to him when Jahir left. More research, of course. A classroom eventually. Would having years and years of students to mentor make up for the friendship he'd never expected to make, and the mindline he'd never dreamed he'd be capable of?

At the end of their visit, Vasiht'h finished tucking in his two volunteers alongside the already sleeping Meekie and left Jahir to the remaining three. Jill looked up as he stepped outside the room and said, "Ah, here you are. So when can I sign up for your study?"

Vasiht'h managed a chuckle. "Since you already know what I'm testing, I can't use your results, alet."

"Can I pretend otherwise?"

If he hadn't known better, he would have wondered if she

was wheedling. Was she really serious? He peered at her. "I'm afraid it really would prejudice the results."

"It figures," she said and sighed. "Everyone's been talking about it. They're hoping to get into your next group."

"They are?" Vasiht'h said, startled. "Really?"

"Oh yes," Jill said. "The people who went through it this semester are so much better off. *And* they can't stop talking about it, the bastards." She wrinkled her nose. "I swear they want to see the rest of us squirming in envy."

Jahir closed the door behind him and joined them.

"You're making a joke?" Vasiht'h guessed.

"Oh no," Jill said. "Absolutely not. There's not a person who's gone through that study with you who wasn't glad they did it. When you repeat it—you're going to, right? Twenty people isn't enough?" She waited for his nod before finishing, "you won't want for volunteers. Assuming you're conducting it here. Please say you are?"

"I . . . I hadn't thought that far ahead," Vasiht'h stammered.

"Well, do it here!" Jill said. "You can expand it to some other hospital another year." She grinned. "Not that I'm biased or anything, but we make good subjects, right?"

"You do, yes," Vasiht'h answered, though whether the children's hospital staff would be any better at sleeping than the general hospital's was beyond him. "I . . . could probably conduct at least one more survey here, sure. I didn't get all of you yet. But I really should talk to my major professor about it, see what he says."

"Do that," Jill said. "And if you decide to start using that technique on normal, paying clients, tell me so. I'll be your first customer."

He wanted to protest that he had no license and in fact would not be earning one given the track he was on, but he couldn't find the words. Instead he said, "I will," and let Jahir shepherd him away. They passed through the lobby, out into the sun, and the Eldritch stayed behind him and beside him the entire way, guiding him by forcing him to move or bump their sides.

"Your technique works," Jahir observed once they'd gotten to the sidewalk.

"Twenty people isn't a useful sample size," Vasiht'h said automatically, but he was still reeling and he knew his roommate could tell. He said nothing, and left the Glaseah to his thoughts.

What Palland said after hearing Vasiht'h's report—his brows lifting with each passing word—was, "Get a post-study follow-up done."

"Sir?" Vasiht'h said.

"I can get you some permission forms," Palland said, tapping his lip and frowning. "I have some with relevant verbiage. The consent forms you had them sign didn't mention a follow-up, and since everything else was set out in detail it's not going to work for this application."

"Sir?" Vasiht'h said again. "You mean even the contaminated subjects?"

"Especially the contaminated ones," Palland said. "Keep all your bases covered, alet." He glanced at Vasiht'h over his desk. "You look flustered."

"I am," Vasiht'h admitted, rubbing his forepaws together where he hoped the professor couldn't spot them. "I had this notion that the research would be . . . tidier. Instead, it just keeps getting messier and harder to get my arms around."

"That's to be expected when you're embarking on something no one else has studied yet," Palland said. "Think of it like being in the wild, woolly woods. No tracks yet to follow, and you and your machete have to start cutting a space big enough for you to even look at your surroundings and decide where to start hacking out a path."

Vasiht'h grimaced. "That sounds . . ."

"Yes?" Palland said, waiting.

"Overwhelming," Vasiht'h finally said.

"Some people would find it exhilarating," his professor said, with a little too neutral a tone.

Vasiht'h folded his arms. "I'll get a handle on it. And before you say anything, when was the last time you mentored a student who decided to tramp into woods so woolly no one had been there first?"

"Admittedly it's a rare thing for students to do work this groundbreaking."

"Then maybe you should let me feel overwhelmed about it," Vasiht'h said. "I'm going to have a lot of people examining what we're doing, given how new it is. That's got to be intimidating even for people used to it."

"Depends on the person," Palland said. "Some people have egos so immense they can't function without that level of attention. Speaking of which . . . how did that hypothetical situation resolve itself?"

"The what?" Vasiht'h asked.

"The hypothetical professor with the problem student?" Palland said, resting his laced fingers on his chest and quirking a brow.

"Oh! That hypothetical situation," Vasiht'h said, chagrined. "I don't know. I think—hypothetically—that the professor hasn't done anything more."

"I see," Palland said. "And the term's about to end. I trust this hypothetical professor isn't going to flunk your friend because of it."

"I never said it was one of my friends' teachers!" Vasiht'h said.

The Seersa chuckled. "Of course you didn't. But you don't get worked up over your own problems the way you do when they involve people you care about. Should I tell you my hypothesis?"

"I won't confirm it if you guess right," Vasiht'h said warily.

"My hypothesis," Palland said, "is that you're talking about your roommate, because you're very protective of him. And since your roommate is a new student, I'm guessing he's going through the core classes, and that means he's run into Sheldan. I'm betting that describes your hypothetical situation very well."

Vasiht'h stared at him, agape.

"I'll be nice and ignore that your expression is confirmation enough, even without words," Palland said.

"How . . . how did you . . ."

Palland shook his head. "Let's just say we know about Sheldan. He's brilliant and he's got his partisans, so we keep him around. But he's on the misanthrope team and this isn't the first time he's been rude to a student."

"There's a misanthrope team?" Vasiht'h asked, aghast.

"Oh, sure," Palland said. "Alet. This is the psychology faculty we're talking about. Half of us teach because we love helping people, and teaching is a way to intersect a vulnerable population and help them get through a critical time in their lives. But the other half teach because they like knowing how people work, and they like proving it to themselves and others. Psychology for them is a weapon, a way to give themselves power over others. They don't actually like people at all." His smile was crooked. "So, you see why I'm fine with you pursuing the research even though we both know you're not enjoying it. You'll end up on the good team if you make it through, and Speaker-Singer knows we need more good teachers."

"I had no idea," Vasiht'h said, ears flattened.

"Now you do," Palland said. "So, should I find you those permission forms?"

"I . . . yes. Please," Vasiht'h said.

"Very good."

As the Seersa reached for his data tablet, Vasiht'h said, "I never had problems with Sheldan."

"Of course you didn't," Palland said. "You're third-generation Pelted. For people like Sheldan, there are only two types in the worlds: the victims of engineering, and the ones doing the engineering."

"Doesn't seem very nuanced," Vasiht'h muttered.

"Hate rarely is."

CHAPTER 25

T HE DAY OF THE REDEDICATION was hot enough to please even his roommate; Vasiht'h marked his enjoyment by the occasional blink that lasted too long, even caught him tilting his face up to the light. He wondered if Eldritch tanned—or burned, for that matter—and had to guess not, given the way Jahir soaked in heat.

"Have you been to this part of campus?" he asked. "I know you've been taking more walks."

"I confine myself mostly to the medical campus," Jahir said. "So I have not yet seen the shrines."

Vasiht'h smiled. "I think you'll like it."

"Shall I?" Jahir asked, and that was a good flavor in Vasiht'h's mouth, like festival candy and the hope of new experiences.

He just smiled again and said nothing, and that flavor deepened until he could taste it in the back of his throat, something warm and good. It felt of one piece with the sunlight, and in it there was a hint of contentment from his roommate at the mind-touch itself. Goddess help them.

The university had built up a semicircular hill to serve the various religious needs of the student population, and surrounded it with old trees that draped the buildings with enshrouding limbs. The path led to a roundabout in the hollow, and from that roundabout little trails wound up the banks to the different shrines and temples. It was a very Alliance sort of place, Vasiht'h had always thought: so many different architectural styles, each in a cozy little subplot side by side, with the trees a unifying element that everyone could enjoy. The shade they cast, shifting with the breeze, was welcome as they stopped in the center of the roundabout.

"Is every religion represented, then?" Jahir asked, fascinated.

"Oh Goddess, no." Vasiht'h laughed. "You'd need a lot more space for that. Even the most homogeneous of the Pelted races have multiple religions. These are just some of the majors. The siv't for the Goddess is over that way, in fact." He pointed at the end of the hill. "But we're going to Iley's shrine. This way."

They went up the hill, joining a few Tam-illee who were heading for the ceremony. Kievan was at the door, greeting people as they entered; he beamed when he saw Vasiht'h and clasped his arms. "You came! I'm so glad!"

"I couldn't not come," Vasiht'h said, smiling. "I brought my roommate, Jahir, as my guest—"

"Ah, the Eldritch prince," Kievan said. "We've heard all about you and the girls in the ward." He grinned. "Go on in! Make yourselves at home. There will be food later, so I hope you're hungry."

They passed into the coolth of the shrine side by side. The sun fell in from the skylights on the slanted roof, bright on the splashing drops of a central fountain. The back of the room had another window, stained glass this time: Iley the laughing god, hands spread and ears pricked.

"I did not expect to be recognized," Jahir murmured to him after he'd taken a seat on one of the benches lining the walls. Vasiht'h had sat next to him on the floor at the bench's edge.

"I think it's asking a little much for us not to have been noticed," Vasiht'h replied. "We're in the hospital every week, after all."

"It is a large facility . . ."

"But a small family. The staff, I mean," Vasiht'h said. He

glanced at his friend. "You know it's always going to be that way, right? People are going to remember you no matter where you go or what you do."

"I suppose so," Jahir said. And, with a touch of amusement, "I wish I were a more exemplary sort of Eldritch, since I must serve as their ambassador due to scarcity of more official representatives."

"You're fine," Vasiht'h said. "And if other Eldritch aren't like you, I'm pretty sure we don't want to meet them."

He thought that won him a sharp look, but the ceremony was starting.

⸙

The ceremony had a joy to it that Jahir would previously had ascribed only to weddings; but naming, it seemed, was an important milestone in the life of a Tam-illee, implying as it did a life purpose. Rededications in particular merited celebration for representing a challenge overcome. He could appreciate such sentiments, as well as the elegance of the ritual itself: Kievan sat with the rest of the audience until a priestess called for him, and he protested that he no longer answered to that name. She asked him by what name he would be known, then, and he stood and declared for himself: Kievan StrongHeart, after a poem his father had been fond of reciting about the virtues of staying one's course.

The priestess presented him to the congregation then, announcing him by name, and they were done.

The only duty of the celebrants involved writing an aphorism or piece of advice for Kievan and leaving it in a wooden box for him to read later. Jahir wrote on the slip given to him, "Our choices shape our lives, and until we die we can make new ones." Then he joined Vasiht'h on the lawn for a tremendous picnic, spread out on summer-lush grass beneath the green shadows of the trees. And it was a delicious meal: roasted birds on a bed of toasted grains with julienned vegetables he couldn't identify but were perfect anyway, and baskets of rolls, both savory and sweet—filled with cream cheese, he thought, and honey and something else that he applied to Vasiht'h for enlightenment: "toasted walnuts, maybe."

He ate enough to satisfy even his roommate and then sat cross-legged on the grass, turning his face outward, toward the spread of the campus.

"What are you looking at?" Vasiht'h asked, offering him a champagne flute.

"Ah? Thank you," he said, receiving it from a hand that was careful not to brush his. "The world. And the endlessness of it."

Vasiht'h canted his head and looked toward the horizon with him. "You're looking in the wrong direction," he said at last.

"Am I?" Jahir glanced at him.

Vasiht'h nodded toward the sky. "You want real endlessness, look up. Look up, and know that out there are a thousand thousand worlds and billions of people, and it's all open to you."

Hearing it he felt it. The celebrating aliens at his back became part of a sweep all the way out to a crown of stars and he closed his eyes, humbled by the power of it, and by his own elation at the thought of embracing it all. For once, his lifespan did not seem a burden, but an opportunity . . . and while he knew that feeling would fade, he was grateful to have had it. Every joy he could use to balance the bittersweet, he would take.

"Do you feel it too?" he asked, because he realized he couldn't sense Vasiht'h's answer, and that this had become something strange.

His roommate lifted his chin and looked up, and in his eyes was something noble and true and good, something that made sense of his face. He smiled at that vista, and Jahir felt it then, the tranquility of spirit that was the Glaseah at his best, his most authentic.

So much of the Alliance had come to him mediated by this male, Jahir thought. Music and food, ceremonies and gatherings, language and culture, wisdom and understanding. Would he have loved the outworld as easily without this self-appointed guide?

"It's a good life," Vasiht'h said, quiet.

"So it is," Jahir murmured.

———∞∞———

"So let me see if I understand this," Sehvi said, pursing her lips. "Your actual research study is useless, but your post-research survey indicates that everyone who participated is less stressed? To the point that they're recommending you to their peers, who are now eager to sign up for your second study?"

"That's . . . about the shape of it, yes," Vasiht'h said, rubbing the side of his muzzle. When his sister didn't immediately reply, he looked up at her and found her eyes sparkling. "Oh, come on, Sehvi. It's not funny!"

"It is funny," she said. "It's comedy routine funny, ariihir. You're obviously useless as a researcher and brilliant as a therapist."

"I am not useless as a researcher," Vasiht'h said, flattening his ears. "I'm just new to it, and not very good at it yet. I need practice."

"Practice does help, sure," she said. "I don't know if it's going to help enough. Seriously, big brother. Why not give it up already?"

"Because . . ." Vasiht'h trailed off. He flexed his paws, realized he was kneading one of his floor pillows like a kit. He pushed it away. "Professor Palland was telling me that there are faculty members who are bad teachers."

"And this is news how?" Sehvi asked. "You've lived with our mother, same as me. You've heard her complaints about the teachers who are in it for the chance to do research, and who can't stand the classroom."

"I know," Vasiht'h said, frustrated. He looked away, tail lashing. "But I always thought it was a matter of them just being . . . thoughtless. Absent-minded. Maybe crotchety, the way Grandfather is when we drag his attention away from whatever he's got on his mind. But Palland says sometimes it's malice."

"Malice," Sehvi repeated, brows up. "That's a strong word."

"He as much said it," Vasiht'h said. "That some psychology

professors hate people. How can that be possible?"

"Same way it is for anyone, I guess," Sehvi said. "They have issues. Everyone has issues, ariihir." She rolled her eyes. "Ninety percent of my professors have issues. They're all hyper about reproductive engineering *because* they have issues."

"That's different," Vasiht'h said. "It's one thing to be afraid of something and then develop a complex about it. It's another to assume your position gives you the license to treat people cavalierly. Especially people who can't fight you about it, or feel they can't." He rubbed his brow. "It's horrible."

"Yes. Yes, it is," Sehvi said, studying him. "But it's not like it's common, ariihir, or there would be the Goddess's own scandals all the time. And I haven't heard anything about scandals in one of the Alliance's oldest universities. That would be big news no matter where you were."

"I know, I know. It just makes me think . . . maybe I really am onto something," Vasiht'h said. It felt like a good reason. It was one, he thought: he felt strongly about it. "Students deserve teachers who care about their success. I'd be a good teacher, Sehvi. I'd care."

"Sure you would," she said. "You care about everyone, ariihir. That's why you keep trying to help them."

"So I'm going to be good about the research," Vasiht'h said. "I'm going to practice doing it well. And when I get my terminal degree after all of this, I'm going to be one of those professors who helps people. Like Palland."

She studied him, then sighed. "It's your life, Vasiht'h."

"Yes," he said. "It is."

"And what about your roommate?" she said. "How's he doing? Still getting the mindtouches?"

Vasiht'h made a face. "Yes."

"Oh, now that's a look. What's wrong now?" she asked. "Other than him also making dumb choices?"

"I heard that," Vasiht'h said, scowling.

"I meant you to hear it," she answered. "So? Mindtouches? What's gone wrong?"

"It's not that things have gone wrong," he said, reluctantly. "It's that they keep going right. I think we're getting past mind-touches and into a primitive mindline. When I feel his feelings, I can tell he senses it. There's a circuit now."

"And he's not offended?" she asked.

"No," Vasiht'h said, drawing the word out. And sighed. "No. I think . . . I think he *enjoys* it, Sehvi."

"And that bothers you."

From her expression she was mystified, and he didn't blame her. He found his own feelings just as troublesome. "Yes. Yes! Of course it bothers me. He's an Eldritch, and he's not supposed to welcome these things—"

"I thought he told you he was fine with it?"

"—and even if he does welcome them," Vasiht'h continued, "what good will it do? He's pushing for his residency and planning to be doing it off-world by this time next year. I'm going to be here for the next six or seven or eight years, finishing my degree. What use is it to develop a mindline, just to have it ripped apart?"

Sehvi flinched. "I can't imagine that will feel good."

He thought of the growing connection and shuddered. "It won't."

"Well, maybe he'll come back?" she said, tentative. "His degree will put him to work in a hospital, and from what you've said he feels pretty strongly about All Children's. Maybe he'll end up there, and the two of you can see each other once in a while?"

"Seeing each other once in a while isn't enough," Vasiht'h said, looking away with bared teeth. "It's getting hard to imagine not having him around, Sehvi. A mindline—a real mindline!—I can't even describe to you what it's like, and we haven't even solidified it yet. The mindtouches alone . . . it's like . . ." He stopped. Swallowed. "It's like finding a twin you never knew you had. It's proof of a benevolent universe."

She looked at him for a long time. Then, quietly: "Have you told him that?"

"What good would it do?" Vasiht'h said. "He's set on this

course, ariishir. He's set on it and there's something driving it, something he has to answer. He's not going to turn from it. And I've got my own path to walk."

"It's too bad you can't walk a path together," she said. "You don't suppose—"

"No," Vasiht'h said, trying not to be brusque, but the idea that things could be different in some ideal universe hurt.

She sighed and smiled wanly. "Well, maybe he'll fail a few classes and have to slow down. You could keep him a few more years that way."

"Maybe," Vasiht'h said. "Maybe."

CHAPTER 26

𝒥AHIR WAS RELIEVED WHEN FINALS put paid to spring term. There was an agitation in him that made him yearn to have his back to the first year of his education. He had enjoyed his first two semesters, but having a clear path before him made him long to be running it. On the final day of the term, he attached the books for summer's classes to his account and spent a quiet afternoon rifling through them. His one 'light' class was on ethics; he had three lecture classes, one on traumatic disorders, another on the psychology of at-risk populations, and a third on derangements and other psychiatric side effects of drugs. His last class was another Clinical Management practicum, and while he wasn't looking forward to the accelerated version he consoled himself that he at least knew what to expect.

It was frustrating not to be able to begin immediately. It must have shown, because his roommate had one look at him when he entered the apartment and said, "Let's go out."

"Arii?"

"You need to keep moving," Vasiht'h said. "So let's go out. Get ice cream, climb trees, listen to music. Something."

"All three?" Jahir asked, hopeful.

Somehow they managed it—or more accurately, Vasiht'h

did, for he knew where to go to make it possible, with it being a night without a concert. The Glaseah led him to the art campus and they walked through the gardens by the music college, where they found several groups practicing in the pleasant evening air. If the music had a rough and unfinished quality, there was talent and energy in it all the same, and he loved it nearly as much as the musicians seemed to love having the two of them there to appreciate it. After that they walked to the gelateria, where the Asanii talked him into the zabajone and it was wonderful. From there, Vasiht'h led him unerringly to the tree he'd climbed that one afternoon. Jahir sat under it, rather than in it, and the Glaseah settled beside him, did not break the silence.

The mindtouches, Jahir thought, had grown more frequent. And he had become accustomed to them. It struck him as astonishing, that in less than a year he could have traveled from a place where such things were always painful and unwelcome to this place here, beneath a tree rustling in the summer evening's breeze . . . where he could get a vague sense of his roommate's steady aura, and find it reassuring. They sat together then, enjoying the easing of the heat, the chirping of insects in the grass.

"It's going to be a rough summer," Vasiht'h said at last. "Will you do something for me?"

"If I can?" Jahir glanced at him.

"Don't spend too much time pre-studying." Vasiht'h met his eyes. "Let me take you to concerts, and out for walks. Let our quadmates feed you. Have some wine—yes, I know you don't drink much, get it hidden in your ice cream if you prefer. Because when all this starts . . . you won't have time for any of that."

The thought of losing so many of the pleasures of the Alliance was painful . . . but temporary, he reminded himself. Three terms, and he'd be on his way to whatever residency he could qualify for. Another two years there and he'd be graduated and in practice. Surely that was worth the sacrifice. "You wish for me to give you these two weeks."

Vasiht'h drew in a long breath, let it out. "Yes."

Jahir rested his elbows on his knees, leaning forward. He

watched the wind bend the grasses, grown purple with the deepening eve. "A little like a bridegroom before his marriage, yes?"

"If the Eldritch have wild nights of celebration before they settle down," Vasiht'h said with a chuckle that sounded reluctant to Jahir's ears. "Yes."

"I would like to think I will not lose myself entirely to the work," Jahir murmured.

Vasiht'h surprised him with a snort. "You have no idea what you're getting into, arii. Not with school, and not with after it. This is a work that consumes you, now and forever."

Jahir glanced at him, surprised. "This from the person of no passions?"

"Maybe I wasn't completely right about that," Vasiht'h said. "Because I feel very strongly about helping people. So," he squared his shoulders. "Will you let me help you?"

"Always," Jahir said, and meant it.

Vasiht'h breathed out, seeming to lose some tension in his shoulders and withers. Not all of it, but . . . some. "All right," he said. "All right."

"So where shall we start?" Jahir asked, after the silence had grown ripe with his roommate's unshared thoughts.

"With the orchestra," Vasiht'h said, firm.

Jahir frowned. "Did not the student season end just now? With the conclusion of spring term?"

"The student season did," Vasiht'h said. "But the orchestra downtown plays all year round."

<hr />

For the performance downtown, Vasiht'h shook out his sari, crimson silk edged in gold swirls intended to evoke the breath of the Goddess, and carefully pleated it over his second back and between the wings before arranging it over his upper shoulders. He had a strong premonition about the coming months: that he would lose his roommate to the work, and that his roommate would not fail as Sehvi had suggested. He wasn't sure if what he was feeling now was mourning; maybe it was more preparation

for it. But he wanted Jahir to take something into the school year
with him, as much of the Alliance as Vasiht'h could roll into two
weeks.

He didn't know why this was necessary. He just knew powerfully that it had to be done, that it was the groundwork for
something important, and he trusted the instinct. When his
roommate joined him at the door, he asked, "Ready?" and they
both knew he was referring to more than one evening. It made
Jahir's steady, "Yes," all the more satisfying.

The capital's downtown concert hall was a sweep of silver
walls and vast black windows—on the top floor of one of the
capital's tallest buildings. The glass was so clear there seemed no
interruption between the plush wine-colored carpet they were
standing on and the night sky with its scattered stars and the
shimmering spread of lights from the buildings below them. It
was enough to give Vasiht'h vertigo, but his roommate stood
near the edge, so intent the mindtouches came in pulsing waves:
awe and a fascination so powerful it felt like need.

The Kavakell Symphony Orchestra was only slightly larger
than the university's, surely by no more than six or seven people.
But even Vasiht'h, who was not well-schooled in music, could
tell the difference between their skills. Usually he spent performances like this watching the musicians play, something he
found easier to enjoy than straining for the aural nuances he was
less equipped to hear. But the mindtouches raveled into a thin
line, and through it Jahir's enjoyment washed into him in gleaming waves, an undertow that made sense of the power of music.
He closed his eyes, and the fur on his shoulders rose.

Jahir didn't speak after they left the hall. Vasiht'h let him
keep his silence, sensing the distance his roommate was traveling to return from the world created by the performance. Truth
be told, having shared some part of it with him, he needed some
of that time himself, and marveled at it: how art could make the
real world seem alien. When they were both present again, he
said, "More?"

Jahir breathed out, then laughed, quiet. "More," he said.

———◦◊◦———

So they did more. Sometimes more was less, was easy: they cooked a celebratory dinner for their quadmates, during which they laughed at the vicissitudes of the student life, ate too much and drank too much, then cleaned up afterward in the quiet of their apartment with great contentment. But Vasiht'h also took him out to the city, to eat at tiny family restaurants maintained by generations of Seersa and ringing with the every-accent sound of their broad language; and to fancy restaurants with transparent floors set over fish ponds that allowed the discerning diner to choose their meal from beneath their feet. They walked through historic districts, took tours of museums and visited the Landing park, where the Seersa had first touched down: there were crete pawprints set on the lawn where the first few individuals had walked, and a reproduction of the shuttle they'd used to reach the surface from the great sleeper ships that had carried the Pelted away in the Exodus from Earth.

Vasiht'h felt Jahir's fascination like a cup he could fill and fill and never be done, and he loved every moment of it, and found himself beseeching the Goddess to let the days go by more slowly. But they came home from their final excursion—this one a whirlwind tour of the temples of the capital—and the holiday was over. Vasiht'h made himself kerinne and Jahir coffee and brought their cups to the little table in the great room.

"That was a proper vacation," Jahir said. "I feel glutted with it."

He looked it too: eyes bright and prone to an excited distance when not engaged. Vasiht'h smiled and said, "And we didn't even get to everything!"

"Ah?" Jahir said. "You cannot tell me you could have gone on like that!"

"It's a big world, arii," Vasiht'h said. "We didn't even get out of the capital! The sea's a big draw this time of year. And there are some amazing natural parks . . . there's a place on the western continent where the wind has shaped rocks into these natural flutes. When you walk through them, you can hear music."

Jahir laughed. "Enough, arii! Enough. There are only so many hours."

"Mmm." Vasiht'h sipped his kerinne.

"There will be time," Jahir said. "But duty first."

"Is this your duty, then?" Vasiht'h asked.

"To be useful?"

Vasiht'h glanced at his roommate, wondering at the gleam that had flashed between them, like the reflection off steel. "Is that what this is about?"

"Is that not every person's purpose?" Jahir asked. "To be useful? What more is there?"

"I don't know," Vasiht'h said. "Is love useful?"

"I would think your goddess would have an opinion on that."

Vasiht'h smiled and rubbed his thumb against the wall of his cup. "And what do you think She'd say, if you're so sure?"

"That to make something, one must feel something," Jahir said. "That there is no creation without a motive force. And that such forces should be positive, or the results become twisted and strange. Which would suggest that love creates the universe, or should." He grinned and set his cup down, folding his hands together on his knee. "So? Did I guess well?"

Vasiht'h gestured with a flourish. "I hereby induct you into my religion. In an honorary sort of way."

Jahir's expression turned mischievous. "I will be sure to eat a cookie for her."

"Do you really think we'll be useful?" Vasiht'h asked more seriously. "When this is over."

His roommate glanced at him, didn't answer immediately. Then he looked away and said, "Do you think there's some reason we might not?"

"I just wonder, that's all," Vasiht'h said, thinking about being a good teacher, a good mentor, a good role model to students. What kind of role model would he be? He couldn't imagine what he'd have to teach them. Would his path grant him the wisdom he'd need to be a good example? Or would he fall prey to bitterness and exhaustion?

"Our textbooks would tell us it is natural to feel anxiety about the future," Jahir said.

Vasiht'h snorted. "And does that make you feel any better about it?"

"No," Jahir said. And glanced at him with a rueful little smile that felt like a gift because of the insight it granted Vasiht'h into the Eldritch's vulnerabilities. "No, not at all. And then I just tell myself: one step, then another. Eventually, one reaches the destination."

"And if it's the wrong destination . . ."

"Then we re-orient and try a new path," Jahir said. And sighed. "It sounds the worst sort of pablum, doesn't it?"

Vasiht'h laughed. "Yes. Yes, it does. Why does it work?"

"I'm not sure it does!" Jahir said. "Save that, perhaps, we make truth out of the things we believe to be true. So it is well for us to listen only to good things."

"To your path," Vasiht'h said, and held out his cup.

There was a hesitation so slight Vasiht'h would have missed it had a mindtouch not hinted at Jahir's surprise, that this custom was shared. Then the Eldritch tapped his cup against Vasiht'h's and said, "And to yours. May they lead us where we belong."

CHAPTER 27

*T*AHIR HAD THOUGHT HE'D HAD no illusions about the difficulties of what he was undertaking; certainly he'd received warnings from so many quarters it was hard to imagine *not* being
prepared. But knowing something was very different from living
it, he thought the first day of class when his ethics professor
gave him twice the amount of reading to do, and a journal to fill.
The at-risk populations class, which came on its heels, was no
less enthusiastic with assignments. Three days into the semester, he found himself again in a simulation hall with Lasareissa
Kandara, the healer-assist instructor from spring term. She had
one look at him, put up her brows and splayed her ears. "You
back for more already? I thought you'd want a few months to
recuperate."

"I have not yet learned all that I must know," he said, and
couldn't tell if this was an apology or an explanation.

She huffed and shook her head. "Your skin, not mine, alet."

By the end of the week he was nose-deep in books. His intention had been to finish his work in time to help Vasiht'h put
together something to bring to the quadmate gathering, the first
of the new term.

He discovered he'd missed the gathering when he woke up on

his data tablet and books. At his elbow was a note: "There is soup in stasis. Please eat. –V."

"Not so sanguine about this now, are you," KindlesFlame said when they met for lunch several days later.

"I am still grateful for the challenge," Jahir said. "And I intend to meet it."

"Mmm," was all KindlesFlame would say, and pushed the menu to him.

⸺∘∞∘⸺

Vasiht'h had no lectures in summer; both his classes were directed studies, to be spent working with his major professor on his research. With Palland's help he adjusted his methods, and returned to the hospital determined to come out of it with a study he could use without discarding half its results.

At least, that was his plan.

"What do you mean there's too many people in the room?" Palland asked, squinting. "I thought the nap rooms were designed for privacy."

"They are if you tuck your body into them with your head in the alcove," Vasiht'h said. "If you lie down in the opposite direction, your head is exposed. I asked; they do it that way so that if someone thinks they're going to be needed they're easier to spot from the door." He sighed and rubbed his face. "In practice, though, no one does that, because the computer will alert you if someone's looking for you. It's a quiet little chime near the pillow, and a low light. So everyone sleeps facing in."

"Except your subjects, who were sleeping with their heads hanging out," Palland said.

"Not just hanging out, but pointing at one another," Vasiht'h said. "There were people in there who shouldn't have been in there, and they were all clustered together in a way that their heads were near one another."

Palland rubbed a finger beneath his nose, looking at Vasiht'h. "So . . . you are drawing what conclusion from this?"

"I think they're hoping to get a backwash off what I'm doing,"

Vasiht'h said, trying not to be exasperated. It didn't help that his professor's ear was beginning to twitch. "It's not funny, sir! I didn't get consent forms from those extra people. What if I do accidentally affect them?"

"Could you?" Palland asked.

"I don't know!"

"Then maybe you should get them those consent forms," the Seersa said, and chuckled at Vasiht'h's expression. "If they're working so hard to get into the study—"

"—but they know what I'm trying to do! Isn't that going to game the results?" Vasiht'h said.

"Not necessarily," Palland said. "As long as they don't tell the people who don't know . . ."

Vasiht'h dropped to his haunches and covered his eyes.

"We'll work it out, alet," Palland said. "But first you've got to breathe. You do that for me? Breathe in."

"I am breathing in," Vasiht'h said, hoping he didn't sound petulant. "It's not changing that I'm upset with them for messing with my research project. Which means I'll have to redo it. Again!"

"It probably won't be all that bad," Palland said. "You might just have to move to a new location to do the testing." He held up a hand at Vasiht'h's protest. "Yes, I know, you're already invested in repeating the study where you are. But if you really are that worried about having to throw out the results, then we should stop now and change venues." He quirked a brow. "Your call, alet."

"But I've already started it at the hospital," Vasiht'h said, trying not to look as distressed as he felt at the notion of having to go through all the initial work of advertising for volunteers and sorting through consent forms again.

"It's only been a week and a half," Palland said. "That's not bad. Particularly since you're going to be carrying the project through into winter term."

Vasiht'h folded his arms to keep from fidgeting. He didn't want to change venues. And part of it, he realized, was because he didn't want to leave the healers-assist at the children's hospital in the middle of the treatment course. They'd been so eager to help him, and to feel better . . . could he really just pull out to serve his own purposes, and leave them hanging that way?

"I guess I'll just see how it goes," he said with a sigh.

———∞∞———

The children took one look at him and said to Vasiht'h accusingly, "You aren't taking care of him!"

"Gently, gently, ariisen," Jahir said, lifting his hands. "It's not Vasiht'h's fault that I refuse his aid."

"You do?" Kuriel asked, ears splaying. "Why?"

"Because he's stubborn," Vasiht'h said, settling on the floor in the story corner.

Jahir said, "I'm afraid he has the right of it."

"What's he being stubborn about?" Kayla wanted to know.

"He's taking five classes in summer, and the summer term is much shorter than winter and spring, so it's far more work in less time," Vasiht'h said.

"How come you won't let him take care of you?" Amaranth asked him with an imperiousness that would have impressed the Queen herself. "He likes doing it, and you need it."

"I fear I sometimes forget everything around me when I am deeply absorbed in something," Jahir said, thinking of music. "So, I work, and forget to rest."

"Or eat," Vasiht'h muttered.

"Or eat," Jahir said. "But mostly rest."

"Then, you will rest now," Amaranth declared. She pointed at her bed. "I'm not using it today. You go lie down."

"Ah . . . arii . . ."

"Would you rather have mine?" Persy asked. "I guess they're all the same length, though. Which probably isn't quite long enough, but you should be okay."

"Ladies—"

"Should I give him my pillow?" Persy said to Amaranth.

"No, he should use mine. His family has special ties to unicorns, remember?"

"We should sing him to sleep!" Meekie exclaimed.

"And maybe Vasiht'h-alet can help by suggesting him some dreams the way he does for us," Kayla agreed.

Jahir looked at their faces, saw their absolute adamantine resolve on the subject. When he glanced at Vasiht'h his roommate's expression was studiously neutral . . . but a mindtouch whispered to him of sour worry. He suppressed his sigh and said, "Very well. And I do think Amaranth is correct: I shall do better with a unicorn pillow than with a dragon. However! One condition." He held up a finger and waited until he had their attention. "I do not intend to sleep. I will lie there quietly as so many of you have had to during our visits, and listen and partake. But rest."

"I guess that's fine," Amaranth said, and the girls murmured agreement.

They chivvied him to Amaranth's bed, and he dutifully stretched out on it. It was shorter than he was tall, but not by much; if his feet were hanging over the edge, it was not uncomfortable, and surely wouldn't matter for the short time he'd be lying down. It gave them such pleasure to tuck him in that he couldn't gainsay them, anyway. They brought him blankets, arranged his pillow, fussed over the position of his ankles . . . until at last they were satisfied.

"Shall we draw pictures?" Vasiht'h said, and lured them back to the table. Over their heads, Jahir shared a lopsided smile with his roommate, and wondered at the amusement he felt in return, not quite mischief, and not quite smug, but something like that. As if Vasiht'h knew something he didn't.

. . . which, it seemed, proved true, for he fell asleep on Amaranth's bed and did not wake until it was time for them to leave.

On the way back to the apartment, Jahir said, "Perhaps I am over-extended."

"I don't think there's any perhaps about it," Vasiht'h said.

"No . . ." Jahir said. "No, maybe not." He closed his eyes, aware of the heat on his shoulders and head, of the ache in his joints from too long bent over a tablet. "But, Vasiht'h . . . the learning, that part is glory."

Vasiht'h glanced up at him.

"I love it," Jahir said, and was surprised to say it, and in saying it, to feel how deep that love ran. "And I'm glad to be here."

"Maybe you can be a little more here now," Vasiht'h said. "And eat with me more often."

"Yes," Jahir murmured. "Yes, I have been remiss. You are good to me, arii, and I am neglectful. Will you forgive me?"

"Does apologizing mean you're already thinking you're going to break that promise?" his roommate asked, eyeing him.

"I will do my best to try. Remind me, please."

"All right," Vasiht'h said, and Jahir could taste his resignation like ashes.

CHAPTER 28

THE SUMMER WENT TOO QUICKLY. Vasiht'h spent half his time overseeing the sleep patterns of hospital staff and the other half trying not to hover over his roommate. Jahir's exhaustion was palpable, but so was his elation: more often now the mindtouch brought him snatches of it, the two sensations intertwined like the artificial helices of the Pelted they were both studying. As promised, Jahir ate more often, and with Vasiht'h. And they still saw the children every week—on that count, Jahir was immovable. But everything else fell away: the concerts, the outings, the lazy days beneath perfect trees. The Eldritch made an effort to attend the quadmate gatherings, but more often than not he slept through them, or begged off to study.

Vasiht'h found it maddening, that he could be losing the camaraderie of their friendship at the same time the mind-touches made it feel like they had more of an intimacy than they did. He could imagine what it would have been like to let the mindline ripen with the friendship. He didn't *want* to, but he could. If it hadn't been for his work at the hospital, he would have despaired.

"You mean you're liking the research now?" Sehvi asked, wary. "What's changed?"

"Maybe nothing," Vasiht'h said, sighed. "Maybe everything. I don't know, ariishir. But I go there to help people, and . . . I need to know that I'm helping someone."

"I thought you were helping your roommate?"

"In the sense that I'm keeping him from starving, maybe," Vasiht'h said. His shoulders slumped. "But he doesn't really need me."

Sehvi's eyes narrowed. "You're sure of that?"

Vasiht'h shook his head. "You don't feel what I feel in him, when the mindtouches come. He's . . . he's in love. With the Alliance, with learning, with the challenges."

"That sounds like the sort of infatuation that burns itself out," Sehvi said.

"I don't think so." Vasiht'h looked away. "I think he could give himself to this and be happy. And it might even be safer for him. If he falls in love with science, and with abstractions, then he can't be hurt when people die around him. He said it once to Luci, even: 'Distance makes most things bearable.' "

"That sounds more like avoidance than love to me," Sehvi said.

"Maybe," Vasiht'h said. "But I can't change his mind, ariishir. What else can I do but sit back and watch?"

"So speaks the nascent researcher," Sehvi said. "But there's more than one approach for the psychologist, yes? You could be affecting."

Vasiht'h said, "He's not my client."

"No, he's not," Sehvi said. "No one is. My question is, how do you feel about the role of the observer?"

"I won't take the bait this time, Sehvi," Vasiht'h said. He shook his head. "No matter how I feel about the matter, he's not my client, and even if he was it's not my right to shake sense into him. What if I'm wrong? What if this is what he really needs?"

"What if you're right? What if what he really needs is a good friend?"

"If he did, why would he be so excited right now?"

Sehvi made a face. "I can't believe I'm about to say this to you, who's supposed to be the one who observes these things. But . . . passion is a funny thing, ariihir. A person can be over the moon about something and not be happy. Not in a healthy, sustainable sort of way. Don't you live next door to a Harat-Shar? Haven't you noticed them plunging off emotional cliffs all the time? They're exhilarated mid-flight, but then they smash into the ground."

Vasiht'h reflected that Sehvi probably had not met a Luci yet. "I can see that," he said. "But I don't know that you're right about Jahir. Everything else pales next to the fact that he's going to outlive us all. It's probably safer for him not to have intimate friends."

"I don't care how old you get," Sehvi said. "It's never safer to have no friends."

―――――∞∞∞―――――

While it was not a requirement for summer classes to give midterm examinations, all of Jahir's classes did. Somehow, he passed them all . . . even Kandara's madcap simulation of a bad night at an urgent care clinic. When he staggered out of it, she eyed him and said, "You know, you're a lot tougher than you look."

"Did I pass, then?" he asked her.

"You did, you did."

"Then," he said, with care for the words, because he was tired enough to slur them, "I believe I shall have a seat."

She chuckled. "You do that. You've got two days to recover. Then it's back on your feet."

"Yes, ma'am," he murmured, much to her amusement.

But it was summer, and there was no respite. The teaching resumed immediately: in the case of his lecture classes, the hour after the exam was given. He gave himself to the learning, and discovered a ferocity of joy in it. He had never been stretched so in his life. Everything at home had always proceeded at a stately pace, unhurried, very aware of the hundreds of available years. No one rushed. There was always time. And, ridiculously, there was nothing to fill it with because the culture was stagnant. The pursuits permitted the noble and common both had been proscribed and had not changed for generations . . . and very little new was discovered or revealed.

It wasn't like this. Where he could open a book and feel with aching clarity how much there was that he didn't know. No matter how fast he learned, millions of people were working to expand that pool of knowledge even as he studied. There would be no catching up with it. He could fill all his life with learning and never be done in the Alliance. It was intoxicating.

Summer's end felt as abrupt as a blow. His results came back and he took them with him to lunch with KindlesFlame, who accepted the data tablet without comment. The Tam-illee's thumb flicked through the grades and notes as Jahir waited, sipping his coffee as much for the stimulant as for the flavor. Some small part of his mind could now—was now—cataloging the effects of the drug for him; he ignored it, save to be pleased that he could now do it.

"You survived summer with a five-class course load," KindlesFlame said without looking up.

"I seem to have," Jahir answered.

KindlesFlame looked at him over the tablet. "And you excelled."

"They were not perfect scores."

"Of course they weren't. You've got the handicap of not having started the degree at the undergraduate level here, where you could acclimate to the culture and language while the curriculum was less intense." KindlesFlame put the tablet down. "I have to admit, alet. I didn't think you'd manage."

"Is it the proper time to admit my own doubts, or would that be prejudicial?" Jahir asked.

The Tam-illee huffed a laugh. "You'd have to have a mania to have gotten through that semester without doubts. But you did, and you're on your feet, and even Lasa said you'd do." He nodded. "I'll give you that letter."

Jahir hadn't realized he'd been holding his breath through

KindlesFlame's speech until it ended. He let it out slowly. "I am grateful."

"Have you thought about where you'll want to go?"

"Only a little," Jahir said. "Enough to have learned that All Children's has no medical psychology residency program but the general hospital here does."

"And it's a good one," KindlesFlame said.

"However, I have done some research," Jahir said. "And it is my observation that the most promising students go to Heliocentrus for their residencies."

"Ah." KindlesFlame stared at his cup, then picked up the cream cup and started diluting his coffee. "Yes."

"You know of it, then?" Jahir asked.

"Oh, yes," KindlesFlame said. "It's what I was thinking when I told you, way back when, that the residencies are killers. Heliocentrus's Mercy Hospital is probably the prize assignment for ambitious new healers-assist. It's not a teaching hospital, so there are only a few slots open every year, and everyone wants them."

"Because. . . ."

"Because it's the biggest hospital in the Alliance's winter capital, on the capital world in the Core," KindlesFlame said. "You get every conceivable kind of case there. The population's so diverse, probably the only thing they haven't seen is an Eldritch, and I wouldn't bet my coffee on it. But—" He held up a finger. "—as one of only a very few psychologist-residents, they'll work you to the bone. And they won't cut you any slack for being wet behind the ears, either. They're not there to coddle you or explain anything to you. You figure things out or you fail and they send you packing. The General Hospital here is attached to the university. They take a full complement of students every semester. They're committed to teaching. If you go there, it will be like a continuation of your schooling here, but with real world examples. And you'll be able to go home at night and get eight hours of sleep."

"And I will be here," Jahir said, surprised to discover that this mattered. "Where I already have made connections."

"Yes," KindlesFlame said. "Any notion then, which you'll want?"

"No," Jahir said. "So I had better apply to them both, and several others besides. There being no guarantee of winning any."

"They'll make room for you at General," KindlesFlame said. "That's part of their mandate, to teach. Offworld . . ." He shrugged, a dip of shoulder and ear.

"We'll see," Jahir murmured.

⎯⎯⎯ ∞∞∞ ⎯⎯⎯

"You live!" Brett said when he entered the room behind Vasiht'h.

"So it appears," Jahir said. "Though pray do not apply to my roommate for evidence, or he may prove me wrong."

Vasiht'h snorted. "He's half-dead, he just doesn't have the sense to know it."

Luci said to Jahir, "Oh, you are in hot water now. He's upset at you!"

"I know," Jahir said, contrite. "I have yet to make proper apology. Perhaps I can put the break to good use."

Vasiht'h eyed him as the others chuckled. Mera leaned over and said, "How are you pacifying the grumpy Glaseah? They do not grump easily, so once they have started, you are in the very, very bad place already."

"You're going to need more than cookie dough to fix this one," Leina agreed, snitching one of the chips.

"I am open to suggestions?" Jahir said.

"Maybe a massage?" Brett said to Luci.

"Not so much," Mera opined. "Hard to find someone who can work on us four-feet."

"I am sitting right here!" Vasiht'h said. "You could ask me!"

"What would be the fun in that?" Leina said, grinning.

"Besides, you probably won't tell anyone what you really want," Luci added. "Because it would make you feel bad to ask for something for yourself. Either that, or you'd be hurt that you had to tell us what you wanted, because you'd want it to come from our own heads."

Jahir glanced at Vasiht'h, and for his efforts won one of the mindtouches: a sour yogurt taste that hinted of exasperation, but with a touch of fondness. Fondness in that context tasted like strawberries. He would have to remember that.

"In that case," Vasiht'h said, reaching past Leina for the wine, "I'll let you all keep guessing."

It was late when they finally returned to the apartment; Jahir was only on his feet due to the judicious use of coffee, and by eating sparingly of foods that might have sedated him. He did his half of the chores in silence, allowing his roommate—his friend—to keep his silence. It was for him to break, however, so he did. "You are hurt. And I truly am sorry. Shall I find you strawberries for cake?"

Vasiht'h stopped in the act of reaching for the tea kettle. He made a strangled noise—laughter, Jahir hoped—and said, "It's too late in the season for strawberries."

"I am sure I can find someone importing them," Jahir said. "Or I can have them materialized in that magical box we never use."

Vasiht'h glanced at him. "I'm not angry at you."

"Much," Jahir said.

His roommate grimaced, then said, "All right, fine. Much. But it's just because I'm worried about you."

'That part, Jahir thought, was only partially true. There was something personal there, and he had an uneasy feeling that he knew what it was about. "Tell me what I can do to make you feel better."

Vasiht'h shook his head. "No . . . it's all right." He sighed. "You're doing what you have to do. I won't stand in your way."

And that felt very wrong, and he had no idea how to say so when confronted with such noble sentiment. He looked away, then reached up to the top cabinet and got down the tea.

Vasiht'h accepted it, silent, and together they fetched the cups and saucers. When the tea had steeped, the Glaseah poured for them both. Jahir took his tea to the great room and had a seat in the chair there.

But Vasiht'h did not join him. He took his cup and went into his room, and very quietly closed the door. Jahir stared after him, feeling as if that was the beginning of a very bad trend, and that he should do something about it. But what could he do? If his roommate chose to withdraw, was that not his right? Particularly when Jahir had done so first, by giving himself so completely to his studies?

It was particularly galling to wake up in that chair several hours later, having fallen asleep in the midst of his own debate . . . and discover that sometime during those hours, his roommate had covered him with a blanket.

CHAPTER 29

V ASIHT'H HAD DECIDED THAT it was time for a little careful self-protection. His roommate was going to leave, and take with him the mindtouches that had become so frequent they were beginning to function like a primitive mindline. He was also going to take with him the pleasure of his company, and the first really good friend Vasiht'h had ever allowed himself to make. Sehvi had been right: he hadn't been open to the notion before. It had taken an alien three times his age to break through to him, by having the wonder of a child about all the things that Vasiht'h had long since taken for granted.

But he was leaving, and Vasiht'h was staying, and they both knew it. He tried to be gentle about it, but he knew when he shut the door on Jahir that evening that he was drawing a very clear line.

Jahir ignored it.

The following morning, he came out of his room, rumpled, and found the Eldritch waiting for him on the couch. He was still in his nightshirt and pants, and was sitting cross-legged, and though Vasiht'h had never seen him look disheveled, there was something about seeing the white skin at his wrists and over his bare feet that made him look vulnerable.

"Good morning?" Vasiht'h said, surprised. "I thought you'd be up and out by now."

"I know," Jahir said, sheepish. "I slept through the farmer's market, however. I thought I'd ask you to go to Tea and Cinnamon with me instead since I bought nothing for us to make for breakfast."

"Jahir," Vasiht'h began, because he felt like his forepaws were on the slope of something and he was just a hair's breadth from skidding down it.

His roommate didn't say anything, just looked at him with his usual careful expression. But Vasiht'h had long since learned to read the subtleties in those eyes, and the mindtouch whispered to him of so much cautious hope that he sighed. Sehvi had talked of other people tossing themselves off cliffs in their passions, whether it was a good idea or not. He could see the ground rushing toward him and yet, here he was—"I'd love to. Let me just brush myself and wash my face."

"Very good," Jahir said. "I'll dress."

The relief felt like the first warm breeze after winter. It made Vasiht'h's fur stand on end. He petted it down on his way to the bathroom.

⸎

The break between summer term and winter's was a month long. Their last vacation had been Vasiht'h's in execution. This one was Jahir's. It involved a lot of walking on campus, but the university was huge and Vasiht'h hadn't explored it all. Neither had Jahir. So they did it together, and found the gardens and fields, the art installations and fountains that they would otherwise never have known about. The business school had an amazing outdoor restaurant, and eating there at the end of the season, with the air still warm but the breeze beginning to cool, was sublime. The humanities building was adjacent to a hedge maze, which startled them both . . . Vasiht'h started laughing the moment they entered, for the thing had been sized for typical Pelted, and Jahir's head and shoulders were visible over the tops of the bushes.

"Not much of a mystery for you," Vasiht'h observed.

"At least we won't get lost," Jahir replied, amused.

Their excursions at night brought them to a pool near the engineering complex stocked with softly glowing fish, each smaller than the length of Vasiht'h's thumb; the students had accessorized the pool with dim colored lights set in the surrounding pavement that rippled on and off in patterns like waves under moonlight. There was something similar near the theater building, but with pinwheels that glimmered when the evening breezes blew. When it was dark enough, they blazed like fire as they spun.

They also ate ice cream, and visited the children, sat under trees and watched the wind blow over the grasses, had coffee and kerinne at home. Jahir dusted the fireplace and brought home wood, 'as it will be growing cold soon enough.'

At the end of the break, Vasiht'h struggled not to feel morose. It was unreasonable to think something like this could last forever, but he wanted it to. He thought about telling his sister, but her pity, he thought, would have been far harder to bear than her teasing. And this situation had definitely crossed into the realm of pity.

Kandara surprised Jahir by stopping him outside his Advanced Diagnostics and Procedures lecture during drop/add week, the first week of the winter semester.

"I hear you're mad to wreck your health on our profession," she said, falling in step alongside him.

"One could construe it that way," he said, guarded.

"And how would you be construing it?" she asked, and he detected a twinkle of amusement in her eyes.

"As dedication to a cause," he answered, and was not at all flippant about it.

"Mmm," she said. "Well, you need a major professor. Have you chosen one yet? Because if not, Lafayette and I have put our heads together and decided I should take you under my wing. He'd do it himself, I suspect, except this isn't his specialty."

"Healer KindlesFlame is already generous with his time," Jahir said. "And I learn a great deal from our talks together."

"He and I have been friends for over twenty years," she said, tail swishing. She was never still; he only wished he had her burning energy. "He asked me to keep an eye on you in spring, and to be honest, I didn't think you had it in you. But you proved me wrong." She grinned at him. "I like that in a student. I hate being right all the time. Gets boring."

Jahir said, "And what would my new major professor say if I told her my course load for the semester?"

"I don't know," she said. "Hit me."

So he told her, and she walked alongside him for several minutes, wordless. He had shocked her, perhaps? But then she spoke. "Drop the Health Management of Adults course and replace it with . . . mm . . . Skills for Psychological Intervention. You're going to need that first, if you want to get through the labs next semester."

Fascinated, he said, "The advisor suggested the schedule?"

"The advisor thinks you're going to fail one or two classes this semester, which would put you in school for an extra term." Kandara grinned. "She wouldn't have done it that way otherwise. But you're not planning on failing anything, are you?"

"No, ma'am."

"Then go rearrange your schedule. And I want to see you weekly. Pick a time, my office hours are online."

Fall brought with it a sense of unreality. This was his life, Vasiht'h thought, and yet it didn't feel like it. He had never been so troubled, and it went with him everywhere . . . except to the studies, which he had moved to the general hospital adjacent to All Children's on campus. The staff there was larger and didn't know him; somehow that made it more comforting when he realized his methods worked on them. There was something important here, and even if he didn't know who'd be using the methods he was pioneering, at least he was, for now, for the length of his research.

After the halcyon month of break, Jahir had vanished back into his workload. The only thing the Eldritch didn't miss was their weekly visit to the children, even though he often drifted off during them. Vasiht'h had been telling a story during one such session, and Jahir had fallen asleep with his back to the wall and Meekie in his lap. The Glaseah lowered his voice so as not to disturb his roommate and carried the story to its conclusion, and then fell silent, just looking at Jahir.

"You're sad about it," Persy said, somber. "Is it because he's making himself sick?"

"No," Vasiht'h said, startled. Was it so obvious? "No, other than having a tendency to fall asleep when he stops moving, he's in fine health as far as I can tell."

"Then what is it?" Kayla asked. "Every time you look at him now, there's something in your face that says you're sad."

"Is there?" Vasiht'h said, dismayed. "Goddess, I hope not." He passed a hand over his face, as if that would wipe the expression from it, and grimaced. "No, it's nothing like that, ariisen. It's just that . . . he's going to be done with school soon, and then he'll be gone."

"You could write, maybe?" Amaranth said.

Persy shook her head. "That didn't work with the girls who were here before you all. I mean, it started off okay, but after a few months they just got too busy."

"I'd write you!" Meekie said.

"Is that it?" Kuriel asked Vasiht'h.

"That . . . yes. That's it," Vasiht'h said. He sighed and tried to smile. "What would you do if you were me?"

"Can you do what he's doing?" Amaranth asked.

"No," Vasiht'h said. The thought of going medical was overwhelming. He didn't want to spend all his working hours ministering to the desperately sick. He needed more balance in his life than that.

"Can you go where he's going?" Kayla asked.

"No," Vasiht'h said.

The girls contemplated this in thoughtful silence. Then Kayla crawled into the circle of Vasiht'h's forelegs and stretched herself up to hug him. "I'm sorry," she said.

He rested her head against his shoulder.

⁂

Outside the room, Jill asked, "How's Sleeping Beauty?"

"Drowning in academia, and loving it," Vasiht'h said. "He's putting them all to bed, as an apology for missing half the visit."

"Mm," she said. "And how's the research going?"

"Well," Vasiht'h said.

She laughed. "And that surprises you?"

"I was a little nervous, moving next door," he said. "But the methods seem to work on people who've never heard of me." He smiled, lopsided. "By this time, everyone here seems to know who I am."

"I wonder why," Jill said, chuckling. "So, can I come to you for a private session?"

"I don't know how, since I have no license!" Vasiht'h said.

She pressed her fist against his shoulder, gentle but firm. "Yes? And? This is a serious question. When can I schedule a visit? Do I have to wait until you get a doctorate, or will you still not have a license to practice then?"

"A doctorate in research psychology doesn't come with a license to practice therapy," Vasiht'h said. "At least not on the Core worlds."

"Then maybe I can be part of a private study?" she said. At his expression, she said, "I'm serious. I want a chance to go through your therapy. It works. Hell, if it worked on Kievan, it'll work on anyone."

Vasiht'h glanced up at her, frowning. "You really mean that."

"Yes?" she said.

Jahir joined them, looking wan but upright. "They sleep and dream of unicorns. Hopefully."

"Hopefully?" Jill asked.

"Either that, or of the rudiments of reading medical displays in critical care units," Jahir said.

"At least that won't be a big surprise for them," she said, shaking her head. "You really that eager to join us, alet?"

"Time," Jahir said, "is wasting." He inclined his head to her and headed to the stairwell.

Looking after him, Jill said, "That sounds like a problem waiting to explode."

"Implode, more likely," Vasiht'h said and followed. As he reached the stairwell, he heard Jill call after him, "Just tell me when and I'll be there! Bells on!"

"Arranging something?" Jahir asked as the Glaseah caught up to him on the stairs.

"She wants to know if she can do the therapy I'm testing," Vasiht'h said, trying not to sound as testy as he was. "I've told her I have no license to practice. I think she keeps forgetting on purpose."

"It is difficult to blame her," Jahir said. "The approach is novel, it works, and you are singularly well-suited to its application."

"I am?" Vasiht'h said, startled.

"You have a gentle touch," Jahir said, and then they were in the lobby. By the time they'd navigated the crush of people, they were outside and the moment was gone, and with it Vasiht'h's desire to pursue it. What would he do if Jahir was right? Wasn't it better not to know? Why did he feel like that described most of his life by now?

The weather grew colder, and brought midterms: Jahir felt as if he was living between the covers of books in the weeks immediately before the exams, but they came, and he passed them, and their passage brought a respite from lectures. He had the time and energy to help Vasiht'h prepare buttersquash soup for the quadmate meeting, the first he'd attend since the semester's beginning. There was something supremely calming about cutting the vegetables while his roommate worked at the sink behind him. The mindtouch brought him hints of harmony, and they smelled like the Glaseahn goddess's incense.

That night he endured the good-natured teasing at the table, and reflected as he bore it that he had . . . friends. More friends than he'd anticipated making here. KindlesFlame and Kandara among the faculty; the quadmates here; the children at the hospital, and Berquist . . . and Vasiht'h, chief and best among them. It was on his mind as he prepared for bed later, his movements slowed by the weight of his thoughts. It was not so easy, making friends among his own kind. The people who'd sworn fealty to him would never have felt easy enough in his presence to befriend him, and it was his responsibility not to discomfit them with overtures they would feel unable to reject. The people of his own station were deeply entrenched in the politics of scarcity that afflicted them: they were all too busy protecting their scant resources to trust one another.

The people here, though, made friends as easily as breathing. And he'd expected his aloofness to protect him from that, and it might have . . . had he actually wanted to be protected.

He sighed and put his head down, and thought that he had brought all this on himself, and gladly, and had no idea yet where it might lead.

When the dream garden returned that night, he was not frantically trying to save the flowers that were growing from it already decayed. He was sitting on a stool in the middle of it, and all around him were the corpses, already decomposed, gone to gray dust. The greenery at the garden's edges was creeping inward, felting the bones, subsuming them, and soon enough he was left there, with nothing, not even clear memory of what he'd lost.

I am alone, he thought.

No, you're not.

He woke slowly, without violence. His parted lashes were damp, but his melancholy had been brushed away by a gentle hand. He was not surprised to find Vasiht'h sleeping on the ground by the door. Setting his head back on the pillow, he sent a surge of wordless gratitude, and felt an equally wordless reply, muzzy with sleep. Jahir closed his eyes and dreamed no more of gardens.

CHAPTER 30

𝕴T HAD NOT BEEN VASIHT'H'S intention to intrude on his roommate's sleeping mind, but he'd done it so often for subjects
that he'd reacted without thinking, and insinuated himself into
the dream just deeply enough to dispel it. He'd slipped to the
floor, too exhausted for worry, and had slept until he'd felt the
gift of Jahir's gratitude. That had soothed him in a place he
hadn't known he needed it.

But what he'd seen and felt in those moments stayed with
him, from the moment of waking, kinked up on the floor of his
roommate's room, to the weeks after as fall gave way to winter
and the semester neared its close. The flowers, the sense of being
surrounded, and yet isolate . . . the melancholy of it. He stayed
vigilant, but Jahir did not have another nightmare, not that he
knew of . . . but Vasiht'h woke several times from dreams where
he wandered the Eldritch's garden, looking for something and
failing to find it. As the weeks continued, his own dreams grew
more urgent, until he began waking from them panting and mis-
erable. He knew then what he was looking for, but even knowing
didn't make the dreams go away.

Near finals week, he came home from one of the quadmate
gatherings with Luci. The Harat-Shar followed him into the

kitchen, holding one of the trays, and glanced at the dark, still rooms, the unlit hearth. Wrinkling her nose, she said, "Nothing says trouble like a quiet house."

"Jahir's asleep, that's all," Vasiht'h said, taking the tray from her and finding a small bowl for the last of the cobbler.

"Uh-huh," Luci said, hopping onto one of the stools at the counter.

Vasiht'h glanced at her over his shoulder, and she lifted her brows slowly. He made a face. "Luci. Really."

"Don't really me, arii. I've cried on your shoulder, and I don't cry on anyone's shoulder. If you can't tell me your woes, who can you tell?"

"There's no woe to share," Vasiht'h said, stubborn. "Jahir's not avoiding us, he's just busy with school."

"Mmm."

He started making an herbal tea, more because he needed to calm himself than to be hospitable. "I mean that. He's taking six classes this semester. Anyone would be overloaded. He needs his sleep."

"Right."

"And he's doing well, so obviously the studying's working," Vasiht'h continued, getting out one cup, then remembering Luci and pulling down another.

"Of course."

He eyed her, then scowled.

"What? I haven't said anything!" she said.

"It's what you're not saying that's getting to me," Vasiht'h said. He poured for them both and handed her the cup.

"If you love him," Luci said. "You should tell him."

He put his cup down hard enough to rattle the saucer.

This time she only lifted one brow.

"I don't love him," Vasiht'h growled.

"Not the way you think I'm intimating, no," Luci said. "Not like romp with him in the sheets love. But you do love him. Don't make the mistake of assuming that just because I'm Harat-Shar I'm not aware of those other kinds of love."

She wrinkled her nose. "You of all people should know better."

Vasiht'h looked away.

"Right?"

"I know," he said. "I know you know. I know you weren't suggesting . . . anything like that. But I don't—"

"Love him?" Luci snorted. "You don't believe in lying to other people, from what I've seen, so this must mean you're in denial."

"Luci, I can't be in love with him," Vasiht'h said, pained.

"On that count you're absolutely wrong," Luci answered. "You can be and you are, and we both know it. And you're upset because at the rate he's chewing through school he's going to be gone soon. Yes?"

He massaged his temples. "Luci—"

"Yes?"

"Yes!" he said. "Yes. But I don't see what good it will do to tell him!"

"Because he can't change his plans unless he knows what he'd lose if he didn't," Luci said, exasperated.

"And you think I'd have a problem with saying this sort of thing out loud," Vasiht'h said, ears flattening. "He's Eldritch. For all I know, they think of love so narrowly that he'll completely misinterpret it, or discount it, or Goddess knows. We don't know their customs, Luci. *I* don't know *his* customs. All I'd probably accomplish is to make him uncomfortable."

"But what if you're wrong?" she said. "What if they have a tradition of platonic love? For all you know they revere agape, or even prefer homosexual—sorry, homosocial—attachments."

"Somehow I doubt that," Vasiht'h muttered.

"Vasiht'h," Luci said, and sighed. "Vasiht'h. Isn't it worth trying for what you might gain?"

"Say I tell him I care about him. And he agrees that he really cares about me. What then? We're still planning very different lives." He looked at her across the counter. "Can you honestly sit there and tell me that just loving someone is enough? It's not! It's not. You have to want the same things out of life. You have to be willing to walk the same path."

She deflated visibly.

"Luci . . . Luci, I'm sorry." He rubbed his face with one hand, and it was trembling. "I don't mean to be harsh. I just . . . I never thought I'd be sitting on this side of the fence."

"I know," she said, quietly. "And maybe . . . maybe I'm telling you to do it because I hope you'll have a happier ending than I did."

He walked around the counter and hugged her.

"But what if it worked?" she asked against his shoulder.

"And what if it didn't?" Vasiht'h replied.

She sighed.

—⚬⚬⚬—

Finals came and went, and took what few hopes Vasiht'h had with them; his roommate shared news of his triumph before tottering to the couch and falling asleep there in front of the cold hearth. For a long time, Vasiht'h sat across from him and stared at him, thinking about Luci's observation—accusation, more like. Was it love, to hate the thought of losing someone? To want their company? To feel so easy around them? He studied Jahir's face and had no desire to touch it, to caress it, to write poetry about it the way he'd observed some of his classmates doing when they'd fallen in love. Was trying to decide whether Jahir's eyes were the color of spring's wildflower honey, or summer's clover honey, the same impulse? He went to his room and opened the topmost drawer of his table, withdrawing the folded paper Goddess. Setting Her on the surface, he said, "I know what You would tell me to do. But Your words shape reality. The rest of us don't have that guarantee."

He sighed and put his head down on the table.

Jahir spent most of the winter holiday recuperating, and there was something charming about that, too, something that managed to wring Vasiht'h's heart. Maybe it was how casually the Eldritch let him see that imperfection. When he left the apartment, he was impeccable: never a hair out of place, all the folds of his clothes crisp, his shoulders and back straight. To have him limp on the couch in front of the fire, in rumpled nightclothes, with his head on an arm as he drowsed in all evidence of contentment . . .

"When do we start the cooking?" Jahir asked as the end of year approached.

Vasiht'h padded to the great room and sat across from the Eldritch, who hadn't even raised his head to ask the question. "This year, Mera and Leina are hosting. She has some recipes she wants to try out."

That won him the Eldritch's attention, and Jahir looked up with narrowed eyes. His puzzlement felt like a breeze humid with disappointment. "I thought you liked to host?"

"I do, but it's a lot of work, and you're tired," Vasiht'h said. "I thought it would be easier on us both to let someone else do the heavy lifting this year."

And as clear as the taste of that breeze, he heard the words hanging between them: *But this is the last time*—and then Jahir shook himself, a minute twitch of chin. When he opened his eyes, he had composed himself. "We should at least bring something."

"Mera asked for the mulled wine again," Vasiht'h said, fighting the tension in his breast. "And I'll bring some dessert. You know me and cookies."

"I do," Jahir murmured. And smiled, though the smile didn't lighten his eyes. "I'll see to the wine, then."

Later that evening, Jahir sat in his room, reading his mother's correspondence. She did not write with the frequency his roommate's family seemed to, but now and then she sent him letters on how matters fared at home on the estate. She'd also told him about the summer spent attending the Queen, and that letter had included some frank mention of the difficulties in court. He in turn had told her about the children and his mentors, about his decision to pursue a course that would see him working in a hospital . . . and about Vasiht'h.

He opened her latest, hoping to quiet his heart with the

details of management, and their implication of the pastoral and unchanging life he'd left behind. It soothed him admirably until he reached the end:

> *How wonderful it is to hear you have made such a fast friend in your alien roommate. Despite Galare being home to the staunchest advocates for the Alliance, we have yet to secure the honor of House Jisiensire. Fasianyl Sera Jisiensire was the last Eldritch to have a strong relationship with an outworlder, and that was centuries ago, when Liolesa was new to her throne. Perhaps you will be the next, and the Seni Galare will be able to take up the Queen's banner, and advance her cause.*

Jahir turned from the projection and pressed his thumb under the ridge of his brow, working at the nascent headache. Fasianyl's friendship with Sellelvi was famous; one could hardly walk at court without hearing of it, given Liolesa's sympathies for the Alliance. The people who supported her were proud of how she'd welcomed the alien, how she'd even found a way to have her adopted into Jisiensire. The people who hated the Queen held it up as an example of the unnatural policies she would foist on them if given free rein.

But no one had talked about what became of Fasianyl after solidifying her famous relationship with Sellelvi . . . because she'd withdrawn from society following Sellelvi's death, so completely, in fact, that no one knew where she was. Not even Liolesa's detractors would speculate on the matter; perhaps they did not want to admit that the death of a 'mortal' could affect one of their kind so powerfully.

Perhaps, he thought, Fasianyl had gone to the Alliance, and that was why no one had heard from her. Or perhaps she had died young of a broken heart. Jahir glanced at the door leading out of his room and felt a frisson of apprehension.

CHAPTER 31

LEINA'S END OF YEAR FEAST was nicely done, Vasiht'h thought; scheduled before the new year, but that was the Seersan custom. He brought a tray of peppermint crinkles and fancy cookies; Jahir brought the wine and a stack of firewood, guessing that Leina and Mera didn't use their fireplace—which they didn't, so they were delighted by the gift. They spent a pleasant evening eating, talking, and eating more, and if there was something missing from the experience, it was still good to spend time with friends.

Vasiht'h wasn't expecting to wake to the smell of baking bread on New Year's Day. He lifted his head and sniffed, licked his teeth and then heaved himself off the pillows to investigate. The feast bread was in the oven: he peeked inside and saw that Jahir had woven it into a wreath, and a far more credible one than his mother had ever managed. The coffee cups had been set out in anticipation of breakfast, and there was jam in stasis, and fresh-ground nut butter—Vasiht'h uncapped it and smelled, and got back the ambrosial scent of more-almond. He couldn't imagine how much that had cost . . . no, he could, and it was extravagant as a condiment for a single meal.

The author of this feast was sleeping in his room, sprawled

on top of the sheets as if he'd only just returned there. Vasiht'h paused at the door, noting the lines beneath the eyes and the shadows too distinct beneath the cheekbones. His roommate might be passing his classes, but it was taking a physical toll. Did he notice?

And yet, he had made Vasiht'h breakfast again.

He padded back to the great room and applied himself to the hearth, in the hopes of figuring out how to make a fire work in it.

Jahir woke with a start. He hadn't planned to fall asleep, but he'd been unable to fight it either. As a youth his mother had put him to bed early despite his complaints, saying that only half of learning was done while wakeful; the mind completed the process during dreams. To be sure, he was exhausted often, and when he slept long enough he woke feeling more confident of the knowledge he'd been studying. He pushed himself upright and was contemplating getting to his feet when his roommate peeked in the room.

"The bread's done," he said. "You should come eat with me."

"I didn't burn it?" Jahir asked.

"Not at all," Vasiht'h said. "You set the cook-timer perfectly." He wrinkled his nose. "I wish I'd done as well with the fire. It's harder to make one than it looks."

Jahir laughed, quiet. "I'll take care of the fire, if you will make the coffee, arii."

"Fair and good."

So he repaired Vasiht'h's attempt, and his roommate made the coffee, and they sat down to the first meal of the first day of the new year. He drew in a deep breath, smelled honey and almonds and springfruit jam. By summer, God and Lady willing, he would be practicing on real people: under supervision, certainly, but still. The thought was unbelievable.

Vasiht'h broke the bread and handed him a piece. "To the new year."

"To all our endeavors," Jahir said. He opened the jam pot.

"You have not said how your latest study concluded at the new hospital. Were you able to keep the results?"

"All of them this time," Vasiht'h said. "Or at least, Palland said they should be fine. This coming semester I'll repeat it there and then we're going to discuss how to increase the scope of the study with me being the only one running it. And I'll have to start writing my thesis." He shook his head. "I am not looking forward to that."

"Not fond of writing?" Jahir asked.

"Not really, no," Vasiht'h said. "Not this kind of writing anyway. Writing letters to my parents and cousins, sure. Writing dry and factual?" He sighed. Smiled. "Well, I'll learn." He tapped the more-almond butter with the tip of his knife. "Isn't this a little expensive for one breakfast?"

"I am sure what remains will go into cookies at some point," Jahir said, amused.

"Augh!" Vasiht'h winced and laughed. "I can't imagine using something this expensive to make cookies!"

"It is there to be used," Jahir said.

"Better to eat it straight with a spoon," Vasiht'h said. "It's that good." He glanced up at Jahir. "You didn't—"

"Have to do it, I imagine you are about to say," Jahir said. "Can I not be a touch indulgent? At least once? We are not exactly spendthrift."

"No, we're not," Vasiht'h said, toying with the handle of his cup. "Jahir . . . you'll write? When you're gone?"

So casually said; the Glaseah wasn't even meeting his eyes. But the words struck him, sharp as spears. "I may not leave," he said.

Vasiht'h looked up at him sharply. "What?"

"Only one of the residencies I am applying for is offworld," Jahir said. "The other is here, at the campus teaching hospital."

"Oh," Vasiht'h said softly. "I didn't know. Why . . . why would you stay?"

Jahir looked down at his plate, at the fire, at the great room, which had become so familiar. He returned his gaze to his roommate and said, "I have friends here."

"Short-lived friends," Vasiht'h murmured.

That could not be borne. "I miss Nieve," Jahir said to him, willing him to believe. "But I would not elide her from my life for the brevity of her passage through it. I don't regret knowing her."

Vasiht'h looked up, eyes wide.

Jahir refilled his cup. "Now. Shall I bring out my gift for you? I hope you do not mind that I bought you one, despite the uncertainty of the year."

"The point of the gift is to help shape the uncertainty," Vasiht'h said. "Not to suggest we can control it."

"Good," Jahir said. "Wait you here, then."

In his room, as he found the small box he'd hidden, he thought of how much it bothered him: that Vasiht'h might consider himself a burden, that he thought Jahir might prefer not to have known him, when the truth was so very far opposite. Was he failing to express that in a way an outworlder might recognize? Perhaps, as Sheldan had suggested, his body language was too restrained. And yet, he couldn't change it. He looked at his box and hoped it was enough to express some part of his fondness. It had seemed a good idea at the time, and now it seemed too minor to communicate the depth of his feeling.

Perhaps it was always so, with gifts. With speech. Even with actions. Perhaps the only thing that made such things completely incontrovertible was the mindtouch.

He brought the box back with him and found Vasiht'h waiting at the table. Instead of setting it there, he held it out. "For you."

Vasiht'h glanced at his ungloved hand and then up at his face, then carefully took the box. A whisper of a mindtouch: a shivery feeling, like a nervous stomach. To calm it, Jahir said, "I do not fear your touch."

"I still don't want to do you any discourtesy," Vasiht'h said.

That didn't sound right; the mindtouch welled forth as if specifically to suggest that his roommate was trying to hide something. But Vasiht'h was opening the box, so Jahir didn't pursue it. He watched, hands folded in his lap.

"This is . . ." Vasiht'h squinted at it. "Cream?" He frowned. "For foot leather?"

"Some of my classmates in Clinical Management are digitigrade and wear no shoes," Jahir said. "They often talk about proper care of their paw pads, to keep them from cracking. I have seen that yours are dry and thought . . ." He trailed off.

"You noticed my feet," Vasiht'h repeated, eyes wide.

"We do a lot of walking," Jahir said.

"*I* don't even notice my feet!" Vasiht'h said with a laugh.

"You are not the only one who can take care of others."

Vasiht'h sobered. "No . . . no, I'm not." He set the jar on the table and said, "I'll try this after we're done. But first, this is for you." He handed over a box not much larger than Jahir's, and hesitated before maintaining his grip on it and waiting for Jahir to take it.

Inside the box was a book, a small and beautiful book with soft covers—surely not leather; did the Alliance use animal skins? It seemed unlikely. But something brown tooled in gold leaf, and the title a looping swirl of calligraphy that any illuminator at home would have been proud to have produced. It was entitled *Major Poets of the Exodus,* and he paged through it with reverence. Many of the poems were in Meredan, the secret language of the Pelted, but they were translated. Some of them were lyrical, rhyming things that rolled off the tongue; others were a staccato rhythm, as visual as they were aural. He stopped on one.

> there is freedom in the stars
> there is somewhere
> out there
>
> looking up we see a dome
> but it is only
> illusion
>
> if we could fly up past it
> we would find

out who

we were

when we were finally alone

"Vasiht'h," he said, softly. "This is a marvelous gift."

"It was that or a book of songs, but I thought you might already have bought yourself some of those. And you read so well," Vasiht'h said, sounding sheepish.

Jahir tilted his head. "Maybe after breakfast, I might read some of these for you?"

"Would you?" The Glaseah's ears perked. "I didn't think . . . that is . . . I thought you might want to save them for—" He stopped and chuckled. "Listen to me, I sound like I've been knocked on the head. Yes, I'd like that."

And that is what they did, after breakfast, while nursing their drinks by the fire. Jahir read from the book, pausing when they found a poet that intrigued them so they could consult the u-banks for biographical data. That led inevitably to discussions of the Exodus, of the cultural issues at the time and the evolution of the races and how that might have affected the poets. And Vasiht'h tried the foot cream on his paws, a process Jahir watched with interest: his roommate could twist his paws far enough to reach them with his hands, but it looked awkward. He wondered if he should offer . . . ? But no. Surely that was too much. After Vasiht'h had finished, and they'd had enough of poetry, they dressed and went for a walk.

Jahir did not have to wonder if, like him, his roommate was wondering what the year would bring. The mindtouch whispered hints like uneasy skies before a storm.

Would the full mindline have made those feelings plain to him?

Was it strange that he wished he could find out?

CHAPTER 32

"**THIS IS IT, YOU KNOW,**" KindlesFlame said to him over lunch. "Your practicum this semester is going to involve real people, not simulations. You'll be observing, not affecting, but it's going to be the first real test for you."

"I know," Jahir said, warming his hands on his mug.

"Have you told Lasa yet about your issues?" the Tam-illee asked, watching him.

"I have," he said. "Though I have not made much of the problems involved. She seems to have intuited the ramifications on her own."

"She would have," KindlesFlame said. "Smart as a whip, Lasa-reissa. How are you feeling about the workload?"

Jahir lifted a shoulder just enough to convey his ambivalence. "It should be similar enough to last semester, which I weathered. The practicum is the only new element, and I cannot predict it. So . . ."

"So, back to where you started," KindlesFlame said. "With it being a challenge."

"Just so," Jahir said. He added, "Healer-assist Kandara has been a great help to me. I thank you for the recommendation."

"She told me she would have tracked you down on her own,

even if I hadn't pointed her at you." The Tam-illee waved it off. "I was just accelerating her own process."

"Still," Jahir said. "You did not need to watch over me so. You're a busy man, to be taking such interest in a single student."

KindlesFlame chuffed a laugh. "Don't start talking like you're already leaving, alet. You've got a long ninety days ahead of you before you can shake the dust of Seersana off those boot heels of yours. Pass all your classes this term and then you can start telling me how much you'll miss me."

"I will," Jahir said.

"Eggs. Chickens. Counting," KindlesFlame said. He tapped the table. "Stay in the now, alet. You can express your undying gratitude when you're packing for your residency."

Jahir smiled. "Yes, sir."

"Better."

"These are good results!" Palland said. "How are you feeling about the study design now?"

"I think it might be better, at least from a methodological perspective," Vasiht'h said. "From a personal perspective . . . I don't know. I've only got twenty results using the dream-affecting without the talking, and it looks like the two together are far more effective than the dream-affecting alone."

"Mm." Palland pushed his chair back and folded his arms behind his head, frowning. "It's hard to design good studies around the efficacy of talk therapy, though. So much depends on the personality of the therapist. You can give twenty people the same twenty questions to ask their subjects and you'll get twenty different deliveries that affect people completely differently."

"But we know talk therapy works," Vasiht'h said. "How did we find out?"

Palland laughed. "By doing it since the beginning of time?"

Vasiht'h frowned. "Not very—"

"Sciency, I know," Palland said. "But we're getting into seriously tetchy waters there. Stick to the methodology that's working to do the second batch this semester. After that . . ."

"We try something different?" Vasiht'h said, hopeful.

"You write a thesis," Palland corrected.

Vasiht'h's shoulders fell. "Right."

"Have you considered what it says about the therapist conducting the study that his novel approach to therapy is more effective when he's personally involved?"

Vasiht'h eyed him, but his professor remained the picture of nonchalance. He rubbed one of his forepaws against the other and said, "May I ask you something, sir?"

"Go on."

"Have you ever wondered . . . how viable this is outside the lab? You keep suggesting I go practice with these techniques. But who's honestly going to let a stranger adjust their subconscious while they're unable to supervise the process?"

"It's been done before," Palland said, and at Vasiht'h's incredulous look, said, "Hypnosis."

"Hypnosis!" Vasiht'h said. "And we see how common that is."

The Seersa held up a hand. "Granted. But recall my comment about the personality of the therapist. You did this study twice at All Children's. You told me the second time you had more volunteers than you had time. They knew what you were doing. So why did they let you do it? Why were they so eager to be chosen?"

"Because their peers told them it was working?" Vasiht'h said.

"Because they trusted you." Palland shook his head. "They trusted *you*, Vasiht'h. To help them."

"But why?" Vasiht'h asked. "Why me? Why does everyone keep telling me that I'd be so good at this?"

Palland's brows lifted. "You really don't know."

"No!"

"Because," Palland said, "you care about them."

Vasiht'h sat back on his haunches.

"That's it. It's that simple. You care about people. You want them to be happy. And we're wired, instinctively, to look for that in other people, to read the cues that say someone cares about our welfare. You give off those signs, alet." Palland gave him a lopsided smile. "That's all. In therapy, that's everything."

Vasiht'h thought about that all the way home. When he got to the door, he looked down at his feet; brought up one paw to have a look at the pads. They were supple and glossy, and when he flexed his toes he felt no nagging aches from cracks. People who care about people, he thought . . . take care of each other.

Resting his brow against the door, he thought: *What are we doing?*

CHAPTER 33

THE WOMAN SITTING IN THE CHAIR had weight, breath, warmth, presence . . . and most importantly, a real aura. Jahir sat by the door as the healer-assist he had been assigned to shadow joined her by her hospital bed. He'd been introduced before his relegation to the far end of the room; the patient had indicated previously that she was willing to have a student there, but once she'd greeted him she ignored him to focus on her visitor.

He could see why she'd agreed. Her resignation was so deep it had become a species of apathy. The addition of one more stranger to the host of strangers who were importuning her didn't matter at all to her. He rested his hands on his knees and listened as the healer-assist asked her how she was feeling. She replied to all his questions in a monotone, but her hands . . . her hands were knotted in the shift over her knees. Occasionally she would notice their disposition, and smooth the fabric out self-consciously. Then her hands would curl into fists again, and the process would repeat.

She was speaking about her miscarriage. Her sixth, which had happened a week ago, and for which she was still under sur-veillance . . . for some reason relating to her physical health, he assumed. He remembered reading about the Tam-illee and their troubles having children and tried to imagine what it would be like, to long for a family and fail in the endeavor six times . . . in a row? Yes, in a row. She had no children yet, and it seemed unlikely she would.

When they left, the healer-assist said, "In a couple of weeks, I'll let you talk to her instead."

"Weeks?" Jahir replied, hiding his surprise. "Will it take her that long to heal?"

His guide glanced up at him, ears flipping back. "Her body's fine, alet. She's here on suicide watch."

So it passed, that class. They visited a Seersa who had lost an arm—an entire arm, Jahir noted with astonishment—and had it reattached. But the duplicate had been rejected, a rare complication in a routine operation, and it had taken the surgical team a day to discover why, amend the process and redo it properly. The patient once again had two functional arms, and was in the hospital until the nerves finished knitting . . . but he had become anxious about the arm, and had begun evincing panic attacks at the least twinge in the new limb. And there was the human who came for regular treatments for a chronic disease that could only be managed, not cured, who struggled with feelings of inadequacy and resentment; she lived badly with the despair of lying beneath a Pelted halo-arch because the human versions were not as advanced, and wished she could go home.

Glad there was nothing scheduled after the class, Jahir walked to the apartment. He found it empty when he arrived and hung his bag by the door, and his coat and scarf—pulled his boots off, leaning against the wall for balance in a way he would have avoided had he been in company. Then he sat on the couch and let his head rest on the back. Grief had a taste. Like licorice root: glutinous and too thick, as if one could choke on it. And the pall . . . it was distinct from the grief. Not a flavor, but a weight on the back of his neck, so that the muscles of his throat tightened in reaction. He would have a headache soon, if he didn't take care.

What the matter wanted was a cup of tea. Or coffee. No . . . alcohol. He forced himself to rise and go through the kitchen cabinets. There was one bottle of wine left from the holiday, so he opened it and brought a glass back with him to the couch.

Did it help? After a few sips on an empty stomach, it gave him some distance. It left him staring at the glass. Then he rose and poured the rest of the bottle out. He could see drinking becoming a bad habit and didn't want to leave the temptation.

The glass was the first thing Vasiht'h looked at when he entered. He frowned and met Jahir's eyes across the room.

"Rough day," Vasiht'h said. "You had the practicum?"

"I must imagine it becomes easier with practice," Jahir said.

"Either that, or you get jaded," Vasiht'h said, voicing the fear Jahir had left unspoken. The Glaseah came near, and brought with him the smell of new flowers, a distraction that felt like a breeze that carried whispers of conversations Jahir couldn't decipher but felt healthy. When his roommate began to sit on the carpet, Jahir said, "No, please. Closer?"

Bemused, Vasiht'h padded to the couch and sat on the floor beside it. He began to speak and the mindtouch stopped them both: it raveled into the line and sprang alive between them. The weight of Jahir's melancholy met Vasiht'h's energy in the center and shivered apart, leaving only a vague sense of disquiet.

They stared at one another, and their mutual shock sang sympathies, like a harp-string plucked hard enough to cause its neighbor to resonate.

"Did you know . . ." Jahir trailed off, still astonished.

Vasiht'h didn't immediately answer, staring at the space between them. He lifted his eyes and said, "That it could do that? No. No! Of course not. What do I know about mindlines? I've never had one!"

"Perhaps there is Glaseahn literature on the matter?"

"If there is, I haven't read it," Vasiht'h said. He licked his teeth and made a face. "And what is that awful taste? It's like it should be sweet, but it's not, and it clings to your throat. What are you drinking?"

"Wine," Jahir said. "But you are tasting licorice tea."

"Let's never have that, ever," Vasiht'h said.

"You will have no arguments from me." Jahir cleared his throat and said, "How long will it last?"

"I don't know," Vasiht'h said. "Until we break it, or pull apart, or it fails on its own."

They fell silent again. Jahir said finally, "Do you see it with your eyes?"

"Do you?" Vasiht'h asked.

"Yes. Though when I do not concentrate on it, it falls out of sight. When I do it looks like . . ." Jahir stopped, watching the gleam of the thin rope. "Like a ferroniere." At Vasiht'h's blank look, which he heard as a subconscious white noise, he elaborated. "A very delicate chain across the brow. For decoration."

"To me it looks like DNA," Vasiht'h said, voice low. "Like a gold helix, made of sparkles." He paused, then laughed ruefully. "Sounds ridiculous, doesn't it?"

"Not at all," Jahir said. "If DNA carries all the possible information that might make a person unique, why would a mindline not look like one when it carries all the possible information that might be shared between two people?"

Vasiht'h glanced at the wine. "Like the information that you haven't eaten, but you're already halfway through that?"

"I discarded the remainder of the bottle," Jahir said, and knew the sheepishness that was usually betrayed only by a slight change in his voice was obvious to the Glaseah. That would ordinarily have disquieted him, but the look on Vasiht'h's face . . . he started laughing. "What?"

"That emotion . . . you're making me feel like I've been caught stealing cookies," Vasiht'h said, and laughed too. "I haven't felt like that since I was too young for the size of my paws."

"Too young for the size of your paws," Jahir repeated, and his roommate gave him an image—gave it to him, through the mindline—a Glaseahn kit, short-legged, with the large feet he'd grow into. He looked up, eyes dancing. "Oh, how marvelous!"

"It is, isn't it?" Vasiht'h said, and then flushed. The mindline's gleam faded, took with it the sense of easy companionship. "Ah, there it goes. It probably wouldn't have survived me walking to the kitchen anyway."

"Perhaps," Jahir said, and closed his eyes. "Ah, but I feel . . . much more hale. Thank you."

"You're welcome," Vasiht'h said. "But let's get some dinner in you before that cup goes to your head."

"I am not an unpleasant drunk," Jahir protested.

"No, because you're an unconscious one," his roommate answered, wry. "So if I don't feed you now, you won't eat until breakfast. Come wash vegetables. You can do that without cutting off a finger."

"I am not that tipsy," Jahir said firmly.

"Mmm-hmm."

"I am not, I assure you—"

"Just wash the vegetables."

That became a pattern: four times a week, following his practicum classes, he returned to the apartment and waited for his roommate. He restricted himself to tea, knowing that Vasiht'h's arrival, his presence, would soothe away the distress of the sessions. Sometimes the mindline raveled, and sometimes there were only mindtouches. But it became rare not to have at least those.

Those were good evenings, spent tentatively exploring something new to them both, consulting one another over the sources of some of the less decipherable impressions. Jahir was careful never to break the Eldritch Veil, but if he could not be generous with his memories, he could with his feelings, and he shared those with his roommate with a gladness.

One night, preparing for bed after one such session, it struck him that he had never been suited to the reserve cultivated by his people. To hold himself apart from the alien had never been in him. His going to the Alliance had probably been an inevitability.

Jahir found himself grateful that there was an Alliance to escape to. He did not like to think what he would have become had he been trapped at home. Like Nieve's grandmother's tree: a thing warped by its need to reach outward, to grow. He suppressed a shiver and went to bed.

Vasiht'h didn't enjoy it, but he was scrupulous in observing the necessary distance from his new crop of subjects. The last thing he wanted was to repeat the study because he'd had to throw out the results, even though he was resigned to having to repeat it again in summer to harvest more data. So he waited for his subjects to fall asleep before entering their cubbies, touched their dreams and then removed himself before they woke. They responded to him via survey afterward, to maintain the separation.

Several weeks later, he was surprised by one of his subjects, who appeared at the door to the cubicle he'd been using to note his observations before leaving the hospital: Deniel, one of the doctors, a Seersa male with ash points and black mottles on a lighter gray coat. He had dreams of the hospital, Vasiht'h recalled.

"Do you have a moment, alet?" the Seersa said.

"Sure. Have a seat?"

The Seersa nodded and hooked himself one of the ubiquitous rolling stools. He perched on it and said, "You always lead me out." At Vasiht'h's perplexed expression, he said, "I dream I'm here and I can't find my way outside, or to my station, or to a patient. And you always show up in my dream, and I follow you and you get me to where I need to go."

"You see me? Me, literally?" Vasiht'h asked, interested. He didn't try to insert himself in his subjects' dreams. In fact, most of the time he didn't see them for himself. Once in a while, someone's mind was so powerfully involved in the narrative that Vasiht'h caught images or scents. He tried to minimize those incidents, to keep from being intrusive, but Deniel was one of the dreamers who projected.

Still, even knowing the Seersa's dreams, he didn't try to rewrite them: just project a sense of motion if things felt constricted, or stillness if they seemed agitated, and a well-being overall.

"I see you," Deniel agreed. He smiled a lopsided smile, one that went all the way up to his ears, which splayed unevenly. "I was hoping since you were so good at helping me find my way while asleep, that you'd have some ideas how I'd do it when awake."

"You . . . know what the dreams are about, then," Vasiht'h said.

"About my younger sister," the Seersa said. "She's marrying too young, and I think the boy she's with—" He paused, grimaced. "No, I don't think. I *know* he's no good. I've tried to tell her, but she won't hear it."

"So you end up in the hospital, but unable to move or find your way. Because you can't with her," Vasiht'h said.

"I have to guess that's what it is." Deniel's hands were resting on his knees; he opened them without lifting them, as if he couldn't admit to enough loss of control to spread his hands in entreaty. "Though why it would be the hospital that it shows me, I can't figure. I know my way around here."

"That's probably why," Vasiht'h said. "It's the feeling of helplessness when you feel like you should know what to do that your mind is struggling with."

The Seersa looked up, frowning. "Huh. Yes. I can see that. But you put it that way . . ." He chuckled. "I guess it's unreasonable to expect you can be that certain of things everywhere."

"You certainly can't control your sister's life," Vasiht'h said. "That's for her to do. And if she makes a mistake . . . well, we all make mistakes. As long as we're breathing, we have a chance to fix them."

"And that's her job, not mine," Deniel said. He sighed. "But, Speaker-Singer, I want to help her. What do you do with that? How can I . . . how can I—"

Vasiht'h held up his hands. "You're about to say 'fix her' or 'stop her' or 'change her'."

The Seersa paused, then flicked his ears back. Rueful, he said,

"Yes."

"You can't," Vasiht'h said. "The only thing you can do to help her is to listen to her. And be the big brother who loves her, and to whom she can turn when things get bad."

The Seersa considered that, head bent, elbows on his knees and hands laced. Then he sucked in a breath and nodded. "You're right. She'll need me if things go wrong, and she won't trust me if I try to run her life for her, will she? Hells, I wouldn't want her running mine! Can't blame her for that." He stood. "Thanks, alet."

"Any time," Vasiht'h answered, meaning it.

"And maybe I'll stop dreaming about being lost in my own hospital, ah?" Deniel said with a grin. "See you next nap, alet."

Vasiht'h waved . . . and then covered his face with a hand. Had he just? He had. Contaminated his own study . . . again. Grumbling, he returned to his notepad, but he was aware of a spark of rebellious pleasure beneath the exasperation.

"We're leaving!" Meekie said as they entered. Jahir paused at the door, then stepped aside so Vasiht'h could enter. That gave him a moment to compose himself against the jolt of adrenalized worry the girl had inspired.

"Leaving?" he said, noting the despondency of the humans sitting at the table.

"Yes," Meekie said. "Kayla and me. In two weeks we're going to that doctor who came to see us. He's all the way over on Selnor! Our families are moving!"

"But he thinks he can make us better," Kayla said. "And the doctors here think whatever he's doing is new and might work, so . . ."

"Two weeks," Jahir said. "That is . . . not so much time."

"I don't want to go," Kayla said, ears drooping.

"We don't want you to go!" Persy said.

Jahir could see where this was heading. He shared a glance with Vasiht'h, felt the warmth of agreement from a passing mindtouch. "Do you know, ariisen, that it is a fine and pleasant day out? For early spring, positively hot. Perhaps we might ask Hea Berquist if we can go to one of the gardens."

"Oh, the fish!" Amaranth exclaimed.

They asked, and the excursion was approved. With Berquist bringing up the rear, they made their way to the garden with the fish pond, and the air of melancholy eased as the children sat at the ledge and watched the colored koi laze in their cool waters. Jahir sat on the end of one of the benches, and Vasiht'h joined him, sphinx-like, on the ground alongside. To his surprise, Berquist paused in front of them and said, "Would it be too much if I . . ."

"Please," Jahir said. "Join us."

She sat close enough to be heard, but far enough that they could have fit another person between them. "I guess they told you?"

"The Tam-illee are leaving," Jahir said. "This new treatment is promising?"

"I think it might work." She nodded to herself, tucked a strand of blonde hair behind an ear. "It's a long ways, though, and their parents are uprooting themselves to go. Selnor's not an easy place to find work. So many people want to live there."

"Will the other girls be all right?" Vasiht'h asked, looking past Jahir's knee. His concern felt like a cool fog.

"They'll get used to it," Berquist said. "There will be new kids assigned to the room and they'll be distracted by that. Not to say they'll forget Meekie and Kayla, of course, because they won't. But the kids here . . ." She frowned. "It's hard to see, but they get used to this. To losing people."

"And you?" Jahir asked, gentle. "Are you taking care of yourself, alet?"

"Me?" Startled, she looked at him. And then managed a self-conscious laugh. "I hope I don't look too tragic!" She shook her head. "No. I'll miss them, but losing them to the hope of a cure is much better than losing them because they get worse."

"It is still," Jahir observed, "a loss."

Her glance then was thoughtful. She smiled. "You have to

make the whys matter. Otherwise, you suffer too much."

Kuriel detached herself from the group and padded over. She paused in front of Jahir, wringing her hands, and the sight of her rare uncertainty made Jahir hold out an open palm to her.

She sighed and climbed into his lap, bringing her grief with her, and he said nothing as she rested her head on his chest. She also reached down and petted Vasiht'h's shoulder, squeaked when he lifted a wing and rested it on her foot. "I forget you have those until you move them!" she said.

Vasiht'h looked up at her, solemn. "Kuriel . . . *I* forget I have them until I move them."

She giggled, and if it was a half-hearted sound it was still a giggle.

"Sometimes," Jahir said, sorting through her feelings and letting the words come, slowly, "you feel like you will be the only one left at the hospital. Everyone else will come and go, but you will always be there."

Kuriel kept her head ducked against his chest, but nodded against it.

Jahir wrapped his arms around her and held her, felt Vasiht'h rest a hand on the girl's knee, and the closeness knitted the mind-line back together. They were in accord, and Kuriel sank into their wordless reassurance. So strong was that union that when Berquist added her hand to the girl's back, Jahir felt the woman's presence as a sweet concern—and nothing else, no whelming, no unpleasantness.

He tried to remember when he had felt anything like it, and was sobered to realize the answer was that he had . . . but only with his roommate.

At last Kuriel sat up and rubbed her eyes. She looked better, though she seemed abashed from the dip of her head.

"You know what, Kuri?" Berquist said. When the girl looked up, she finished, "You're not going to be the last person standing up there. I am!"

It was just the right combination of rue, resignation and teasing. Kuriel blurted a laugh and then covered her mouth.

Berquist just grinned and tweaked her nose. "Oh, go ahead and laugh, I don't mind."

Kuriel giggled again and hugged the healer-assist, then popped off the bench and went back to the fish. The children scooted over to make room for her.

"I don't know how the two of you do that," the human said softly. "But it is amazing. And I kind of want to be near it all the time."

"Alet?" Vasiht'h said.

Berquist shook her head. "That thing with the . . . the soothing. Like a crack in the universe opens and you can see God's love in it." She shivered. "Like sunlight."

Jahir glanced at his roommate, who said finally, "We care. That's all. That's what you're feeling."

"I care," Berquist said. "But I can't do that. But the two of you . . ." She shook her head. "You know, if I look out of the corner of my eye, it's almost like you're one person." She laughed. "Isn't that ridiculous."

"No," Jahir said, struck to the quick. "No . . . it's not at all ridiculous."

"I'm glad you think so," she said. "Would you mind if I just . . . sat here? And . . ." She trailed off, sheepish, then said, "Well, if I basked in it."

"You can still feel it?" Vasiht'h asked, his incredulity in his voice.

"Yes," she said, nodding. "And it's good."

"Then by all means," Jahir said. "Stay."

The mindline lingered throughout the visit and accompanied them out of the hospital. They did not speak, but then, they didn't have to. They were aware of one another, and if the emotional information they received from the line was lacking in granularity, there was enough there to sate them, for it was still so new . . . and there was a perfume in it like the resin-sweetness of incense, touched with awe and gladness.

When at last it dissolved halfway to the apartment, they were silent a while longer. Then, Jahir said, "The mindline is something very special."

"Yes," Vasiht'h said.

Jahir dared say nothing more, lest he grow too attached to what he was feeling. He knew that Vasiht'h was doing the same.

CHAPTER 34

"SO, GIVE ME THE NEWS," Sehvi said, muzzle in her hands.

Vasiht'h couldn't help a touch of suspicion. "And you're looking at me like that . . . why?"

She grinned. "You haven't talked about your roommate for three weeks, but today you're back to rubbing your paws, so you must be ready."

"My—how can you see my feet??"

"I can't!" she said, laughing. "I can see your withers. They're twitching."

Vasiht'h folded his arms. "I thought I was supposed to be the body language expert."

"You are! But I've lived with you all my life, remember?" She leaned toward the screen. "So. Talk."

"Sehvi . . ."

"No, I mean it," she said. "You're dying to talk about this, I can tell. It's almost midterm there, isn't it? So you've only got two months left of his company. He hasn't failed, has he."

"No," Vasiht'h admitted, and dropped back onto his haunches. "No, Sehvi, he hasn't. He's doing amazingly."

"He told you so?" she asked, lifting her brows.

"Nooooo." Vasiht'h drew out the word. At her inquisitive

look, he said, "I might have done some snooping. They post class lists for half the courses he's taking, so I looked up his student number, so I could see how he's doing."

"Isn't that—"

"He leaves it on his data tablet!" Vasiht'h said, ears flush to his head. "And I wanted some warning if I was going to lose him at the end of spring, or if we'd have summer together."

"And you're not," she said, quieter.

"No," Vasiht'h said. "No. He's going to leave. But Sehvi . . . he needs people."

"This is new," his sister said, and sat up. "I would have thought he was the opposite of someone who needed people, what with the Eldritch being so xenophobic."

"That doesn't have anything to do with it," Vasiht'h said, frustrated. "Or at least, being xenophobic doesn't mean you hate all people, you just hate unlike people. And he doesn't hate unlike people. He seems to thrive on them." He shook himself. "No, what I mean is . . . he's seeing patients now, as part of his shadow rounds. And he comes back from that completely drained—"

"—I can't imagine why," Sehvi interrupted. "Hospital rounds of people in serious enough trouble to need specific psychiatric assistance?"

"Exactly," Vasiht'h said. "It's non-stop pain and it uses him up. But he comes home and he waits for me, ariishir. And we talk and . . . he revives. And he knows it. He knows that he needs it."

"That he needs *you*," Sehvi corrected.

"He's back to coming to the quadmate gatherings," Vasiht'h began.

"But it's you he waits for, isn't it," she said.

He rubbed his arm, feeling the fur chafe against the grain. "We talk," he said, low. "And . . . there's the mindtouch."

Something in his tone made her eyes widen, then narrow. "You do it on purpose."

"*We* do it on purpose, yes," Vasiht'h said, struggling not to sound as unhappy as he was.

"And it's amazing?" she said, her voice soft.

"Oh Sehvi," Vasiht'h said, head drooping. "Sehvi, I can't tell you. I want it forever. All the time."

She was silent, and in that silence Vasiht'h found himself thinking of Luci and her failed affair. And he had told the Harat-Shar that she had to withdraw and find someone else, that there were plenty of potential mates in her future! Why hadn't she thrown that advice back in his face? Now that he knew how ridiculous it was, he couldn't fathom how she hadn't. You never stopped wanting a relationship that made you happy, even if there was no way to make it work.

"Does he realize that this is going to hurt when the two of you rip it apart?" Sehvi said. "No, wait, back up. Is the mindline permanent yet?"

"Not yet," Vasiht'h said. "And . . . I think he knows, but he can't help it. He wants it too."

"Don't you think that's something you should discuss?" his sister asked. "This is serious."

"It's only two more months," Vasiht'h said, shoulders slumped. "Two more months and it won't matter anymore. We'll all go our separate ways."

"I really think you should talk to him," Sehvi said.

"And make it harder on him?"

"I don't think it has anything to do with making it harder on him!" Sehvi exclaimed, irritated. "I think it has everything to do with you being unwilling to take the chance! What have you got left to lose, ariihir? If he's leaving in two months, and you tell him you don't want him to go . . ."

"It's not just that I don't want him to go," Vasiht'h said. "I really think . . . he's going to burn himself out on this. He's leaning on me to get through it. And—" He stopped abruptly, feeling as if he'd been struck.

"Ohhhh," Sehvi said, quieter. "And you're afraid he might figure out how to lean on other people."

"The quadmates—"

"Aren't you, and don't have a mindline building to him," she said. "You're afraid that he can replace you. And you don't want to know if that's true. Better not to know that you mean something to him, if it means he can move on from you. Right?"

"He'd have to anyway," Vasiht'h said, shaking. "He'll outlive me by several orders of magnitude."

"He's not a main sequence star, ariihir—"

"He might as well be," Vasiht'h said, curt. "Ten centuries or ten million, it'll all be the same to me, Sehvi. I'll be dead. And he'll have to keep moving, keep finding people to make living worthwhile. In the end I have to be replaceable, or he'll go crazy from grief. And he knows it. We both know it. He even said it, that distance makes things livable. So no, I'm going to say anything. I'm not going to make this harder for us both."

She leaned back. "Vasiht'h. . . ."

"No, Sehvi," he said. "I can't see it ending well. So why get invested?"

"Because you already are?" she said, soft.

"I'm—"

"Love, you're crying."

He touched his cheeks, found the fur damp. So this was what it was like, to cry for something other than physical pain. And he'd wondered that he was capable? He rubbed his fingers together, curled them into fists.

"I can't spare myself," he said, when he was sure he could talk. "The least I can do is spare him." His eye was still leaking. He wiped at it with a rough gesture and said, "So tell me how school's treating you. Did you get through the deadly dull class on pre-natal nutrition?"

She looked at him for a long time, but to his relief she answered, and let him direct the conversation away from things that hurt. That they hurt so much was a surprise to him, but undeniable. When they'd said their goodbyes he curled up on his nest of pillows and fought the tension in his chest that wanted to become another crying fit. Jahir did need him—he knew that, knew it in the way only the mindtouches could make clear. When the Eldritch left for his residency he'd come apart at the seams without someone to ground him in the familiar and the gentle and the normal. And what's worse, they both saw it. And if they both saw it, then why was Jahir still so determined to pursue that course? It had to be that he felt confident he could manage without Vasiht'h.

Or was his roommate not thinking that far ahead? It seemed ridiculous that someone as long-lived as an Eldritch wouldn't, but Jahir was so good at living in the moment. Maybe that was his defense against the inevitability of loss?

He could ask . . . but that would involve talking about all the rest of it, and Sehvi was right. He wasn't prepared to hear that he was replaceable to someone who was—he understood with painful clarity—not at all replaceable to him. He could consult the mindtouches; they would probably reveal something. But increasingly the mindtouches were reciprocal, and he didn't want to chance his roommate sensing what he was hiding.

He would have to keep going, and hope that he recovered from his first real love. Because that's what he was forced to admit it had become.

—————∞∞∞—————

"I trust I acquitted myself well," Jahir said to Kandara after class. Hers had been his last midterm examination, and he was feeling the strain of it—the strain, and the pleasure. He didn't need her nod to know he'd done well.

"You were a bit wobbly at the beginning of the semester," she said, tail swishing, still with that boundless energy he'd noted at their first meeting. "But you straightened out and you've been sailing smooth since. You figured out some coping mechanisms, I assume?"

"I believe so," he said, even as he started. He hadn't thought of his conversations with Vasiht'h that way, but . . . she was right. "Yes, I think I have. Though it's debatable whether I can maintain it."

"Don't let it panic you," she said. "You can't rely on any one single thing. Spread your needs around, that's the best way to keep yourself healthy. How's the touching going? Farrell told me you've been letting the patients grip your hands."

"It was disconcerting at first," Jahir said, "but it has become . . . less so."

"Less so," she repeated, lifting a brow.

"Less so," he said. "I can handle it."

"Mmm. Well. Half the semester down, half to go. Go enjoy your off-day, alet, and then it's back to work next up-week."

"Hea," Jahir said, inclining his head to her.

Heading home, he thought back to those first few disconcerting touches. He had not shared with the Seersa that they had been unsettling because they hadn't deranged him as completely as he'd expected. He remembered the fall he'd taken in his first Clinical Management class, and the disorientation of having so many minds forced on his. What had changed, he wondered? Had he desensitized himself to the contact by being with the children?

Or was it the mindtouches that had given him some form of armor? Because there were times he thought that he was carrying Vasiht'h with him when they were apart.

Jahir glanced up at the sky, a creamy blue pierced with the trail of rising birds. Spring was half-sped. It seemed incredible to him that he was almost done with his time as a student. He found himself wishing otherwise, and there was a heartache in him that he did not like to contemplate. If distance made things bearable, why did the coming end of his tenure here make things feel so much harder?

Seeing Meekie and Kayla for the last time was painful, but Jahir thought of Berquist's comment and could feel the truth in it as he hugged each girl. To know they were leaving to go to a possible cure was much, much better than to lose them for some other reason; there were gradations of loss, he saw now. Surely that would make things easier. He found them gifts to suit their interests: art kits, one designed for a calligrapher and one for a painter, and unlike his previous offerings, these were meant for adults. It was his way of expressing the hope that they would live to use them; perhaps Vasiht'h's goddess would notice his attempt to shape the future, and grant the two those years.

He applied himself to his remaining coursework, and also to maintaining the social connections he now understood to be vital to his ability to work with the severely affected: his weekly talks with KindlesFlame and visits to Kandara's office, the gatherings with the quadmates, the time spent with the remaining children.

He relied on them all . . . but knew that his first anchor, and surest, was Vasiht'h.

"Congratulations are in order, I see," KindlesFlame said as he joined the Tam-illee at their usual haunt.

"Pardon?" Jahir said, stopping with a hand on the back of a chair.

"Ah, so you haven't heard." KindlesFlame grinned. "You got into the Heliocentrus residency. And you were one of only two people they accepted this year."

"I did?" Jahir said, stunned.

"Not only that, but you were the only student from this university. This planet, at that. The other's from some school on Asanao." KindlesFlame chuckled. "Sit, alet. You know you stop moving when you're overwhelmed? Relax. You're going to pull a muscle freezing like some wild animal."

Jahir sat across from him, fighting his bewilderment. "The semester's still two weeks from its completion. I haven't taken my finals—"

"And if they waited, you wouldn't have time to get there before they needed you to fill the roster," KindlesFlame said. "No, they make their decision based on your academics up to that point, and from recommendations. Which Lasa and I sent a while back. You should be hearing from General here on campus soon, too; they do their paperwork the week before finals." He cocked his head. "Did you really think you wouldn't get in?"

"I didn't, no," Jahir said. "They seemed too exclusive."

"And they are," KindlesFlame said. "I've been friends with the program director over there since . . . ah. Time out of mind. And even so, he doesn't take every person I recommend." He grinned. "You got in on your own merits, alet. Beat out some fairly impressive competitors at that."

"I don't even know if I'll go," Jahir said, and the words surprised him.

They surprised KindlesFlame also. Not in a disapproving way, he noted; his mentor seemed more interested than upset. "What's this now?"

"It has been my observation this semester, now that I have been working outside simulations, that it is important to have friends," Jahir said. "I don't relish the thought of leaving the ones I've made behind."

"You'd set aside a promising residency for your friendships?" KindlesFlame asked, his voice neutral.

Jahir studied him, wondering what the other man was thinking, but the Tam-illee's control over his ears, his expression, his shoulders . . . flawless. So he gave the candid answer. "I did not come to the Alliance in search of a career, alet. I came to immerse myself in the Alliance culture. It has taught me to value diversity, and interdependence. That culture is carried by people. So yes. I consider it a difficult choice. I don't know that I will privilege it above the opportunity on Selnor but . . ." He drew in a breath slowly, through his nose. Then inclined his head and said again, "But it is a difficult choice."

"Good," KindlesFlame said. When Jahir looked up at him, surprised, the Tam-illee continued, "When you first arrived, you fainted in your apartment and fought very hard against anyone helping you. I don't think you'd make that choice again, would you."

Thinking of Vasiht'h catching him on the sidewalk, Jahir said, "No."

"Then I'd say you're doing very well." KindlesFlame beckoned to a server. "Lunch is on me, and be extravagant, eh? The Heliocentrus residency is worth celebrating."

"Even if I turn it down?" Jahir asked.

"Especially if you do," the Tam-illee said with a laugh. "How many people can say they've done that? Not many!"

CHAPTER 35

T HE WEEK BEFORE FINALS, Palland canceled their regular meeting with apologies—something had come up—and hoped that Vasiht'h would send him mail if there was anything urgent he needed.

But Vasiht'h read the cancellation note with gratitude. He'd been due to report his conclusions on the semester's study at the hospital, and while he had the numbers he hadn't been looking forward to divulging just how little useful research he'd done. Deniel had not been the only person to seek him out for a quiet talk . . . and though Vasiht'h had known he was prejudicing his own results, he couldn't turn them away; more than that, he hadn't wanted to. He'd derived a fierce happiness from helping them, and he hadn't been able to give that up. Even knowing that he'd probably have to toss the entire semester's work, he would still have done it again.

That was why he'd used the free hour to visit the campus siv't. The shrine to the Goddess was empty, strangely; he would have thought that the week before finals would have been a perfect time to beg divine aid. But it was just him, and he padded to the altar and sat in front of it, haunches neat and paws facing forward where, he hoped, the Goddess would not notice the bare patches he'd chafed on the insides of his lower wrists. The shrine was made of black stone, polished smooth: the altar too, and the panel behind it, which had been carved with the Goddess's face in profile, blowing the breath of life from Her lips. There was slow-burning incense lit on the altar, and from time to time the draft from the overhead windows blew it into arabesques that mimicked the forms of that divine breath.

He traced the lines with his eyes until his heart slowed, and his breathing with it.

"I'm not where I'm supposed to be, am I," he said at last to Her. She was listening, he knew it, in the same way his mother had been listening to him while measuring chemicals into a machine, or flour into a bowl. "I've been so proud of myself for coming here, daring to do something different from my family. But I've been living in fear ever since." He inhaled, disrupting the plumes of smoke. They tasted like something out of Jahir's mindtouches, and dried the back of his throat, the inside of his nose. "Well, I'm going to stop. You tell us we have to be responsible for shaping our lives, or they will be formless, and subject to the whims of circumstance. So I'm going to take responsibility."

He lifted his eyes to Hers. "I was never meant for a classroom. I'm going to do what I obviously love doing. Helping people."

The silence in the siv't seemed to ring. His fur lifted and he bowed his head. The sense of relief that flooded him . . . ah, Goddess! To be free of the tedium of years of something he had never wanted to do. He was glad, glad that he'd made the decision before he wasted that time.

Standing, he bowed to the altar and then padded away. But at the door, he hesitated and looked over his shoulder. "He's not where he's supposed to be either, is he?" he whispered.

She did not answer.

Perhaps the rarified air of the shrine had made him more sensitive; when he reached the apartment and found Jahir there, he stopped abruptly at the door. That tension . . . was it real?

Some artifact of the mindline, now dormant? But his roommate lifted his head and smiled, just a touch of a curve, one Vasiht'h had long since learned to read as self-deprecation. "Arii. You find me at perhaps the most pivotal of crossroads, and in grave uncertainty."

Cautious, Vasiht'h padded into the great room and sat across from his roommate. "About . . . ?"

"I have been accepted to both my residencies," Jahir said, lifting the data tablet he'd been holding.

"The one off-world—"

"And the one here, at General," Jahir agreed. "And I must decide by the end of the semester which I am to attend, because if I choose Heliocentrus I have to be on my way by the first week of intersession."

Vasiht'h pressed his forepaws into the rug to keep from chafing them together. "And you don't know which one you want? I would have thought you'd be mad for off-world. Especially since it's on the capital. You'd learn a tremendous amount there."

"I would, and I won't deny that I find the opportunity compelling," Jahir said. He slowly rubbed his thumb along the edge of the data tablet, his gaze lowered, distracted. Was he really that uncertain? Vasiht'h bit his lip as the Eldritch looked up and continued. "But staying here has its advantages as well, chief among them that I wouldn't be learning my way around a foreign city and culture at the same time I'd be engaged in a residency even my mentor deems arduous."

"I've heard some of the medical track residencies are hard," Vasiht'h murmured.

"Yes," Jahir said. "It may be prudent to minimize my risks."

Vasiht'h studied his friend, who was again staring at the data tablet, this time with a slight frown. The mindtouch woke to give him the sensation of his heart skipping, the translated impression of a queasy hesitance.

So his roommate really didn't know what to do. And oh, how Vasiht'h wanted him to stay! Jahir could go to the hospital and come back to him for help staying grounded and sane. Vasiht'h could go back to school and wrap up the last of the clinical classes he needed to graduate. They could live together for another two years. . . .

But if Jahir stayed on Seersana, he'd never know whether he could survive the medical track on his own. He'd never have a chance to learn—as Vasiht'h had learned—that maybe he was in the wrong place. That maybe he needed the more normal ups and downs of a practice outside a hospital setting. If he went to Heliocentrus, Vasiht'h would lose him. But he might come out of the experience wiser about his own needs, and whether work in a hospital was the only way to fulfill them.

But he would lose him.

"I think you should go," Vasiht'h said softly.

"Arii?" Jahir said, looking up in surprise.

"If you're going to give yourself to medical," Vasiht'h said, his chest growing tight and painful, "you should know if you can handle it at its roughest."

The mindline began to coalesce between them, whispering. Vasiht'h closed his eyes and pushed it away; it unraveled and took with it the hint of loss, bitter in his mouth like tannin. When he could open his eyes again, he said, "You need to know. Better to learn before you graduate and get your license."

"Yes," Jahir said after a moment. "I can see where that would be the better part of wisdom."

When his roommate didn't go on, Vasiht'h frowned. "Arii?"

Jahir looked up, and there was what looked like beseechment in his eyes. Eyes like honey in sunlight. "I am not sure I wish to be wise," he said.

Vasiht'h cleared his throat. The pressure in his chest was so intense he thought he might cry. He carefully flexed his toes and fingers, crossed his arms. "We have to be brave enough to make the mistakes that teach us. Right?"

The silence then was painfully empty without the mindtouch to tell him what his roommate was thinking.

"We do," Jahir said finally. Quieter, "Vasiht'h. Thank you for the advice."

"Anytime," Vasiht'h said, and padded into his room before Jahir could ask if he wanted dinner. The last thing he wanted was to eat. That sense of loss he'd felt in the mindline before he had pushed it away . . . Jahir had already made his decision. They both knew it.

CHAPTER 36

T HE LAST TWO DAYS OF THE semester were too, too full: his final few sessions with the patients he'd come to know during the practicum; the examinations with all the attendant studying; one last meal with the quadmates, all of whom were staying on at the university but him. Somehow he managed.

At their table, KindlesFlame asked, "So, did you decide?"

"I'm going to Selnor," Jahir said.

KindlesFlame smiled and said, "Tell me how it goes, ah?"

"I shall," Jahir promised, and then they were joined by Kandara, who'd been invited by KindlesFlame for this last lunch. The two of them regaled him with stories from their own residencies; though the healer residencies were treated very differently from the psychiatric ones, he still found the anecdotes delightful, and full of the wisdom of people looking back on their mistakes from years of perspective.

And yet, even more than their stories, he felt their camaraderie, the ease they had in one another's presence, the common context they shared in their backgrounds. How many years had KindlesFlame said he'd known Lasareissa Kandara? Long enough to have grown into a union he could sense at the edge of his mind.

He was aware, distantly, of a yearning toward that, and gently

put it away. Distance. He would respect the distance. Did not
Berquist tell him that the people who cared for him would have
to be willing to live with the inevitable hurt they would consign
him to? And who was he to object, if they withdrew?

Saying goodbye to the girls was difficult. That day he sat in
their story corner with Persy in his lap and Amaranth and Kuriel
leaning against him, and Vasiht'h had settled across from him,
still observing their mind-silence. That hurt, but he thought—
he hoped—he was growing accustomed to it. He would be doing
without when he reached Selnor.

"But where are you going?" Persy was asking.

"To Heliocentrus," Jahir told him. "To one of the hospitals
there."

"Oh!" Amaranth said. "You'll be on Selnor! Maybe you'll see
Meekie and Kayla. You could tell us how they are."

"I could," Jahir agreed, and gathered them all close. Their
sadness welled into him, and their uncertainty and resignation,
and he paced his breathing, taking it in and letting it out. When
he opened his eyes, he found his roommate concentrating, and
his chest was rising and falling in synchronicity, and the children's sadness was passing through him and out of them both.
He thought, but did not allow out of his own mind, *You're still
there.*

Shivering once, Jahir rested his head against Persy's. "I will
miss you all, ariisen." They smelled of antiseptic and the slight
sour scent of sickness, and his eyes watered. He waited until he
had his composure before straightening and saying, "But let us
not dwell on it. What shall we do?"

"Read to us?" Amaranth asked.

"Come closer, manylegs," Kuriel added, reaching over to tug
on Vasiht'h's paw.

So the Glaseah curled closer, and Jahir brought forth the
book and read them poetry, about birds and trees that saw the
passing of the years.

When it was time to go, Persy said, "Jahir-alet? We made you
something."

"You did?" he said, surprised.

Amaranth went to the table and fetched back a folded paper card. Hearts had been pasted to it, and drawings of plump unicorns frisking, their tails decorated with flowers and butterflies and rainbows. On the inside, they had signed their names; not just theirs, but Meekie and Kayla's too, in Kuriel's writing.

"For me," Jahir asked, throat tight.

"For you! To remember us," Kuriel said.

Jahir went to one knee and offered his arms, and they poured into them. He fell past their sadness and into their love, and could not believe that he had earned it . . . and that he was choosing to leave it.

Outside, he found Berquist waiting. "So did they—ah, they did. They worked on that for two days, if you believe."

"I do," Jahir said, and cleared his throat. "I am honored."

"Mmm. Well, there's one thing missing from it, and the rascals gave their okay. If you mind?" She held out her hand, and he gave her the card, mystified.

She found a pen and wrote her own name alongside her charges' and then gave it back. "I'll never forget finding the two of you jumping rope for them in the parking lot. Thank you for being part of their lives. And mine."

Jahir bowed to her, and she seemed to find that an appropriate farewell. When he rose she had taken a step back and turned away. She was wise, he thought. She had learned how to hold a thing apart.

"I guess you're leaving soon," Vasiht'h said as they walked to the apartment.

"Tomorrow," Jahir said. "I am almost done packing." He glanced at his roommate. "I thought we could make dinner."

"I'd like that," the Glaseah said. He frowned. "I'm not sure there's food, though . . ."

"I bought groceries."

Vasiht'h smiled. "I guess you had this planned."

"I had hoped you would be agreeable," Jahir said. Quieter: "I will miss our meals together."

"So will I," Vasiht'h said softly.

It was good, working together in the kitchen; as they did, Jahir noticed how easily they moved around one another. He reached over Vasiht'h; Vasiht'h ducked under his arm. He dealt with the preparation, and Vasiht'h cooked. They did it without consulting one another, and the mindtouches lapped against his mind, trying to bring the mindline back. He knew that Vasiht'h was blocking it, and even wishing to feel that connection again he couldn't bring himself to ask. Their parting would be difficult enough without adding that much more weight to it. Some things came and went; was that not the Alliance's lesson? He would have to grow accustomed to the ephemeral joys, and make his peace with their passage from his life.

"You have not told me how the research went this semester," Jahir said over dinner.

"Oh!" Vasiht'h said. And softer, "Oh. No, I didn't, did I." He looked up. "It went awfully."

Jahir set his fork down and gave his roommate his attention.

"Contaminated, completely. Not a single result I can use," Vasiht'h said, without the distress Jahir had been expecting. "And my thesis . . . I never did write a good draft. In fact, I never got past the first paragraph of my abstract."

"You gave it up," Jahir said, understanding.

"I did," Vasiht'h said, meeting his eyes. "I was trying to do something I wasn't suited for. Instead, I kept helping the people I was supposed to be studying. And I was doing that because . . . I enjoy it."

"You no longer fear you will be incapable of rising to the demands of practice," Jahir said.

"No." The Glaseah breathed in, shook his head. "No. I've had enough experiences lately to prove otherwise. I'm steady on these feet, even when I feel like I'm dying inside." That startled Jahir into looking at him sharply, but he was still speaking. "So I'm going clinical. I'll take some practice management and business classes too. It should help. I've never run a business before."

"Sensible," Jahir said, surprised at his own relief.

"You're glad," Vasiht'h observed, brows lifting. "About this."

"I am. I did not think you suited to research," Jahir said. "You have such a natural talent for helping others. You put them at ease."

"And you told me so when I decided to go research," Vasiht'h said. "I would have saved a lot of time if I'd just listened to you, but . . . I guess some things we just have to figure out on our own before we actually believe them."

"Change must come from within," Jahir murmured.

"Yes."

"But it can be influenced by the opinions of someone we trust," Jahir finished, and saw Vasiht'h's surprised glance. He stood and said, "We should make more-almond cookies."

Shaking himself, Vasiht'h said, "Well, you certainly won't get any argument out of me."

Over cookies and kerinne—and tea—Jahir said, "Vasiht'h . . . I will write. You know I will."

"I know," Vasiht'h said, and swallowed. "And you know me. I'm always corresponding with family."

Jahir nodded. "I will look forward to that, then."

"When does your shuttle leave?" Vasiht'h asked, toying with the handle of his cup.

"I must be at the orbital facility by dawn, I'm afraid," Jahir said. "My trip to Selnor requires several transfers, and if I miss any one of them I might not arrive in time to report for the residency."

"Interplanetary travel's messy that way," Vasiht'h said. "You . . . you should get some rest, then. Go to bed early."

"I should," Jahir said. "After I wash the cups—"

"I'll wash the cups," Vasiht'h said. "Don't worry about it."

Jahir studied him . . . this alien who'd taken him beneath a wing from his first day on Seersana. He no longer seemed so strange to the Eldritch's eyes: the feathered ears and wings and the centauroid body. He had become Vasiht'h, known . . . friend. Perhaps better than a friend: one of those rare people one knows only once in a lifetime. The thought was impossibly painful to contemplate. To lose that? And yet, he would.

But in the name of what they had shared, if only briefly, Jahir went around the table then and down to one knee. "If it would be no imposition?"

"No imposi—you want to . . . hug me?" Vasiht'h asked, voice thin.

"You have been my closest friend," Jahir said. "And the embrace is custom here. I gave it to the children, and I would not withhold it from you. If . . . you wish it."

Vasiht'h stared at him, so still that Jahir remembered KindlesFlame's comment: 'you stop moving when you're over-whelmed.' But he remained where he was, willing the Glaseah to allow him to make the gesture.

"You're sure," Vasiht'h said, hushed.

"Completely."

His roommate took one step toward him, and another, until he was close enough that he could brush Jahir's chest by breathing deeply. And there he froze. But that was well: it was for Jahir to show the Glaseah that he'd meant it, and so he drew Vasiht'h into his arms and with him, the complexity of his feelings. So dense! Loss and sorrow and other things, raw like wounds. And over them, shock and elation and wonder at the touch. Jahir sympathized. He found the revelation of the glossy fur astonishing, and liked the incense-musk scent of his roommate's shoulder, and found it satisfying that the steadiness of the Glaseah's personality was matched by the weight and stability of his short, solid body.

Slowly, Vasiht'h set one of his hands on Jahir's back and rested his cheek on Jahir's shoulder. He was shaking, or Jahir was. Perhaps they both were.

When they parted, Vasiht'h said, "If I don't see you in the morning . . . Goddess keep you, Jahir Seni Galare."

"Vasiht'h," Jahir answered, his hand on the Glaseah's shoulder. He let it slide off as he stood, and took himself to his room.

One final night, he thought. And then . . . what? To leave all this behind?

To leave this behind, in particular?

He thought of the mindline and closed his eyes, and gently put it away. He would have to learn to put all such things away.

⸺⸻⸺

Vasiht'h went to bed in a roil of conflicting emotions so powerful he found himself pacing, as if he could release them in movement. Oh, Goddess, that hug. He threw himself on his pillows and buried his face in one of them. This was the last night. How could this be the last night? And he had brought it on himself, suggesting that Jahir leave!

But he had made the suggestion, and his roommate had taken the advice, and now they'd both have to live with it. He'd spent the night suppressing the nascent mindline, and he knew Jahir had felt him doing it, and accepted it. They both understood what had to be done.

So why did it hurt so much?

⸺⸻⸺

He had planned to wake in time to see Jahir off. Had even set an alert, so he wouldn't sleep through his roommate leaving. There was so much he hadn't said, so much he wanted to tell him about the two years they'd spent together, and how much they'd meant; how grateful he'd been to experience the mindtouches, and how wonderful it had been to see the Alliance through fresh eyes. He wanted to tell Jahir that he'd never had a real friend until the Eldritch had arrived and taught him that friendship was sometimes more than just idle companionship. That it could be fierce and joyful, too, that it could be laughter and quiet. That it could be sharing a hearth as well as sharing, sometimes, thoughts.

But he slept through the alert, and woke abruptly to the

light of a bright summer morning in his eyes. He jerked upright, pillows gliding from his limbs and there was . . . a smell in the air, cinnamon and nutmeg and honey. Bewildered and in pain, he stepped out of his room.

There was bread in his oven.

He stared at it for a long time before he thought to check the counter. There was a note on it, of course.

I know it is not a holiday, but I hope you enjoy it all the same.
Be well, my friend.
—J

Vasiht'h sat because his back legs wouldn't hold him up anymore. He pressed the note to his chest and dropped his head on the counter, in his arm. Was he crying? He was, but it was a stifled, hot thing, so small. He didn't want to smell his own tears and acknowledge what he was mourning. He forced himself upright, forced himself to make dark, strong coffee and set out the jam and more-almond butter. When the bread came out of the oven, it was not lumpy, but a beautiful ring, braided in three parts and glistening with melted sugar.

There was enough for two. Vasiht'h tore off a piece and had a bite, but it was too hard to swallow. He managed the one piece and sat staring at the table and the empty chair across from him. Forcing himself to rise, he put the bread in stasis, washed up the plates, returned the jam and butter to the refrigerator. Then, despondent, he went back to bed. He fought the first sniffle, but the second one won, and he cried himself to sleep.

———— ∞ ————

He dreamed of gardens, as he knew he would. The stool in the center, the one Jahir would have been using, was empty. All around him were flowers: beautiful flowers that he couldn't touch no matter how he reached for them. He denied that dream and backed away from it, and for a while there was nothing in his mind. But it returned, and this time he saw flowers . . . flowers that were dying even as they broke free from the earth. He felt the desperation of it, dove for them and did everything in his power to make them live before they died . . . and he failed, over and over.

His hands, he suddenly realized were white, and had one finger too many. They weren't his hands, but Jahir's.

Vasiht'h woke on a gasp. It was late afternoon, and his heart was racing and his pelt sticky with sweat. And in his mind the words resounded: *I was wrong.*

So long ago, Jahir had told Luci that distance made most things bearable. It was a common wisdom, certainly. But the answer to pain wasn't distance, but a deeper connection, with others, with life, with people who could stay and sustain one's heart when it faltered. And somewhere inside, Jahir had known that. Known that none of them was replaceable.

That was what had driven him into the medical track. Nieve's death had shown him that he couldn't stop loving the people around him, and that they would inevitably die. And he was reacting out of an anguished need to make it stop, to make it stop happening, because before he could admit to loving any of them he had to make them stop dying, make them stop receding into the distance, out of reach, beyond his grasp. The hospitals, the society of the healers, it was all his defense against loss. And it was too late for him, because he already loved them.

Vasiht'h, who had spent a year researching the use of dreams to heal, had not paid close enough attention to his roommate's. Jahir had told him his grief himself:

I'm alone.

Vasiht'h went to the window, gripping the sill so tightly his palms ached. That night he'd soothed that dream by telling Jahir that he wasn't alone, and it had worked because that was the core of the Eldritch's grief. Not that he would outlive them, but that he was to be forever held apart, and that he must be complicit in his own abandonment by those who sought to protect him.

Sought to protect him! When all he wanted was to fully engage the life he'd chosen, and the people he'd taken into his heart?

And he had encouraged Jahir to leave . . . had all but sent him away!

"Oh Goddess," he whispered. "What did I do!"

She seemed close, so close he could feel Her breath on his shoulders. "No," he said. "No, You would say the past is in the past, and not to dwell on the mistake. So what do I do now?"

And asking made it obvious. The temerity of his plan didn't matter. Trembling with the need to fix it—fix everything, now—Vasiht'h lunged for his data tablet and started writing messages. He left one for Palland, requesting an emergency meeting. He left one for Sehvi, telling her he might be out of contact for a while. He researched schools he could transfer to, and academic leave requests in case he wasn't accepted at any of them. And he looked up shuttle itineraries. Too much to do, and so little time . . . he didn't think he could put it all to bed for a week at least. Probably two. Goddess! Two weeks! Luci would help, surely, when he explained it to her, and the quadmates. Palland, too. Maybe he could continue his studies through correspondence . . .

He didn't know how he would work it out, but he knew he would. And before intersession was over, he was going to be on a ship bound for Selnor.

"Hang on, arii," he whispered as he worked. "I'm coming. And this time, I'll listen more carefully when you tell me what you need. We'll get through this together . . . and we're going to end up where we belong—

"—I promise."

Brief Glossary

Alet (ah LEHT): "friend," but formal, as one would address a stranger. Plural is *aletsen.*

Arii (ah REE): "friend," personal. An endearment. Used only for actual friends. Plural is *ariisen.* Additional forms include *ariihir* ("dear brother") and *ariishir* ("dear sister").

Dami (DAH mee): "mom," in Tam-leyan. Often used among other Pelted species.

Fin (FEEN): a unit of Alliance currency. Singular is deprecated *finca,* rarely used.

Hea (HEY ah): abbreviation for Healer-assist.

Kara (kah RAH): "child". Plural is *karasen.*

Tapa (TAH pah): "dad," in Tam-leyan. Often used among other Pelted species.

Kerinne

Like coffee and tea, kerinne has as many variations as it has drinkers. It's always based on milk and cinnamon, but every other variable can (and has been!) messed with. I've seen molasses-sweetened kerinnes, or kerinnes with extra spices; restaurants will often have house variants or even kerinne cocktails! Vasiht'h's recipe is a very common one, and begins with creaming butter, as if you're making a cookie.

Vasiht'h's Kerinne

- 1 tbsp butter
- 1 tsp cinnamon
- 1 tbsp honey
- ¼ cup cream
- pinch of salt
- milk to taste

Over pot set to medium-low heat, stir butter, cinnamon and honey until combined and warmed through. Add cream and stir until combined. Leave on burner until steaming, then season with salt and add milk to taste. (Steamed or warmed milk integrates more easily.)

Yield: 1–3 servings (depending on how much milk used)

MINDLINE
BOOK 2 OF THE DREAMHEALERS

AT THE ADVICE OF VASIHT'H, his first and truest friend, Jahir
Seni Galare has accepted one of the most coveted residencies in xenotherapy, even though doing so has severed him from
all the relationships he's fostered since leaving his cloistered
homeworld. But not all the simulations at school have prepared
him for the reality of being an esper in a hospital large enough to
serve the winter capital of the entire Alliance, and it's not long
before he's questioning the wisdom of having left the university for the tumult of one of the largest port cities in the known
worlds.

When Vasiht'h follows Jahir to Selnor, he's not sure whether
his plan is to help his friend survive his residency, or to drag him
back to Seersana University and into a less strenuous residency
program. But a storm is coming to Heliocentrus, one they're
uniquely positioned to address, and their nascent mental link is
about to receive its first test in the crucible that will either forge
their lifelong partnership—or kill them both.

About the Author

DAUGHTER OF TWO CUBAN political exiles, M.C.A. Hogarth was born a foreigner in the American melting pot and has had a fascination for the gaps in cultures and the bridges that span them ever since. She has been many things—web database architect, product manager, technical writer and massage therapist—but is currently a full-time parent, artist, writer and anthropologist to aliens, both human and otherwise. She is the author of over fifty titles in the genres of science fiction, fantasy, humor and romance.

Mindtouch is only one of the many stories set in the Paradox Pelted universe. For more information and additional stories about Jahir and Vasiht'h, visit the "Where Do I Start?" page on the author's website.

Twitter: twitter.com/mcahogarth
Website: mcahogarth.org